DESIRED

DON'T JUDGE ME

C C CAMPBELL

To:

Jo, Jilly, Ros, Ruthie, Rich, Helen, Hannah, Harry,
Kath, Sal, Sarah, Charlotte, and Angie, thank you all so
much for baring your souls.
Also, special thanks to Jacqueline for her devotion
to the cause.
Love, as always,

C C xx

PROLOGUE

Many of the women in the room wore negligees so loosely tied that their breasts and nether regions were on show.

My eyes were drawn to their faces first and then to the sensual curves of their chest, where my gaze rested momentarily. Thereafter, I followed the soft contour of their tummy down to between their legs. After lingering there for a moment, I then studied the complete picture to take in as much of their sexiness as possible.

With my discreet survey of the thirty or so women in the lounge complete, I took a closer look at the men. They slightly outnumbered the women. Roughly half were smartly dressed – collared shirts, trousers, and polished shoes. The remainder had towels wrapped round their waists. There was a lot of tactile flirting in amongst the conversation and laughter. As you can imagine, the sexual excitement which pervaded the atmosphere was palpable.

Having put the drinks on his tab, Marcus turned away from the bar and cast his eye around the room. At six two he was just a bit shorter than me, and was also well toned.

'There they are Rich,' he said, nodding to his left.

He then led the way to where Natalie and Angie were sitting. Our wives looked up at us and smiled. Marcus set the tray of drinks down on the table, and we sat on the leather sofa opposite. We all raised our glasses and said cheers.

Perched on the edge of his seat, Marcus ran his fingers through his wavy dark hair. My wife Angie also sat forward. The pair of them looked pretty cosy chatting to one another, with just a low drinks table between them.

Does she want sex with him? I wondered, as I discretely observed their interaction.

It was plain to see that my wife literally oozed sexiness from every inch of her being. At forty-six, she was roughly in the middle of the age range and, to my mind, she was the hottest woman there. There was just something about her. Her hourglass figure, her naughty blue eyes, her blonde bobbed hair, and her pretty 'girl next door' heart-shaped face.

I then turned to look at Natalie. As I dropped my gaze from her face to where her auburn hair rested on her shoulders, she turned her head to look at me. I immediately looked up. Her big brown eyes locked onto mine for a moment. I felt a little self-conscious and smiled awkwardly. She beamed at me and then tipped her lovely round face to the side.

'You alright?' she mouthed.

I nodded in response and then looked over to Marcus and Angie, like I was going to join their conversation. Natalie did the same.

Whilst they all chatted, I returned my gaze to Natalie. By this time, she had uncrossed her legs and had left them tantalisingly open. Her negligee was unfastened, revealing her see-through babydoll. Very little was left to the imagination, and my eyes were on stalks, despite my attempts at discretion.

Jesus, what am I doing disrespecting my wife and Marcus by lusting after Natalie? My feelings of impropriety soon faded though, when I followed Angie's gaze to Marcus's manhood, which was on show through the split in his towel. She was smiling and happily chatting away. Her eyes flitted between his gaze and his package. You could kind of tell she was trying to maintain eye contact but couldn't stop herself from constantly glancing down.

As I watched the proceedings, Angie parted her thighs so that her stocking tops and skimpy lace knickers were on show. At this moment, I sensed movement and turned to see Marcus's cock grow completely hard right in front of me. I was reluctantly impressed by my wife's incredible sexiness, but also jealous and insecure at the same time.

God, a man has his huge erection on display, yet the polite chit-chat continues, as if we were just having drinks at a dinner party.

Realising that I'd been staring for way too long, I immediately lifted my gaze and looked at Angie. Her head was tilted down, and her eyes were wide and unashamedly excited. She then looked back up at Marcus wearing an almost smug smile at a job well done.

With my own hard-on throbbing away in my trousers, turbo charged by sexual jealousy and a big shot of adrenaline, I tried to calm my quickened breathing. Despite my reaction, I bizarrely felt a sense of pride at having a wife so hot, that she'd excited a really good-looking younger man.

Jesus, a beautiful woman just has to flash her knickers, and us blokes turn into puppy dogs, waiting for the mistress's command.

At this point I suddenly became anxious, as the sinful arousal and immorality of my actions hit home. Unwilling to deal with that at this time, I left my morals and emotions to battle it out with my debauched demons.

As I stared intently at my wife, another bizarre sense of pride came over me. I liked that she was sexually assertive. She was powerful, and that was a turn-on. But even so, watching her control Marcus with her womanly ways, made me resentful and a bit possessive.

To me, looking at forbidden fruit is one thing. Eating it is another, and Angie was primed and ready to devour as much fruit as she could lay her hands on. This made me think that her *forgotten me* had gotten out of control, but I wasn't entirely sure what I could do about it.

My wife's *forgotten me* came about after we lost everything in the recession. Her confidence was shot to pieces, and she was emotionally battered. Having had a sudden epiphany, she realised her identity had been overwhelmed by being a wife, mother, and career woman. She had lost sight of the person she was meant to be, and wanted to feel attractive and desired. This foray into The Hub was supposed to help with that.

But before we get to the good, the bad and the ugly of my wife's self-discovery, I need to retrace my steps. I need to take you back to the events which lit the blue touchpaper of dramatic change, in the lives of an ordinary middle-class, middle-aged, married couple …

CHAPTER 1

The day of our departure from Surrey to Hope Harbour …
My footsteps slowed as I approached my bedroom window. I drew in a faltering breath, and then eased the curtain aside. As I peered through the small gap with a sense of foreboding, my heart raced.

'Thank God,' I whispered. 'No bastard lying in wait.'

Over the last few months, I had come to realise that I couldn't afford to drop my guard for a moment, because, just when I thought it was safe, yet another devastating blow would send me crashing to the ground.

With my fears momentarily allayed, I headed downstairs, shaking my head in disbelief. How had it come to this bittersweet farewell to our lovely family home? Bitter, because we were leaving the home we had happily built up over the years. And sweet, because we were fleeing thugs and bailiffs who were pursuing us like a pack of hounds in a fox hunt, driving us into the ground, financially and emotionally.

As I paused for thought at the top of the curved, sweeping staircase, my gaze was drawn to the vacant dusty outlines left by the beautiful family photos which once adorned the walls. Each empty space now created a new and profound work of art in its own right. This highlighted the stark contrast between the happy days we once knew, and our current situation. That in turn triggered a flood of thoughts which unexpectedly brought tears to my eyes. Shaking my head like a wet dog to snap myself out of my sentimental reverie, I pounded down the stairs and headed outside to bring myself back to the here and now.

With a running jump, I latched on to the top of the huge oak entrance gates at the beginning of our driveway and pulled myself up to peer over. All clear. I dropped to the ground, wiped the cold sweat from my brow with the back of my hand, and then pressed the remote control. I took a big nervous breath and quickly slipped through the tiny crack as the gates slowly swung open. Frozen for a moment, I confronted the letter box with trepidation. There it was, mounted on a substantial wooden post, intimidating me.

It was, as usual, overflowing with official-looking threatening letters. Even though I'd now come to expect this, I hadn't yet come to terms with it. Just a few short months ago, I cheerfully extricated copies of *Golf World, The Economist* and *Cosmo* from this very letter box. But now, I faced notice of bailiffs, court papers and, worst of all, menacing handwritten notes from barely literate thugs. It was intimidation: we know where you live, and we want our money! On more than one occasion, underworld debt collectors menacingly tapped their concealed guns without actually pointing them at me, and asked after my wife and children through sinister smiles. Even though I knew they probably wouldn't harm my family, I couldn't take any chances. I had to get out! Being a lean, powerful six-foot-five lad was no match for these guys.

And of course, I was also scared for my personal wellbeing. Avoiding the shadows and constantly looking over my shoulder, fearful that I'd have the crap beaten out of me, didn't appeal.

I was completely taken aback by the dramatic change I saw in some people. Certain business associates once eagerly courted me and appeared to be my friends, but now they wanted to rip me apart like a pack of wolves.

Drawing in an anxious breath, I unlocked the letter box, plunged my hand deep inside and drew out the mass of crumpled post. I hoped for just one piece of good news somewhere in this heavy bundle. Looking around like a fugitive, I slipped back through the gates and breathed a sigh of relief as they closed behind me.

Pausing in the late morning sun of a crisp January day, I thoughtfully admired our, or should I say the bank's, imposing Victorian farmhouse one last time. I lowered my gaze from the red brick façade and focused on the middle of the long driveway, flanked by manicured lawns and substantial hedging.

Looking up at the house once more, I nodded with pride because I'd rescued this grand old lady from the brink of extinction. At least I could be proud of that. It had all but tumbled down when I bought it for just over two million at auction, together with thirty odd acres and a handful of derelict farm buildings.

As I continued towards the house, I recalled the risk I'd taken to acquire it. I hadn't arranged funding for its purchase at the point the auctioneer's gavel fell. My arse was bubbling to say the least, despite my near unshakable confidence. That had now, without doubt, taken a huge hammering.

'Goodbye, lovely house,' I said, before walking through the front door.

There was Angie stacking a box in the entrance hall.

'What were you saying, Rich?' she asked, looking at me quizzically.

'Nothing important,' I muttered, as I held the post behind my back. 'I was just saying goodbye to our lovely old house, that's all.'

'Aw,' she sighed. 'You're such a softie behind that macho exterior.'

I nodded and smiled in response, and then watched intently as my wife walked towards me. I loved looking at her. She was tallish, with a few pretty freckles on her pale heart-shaped face. As she drew closer to me, I could smell the perfume I'd bought for her: Poison by Christian Dior. She loved diamonds and wore four carats on two rings which I'd given her. They were complemented by a gold Rolex watch, complete with the diamond face she'd insisted on.

Having wrapped her arms round my waist, my wife immediately buried her head in my chest. With nearly a foot between us, I was the perfect height to envelop her. She loved that. Said it made her feel protected and secure. I have to say though, I wasn't sure how well I was protecting her since the business went bang, and I lost our fortune.

Easing herself away from me, my wife regarded me at arm's length.

'Today's the day big man!' she said.

I nodded thoughtfully and smiled.

'Thank you for agreeing to Devon,' she continued.

'Don't be silly, sweetheart!' I drew her back to me. 'Whatever makes you happy.'

If the truth be known, I'd told everyone I was supporting my wife's need to move to Devon, but deep down, I knew

I was running scared. I really didn't want to leave my hometown, the place where I grew up and the place where all my family and friends lived, but I couldn't admit that to anyone. I'd never run away from anything. I'd always been the protector and confronted things head on. Always fixed everything, no matter how difficult. But the thugs and the recession were just too much for me. I'd been lured by the banks. Their traps were baited with pound signs, but when the party was over, they tightened their snare round my neck, gradually throttling the emotional and financial life out of me, whilst I desperately kicked, screamed and punched to no avail.

Although I had a plan, I sensed my Angie felt exposed, under attack and tortured by uncertainty. Yet despite all her misgivings, she put on a brave face. I admired her for that, but also realised her stoicism was very delicate. So, for her sake, I had to appear totally confident that my plan would work. I needed to convince her that I was reinventing myself, ready to rebuild our family fortune.

My brooding was suddenly interrupted when Angie eased away from me.

'Best be getting on,' she said, before accidentally catching sight of the post I was trying to hide from her.

'Give me that pile of shit, Rich!' she insisted sharply.

I knew her anger wasn't directed at me, it was just her way of coping. Nevertheless, it saddened me to see my wife so upset, especially as I knew I was to blame.

Holding the bundle to her chest, she quickly sorted through all the envelopes, contemptuously tossing the official-looking ones to the floor to be dealt with later. This left just two which were potentially good news; or at the very least, not bad news.

'Ah huh!' she exclaimed, as she ripped open the auctioneer's envelope. 'Woohoo! Fifteen grand!' She waved the cheque in front of my face. 'Good, you put it in your sister's name like I said,' she added with a smile, and stepped forward to peck me on the lips.

'C'mon, sweetheart,' I said with a grin. 'Let's get this show on the road!'

I led the way to our huge forty-by-thirty open-plan kitchen, dining and family room. We'd specifically designed this area so that the whole family could be in the same space together.

Angie, dressed in her tight-fitting blue jeans and yellow V-neck jumper, peered into a large carrier bag she'd placed on the breakfast bar, and announced that she'd got all the essentials for the journey.

'I'll take this with me in the people carrier,' she added.

'I love you, Angie,' I whispered, beaming at her. 'You're amazing!'

'A domestic goddess,' she replied.

Leaving my wife to it, I drifted over to the French doors. As I observed my four children playing in the garden, I contemplated the enormity of what we'd achieved. In just six short days, we'd found a place to rent in Devon, secured school places, and packed up a substantial six-bedroomed house. This was down to the incredible synergy Angie and I had as a couple. She was my love, my friend, my colleague and my inspiration. Yet unexpectedly, at low points in my marriage, and sometimes even at high points, Black Dog, my jealous and insecure response, would rear his ugly head. I was always surprised by my negative feelings when everything was rosy in my marriage garden, until I realised that the incredible joy of being married to Angie, highlighted what I'd lose if it all went wrong.

* * *

It was late afternoon when I swung the huge seven-and-a-half-ton lorry into the drive, and watched the electric gates close behind me. Connor, aged twelve, was excited to be riding in the cab with Daddy and asked if he could operate the tailgate.

'Of course, son,' I replied, regarding his big blue-green eyes with pride as I tousled his dense mop of brown hair affectionately.

He was my Braveheart, because he stood up for the underdog, perhaps helped by the fact he was just shy of six feet. I guess he got his height from me and, like any dad, I was proud that my lad was tall and could look after himself. He'd passed the exam and interview for Charterhouse, but that wasn't going to happen anymore, because I was arsehole broke.

Just as I drew to a halt, the lorry's air brakes let out a big 'pshhh' sound. Angie appeared at the front door with a smile so big her eyes disappeared. Our three other children, Olivia, Phoebe and Archie were gathered around her. I opened my door and beckoned the excited ensemble to join me. Olivia, or Livy as she was mostly called, made her way round to the passenger side and jumped in beside Connor. Angie helped Archie and Phoebe up to my waiting hands, took a couple of steps back and looked the lorry up and down.

'Mmmm, that's a big one,' she said, smiling a wicked smile and licking her lips. 'Just the way I like it!'

'You really are a *naughty* girl, Angie,' I replied through

a growing smile.

'I'm operating the tailgate!' Connor suddenly announced.

'Can I too?' said Archie, as he plonked himself on my lap. 'What is the tailgate, Dadda?' he asked, making pretend turns of the steering wheel, accompanied by a chorus of 'vroom, vroom, vroommm'.

As I explained about the tailgate, I admired my bright-eyed, extrovert and confident fourteen-year-old Livy, who was taking everything in. Angie and I did an excellent job of raising our kids. Lots of love, hugs and understanding, alongside a firm but fair approach. Also, teaching them self-reliance was important to me, although I sometimes thought I was a bit too strict and impatient with them. The never-ending stress of my business had doubtless played its part in that. Thankfully, being more relaxed would be a welcome by-product of escaping the financial and emotional trauma we currently endured.

Seven-year-old Phoebe was almost choking me as she hung onto my neck for support whilst standing on the edge of my seat. She was Daddy's little princess and stuck to me like glue. She looked like her mother, with her striking china-blue eyes and lightly freckled face.

Smiling to myself, I revelled in the joy of being surrounded by my beloved children, all happy and excited. This reminded me that they were innocent victims of my financial catastrophe, and strengthened my resolve to provide them with the wonderful life they deserved.

That thought was suddenly interrupted by the sound of a car horn which immediately brought me out of my reverie. Returning my attention to my increasingly unruly mob, I bellowed at them in faux military style…

'Right, you 'orrible little lot, the boys are here. Everyone out!'

Having zapped the gates open with my remote control, I jumped down from my cab and deposited the little ones on the driveway beside me. My three nephews drove in and, as the gates swung closed behind them, I walked over to greet them.

Alex, Conrad, and Mark all hugged me in turn. We then immediately began loading the lorry, starting with the heavy furniture first.

* * *

It was past midnight when we finally finished filling the lorry with our remaining worldly possessions. That accounted for about ten per cent of what we'd accumulated over the years. Ruthless reduction was necessary for both space and sale proceeds to survive on, and to pay off the most menacing creditors.

Having shut the lorry's big rolling shutter and secured the tailgate, I ventured into the sitting room and picked up Phoebe, who was fast asleep in a sleeping bag beside Archie. I gently deposited her into the VW, before returning to collect Archie, complete with sleeping bag, to put him in the lorry next to Connor. Livy was riding with Mum in the VW and was ready and waiting in the passenger seat.

Leaving my nephews and Angie chatting in the drive, I walked round the empty house, checking to see if we'd missed anything. We had cleaned and vacuumed. We couldn't bring ourselves to disrespect our home even though it was about to be repossessed by the bank.

As I began my rounds, I had a kind of outer body

experience, where I seemed to be moving in slow motion. As I surveyed the big kitchen-living-dining room, I saw so many happy memories play out in front of me: noisy parties with loud rock music and deranged dancing; big family meals at the huge pine dining table; me ensconced on our sumptuous sofa watching *The Sound of Music* with all the children whilst Angie prepared lunch.

As I walked into the sitting room, I saw a roaring fire burning brightly in our massive inglenook fireplace. Angie and I were sitting on our treasured Persian rug, wrapping Christmas presents and drinking too much mulled wine. I continued watching the lovely Yuletide scene play out as I slowly pulled the door closed.

Once it had symbolically clicked shut, I sighed heavily and ventured upstairs to check the children's rooms, just like I used to before retiring to bed.

First, I walked into Archie's room. There he was, sprawled out on his bed fast asleep with the covers kicked off. I watched myself remove the plastic dinosaur from his chubby little hand. I then tucked his blanket in, and kissed his forehead ever so lightly so as not to disturb his slumber. As the movie played on, my emotions played out, bringing reluctant tears to my eyes. I then headed to Phoebe's room. Here, I saw myself carefully removing numerous grips from her hair, before gently kissing her goodnight. In Connor's room, I eased his book away from his face and kissed his forehead.

On the top floor, I walked into Olivia's bedroom. I stood at the door and smiled as I saw myself gingerly re-covering her with the duvet she'd half kicked off. As the film rolled on, I visualised myself softly transferring a kiss to her forehead with my fingers. I slowly shut the door on another precious memory, and quietly descended the stairs back to the first floor.

I again sighed heavily as I walked across my bedroom to the Juliet balcony. Here, I looked out over my golf range, where I'd spent many a happy hour practising whilst the children played nearby. Having turned to look at where our bed once stood, I pulled a bittersweet grimace as my eyes welled up at the memory of Angie and I blissfully entwined after making love.

A second or two later, I suddenly came to my senses and stopped wallowing in my own self-pity. I then wiped my tears away with my hankie and ran down the stairs at speed, putting on a contrived smile as I went. As I emerged from the front door, Alex asked me what had taken me so long.

'Just checking every nook and fanny!' I replied, trying to disguise my sadness. 'I mean cranny!' I added, like a bumbling fool, for comic effect.

'We don't want to hear that you've been checking new fanny,' retorted Conrad.

'Don't even think about it, Rich.' Angie chuckled. 'Or I'll chop it off!'

'Ouch!' The boys winced in unison.

Our laughter subsided and a momentary quietness befell us. It was time to go. Mark approached me with arms wide open. Our man-hug was very dramatic and over-emphasised. It was our way of diverting from the real emotion, which in this case was sadness.

Putting on a brave face, I eased away from Mark and said goodbye.

'Bye Rich,' he replied. 'And remember,' he added, 'you built up a fortune in just a few years. Not many can do that, and you'll do it again.'

'I'll be back!' I retorted like Arnold Schwarzenegger.

Then, forcing a big smile, I said my goodbyes to Alex and Conrad. Angie did the same, and then jumped into the VW Sharan. I climbed behind the wheel of the lorry, where Connor waited excitedly beside a zonked-out Archie. As I pulled out of the drive, we waved at the boys, shouting 'byeeee!' at the top of our voices.

With Angie in tow, I slowly picked up speed in the lumbering lorry. All that was familiar to me faded into the history of my life as I drove by. I could now only hope that things would get better, and looked forward to a simple new beginning in Devon.

CHAPTER 2

With the low, soporific hum of the engine in the background, Connor soon drifted off to sleep, and I gradually began to unwind. Tired and emotional, I took a deep breath, and exhaled long and hard. I then became aware of tears running down my cheeks.

'What's the matter with you, Rich?' I snapped under my breath. 'Why are you crying? Get a grip man!'

My pep talk did nothing for me. Tears kept coming as my head quietly bobbed up and down. After a while, I sat up straight and wiped my eyes with the back of my hand.

They say everyone knows where they were when they heard the sad news of Princess Diana's death. Well, I knew *precisely* where I was when I heard the sad news of my financial demise. I was sitting in my Range Rover listening to the radio as I waited to collect Livy from ballet. The BBC's Robert Peston reported that there was a 'run on the bank' at Northern Rock – the first run on a British bank in over a hundred and fifty years! So, what did that actually mean? It meant that depositors wanted their money back because Northern Rock had severe liquidity issues. Plus, high-risk subprime mortgages were beginning to default. These catastrophic events were the thin edge of a very short, very fat wedge. Even with my A-level economics, I knew the housing market was going to free-fall and crash, rather than just make a small downward correction, because subprime mortgage lending had started to implode.

At that point, I chose to ignore the reality of the situation. Why? Because I was in too deep to get out in time and I couldn't face the alternative – financial ruin. Family home gone, cars gone, private schools gone, status gone, reputation in tatters. I had no alternative but to hope the inevitable wouldn't happen. A bit like you do when a loved one is diagnosed with terminal cancer. You know the outcome, but early on, you somehow refuse to accept it.

And I couldn't even batten down the hatches – there was nothing to cover them with. I had set sail in calm, warm waters and reckoned to squirrel away a large contingency once I'd reached a net asset value of around ten million pounds. This was the critical mass needed to secure the future of my business, but alas, the financial shitstorm hit me just before I got there. The water poured into the hatches and sank my ship in double-quick time. So why didn't I just go steady, I hear you ask. Because, if I was going to grow quickly, I had to take the risk; but it didn't pay off.

Ah, but the banks, I consoled myself, they nearly went bust too. But they got bailed out by the government! I didn't, and my property empire crumbled fast. I had ducked, dived, bobbed and weaved every which way to save my business, but there was no more to be done. It was over. Then, as I stared at the road before me, I asked myself if I even knew where I was going. Resigned to my failure, I reluctantly conceded that I probably wouldn't rise above the ordinary again as I'd always striven to do.

Having drawn a massive breath, I exhaled long and hard before turning the radio on to distract myself from my negative thoughts. As luck would have it, the news was about to start. That would focus my attention. The news reader began …

'It's one a.m. on the fifth of January and here are the headlines …'

Although a welcome distraction, the radio eventually made me sleepy, so when the services appeared, I pulled off the motorway and parked up directly outside Costa. Angie parked next to me. I jumped down from the cab and watched her alight. The yellowish car-park lights discoloured her face and made her grumpy, tired expression look almost menacing. The wind-driven cold drizzle didn't help her look.

'I'm knackered,' she declared through a big yawning stretch.

'I know what you mean,' I said, mimicking her stretch.

I asked her if she needed a nap.

'No, just the loo,' she replied sharply. 'And then let's just get there, shall we?'

'Sure,' I said with a nod.

My wife shook her head whilst telling me she couldn't believe I'd made her do a midnight flit.

'You put everything on the line,' she added angrily. 'And now we're running away!'

'You wanted to go to Devon,' I countered.

'Only because we're bankrupt and can't show our faces anymore.'

'Let's just grab a coffee and get on!' I scowled.

'You've put the whole family in jeopardy!' declared barrister Angie. 'And I'm picking up the fallout for your mistakes.'

'It's not about mistakes,' I replied through a heavy sigh.

'It's about stopping debt-collector thugs attacking us and protecting our arses as best we can.'

I looked away from my wife because I knew she was right. I was to blame. I felt worse than shit when the business went tits up. The ignominy and sense of failure were soul-destroying.

As I was thinking of a way to calm my wife down, she thrust her head towards me and reminded me that she was a high-flying barrister.

'I gave up my job to work in your stupid business,' she continued. 'And now I'm ruined.'

'You worked in a provincial chambers for heaven's sake,' I replied dismissively. 'That's hardly high-flying.'

'You bastard! How dare you?'

'I'm not doing this conversation, Angie!' I said, raising my voice, desperate for the solitude of my cab. 'Let's just get our coffees and fuck off.'

I locked the lorry and headed for Costa. Seconds later, I heard Angie's hurried footsteps heading my way. To avoid further argument, I veered sharply off to my left and watched her stomp over to the loo.

Whilst keeping an eye on the children through the glass doors, I purchased the coffees and then immediately went back to the lorry. Angie soon returned. Her face was tense and angry. I just knew she was going to pick up right where she'd left off. True to form, before I could even draw a breath to speak, she announced …

'Just getting our coffees and fucking off isn't gonna fix anything. Nothing! You got that? Nothing! You screwed up!'

'Don't you worry your pretty little head,' I retorted haughtily, keen to disguise my considerable self-doubt, 'I'm gonna make it all back again trading!'

Angie made no reply. Instead, she just stared at me. As I handed her latte to her, I braced myself for a tongue lashing. Mercifully though, she just sipped her coffee. I too sipped my coffee and was thinking of getting going when she suddenly insisted that my trading wasn't going to happen.

'You win, you lose, you win, you lose,' she scowled, 'and you spent money we could ill afford training in Chicago and Texas, and it hasn't paid off!'

'It will pay off,' I retorted. 'And I will make my millions back.'

'Only *your* millions?' said Angie, screwing her face up.

'Yes, *my* millions, because you always say I lost *my* business. So, *my* business, *my* millions!'

'They were *our* millions,' insisted my wife. 'I was a director of the company too,' she added, 'and I worked my arse off.'

I wanted the arguing to stop, but I knew it had to run its course, because when Angie and I started, we had to finish. I was always surprised at how we could both go from incredible feelings of love and adoration one minute, to attacking each other like scrapping dogs the next.

'I take full responsibility for losing the business,' I announced, filling the momentary silence. 'Does that make you feel better?'

'I'm cleverer than you and you don't like it,' retorted Angie. 'You feel inadequate.'

'*You're* the inadequate one,' I insisted, 'because London law firms rejected you. You think you have to prove yourself because your family's working class, your grandfather was a coalman and your grandmother thrice removed was in the workhouse. You've got a chip on your shoulder, woman.'

'You bastard!' yelled Angie, glaring at me angrily. 'You think you're so superior with your public school education, don't you?'

I made no reply. I just stood still and observed my wife's horrid, contorted face with contempt. After a short festering pause, she lunged at me and grabbed my collar.

'You've never loved me properly,' she growled, having pulled me down to her level. 'I wasn't good enough for you. I didn't speak right, but you were always very nice to that silly bitch Liz. Weren't you?'

'Not particularly.'

'You better not have fucked her,' added my red-faced wife, before pushing me away with her clenched fist.

'I never fucked Liz,' I retorted crossly, 'and I certainly don't wanna fuck you.'

'That's because I'm soiled goods,' responded Angie, with a look of disgust on her face, 'and not virtuous. And FYI,' she added, 'I was free to sleep with whoever I wanted to after Dom died!'

I didn't reply to my wife's statement, instead I just looked at her through unbelieving eyes as I again drew in a huge calming breath and let it out slowly. During that momentary silence, I contemplated our needless argument, which, as was often the case, had literally come from absolutely nowhere. It seemed like pent-up stuff was coming out – "tired and emotional" the catalyst.

'Sweetheart,' I eventually whispered, 'your husband died, and you went with another man, you really mustn't ...'

'You don't understand Rich,' interrupted Angie, her voice now anxious and pleading, 'I was in a terrible state after Dom died!'

'I'm sure you were,' I replied warmly, having realised it was time to stop all this nonsense.

'His family were horrible to me when he was dying,' she continued. 'They said I didn't care about him.'

'I know Angie, and they were bastards for saying that.'

'And Dominic's bitch of a sister said I was eyeing up other men to take his place.'

'That was just plain nasty of her. She had no right to suggest you'd go on to disrespect Dom's memory.'

At this point, Angie got in my face and glared at me with Robert De Niro style contempt on her face.

'Go on to disrespect Dom's memory?' she growled.

I swallowed hard, and then tried to explain that my words came out all wrong.

'I simply meant that they had no right to suggest that you *had* disrespected Dom's memory,' I said, 'because you actually hadn't done anything wrong at that time.'

'At that time?' repeated my wife, 'you're judging me, you bastard, aren't you?'

'If you say so,' I retorted, now fed up with having my words twisted.

'I was free to see whoever I liked,' countered my wife. 'I'd just lost my husband for God's sake, what was I supposed to do?'

Probably not sleep with another man before Dom was even cold in his grave, I thought to myself.

Desperate to hold my tongue, I just stared back at my wife and said nothing.

'I needed someone!' she suddenly announced, filling the momentary silence.

'Of course you did,' I retorted sarcastically, as my emotions got the better of me, 'some expert planning wallah you worked with on a case – must have been very cosy.'

I now braced myself for an earbashing, but to my surprise, Angie just looked down at the ground and sipped her latte. There was silence. Then, as I drank my Americano, I observed the depressing, wet car park, and shook my head in disbelief at the raging argument which had literally come from nowhere. Yet I knew that talking about my wife's past always turned nasty. Why? Because, despite getting on her moral high horse about other women's reprehensible sexual behaviour, she couldn't admit her own moral failing to herself, even though she desperately wanted to. The net result of all this, was that my wife cornered herself into defending the indefensible, i.e. her own transgressions.

With my psychoanalysis complete, I refocused my attention on Angie. She looked up at me through warm eyes. Her loving self had now suddenly returned. Having reached up to stroke my cheek with the back of her hand she said …

'We always stumble over this Rich, and we don't have to.'

'I'm not stumbling Angie.'

'But you *do* stumble Rich. Your Black Dog always comes out when we talk about my past.'

'Well then why bring it up?'

'Because it's there in the background.'

'What do you want from me exactly?' I demanded, feeling frustrated.

'I need you to love me without judging me,' replied my wife, as she continued to stroke my face. 'I need you to love me unconditionally.'

'This is a conversation for another time Angie,' I replied flatly, removing her hand from my face.

Then, without saying another word, I jumped into the

lorry and drove off as fast as I could, leaving Angie to catch up. I pulled onto the motorway wound up like a spring in a clockwork toy.

Why did she have to bring all this shit up now? I asked myself.

The upset had produced enough adrenaline to turbo charge me all the way to Devon, making my Costa caffeine completely redundant.

Changing into fifth gear, I wriggled my bum into the back of my seat before taking a deep breath to calm myself down. Having dismissed all thoughts about my wife's past, I looked over at Connor who was fast asleep with his head on a cushion pressed up against the passenger door. I then nodded in thoughtful appreciation of the lovely vista of my Archie resting against his brother, also fast asleep.

With my attention fully back on the road, my mind quietened for a moment until the demon voice inside me reared his ugly head.

You idiot, he scowled, in his grating cockney accent, you could've retired three years ago with a couple of mill in the bank. But no, you wanted to creep into The Times Rich List. You wanted to prove you could do something if you put your mind to it, but you failed and let your wife down badly. And now she's never going to have faith in you again. She's gonna lose interest and leave you for a better man.

'But she's my inspiration,' I whispered out loud. 'What would I be without her?'

I swallowed hard at that thought and then flashed my hazards to say hi. My Angie flashed back. I was pleased she did, I desperately needed to know we were still okay.

* * *

At close to five in the morning, I parked up in the driveway of Hope House and turned the engine off. As I looked out into the darkness, I suddenly felt uneasy about this new chapter in our lives, but I didn't know why exactly. Keen to distract myself from my negative thoughts, I jumped down from my cab and stood next to Angie who had parked up alongside me.

'Bloody hell!' I said, through a big yawn. 'That was a hell of a drive.'

'It was,' said Angie, before pulling my fleece open and burying her head in my chest.

Pleased at that, I hugged my wife warmly, even though I was still a little upset with her. My upset was tempered by the fact that I knew her mantra was, "attack is the best form of defence". This meant she often said things she didn't really mean. Even so, it was no fun being on the receiving end of that.

After a few moments of quiet contemplation, Angie suddenly inhaled loudly and then held me at arm's length.

'Can you smell that, Rich?' she asked in an excited whisper.

'Smell what?'

'The sea!'

I sniffed hard.

'Yes,' I replied softly.

She then cocked her head to one side with a look of concentration.

'Can you hear that, Rich?' she asked.

'Hear what?'

'The sea.'

I listened intently and tuned into the sound of breaking waves.

'Oh my God, yes, I can.'

'We're going to be so happy here with the children,' whispered my wife.

'For sure,' I whispered back.

'And I'm sorry for what I said at the services,' she added, taking hold of my hands. 'I know you did your level best and I really do think you'll succeed again.'

I nodded in reply whilst squeezing my lovely wife's hands. And then, after an easy silence, I gazed into her eyes.

'You know what sweetheart?' I said, sotto voce, forcing my uneasiness aside. 'This move is our Golden Ticket to Willy Wonka's chocolate factory.'

'You know what Rich? replied Angie. 'I think you're right.'

CHAPTER 3

As I awoke, my eyes were greeted by the Devon morning light filtering through the curtains of the master bedroom at Hope House. All was quiet, except for Angie's light snoring, and the rhythmical breathing coming from Archie and Phoebe, who were sandwiched between us. Having slowly unzipped my sleeping bag, I got up off the floor, tiptoed to the south window and half drew the curtains aside. As I pulled a huge stretch, I caught sight of the ocean in the distance beyond the rolling patchwork countryside. That made me feel good, despite my lack of sleep.

Letting out a quiet, contented sigh, I nodded my head appreciatively.

'Here we are,' I whispered under my breath, 'a wonderful new beginning in God's own country. Thank you, Lord.'

With my mindfulness musings complete, I looked at my watch and realised I needed to rally the troops to help unload the lorry, so I could return it to the hire company in Surrey before close of business.

Having tiptoed back over to Angie, I knelt down and shook her lightly. It was a perfunctory wake-up. As ever, my ability to "let go and move on" had failed me, so I remained a bit distant. I sometimes thought I was a bit too sensitive, and desperately wished I could toughen up. But sadly, Angie's heart crushing and soul-destroying remarks had an increasingly injurious effect on me. It sometimes took me a couple of days to get over these episodes. She, however, was lucky enough to bounce back pretty much straight away.

'Angie,' I whispered flatly, 'we have to get going. I'm gonna wake Connor and Livy to help unload the lorry. Will you make us some breakfast?'

'Of course,' said Angie, before sitting up to stretch and yawn.

She then extended her hand to me, but I backed away, and slipped into my jeans and rugby top. As I pulled my socks on, I wished I could have woken my wife lovingly, but for that I needed reassurance. My Black Dog, that horrid, fitful insecurity about Angie's love for me, naturally made matters even worse.

As I was leaving the room, my wife called out to me. 'Richie!'

'Yes,' I replied, turning round.

'I love you and I'm really sorry for saying those nasty things – I really didn't mean a word I said.'

My Angie's simple heartfelt apology instantly banished my upset, and I once again warmed to her with all my heart.

'Thanks my love,' I replied softly, before returning to bid her a proper good morning, and welcome her to her new home with a loving kiss.

* * *

At 11 a.m. I stepped out into a beautiful crisp, bright winter's morning with Connor and Olivia in tow. Our house was isolated – no neighbours for half a mile. Fantastic! We could make as much noise as we liked. I valued isolation for that reason, and the acre garden and the open fields which surrounded us on all sides, provided a truly fantastic setting for our idyllic new home.

'Look at the big trees, Dad!' Connor blurted out excitedly. 'Can we climb them?'

'Of course, and I'm going right to the top!' I insisted convincingly.

'No way Dadda,' commanded Olivia. 'It's dangerous!'

'Ahhh … Livy my princess,' I sighed, before kissing the top of her head as I embraced her, 'you really are Dadda's little angel.'

I then suddenly held her at arm's length and screwed my face up.

'Phew! What's that smell?' I demanded. 'Have you farted?'

Olivia gave me "the look". Her head tilted to one side, her striking rich, big blue eyes staring up at me, and her brow furrowed.

'Jeez, you look just like your mother,' I said. 'You're scaring me!'

'Be sensible Dadda,' she insisted, like she was telling a five-year-old off.

I loved my kids telling me to be sensible. I loved acting my shoe size and behaving more like a child than they did. They loved it too.

'Right! You 'orrible little lot,' I barked in my regimental sergeant major's voice, 'jump up on the tailgate and pull the shutter up. And watch out for falling boxes!'

Whilst the children clambered up onto the half-raised tailgate, I sighed with relief and contentment, pleased that my Angie was happy. I then looked skyward, extended my arms out like the almighty himself, and declared …

'The beginning of a wonderful new chapter!'

The children were used to my melodramatic antics, and so paid me no attention whatsoever.

'Mum promised we'd go to the beach today,' said Livy. 'Will we need to unload the whole lorry before we go?'

'Yes,' I replied, 'but we'll be done in a couple of hours.'

'Cool,' said Livy, before eyeing the vista from the tailgate. 'I'm gonna miss my friends,' she added thoughtfully, 'but I guess we can keep in touch on Facebook.'

I nodded in agreement and then jumped up onto the tailgate to begin unloading.

Despite their age and size, my two apprentices proved very capable removers. They made light work of carrying their end of the sofa into the sitting room. It had windows on three sides, a lovely polished wooden floor and a nook, where our Georgian secretaire chest of drawers would go.

Within half an hour, we'd made significant inroads into unloading the bigger items, and decided it was time for breakfast. We all ventured into the kitchen and were enthusiastically greeted by Mum. It was a wonderful farmhouse kitchen with old-fashioned pine units standing on turned wooden legs, a Victorian dresser, and a handsome warm green Aga along the back wall. The red polished quarry-tiled floor completed the rustic look.

I sat on a kitchen chair and watched my beautiful wife mothering our children as they excitedly recounted their morning's work. She congratulated them on a job well done and, as breakfast wasn't quite ready, they skipped off to join Archie and Phoebe, who were playing in the den.

'Breakfast won't be long!' Mum sang after them.

When things were right between us, my Angie was a

very happy soul. She seldom whinged and just cracked on. I loved that about her.

With my eyes fixed on my wife, I walked over to her and drew her close to me. She wrapped her arms round my waist and, as usual, buried her head in my chest. Having breathed in hard she whispered …

'I love your smell Rich; it calms and reassures me. And I feel so protected and secure when you hold me like this.'

'And I love protecting you,' I responded, 'and will *always* protect you, no matter what.'

'I know,' said my wife, 'but if I'm honest, I'm a bit scared right now.'

'Is it the financial uncertainty?' I asked, grimacing with guilt.

'Yes.'

Holding my Angie a little tighter, I told her we were two clever people who could achieve anything if we put our minds to it. But, if the truth be known, I actually didn't believe that. Now, more than at any time in the past, I was fighting with the ever-present demon voice in my head, who was turning more demonic as days went by. And the more I tried not to let him have a voice, the louder he became.

After a short pause, my wife suddenly pulled away from me. Then, holding me at arm's length, she enthusiastically announced that she could get a job in Sainsbury's.

'Only until I'm discharged from bankruptcy that is.'

'Whatever makes you happy,' I said. 'But there's no rush because we've paid the rent upfront.'

'That's true,' replied a thoughtful Angie. 'Maybe we should stop and smell the roses,' she added, 'albeit on a budget.'

I nodded and smiled in response, and then listened as

my wife told me she was happy, but down at the same time.

'I'm happy we've moved,' she explained, 'but my confidence and self-esteem aren't what they used to be. I'm a fat middle-aged woman, who's past her best before date. I'm invisible to men,' she added, 'and I just don't feel good about myself anymore.'

'Don't be silly Angie,' I said, looking deep into her eyes, 'you're gorgeous and sexy with all the right curves in all the right places.'

'*You* think that because *you* love me,' she replied, before snuggling back into me.

'Sweetheart,' I said, 'you've been a wonderful wife for sixteen years, a fantastic mum to our four babies, and a brilliant hard-working business partner. You're amazing!'

'Sure,' she said, 'but I was all of those things for *other* people, but what about me? My *forgotten me*.'

'But what else is there?' I asked.

Easing back a little, my wife took hold of my hands and looked up at me with thoughtful eyes. She then suggested that her time had come, because the business was gone, and the kids were at school.

'Your time?' I questioned.

'Yes,' said Angie. 'Like I said, it's time for my *forgotten me* to blossom.'

'But what is your *forgotten me?*' I asked, wrinkling my nose.

'I just want to be me, for *me!*' responded my wife. 'And as I said before,' she added, 'I don't want to be invisible anymore!'

'But what does that mean exactly Angie?'

'It means,' she replied, 'that I want to be noticed and feel desired as a woman. Most girls like that if they're honest with themselves.'

'But Angie darling,' I said warmly, 'you only have to give me a sexy look and I get a raging hard-on for you.'

'But it's not all about *you* getting a raging hard-on for me,' she responded, 'is it?'

Frustrated at not being able to say the right thing, I thought it best to say nothing, because I clearly didn't understand my wife at all. Instead, I just asked her what else she wanted from her *forgotten me.*

'I'm not entirely sure,' she replied, 'it's just a feeling that there's more to life than just being a stay-at-home mum and wife.'

'Well, whatever it is,' I responded warmly, 'we'll make it happen!'

'Aww,' sighed Angie, 'thank you.'

With that said, she cupped my face in her hands and looked up at me through brimming eyes. She then buried her head in my chest again and hugged me tight. I felt so loved as we embraced each other in comfortable silence.

After a short while, my lovely wife suddenly backed away from me.

'I'll need to lose weight,' she announced, 'if I'm to blossom. Will you be my personal trainer?'

'Of course.'

'Thank you my big man. That means the world to me.'

With the sizzling bacon needing attention, Angie stepped over to the grill, and I rested my bum against the kitchen worktop. As I watched her making breakfast, I noted how these moments warmed my heart and soul beyond words. This was the beauty I craved so much. But just recently, and particularly since our financial crisis, this sublime happiness would disappear quite unexpectedly, and then

BAM! We'd suddenly be at an emotional rock bottom. Angie called me her roller coaster. Desperate to avoid the lows, I hoped I could learn to give her my love the way she wanted me to, *all* the time, so we could live happily ever after. And I sensed that was well within my grasp, now that the stress of running a huge business had gone.

I was brought out of my musings when the children came bounding into the kitchen talking excitedly. I dropped to my knees to embrace the little ones.

'Come see!' enthused Phoebe, as she tugged my hand.

'You're not gonna believe this, Dad!' said Connor.

'Oh wow!' I responded, 'I can't wait.'

As I was led away, I looked back at Angie. She was watching the scene unfold with a beautiful smile made of pure contentment.

Yesss! This is it, I thought to myself, our future is bright, and you can go and fuck yourself demon voice!

* * *

Having set the last of the boxes down in the hallway, I ventured into the kitchen.

'All done!' I announced through a big sigh.

Angie straightened up from the box she was unpacking and smiled at me.

'Well done you,' she said, before grimacing sympathetically. 'Shame you have to return the lorry to Surrey today.'

'It is sweetheart,' I replied, 'but the sooner I get going, the sooner I'll be back.'

'Give me a minute,' said Angie, 'and I'll make you a coffee and a sandwich for the journey.'

I nodded in response, and then disappeared to the loo.

Upon returning to the kitchen, my amazing wife handed me a carrier bag with my flask and sandwich in.

'What's your ETA at Plymouth?' she asked.

'I'm not sure at the moment,' I replied. 'I'll text you when I'm on the train, but it's going to be late.'

'No worries,' said Angie. 'The little ones will be asleep, so I'll leave Livy in charge.'

I smiled in response and then moved in for a hug. After a loving embrace, my wife eased away from me.

'Children!' she called out. 'Dadda's just about to leave. Come say goodbye.'

A moment later, I heard the stampede of children headed my way. With a kiss and a cuddle for each of them in turn, I said my goodbyes and made my way to the lorry. My lovely family followed me out. As I carefully eased the truck out of the drive and onto the track which led to the road, I was sent on my way with energetic waves and cries of 'byeeee!' I called 'byeeee' back and smiled to myself before letting out a long, contented sigh. I then wriggled back into my seat to get comfortable for my three-hour drive back to Surrey.

CHAPTER 4

It was day two of our new life, and we'd already settled into Hope House, which stood on top of a hill overlooking Hope Harbour.

In the morning, Angie and I dropped the children to school and headed into town to pick up a prescription for Archie's eczema cream. As we wended our way through the narrow country lanes with me at the wheel of our trusty Sharan, I sensed that Angie was a little pensive and asked her if she was alright.

'Well,' she said, 'if I'm honest, I sometimes feel judged and that I'm not your priority. That makes me feel like you don't love me properly.'

Reluctant to explain her part in that equation, I simply told my wife that I loved her.

'You know that don't you?' I added warmly.

'True love,' she responded, 'is supposed to be unconditional!'

'But I *do* love you unconditionally,' I replied, 'and I would give my life for you in an instant.'

At this point Angie and I fell silent. I needed to prove my love for her beyond any shadow of a doubt, but how could I do that? Nothing came to mind, so I asked her to think of some extreme thing that would categorically prove my love for her.

'Really?' she questioned, widening her eyes.

'Yes. And make it as weird and as wonderful as you like,' I responded in a cockney voice. 'I can't say fairer than that, darlin'!'

As I negotiated the narrow country lanes down into Hope Harbour, I could hear the cogs going round in Angie's head. A moment later, she suddenly blurted out her answer.

'Let me sleep with another man without judging me,' she said.

'Are you serious?!' I responded through an unbelieving laugh.

'Maybe, maybe not,' replied my red-faced wife.

'Is this part of you finding yourself,' I asked. 'You know, you're *forgotten me?*'

'Maybe, maybe not,' she again replied, before hurriedly turning her gaze away from me.

'I can picture it now,' I said. 'You would get all dressed up and I would send you off with a kiss and say, "have a nice evening darling", just like in the film *Indecent Proposal.*'

'Yes, just like in the film, and *I'd* be the prize!'

'We'd get a million dollars, Angie, and I'd be your pimp!'

'No, you wouldn't!' she insisted. 'Because *I* would get to choose the guy. And the million dollars would be all mine!' she added, as she drew her extended arms into her body, like she was gathering a mountain of casino chips at a roulette table.

'Ooh, get you!' I said in a camp voice, before pressing play on the CD.

As Spandau Ballet's *True* filled the air, Angie sang along.

Would she actually feel properly loved if I supported her having sex with another man? Although I could see why she would think that was the ultimate test of love, it made me question things.

After '*True*' faded out, I reached over and turned the volume down.

'Angieee,' I sang, drawing her name out like a five-year-old wanting sweeties.

'Yesss?' she sang back.

'Wouldn't sleeping with another guy make you feel bad? You know, like you were breaking our marriage vows.'

'Not if you truly supported me,' she replied, having shifted around on her bum to look at me. 'The point is,' she continued, 'that it's something you'd naturally judge me on, like you did with my previous relationships.'

I nodded in response, and then listened as my wife told me that not judging her would prove my unconditional love beyond any shadow of a doubt.

'So, you'd be taking one for the team then?' I suggested sarcastically. 'To prove a point?'

'Ha-ha,' responded Angie.

Sensing that the *Indecent Proposal* scenario was somehow related to our conversation about her *forgotten me,* I asked my wife if her personal training was about her getting ready to go with another man.

'Don't be silly,' she replied dismissively. 'It was one hundred per cent hypothetical. I literally just made that up in response to your question.'

My wife then went on to explain that she had no interest in sleeping with any other man, and that getting in better shape was about her feeling more confident.

'And is feeling more confident connected to what you said yesterday?' I asked. 'You know, about being noticed and feeling like a woman.'

'I dunno,' said Angie, 'probably.'

'So, more male attention makes you feel good about yourself,' I said. 'Correct?'

'Hark at Sigmund Freud,' said a smiling Angie. 'But yes, you're right. And they'd have to be good-looking,' she added, 'otherwise it would be creepy.'

I smiled and nodded in response. Then, feeling insecure, I asked her if she would *actually* take money for sex.

'Not like a prostitute!' she replied, screwing her face up in disgust.

'Shame,' I joked. 'We could use the money!'

'But don't get me wrong,' she continued, 'I love the idea of a sexy man paying a million dollars for me, just because I'm that attractive to him.'

'Yeah?'

'Yeah. And it would be nice to be romanced,' she added. 'You know, dinner on a yacht and being seduced.'

'And then you'd come home to me?'

'Yes of course. And that would be a wonderful homecoming.'

'Why?'

'Because I'd love you all the more for not judging me.'

'Sure,' I said. 'But I couldn't deal with you coming back to me with another man's semen inside of you.'

'Oh Rich,' sighed Angie. 'You're so base!'

As I smiled at my wife's reaction to my primal response, she went on to say that the *Indecent Proposal* thing was just a random thought which came to mind, and that I shouldn't read anything into it.

We then fell silent again, and whilst I watched the countryside fly by, I began to wonder who my wife would choose to sleep with in real life. For the sake of having a bit of fanciful fun, I asked the question. She immediately told me that it would be her old salsa partner Dave, because she liked him, and he *definitely* liked her. I asked her how she knew that.

'Because he always went hard for me when we danced together,' she replied, having gone red in the face.

'No way!' I responded, as my Black Dog of jealousy and insecurity went ballistic, whilst an erection inexplicably appeared in my jeans. 'Why have you never told me that?'

'Because you would've stopped me going to salsa,' retorted my wife.

'So did you actually fancy Dave then?' I asked. 'And be honest.'

'Yes,' she replied.

'So you're being honest now, Angie,' I said sharply, 'but you weren't then.'

'I'm sorry,' she said, before straightening in her seat, 'but I didn't do anything wrong, and I wouldn't have done anything wrong. It was just a bit of innocent flirting – that's all.'

Having inhaled hard, I then released Black Dog into the ether on the exhale, and felt my erection subside. We were both quiet for a moment, until my wife suddenly announced that it was quite normal for spouses to fancy other people, and that it was, in fact, healthy.

'Much better than being deceitful,' she added.

Having nodded in agreement, I then asked her if she thought Dave's behaviour inappropriate because she was married.

'No,' she replied, 'because salsa is a sexy dance, and I was flattered.'

'So did you get tingly and wet when you were dirty dancing with Dave?' I asked through a pained grimace, even though I didn't want to.

'Oh God yeah,' replied Angie, her face now redder than beetroot. 'And I did my fair share of bumping and grinding too,' she added, before telling me that she was being completely honest with me just like I'd asked her to be.

I got the impression that my wife thought her brutal honesty somehow mitigated, or even excused her wrongdoing. It didn't. Outraged, I white-knuckled my grip on the steering wheel. At the same time, I became aware that my penis had gone hard again, but I didn't know why. And then, before I could react to my wife's revelations, she told me she was always horny for me when she got back from dancing.

I guess she thought me getting something out of her twice-weekly bump and grind, also excused her actions. Just as I was trying to get my head round her attempt to minimise her behaviour, we arrived at the chemist.

As I searched for a parking space, I decided not to reproach Angie about Dave, because that would be seen as judging her. And the whole point of this conversation was about *not* judging her.

Having drawn to a halt, I asked my wife if she wanted me to wait for her.

'It's okay,' she replied. 'I've got a few bits to pick up, and then I'll walk home. But thanks anyway.'

With that said, she rubbed my thigh reassuringly, and then, looking down at her hand, she noticed the bulge in my jeans and squeezed it.

'Wow!' she exclaimed widening her eyes. 'Where did that come from?'

With something of a smug smile on her face, she leant over and pecked me on the lips. She then hurriedly alighted from the car and disappeared into the chemist.

Sitting quietly for a moment with the engine still running, I stared into space as the cogs went round in my head. Angie and I had actually had a meaningful, yet extremely disturbing conversation. Still deep in thought, and with my erection faded, I pulled away.

On the drive home, I replayed our exchange. That made me wonder whether Angie had slept with Dave. I mean, she'd danced with him every Monday and Thursday night for three years. Dancing from half seven till ten, with a cosy drink in the bar after. The thought of my wife having cheap sex with Dave sent my heart racing and, to my surprise, my cock went hard, yet again!

'Sleeping with another man was just hypothetical,' I said out loud.

Nah, scoffed my cockney inner demon. First off, your wife wasn't being a hundred per cent truthful with you. She told you just enough to appear honest, to see if you would judge her badly or not. The fact of the matter is that she's probably been shagging Dave on the side for ages. Loads of women get nearly all they want at home, but not excitement. And secondly, it wasn't a hypothetical conversation. Your wife wants to be who she really is deep down. She wants to be desired and wants the wicked excitement which comes with eating forbidden fruit. And now that Dave's off the scene, she wants a new naughty thrill.

I parked up at Hope House and slammed back into my seat with a big sigh.

What was going on in my wife's head? The thought of her *actually* wanting another man really troubled me. And, despite her assertion that this whole thing was hypothetical, I got the feeling she'd be up for a bit of fun on the side.

That made me think that proving my love for her was just an excuse to shag someone else.

With my unwanted erection now gone, I got out of the car and made my way to the outhouse office. Having fallen into my desk chair, I told myself to be grateful for Angie's honesty. Sitting back, I gazed out of the window into the grey January day outside and wondered what my wife's *forgotten me* actually meant for my marriage going forward.

At first, it seemed to be all about rebuilding her confidence after we were forced to go bankrupt when *I* lost the business. I was certainly okay with building her confidence, but the thought of her wanting to sleep with someone else, for whatever reason, suddenly made me anxious.

Quite bizarrely, my wife's desire for another man made me hard again. I now wanted to possess *my* woman sexually. Overwhelmed by my unwelcome, yet incredibly demanding jealous erection, and in the absence of being able to make love to my wife, I lifted my bum off my seat and pulled my jeans down at speed. My raging hard-on pinged up purposefully. With unwanted images of Angie dirty dancing with Dave in my head, I became angry. With my anger, came an even greater sexual arousal. Incredibly, within seconds rather than minutes, I was ready to come. And to my amazement, my ejaculation was more powerful than usual. Semen spurted out of my cock like a fountain, spraying my desk in the process.

I sighed with relief. Relief that Black Dog had been placated by satisfying the sexual need he'd stimulated in me. Then, as I wiped the semen off my desk with a tissue, I again wondered what my wife's *forgotten me* actually meant. And even if sleeping with Dave was just a hypothetical scenario to make a point, I felt that Angie's *forgotten me* was somehow going to bite us on the bum in the not-too-distant future.

CHAPTER 5

Two weeks had now passed since Angie and I had our bizarre chat in the car about unconditional love, and her shenanigans with her former dance partner, Dave. Following that conversation, I became very jealous and insecure. I mean, when you learn that your wife's salsa partner gyrated his hard-on against her nigh-on twice a week for three years, it is something of a shock to the system.

For a few days after Angie's revelations, I viewed her actions as deceitful. I then realised that she simply failed to mention something to me, as opposed to actually lying to me. I know that's a moot point, but all in all, I felt it best to side-line Black Dog and simply accept my wife's actions for what they were – a little bit of innocent flirting, which made her feel good about herself. And on top of that, we all know that salsa is sexy and, like in Strictly Come Dancing, dance partners often get involved. But my Angie didn't – she always came home to me. Plus, she was always horny as hell when she got back, which meant *we* had great sex together. So, my wife's dirty dancing was win-win for us both, as opposed to something to judge her on. A classic case of accentuating the positives, rather than dwelling on undue negatives.

And as to my concerns that Angie had actually slept with Dave, and that she wanted to sleep with someone else to prove I loved her; well, I'd stopped fretting about all that too. I realised that Black Dog and demon voice had created a terror picture in my own mind. And what was it Mark Twain said? I spent a lot of time worrying about things that never actually happened.

So, with all of the above in mind, I now had a clear head, and had stopped to smell the roses. As I did so, I quietly celebrated the fact that the stress of the collapse of my business had now largely faded. Only a little residual fallout persisted, such as bailiffs (but no thugs thank God) turning up at our front door unannounced. We would waive the bankruptcy papers in their faces, and they would tootle off and leave us alone.

It is fair to say that Angie and I had worked hard to build up our business and to raise our ever-increasing family. By contrast, it was something of a relief not to be running around at a hundred miles an hour anymore. On the other hand, it was quite a shock to find that in early middle age, we had no material wealth, relied on benefits, and claimed free school meals for our children. I felt that bringing home the bacon was my job, which hurt; but despite that, we were happy.

All in all, our fresh start in Hope Harbour was wonderful. The only thing that needed work, other than rebuilding our family finances, was Angie's lack of confidence and self-esteem, which I'd seriously undermined by losing my business. I needed to put that right. That meant supporting her in every possible way without question, despite my reservations.

CHAPTER 6

Two months after moving to Hope House …
Upon arrival at the gym, membership of which was a thoughtful housewarming gift from my nephew, we purposefully marched over to the bikes. Acting like you meant business was part of the psyche of working out. I'd designed a tough regime for Angie, and once I got her started, she worked hard and was determined to succeed. Her number one priority was fat burning.

An hour later, a red-faced Angie and I left the gym and skipped across the car park, hand in hand.

We then jumped into the VW and, as we pulled onto the road, Angie told me that I'd worked wonders with her.

'I was looking at myself in the mirror,' she added, 'and I've come a long way.'

'You have,' I said, 'and you've worked really hard.'

'I'd like to think so,' responded Angie.

Having parked up at home, my wife took hold of my hand en route to the back door and swung it back and forth like an excited five-year-old out with daddy.

'Just look at this place Rich,' she enthused, pulling me to a stop before gesturing to the vista over Hope Harbour. 'I'm so glad we moved here and left all that shit behind us.'

'Too right!' I replied. 'And we've never been happier.'

'I know, it's lovely,' said Angie, with a look of contentment. 'And I love being a wife and mum.'

'And what about your *forgotten me?*' I asked.

'Well yeah,' she replied, 'I feel much better about myself, and that's a great start.'

'Not invisible to men anymore then?' I questioned with a cheeky smile.

'No,' said my wife, 'in fact, I've been getting some approving looks, and I'm actually starting to feel sexy again!'

'So, is this the blossoming of your *forgotten me* then?' I asked.

'It's part of it,' replied my wife, 'but like I said before, it's just a sense that there's more to life than just being a wife and mum. But to achieve that,' she added, 'I have to feel valued as a woman in my own right.'

'Sure,' I replied, still none the wiser as to what my wife actually wanted from life.

Then, as we momentarily admired the view in silence, it occurred to me that money would probably play a part in my Angie's blossoming. With that in mind, I told her I'd be ready to start live trading in a few months.

'Great!' she enthused, 'get those profits rolling in Rich, and then we can get our old life back again.'

'Consider it a fait accompli,' I responded enthusiastically, keen not to allow my uncertainty to show.

With that said, I let go of my Angie's hand and told her I was going straight to the office.

'Sure,' she said, 'I'll bring you a cuppa later.'

I smiled in response and then watched her make her way into the house before suddenly calling out after her.

'Yes?' she said, turning round to face me.

'Nothing,' I replied through a soppy grin. 'I just wanted

one more look at that gorgeous face of yours.'

'Aww,' sighed my wife, before smiling her beautiful smile at me.

She then continued on her way, whilst I floated over to the outhouse office, still grinning with delight.

As I waited for my computer to fire up, the huge black and white cat we'd inherited with Hope House, slinked by my half open window. The kids had named him Jack.

'Hey puss puss,' I called out.

Jack gave me a haughty stare and then continued on his way.

Smiling to myself, I grabbed a Post-it pad with my old company logo on, and began writing feverishly to capture my feelings …

High on life with my darling wife
Having come through much trouble and strife

High on life having made safe shore
We don't fight with anyone anymore

High on life with our children so close
My dear Lord gave us a happiness dose

High on life our great future is set
You betcha mate – we've no more debt!

I smiled as I read my infantile poem out loud and added it to a pile of other jottings in my drawer. I then logged into my US trading account and began analysing the markets in readiness to place my first practice trade of the day.

CHAPTER 7

At around 10 a.m. on a school day morning, our neighbours John and Charlotte Fortescue popped over to introduce themselves with a delicious homemade apple pie. We chatted for a couple of hours over coffee. I liked Charlotte straight away. Her blonde shoulder-length bob framed her pretty, round, milky-white face, with its sparkling green eyes and megawatt smile. I loved her ample breasts with matching arse. You'd never know she was approaching the big five-oh. John, her toy boy at five years younger, was a stocky five foot ten. He was a reserved man with a mop of salt and pepper hair which just sat on his head in no particular style. His rugged face was made even more attractive by his bright blue eyes and powerful posh voice.

We all got on very well, and Angie and I took great pleasure in accepting our neighbour's kind invitation to join them at their forthcoming dinner party.

* * *

Having left Livy in charge at home, and with the two little ones tucked up in bed, Angie and I left for Charlotte and John's house. As we walked toward their front door in the light of an early spring moon, I stopped to admire the robust handsomeness of their Georgian stone farmhouse, with its imposing chimneys soaring boldly into the night sky. At this point, Angie stepped in front of me and looked me up and down. She then straightened the collar of my white shirt before undoing the button of my tailored blue jacket.

'Perfect,' she said. 'Your beige chinos and brown brogues were the right choice,' she added, before slipping her Ted Baker coat off, to hang it over her arm. 'How do I look?' she asked nervously.

I stepped back and smiled as I admired my beautiful wife. 'Wow! Sexy!'

'I don't look tarty, do I?' she responded. 'You know, my dress isn't too short, is it?'

'No darling, it's just the right length to showcase your shapely legs.'

'And the black stockings?' she urgently questioned. 'Should I change into the nude ones I've got in my bag?'

'Hell no,' I replied, 'black is perfect with your red frock and black shoes and handbag.'

'It's a cocktail dress Rich!' retorted my wife. 'Not a frock.'

She then wanted to know if she looked too lumpy-bumpy round the middle. In response, I reminded her that she'd told me I'd done wonders with her. 'You look amazing!' I added enthusiastically. 'So please stop fretting and relax.'

My Angie nodded and smiled in reply, before taking a big breath and strutting purposefully on. I was pleased to see her confident persona emerge.

Having banged the heavy brass door knocker against its strike plate, we received a warm greeting from a smiling Charlotte. And then, when we stepped into the hall, John appeared.

'Welcome!' he said in his deep voice, before relieving Angie of her coat to greet her with a hug. He then shook my hand and told me he was going to steal my wife for a moment to answer a legal question.

'Music to my ears!' I replied enthusiastically.

Angie air-slapped me round my ear before latching on to John's arm. They then disappeared down the hall together. I sat on their monk's bench to retie my shoelace.

'So, how's you Charlotte?' I asked.

'Much better thanks.'

'How do you mean, better?'

'Well, you remember I told you I was made redundant when we were chatting at yours?'

'Yes.'

'Well, it knocked me for six.'

'I'm not surprised,' I said, before standing up. 'They say not to take it personally, but it's bloody hard not to.'

'You're not wrong there,' agreed Charlotte, 'my self-esteem plummeted, and on top of that, our tenant wouldn't pay his rent.'

'Jesus!' I said through a grimace. 'It never rains but it pours.'

'You can say that again.'

'At least you have your health,' I suggested. 'I always say health is wealth.'

'Sadly, not my mental health,' responded Charlotte. 'I had to see a counsellor.'

'Did you?'

'Yes. Julia Phillips in Plymouth. She's brilliant!'

'Really? These shrinks actually work?' I said, with more than a hint of disbelief in my voice.

'They do Rich, but she's not really a shrink. She's more

of a spiritual counsellor.'

'Well, she's obviously very good Charlotte, because you look absolutely fabulous!'

'Ahh Rich,' she sighed, 'you know how to flatter a girl.'

'That'll be a fiver then,' I said, holding my hand out with a smile.

'You're a cheeky one!' replied Charlotte, smiling back at me. 'C'mon ,' she added, slipping her arm in mine, 'let's get this party started!'

Having walked into the sitting room, Charlotte and I joined John and his friend Malcolm, who were talking through a legal issue with Angie. Once that boring bit was out of the way, Angie and I circulated and chatted with ease. Lots of banter and jokes. I was the funny guy, and Angie played the stooge to great effect. We were quite the comedy duo.

After a number of pre-dinner drinks, we all gathered around the dining table. In addition to me and Angie, and John and Charlotte, there was Ryan and his wife Amy, who was a bit mousey. There was another couple as well, John's retired colleague, Malcolm, the one with the legal question, and his wife Jenny. They didn't say much at all. Ryan, Angie, Charlotte and I largely held court, with Ryan topping the bill with entertaining stories from his acting days.

With the dinner party in full flow, we munched our way through Charlotte's impressive cooking.

Once we'd finished our pudding, there was a lull in the conversation. At this point John invited us to watch a funny video he'd uploaded to YouTube. Ryan remained seated and continued to chat with Angie.

John's computer was in his small study just off the dining room. We all piled in. I stood by the doorway with a view of both the computer screen and the dining room. I could see Angie merrily chatting away to Ryan out of the corner of my eye. He was about six foot two, good-looking with swept back dark, wavy hair. He was even featured with blue eyes which stood out against his tanned complexion.

I was hoping Angie would look up so I could wave at her, but she didn't notice me. I was nevertheless pleased she was enjoying herself and obviously feeling more confident.

'This is it chaps,' John announced.

I turned to look at the screen and waited for the funny bit. It was a video of a pheasant shoot John was on. It went on for quite a while and wasn't particularly funny. I was getting bored and so looked over to Angie. I saw Ryan step over to John's bookcase to pick out a book. And as he did so, I noticed Angie pull her dress down a bit to reveal her cleavage and the lace of her black bra. My heart leapt into my mouth as I watched intently to see what unfolded. It felt wrong checking up on my wife, but I couldn't stop myself.

Angie was originally seated opposite Ryan but had now moved to sit beside him to look at the book he had placed on the table. She was unusually tactile with him, and tipped her head to the side, whilst running her fingers through her hair.

What's that all about? She's flirting, I thought to myself.

At this point in the proceedings, I was disturbed by a raucous laugh from around the computer screen. I turned round and joined in the laughter giving the impression I'd seen the whole thing.

'Did you see that pig, Rich?' John asked through a chuckle.

'What a mess!' I replied.

Eager to see what my wife was up to, I quickly returned my gaze to the dining room. I was surprised to see her now standing up. She then said something to Ryan, which I couldn't hear, and he then smiled and said something back to her. With that, she then bent over, her legs wide and straight, and tucked her fingers under her toes. Ryan then smiled and clapped. I felt a bit sick in my stomach. This was a side of Angie I'd never seen before. I tried not to dwell on it and put her antics down to excessive booze and over excitement because Ryan was an actor she'd seen on TV.

With the video clip out of the way, everyone returned to the dining table for a liqueur. With Angie still sitting close to Ryan, I had to work hard to fend off Black Dog and to remain present. Then, after she'd partaken of three different digestifs, I thought it best to leave before she got a bit too touchy-feely with Ryan.

I thanked Charlotte and John for a fabulous evening and then set about saying goodbye to all the guests. The usual round of farewell hugs and kisses ensued. I found myself watching closely as Angie said goodbye to Ryan. Her embrace with him was much closer than with any of the others, and she nuzzled her head into his chest. I watched wide-eyed as she prolonged their embrace and ran her hands up and down his back. They then kissed each other on both cheeks, very close to their lips. It was pretty clear that they fancied each other rotten.

A few steps into our walk home, Angie slipped her coat off and hung it over her forearm. She then grabbed hold of my arm with her free hand and held it tight to her chest.

'What was all that about with Ryan, Angie?' I reluctantly asked, trying hard not to make something out of nothing.

'What are you on about Rich?' she questioned dismissively.

'You were pretty cosy with him,' I retorted a little sharply.

'Nah, don't be stupid, we were just chatting. That's all!'

'Do you like him then?' I asked.

'Well yeah,' said my wife, 'I suppose I do. He's a bit of a celebrity and he's quite tall, which is nice.'

'He's not as tall as me!' I insisted, feeling the need to prove myself.

'I never said he was.'

'Why did you um ...' I faltered, '... you know, pull your dress down to show your cleavage?'

'Pull my dress down?' repeated Angie, wrinkling her nose. 'Did I?'

'Yes. And what was all that suggestive bending over with your legs apart?' I asked, the anxiousness in my voice now showing a little.

'I was just demonstrating how I could get my fingers under my toes. Ryan challenged me. Never challenge a Rowe, right?'

'I could see your bare thighs above your stocking tops,' I declared firmly. 'Not to mention your skimpy knickers!'

'Ryan couldn't see!'

'He definitely could,' I retorted sharply.

'Are you Jealous Rich?' asked Angie slowly, as she drew me to a halt, a big grin spreading across her face.

'Nah, don't be stupid!' I replied dismissively, before resuming walking so my wife couldn't see my telling face.

We walked on in silence for a bit until insecurity, once again, got the better of me.

'Well ...' I said, drawing the word out, '... I was a tad jealous. I've never seen you like that before.'

'Don't be jealous Rich,' replied my smiling wife, 'you know you're the only one for me, don't you?'

'Am I really?' I asked.

'Yes,' affirmed Angie. 'But I think I just wanna be more myself,' she added dreamily. 'Like I said earlier, I've been mum, wife and career woman. I've been there for others, but not for me.'

'But what does that mean Angie?'

'I've already told you,' she responded. 'I need to discover what *I'm* about.'

'Your *forgotten me?* Is that it?'

'I guess so, even though I'm not entirely sure exactly who she is.'

'How will you know then Angie?'

'Again, I'm not sure,' she replied, 'but I have to say that I really enjoyed being myself with Ryan.'

'Did you?'

'Yes. It was liberating and empowering,' said my wife. 'Sexually empowering if I'm honest. And you were there, Rich,' she quickly added, 'so I felt completely comfortable.'

'What do you mean sexually empowering?' I asked, trying hard to keep Black Dog at bay.

'Oh, I don't know Rich,' dismissed Angie. 'All I can say is that I really liked feeling sexy; Ryan brought that out in me. Plus, I could see he was interested.'

With that, Black Dog began barking furiously, whilst straining at his leash.

'How do you know he was interested?' I asked.

'Because of his naughty eyes and general demeanour.'

'And did you check to see if he was hard for you?' I demanded to know. 'Like you did with Dave?'

'I didn't have to.'

'What do you mean by that?' I questioned sharply.

'I mean I saw him reposition his huge erection,' said a defiant sounding Angie, clearly annoyed at being called out on her actions.

Driven by some sort of primal force, I pulled her to an abrupt stop and drew her to me. I then kissed her full-on, savouring the feeling of her tongue dancing round in my mouth as our lips melded together.

The thought of her feeling sexy for Ryan and making him hard, made me squeeze her tight to physically secure her for myself. I felt strange and out of control.

As we kissed, Angie's hand slid down my body until she reached my full erection and then massaged it through my trousers.

'Ooh, you're all excited my big man,' she said, having eased back a little. 'So, are you gonna put that big hard-on to good use when we get home?' she asked, with a naughty glint in her eye.

'Damn right I am,' I said, before resuming our passionate snog.

A moment later, I suddenly became aware of a slowing car and looked up to see Ryan leaning out of the passenger window.

'Get a room you two!' he called out, before asking us if we wanted a lift.

Then, as the car drew to a halt, he beamed at Angie, and she beamed back at him.

'Ryan,' I said, feeling awkward as I bent forward to hide my erection, 'thanks anyway, but we only live up the road.'

As he smiled and nodded, Angie pushed past me and leaned into the car; her boobs were well on show.

'What a great evening!' she announced.

'It's alright for you folks,' said Amy, who was driving, 'I've been on orange juice all evening!'

'Aww, poor you,' replied Angie. 'You men have got it made.'

'We have indeed,' said Ryan, as he enjoyed an eyeful of my wife's breasts.

'Ooh Amy!' exclaimed Angie suddenly, before pushing her chest past Ryan to get to the driver's side. 'I was admiring your necklace at Charlotte's.'

Christ, she's shoved her tits right in Ryan's face.

As I looked on aghast, I swear he was squeezing her with his out of sight hand. Black Dog was now going crazy, causing a surge of adrenaline to run through me, accompanied by an involuntary erection.

Shaking, I took a deep breath and tried to let it go. I had to give Angie the benefit of the doubt, because I couldn't be sure she'd done anything wrong. She would give me a right earful if I judged her erroneously.

'Catch you later!' I announced abruptly, as I squeezed past Angie to shake Ryan's hand to force her out of his face.

'Byeee!' came the joint cry from the car as Amy pulled away.

'It was nice of them to stop and say goodnight,' said Angie, as she tugged on my arm to get me moving.

I didn't reply. I was preoccupied with her leaning into the car to get her tits in Ryan's face.

What the hell did she think she was doing? And how could I mention it without any concrete evidence? That would mean a big argument for sure.

'Angie,' I said, as I fought hard to keep my emotions from boiling over.

'Yes.'

'Remember what we said about always being honest?'

'Yeesss,' she replied, drawing the word out.

'So why did you press your tits against Ryan's face in the car then?' I demanded without thinking.

Angie stopped and looked up at me with her big, soft, loving eyes. She then took hold of my hands and said, 'I'm sorry my big man, I didn't realise.'

'Don't Angie, alright?'

'Okay,' she said, 'it was just a bit of innocent flirting because I've had too much wine, and people do silly things when they've been drinking.'

'No Angie!' I retorted sharply. '*In vino veritas.*'

'In wine truth,' she said. 'What about it?'

'Your true self came out under the influence of alcohol. That's what about it, Angie.'

'Maybe,' she replied thoughtfully, 'but I've already told you, I like feeling sexy, that's all. And when I feel sexy, I get horny for *you!*'

'For Ryan more like!' I snapped.

At this point, my wife squeezed my hands and then shook them.

'Rich,' she said, 'I've given you four healthy ten-pound babies, but that has taken its toll on my body image.'

'And is "innocent flirting" with your tits in Ryan's face going to make that better?' I demanded to know.

'I know I shouldn't tell you this,' replied my wife, 'but I really liked Ryan's attention because he's attractive. I'm not a bad person for that,' she said, her eyes pleading not to be judged.

Having resumed our walk along our drive, I tried to rationalise my thoughts. And even though my heart was pounding hard as a wave of jealousy swept through me, I was grateful for her honesty. Honesty, to me, however brutal, was way better than deceit.

'I'm glad you told me that Angie,' I said softly, trying hard to let things go. 'I have to tell you that I felt pretty awful watching the proceedings this evening.'

'I'm sorry Rich,' she said. 'Nothing was ever going to happen. It was just a bit of fun.'

'It made me jealous and insecure.'

'You needn't be. You're my world!'

'Am I?'

'Yes!' insisted my wife. 'I just need to rebuild my self-esteem after going bankrupt when you lost your business – that's all.'

'But a moment ago you said it was your body image,' I countered.

'Yes, that's part of it,' replied Angie. 'But I wouldn't have that problem if my confidence and self-esteem weren't crushed when we went bust.'

As we walked on in silence, an overwhelming sense of guilt hit me for failing my Angie so badly. Bearing that in mind, I told her I would do anything to rebuild her confidence and self-esteem, before adding that she didn't have anything to prove, because she was, without doubt, incredibly attractive and sexy.

'*You* say that because *you* love me Rich,' said Angie, 'but I need unbiased proof.'

'Unbiased proof?' I repeated.

'Yes Rich. And Ryan made me *feel* attractive, *feel* desired and *feel* sexy! I needed that,' insisted my wife, like I'd failed her in some way.

'Did your unbiased proof make you *feel* horny?' I questioned. 'And be honest.'

'Yes,' came my wife's quiet response.

Still erect from jealousy, I drew Angie to a halt by our outhouse office and asked her if *I* made her feel horny.

'You know you do,' she said, before tiptoeing to kiss

me passionately. I searched her mouth with my tongue and felt close to her. I then eased away and asked her if Ryan squeezing her tits made her feel like a woman.

'He didn't squeeze them!' insisted my wife.

'Did you enjoy it?' I demanded, raising my voice.

'Yes, alright,' snapped my wife, 'I did.'

'And is that innocent flirting then, Angie?'

'Well yes Rich, I think it is,' she replied earnestly. 'I mean you were okay with Dave getting hard for me when we danced. And that was innocent flirting!'

'And did Ryan make you tingly and wet like Dave did?'

Angie turned away from me and didn't reply.

'Well, did he?'

'Okay, yes! He made me tingly and wet.'

At this point, Black Dog went berserk at my wife's admission. That gave rise to an overwhelming primal need to penetrate her as a matter of urgency. Shaking with jealousy and anger, I kissed her even harder than before. She responded with unbridled passion.

With our mouths still locked together I pushed the office door open, and we half tumbled inside, coming to a stop by Angie's desk. Having tossed her coat to the floor, I swept her monitor and papers aside with a swish of my arm, before lifting her onto the desk. I hoicked her dress up and then hurriedly dropped my chinos. The sensation of my cock springing up ready for action, made my heart skip a beat.

'I want you for my own, Angie,' I insisted in a gruff whisper.

'Well then take me for your own,' she replied, 'and triumph over Ryan.'

With my woman seated, I pushed her dangling legs open. Then, looking down, I gripped the base of my shaft and pulled her knicker gusset aside before unceremoniously penetrating her … hard! That was my driver. Satisfying my basic instinct to mark my territory, in the knowledge that she was wet from her dalliance with a rival male.

I now furiously pumped in and out of my wife's opening for a short while and then stopped. Whilst remaining deep inside her, I resumed my passionate kissing with a mix of love, anger and jealousy. Then, without thinking, I once again pounded my Angie as hard as I could, whilst she hung onto my shoulders and dug her nails in. I kept this up for a few minutes, all the while loving the sound of her moans of pleasure.

Having momentarily run out of puff, I pulled out of my wife and yanked her knickers off with considerable urgency. I then pushed her thighs apart and stroked myself whilst scrutinising every inch of her animal sexuality. After a moment or two, she took the initiative and kicked her legs up into the air with a sense of purpose. Grabbing hold of her ankles, I opened her legs wider still and once again, studied the very essence of her womanhood.

Then, whilst still standing, I re-entered my wife forcefully. She yelped.

'Arghhh, Rich!'

'Do you want me, Angie?' I demanded gruffly.

'Yes!' she replied, 'fuck me will you, just fuck me!'

I momentarily revelled in my wife's desire for me, but then instantly thought it must be for Ryan.

Enraged, I watched myself going in and out of her stretched open vagina.

Surely that proved she was mine. Or did it?

Despite physically connecting with my wife, I became convinced that her moans and sighs, and the opening of her body were for Ryan. That seriously antagonised Black Dog and made me even more angry.

'You're not thinking of me Angie!' I insisted gruffly, 'you're thinking of *Ryan!* Aren't you?'

'No!' she whispered, '*you're* fucking me, and I'm loving it!'

'But you got your tits out for Ryan, didn't you Angie?'

'No, but I'm getting them out for you,' she said, wearing a smug smile.

Resting her back on the desk, she immediately flopped her soft, shapely breasts out of her dress. I then rested her ankles on my shoulders to free up my hands.

'So, you liked Ryan touching your tits, did you?' I demanded to know, as I excitedly massaged them with both hands.

My wife made no reply. Instead, she just stared at me defiantly, like I was invading her privacy.

'Well, did you?' I asked sharply, as I slammed into her.

'Yes, I did!'

'You're mine!' I insisted loudly, 'you got that?!'

'Yes, I'm yours Rich,' replied my wife. 'And I love that you're fighting for me.'

With an adrenaline-fuelled sense of victory over Ryan, I stopped massaging my wife's breasts and stood up straight. I then got into a slow, deliberate rhythm, my eyes wild and staring. I again looked down at where our bodies were connected. In deep, then shallow, in deep, then shallow. Observing our physical union meant everything to me – the ultimate expression of love, passion and possession, fuelled by a myriad of maddening primal emotions.

'Fuck me, fuck me, fuck me,' chanted my wife, in time to my rhythm.

'You need fucking Angie,' I insisted angrily.

'Yes,' she whispered in reply, 'I've been a bad girl!'

Her words spurred me on to punish her with even harder penetrations for being so naughty. Then, after a short while, she suddenly stopped moaning and went quite still as she locked her eyes onto mine. I felt her tighten for a good few seconds until she let out a series of urgent sighs, whilst writhing in ecstasy. She had come. I felt I'd done my job, even though our sex was about my insecurities.

A few seconds later, the sensation of my penis head rubbing against the inside of my wife intensified. As base and graphic as that is, that was the focus of my entire world at that moment, augmented by the smell, sight and sounds of my woman. Now I was about to come. I went super hard and felt the base of my throbbing cock tighten as I continued to pump in and out of my mate. Then, as my taught muscles finally released, I let out an almighty 'ARGHHHHH!!!' like a wild, rampant gorilla.

With my cock twitching uncontrollably, I focused on the wonderfully wicked sensation of hot semen spurting out of me with each pulsating spasm. Then, when I was ready to release the last of my ejaculate, I pulled out of my wife. Having paused in her vagina lips for a millisecond, I slammed back into her one last time. With my cock rammed up inside my woman, I gripped her thighs and held her tight against me as I discharged the rest of my semen as far up her vagina as I possibly could. That was incredibly important to me.

With my deep-seated, innate response satisfied, I leaned forward and rested my head on my Angie's chest. She then wrapped her legs round my middle, before crossing her forearms behind my neck.

'Oh my God, Rich,' she panted, 'that was just incredible. So passionate and primal, and unlike anything we've done before!'

Still catching my breath, I made no reply. Instead, I just nodded my head in agreement and remained quiet whilst the tension drained from my body, as my debauched high slowly faded.

A moment later, I wanted to be closer still to my wife, and so gently eased myself out of her embrace. Then, whilst looking into her eyes through the warm moonlight which pervaded the office, I lifted her off her desk and gently placed her onto her office chair.

Having dropped to my knees in front of my Angie, I wrapped my arms around her middle and buried my head in her lap under her dress. Her strong scent mixed with my cum was strangely reassuring. To me, leaving my semen inside my mate proved she was mine, and I needed that just now. As that thought left my mind, I felt my wife's forearms sliding over my shoulders until they came to rest on my upper back. She sighed contentedly.

'I love you Rich,' she said, as she began stroking my back lightly with her fingertips. 'And thank you for loving me so beautifully.'

Hearing those amazing words brought a huge smile to my face.

'I love to love you my Angie,' I whispered, having lifted my head up from her lap to speak.

I then kissed her vulva softly before once again resting my head on her thighs. Then, after a quiet moment alone with my thoughts, I wondered how it ever got this crazy. I mean, I'd always made love to my wife; romantic, warm yet passionate lovemaking. Not the mad, debauched sex of a few minutes ago. But, once again, just like when she told me about her dirty dancing with Dave, I'd become incredibly aroused, in an angry, jealous, and possessive sort of way. That felt very strange to say the least.

As I was trying to figure out what was going on with me, my Angie told me that our sex life had gone to an amazing new level.

'I love that you kind of got a bit possessive and fought Ryan off,' she added.

'I'm glad sweetheart,' I responded, lifting my head momentarily, 'because I wasn't sure if I was a bit over the top.'

'You were absolutely great,' insisted my wife. 'I love it when you fuck me like that. Makes me feel desired. And, like I said, when you kind of saw Ryan off, I felt valuable and not taken for granted.'

'I'm so pleased,' I said, before dropping my head back into my wife's lap.

'Your response was kind of like when I mentioned about Dave,' she continued. 'This is good for us.'

Wrapping my arms tighter still round my woman, I nodded in acknowledgement and then listened as she told me that a little bit of flirting seemed to go a long way.

'I like the attention,' she added, 'but I don't want sex with anyone else but you.'

Still nuzzled up in my wife's lap, I suggested that a bit of male attention was good for her ego and confidence. She agreed with me and then leaned forward to kiss the back of my head. I felt utterly loved as I savoured the warmth and intimacy of our embrace.

Then, out of the blue, I was suddenly filled with trepidation. Despite my wife's assertion that she didn't want to sleep with any other men, I kind of felt she'd already slept with Dave, and that given the chance, she would sleep with someone else. I knew this was an unfair judgement and conclusion, but what can you do when a sixth sense suddenly overwhelms you?

Additionally, I knew I needed to support my wife going forward to right the wrong I'd done by losing everything. And on top of that, I needed to love her properly, as she put it, and make her my priority, so she felt secure. With Black Dog at my heel, this wasn't going to be easy, especially if Angie pushed the boundaries. And something deep inside me told me she was going to do just that.

CHAPTER 8

The next morning, we joined my wife's Uncle Jack on the first tee to support his charity golf day. His treat. Angie was my caddie, and this was our big day out. My niece had come down from Surrey to babysit. Alas things didn't go too well because Angie and I ended up having a hushed argument halfway round the course. It was my fault because I was horrid to her for flirting with Ryan. I knew I would be, despite our sublime post-coital closeness of last night. My problem was that whenever Angie and I had a contretemps, there always seemed to be some sort of residual upset within me which needed to work its way out. Once that upset had passed through my immature emotional system, I then worked hard to get back into my wife's good books. Ultimately, I just wanted to make her happy. Happy wife, happy life, as the saying goes!

* * *

With our round of golf completed, we joined the players who'd teed off before us in the clubhouse for a drink. After swapping golf stories for an hour or so, Angie and I made our way to the Downs View Hotel.

We checked into the room Uncle Jack had kindly booked

for us and changed into our formal evening wear. I wore the obligatory blue blazer, white shirt, and beige chinos. I then completed the ensemble with my former golf club tie and a pair of brown leather brogues. Angie looked her usual stunning self in a black knee-length dress with a V-neck showing a tasteful splash of décolletage. A deep-red bolero top was tied under her bust to accentuate her curves. Simple but stylish. She wore a pair of Jimmy Choo red high heels which contrasted nicely with her black hold-up stockings. Her matching red handbag completed her elegant look.

At around 7 p.m. we joined Uncle Jack in the big clubhouse dining room. A grandiose, but tired Victorian space with two huge, glazed cabinets full of sparkling silver trophies. There were about a hundred people seated around a number of circular tables, all with polished cutlery neatly laid out on crisp, white, linen tablecloths with matching napkins. I sat beside another of Angie's uncles, Roy. He was a slight man with an interesting story to tell about everything. I really liked him. To his right was uncle Jack's wife, Paula. A petite, fiery Irish redhead in her early sixties. Next to her was a single guy called Adam. A charming and handsome man in his forties, who was just a bit too full of himself. Completing the circle was Uncle Jack.

After a glass of wine, I slipped my hand under the table and rubbed my wife's thigh affectionately. She took hold of my hand and squeezed it reassuringly. Pleased that all was well between us, I settled down to dinner.

After a call of nature, I returned to my seat to find Adam had taken my place.

'Ahhh Rich,' he said, looking up at me with a smarmy smile on his face. 'I'm just flirting with your beautiful wife.'

Christ! She suddenly seems to be attracting guys like

flies. Disappointed with myself for thinking that thought, I realised that I still wasn't over the Ryan thing yet.

Forcing an agreeable smile, I stood directly behind Adam to pressure him into vacating my seat. I then tried to be funny by saying that I couldn't blame him for flirting with my wife, but that he really ought to get one of his own.

'Sit there, Rich!' ordered Aunt Paula, nodding at Adam's seat.

Paula's command irritated me. Not being one to be ordered about, and not being inclined to be outmanoeuvred by smarmy faced Adam, I stayed where I was. Then, whilst still wearing my fake smile, and with apparent bonhomie good humour, I suggested that I wouldn't be very chivalrous if I let such a handsome charmer move in on my wife.

'I don't mind Rich,' said Angie.

'Neither do I,' quipped Adam.

'Sit there, Rich!' Paula again instructed, whilst pointing at Adam's seat in a dictatorial manner.

'Actually, I'm gonna sit right here in my own seat,' I said firmly, jiggling the back of my chair.

My wife fired daggers at me but said nothing as Adam reluctantly rose to his feet.

Just when I thought all was well, along comes smarmy shit-face Adam to mess things up for me. Unable to get past the seat issue, Angie and I hardly spoke during the rest of dinner. I knew this unfinished indifference would rear its ugly head again, and that a row would inevitably play out in order for us to clear the air. I wasn't looking forward to it.

* * *

Once back at the hotel, I held our room door open.

Angie strode in and tossed her evening bag onto the luggage rack. She then strutted across a sea of blue carpet to the big sash windows at the opposite end of the room, and drew the heavy red curtains together sharply. I shut the door behind me and dimmed the lights. Remaining still, I quietly observed my wife.

Without saying a word, she marched over to the desk and began undressing for bed. At this point, we'd usually be winding down, looking forward to huggles and a catch-up, and maybe even a plug-in cuddle to feel really close. But as you could cut the atmosphere with a knife, there was no chance whatsoever of any intimacy between us at this moment in time.

Having quietly walked over to the bed, I too undressed. Now completely naked, I just sat for a moment and contemplated my position. I looked up at my wife who was still beside the desk chair. She looked deep in thought, standing there, almost naked, in her red high heels and sheer black hold-ups.

With my contemplations complete, I decided to say something about what had pissed me off.

'I sense you're cross Angie,' I said sharply. 'Why?'

'That thing at the dinner table with Adam,' she replied dismissively, 'couldn't you just go with the flow?'

'If I don't like the flow, I ain't gonna go!' I declared churlishly.

'Whatever!' snapped Angie. 'I really don't care.'

Annoyed by my wife's lack of understanding, I told her that she should have supported me, and that I wasn't gonna take orders from Paula. She told me that support for me would have been 'misplaced'.

Realising I wasn't going to get anywhere, I decided to

let things go and just sat quietly.

'You've got a screw loose Rich!' my wife suddenly announced, whilst turning her finger into her temple mockingly.

'I'm feeling insecure!' I called out after her, as she marched off to the bathroom, 'because you want attention from other men. Dave and Ryan to name but two,' I added. 'Not to mention what happened after Dom died.'

Angie didn't reply. She finished brushing her teeth before striding purposefully over to me. Then, with her legs straight and wide, she bent forward at the waist and pressed her forehead against mine. We were literally head-to-head, with me sitting on the edge of the bed inhaling her toothpaste and booze breath, whilst staring at her sexy hanging breasts.

'Not that again!' she growled. 'I'll make it simple for you,' she added, 'my husband died, and I had a fling with a married man. What do you want me to say for God's sake?'

'That you're sorry for disrespecting Dom's memory,' I suggested.

'Sorry for disrespecting Dom's memory?' repeated my wife, having risen back to her full height. 'I was perfectly within my rights to see whoever I wanted to!' she declared, looking directly at me, hands defiantly on hips.

'You were within your rights,' I responded, 'but how do you think that makes me feel?'

'I don't care!'

'I just need reassurance Angie, that's all.'

'Reassurance?' she questioned.

'Yes,' I said, 'reassurance. You didn't even inter Dom's remains. I did. Can you not see why I might wonder what love actually means to you?'

'I'm sick of this, you stupid bastard!' said my wife. 'You need a virtuous girl. I'm not that girl! I shagged some arsehole who wouldn't leave his wife! Get over it!'

'Get over it?!' I questioned. 'You said you adored your husband and now you say you love me, but like I said, what does that actually mean?'

My wife made no reply. She just shook her head and then, as she slowly walked away, I asked her if 'wouldn't leave his wife' meant she wanted to set up home with him two days after Dom had died. Angie stopped in the middle of the room with her back to me. There was a long pause until she eventually spoke.

'It didn't happen like I said,' she whispered, before turning to face me with her eyes downcast.

'What do you mean?' I asked softly, as I slowly rose to my feet and remained by the bed. 'What exactly was the deal with this guy?'

'Martin and I,' she replied, 'had actually been seeing each other for over a year *during* my marriage to Dom.'

My wife's unexpected revelation sent my heart rate through the roof. I stared at her completely dumbstruck, until I finally found the words to ask her why she'd waited sixteen years to tell me this. She didn't reply and just stood there motionless, looking awkward, exposed, and vulnerable. With her head still bowed, she held one hand with the other. She looked like a little girl lost, but I couldn't reach out to her. Lying to me for all those years and her betrayal of Dom, made me sick to my stomach.

'C'mon!' I prompted gruffly, 'tell me why you've waited sixteen years to tell me this Angie.'

'Because,' she began softly, as tears ran down her cheeks, 'maybe you won't think so badly of me, now that you know that I didn't just start sleeping with someone else immediately after Dom died.'

I looked my wife up and down with obvious contempt, and could clearly see her pained expression.

'What sort of woman are you?' I asked, screwing my face up with disgust.

'It sounds worse than it is, Rich,' replied Angie, her sobbing now in full flow.

'And were you seeing Martin when Dom was diagnosed with cancer?'

'Yes.'

At this point, a sudden calm came over me, accompanied by a feeling of being bereft of the marriage I thought I had. After a short pause, I slowly sank back down onto the bed and asked my wife why she originally told me that she took up with Martin *after* Dom died.

'I'm sorry,' she replied. 'I started to tell you the truth on our first date.'

'Started?' I questioned.

'Yes, but when I saw your reaction,' explained Angie, 'I knew that if I told you I'd been seeing Martin for over a year whilst I was married to Dom, there wouldn't have been a second date. Can you …'

At this point in the proceedings, Angie's phone rang. I think she was relieved by the interruption and quickly turned away from me to get to her handbag to answer it. It was her Uncle Jack.

Her voice faded as I looked at her. I could see her lips moving but could hear nothing. Alone with my thoughts, I wondered what my wife's revelations actually meant to my marriage.

It means, Richie boy, answered my cockney demon

voice, your wife's love for you is not what you think it is. She deceived you and she ain't who you thought she was.

Angie soon ended the call and placed her phone down on the luggage rack. She then turned round to face me again, and stood motionless with her gaze directed at the floor. I took a deep, deliberate breath and let it out slowly to calm myself down. This isn't the time to throw a wobbly, I thought to myself, this is a time to figure out exactly who you're married to.

'So you deliberately deceived me right from the start,' I said quietly, whilst remaining seated on the edge of the bed,

'I'm telling you the truth now,' said my wife, 'because I love you, and I want our marriage to work.'

'Yeah sure,' I retorted sarcastically.

'You don't need to be so upset Rich. Martin was before your time, and I didn't have to reveal anything to you anyway.'

'That's all true,' I said, before adding that it was her that brought the matter up on our first date, and then lied to me to ensure there was a second date.

Angie responded by telling me that her past had nothing to do with me, and with us as a couple. I told her that her past had everything to do with me because she lied about it.

'Our past paints a picture of the person we are,' I added, 'and often informs the future.'

'Well, I haven't cheated on you Rich, and I never would. I love you.'

'Love me?!' I repeated contemptuously, looking my wife up and down. 'Like you loved Dom? And that's true love?'

Having composed herself, my wife went on to tell me that she loved Dom in her own way, before then slowly walking towards me. Stopping halfway across the room, she told me that if Dom had known about Martin, he wouldn't have minded at all. He loved her, and he wasn't a jealous guy.

Before my wife tried to justify her wrongdoing, I was ready to make everything better, but somehow her assumption that her dead husband would have approved of her affair, made my blood boil. Such a convenient and disrespectful assumption about a man who couldn't speak up for himself. I felt I had to speak up for him.

'So you're saying,' I began slowly, 'that Dom wouldn't have minded you having sex with Martin?'

'Yes.'

'Of course he wouldn't have minded,' I scoffed sarcastically, 'we all know every husband's cool with his wife cheating on him.'

Looking directly at me, Angie told me that it wasn't like that. Still incensed by her convenient thinking, I demanded to know what it was like. My wife responded by telling me that it was hard to explain. I asked her if she would have left Dom for Martin if he'd left his wife. She said yes, but only when they first started seeing each other.

'But then, when Dom was diagnosed,' she added, 'I wanted to be there for him until the end.'

For the inheritance more like, I thought to myself.

At this point the room fell silent. During this time, I wondered why I asked so many questions. I then immediately concluded it was because I wanted to understand my wife's circumstances, so I could work out what sort of woman she actually was, and what that ultimately meant for my marriage going forward.

'Angie,' I eventually said through a sigh, 'I just want to …'

'I know this is completely against your moral values,' she interrupted, 'most people's values, but I didn't cheat on you!'

'But why cheat at all when you say you absolutely adored Dom?'

'We kind of became a bit like brother and sister,' replied my wife, 'and I didn't really want intimacy.'

She went on to tell me that because Dom seldom initiated sex, they were effectively companions. Apparently, she settled for that without really realising why. But then, when she met Martin, he ignited an unexpected sexual passion in her.

'I just couldn't get enough of him,' she continued. 'He made me feel desired and sexy. I felt confident and empowered, and realised I was married to the wrong man for the sex side of things.'

'Well then why marry him in the first place?'

'Because the sex was okay to begin with, but then it just sort of fizzled out.'

'Why?'

'I don't know,' said Angie, with a shrug of her shoulders, 'but I read up on it, and a lot of wives don't want sex with their husbands. But often, when they come out of their marriage, a new man will awaken their sexiness, and then they go absolutely mad for it. They never thought they'd feel that way, and it kind of takes them by surprise, but it makes them come alive.'

'And is that what happened to you Angie, even though you were still with Dom?'

'Yes,' she responded, before wiping her tears away with the back of her hand and adding that Martin brought excitement to a lacklustre marriage.

Ignoring my wife's play for sympathy, I rose to my feet and asked her if Martin wore a condom.

To my pathetic mind, it felt fairer on Dom if his wife's lover hadn't actually ejaculated inside her body. That special intimacy could have been reserved for him.

'Yes, he wore a condom to begin with,' replied Angie.

'What do you mean, to begin with?'

'Well, when Dom was diagnosed,' she explained, 'we decided to try for a baby so that he could live on through his child.'

'Oh,' I replied softly, 'I'm sorry. So you took precautions with Martin when you were trying to get pregnant by Dom?'

'Actually I didn't,' replied my wife. 'I told Martin I was on the pill.'

Having leant against the wall by the bed, I sighed heavily and then told Angie that it wouldn't have been fair on Dom, if she'd become pregnant by Martin.

'That wasn't the point,' she retorted. 'Because chemo had impacted Dom's sperm, I wanted Martin as a back-up for a baby, which would, to all intents and purposes, have been Dom's.'

'Really?'

'Yes. Just knowing I was pregnant would have made Dom very happy, even though he wouldn't have been around for the birth.'

'So, you were taking one for the team?' I retorted sarcastically. 'Fucking Martin to give Dom an heir?'

'Yes.'

'Huh,' I scoffed. 'Lady Chatterley's Lover revisited with Dom as Clifford, Martin as Mellors and you as Lady bleedin' Chatterley herself!'

With that said, another silence befell the room, during

which Angie quietly drifted over to the desk chair to sit down. Her face was sad.

'Please don't mock me Rich,' she whispered, 'I did genuinely want to give Dom a baby. He so wanted to leave part of him behind for me to love.'

'And if you got pregnant,' I said, 'what would you have told Martin?'

'That it was Dom's.'

'What, and potentially deprive him of his child?'

'Yes. Maybe. I don't know!' shouted my red-faced wife.

I then asked her why she kept seeing Martin when Dom was seriously ill and couldn't have had a baby.

'I don't really know,' she replied through a heavy sigh. 'I was caught up in all sorts of emotions and circumstances. I sort of needed someone,' she added, 'and I wasn't thinking straight.'

'And a cheap fuck was the answer, was it?'

'You need to be sympathetic!' insisted my wife.

'I'm trying to be,' I replied, 'but you've been incredibly deceitful and manipulative, and I don't know where that leaves me. Untrusting of you, insecure and worried is my best guess.'

We fell silent. I contemplated Angie's emotional conundrum. Maybe she was being altruistic and trying to do the best for Dom. Or was she just having a cake and eating it by making 'the baby' a convenient excuse. Or perhaps it was wrong of me to judge her badly.

Lost for a response, Angie just sat there, nearly naked, looking small and vulnerable. Even though I knew I'd been an insensitive bastard, I just couldn't reach out to my wife. Instead, I just asked her if she thought it was wrong to have an affair in the first place.

Say yes, I thought to myself. Say it was wrong, then I'll feel secure.

'I told you Rich,' replied my wife, 'I was trying to get pregnant for Dom.'

Feeling that it would be wrong to judge Angie badly for trying to get pregnant to make her dying husband happy, I told her that her actions were commendable in a twisted sort of way. A kind of fault on the right side. She nodded in agreement and told me she was doing her best for Dom.

'But the thing is,' I said, 'you began this affair before Dom became unwell. Do you think that was the wrong thing to do?'

There was a long pause as the cogs went round in my wife's head.

'It's not a simple yes or no answer to say I was wrong,' she replied assertively, as her "best form of defence is attack" suddenly kicked in.

Then, with a measured look on her face, she stood up and plucked a bottle of water off the desk. It was like she had suddenly morphed into confident "barrister" Angie, who was about to address the court.

'I loved them both I think,' she declared with thoughtful pomposity, standing legs apart. 'Dom in a more platonic sort of way.'

She then tilted her head back and gulped some water down before extending the bottle to me. I shook my head and remained against the wall to gather my thoughts.

After a short pause, I asked her how often she saw Martin.

'Two or three times a week,' she replied, matter-of-factly. 'Mostly at lunchtime.'

'Did you kiss a lot?' I instantly asked without realising.

'Why all the questions?' retorted my wife.

'I dunno,' I replied sharply. 'Just answer Angie!'

'Alright then I will,' she snapped. 'Yes, we kissed a lot. Tongues down each other's throats, his fingers up my wet pussy, my hand wanking his hard cock. Is that what you want to know Rich?'

Hearing that woke Black Dog up with a start. Now erect and angry, I suddenly wanted to know every last detail of my wife's sordid sexual encounters.

'Where did you do it?' I immediately asked without thinking.

'In the back of his car up a farm track,' replied my wife, having dropped her gaze to my erection. 'And occasionally in a cheap hotel.'

'Cheap hotel,' I repeated, 'that about sums it up. And how did you do it?'

'Rich, STOP!' cried Angie, raising her hand in front of her face like a traffic cop. 'You're judging me.'

'I have to work this shit out for God's sake,' I insisted, 'and yes I may be judging you, but you probably deserve it!'

'Well as you're judging me,' growled my angry wife, 'you might as well judge this too; I was fucking Dom whilst I was still married to my first husband Abe!'

Surprised to hear that, I told Angie that cheating wasn't something to be proud of. She immediately countered by telling me that she wasn't going to apologise for who she was, and that I was the one with the problem.

'Me?' I scoffed, as my erection faded, 'I don't think so. Now let me see,' I added haughtily, 'you cheated on your first husband Abe, to get with your second husband, Dom. And then you cheated on Dom with Martin, but he wouldn't leave his wife, so you stayed with Dom?'

'You're judging me without knowing the facts,' replied Angie. 'You need to love me for who I am,' she added, 'or our marriage will be over!'

'And you were still shagging Martin,' I continued, deliberately ignoring my wife's comment, 'when Dom had just weeks to live, because you wanted to get pregnant for him and you weren't thinking straight?'

'You bastard!' shouted my wife, thrusting her head forward. 'It's not as simple as that.'

'And in addition to all of the above,' I continued forcefully, 'you started to tell me that you had an affair with Martin whilst Dom was still alive, but then changed your story to having an affair with him *after* Dom died, so as not to frighten me off.'

'You bastard!' my wife again shouted. 'I wanted us to be together!'

With that said, she then rested her bum on the desk and sighed heavily.

'Rich,' she said warmly, 'we don't need to get cross with each other like this anymore.'

She then told me that I wasn't to take what she was about to say the wrong way.

'Take what the wrong way?'

'I saw you go hard when I told you how Martin and I kissed,' replied my wife, before reminding me that I also got very excited when she told me she'd made Ryan stiff. 'I did say that a little bit of flirting seemed to go a long way,' she added, 'not just for me, but for you as well.'

Before I had a chance to formulate a response to that assertion too far, Angie went on to tell me that her infidelities seemed to turn me on.

'No,' I replied.

'Yes,' she countered, 'because when I told you how Dave rubbed his cock against me, you liked it, didn't you?

'No,' I said, as I fought hard to stop myself from reacting physically.

'I'm just remembering that now,' continued my wife, 'and it's turning me on. Can you imagine,' she added, in a sultry voice, before standing up from the desk, 'Dave grinding his big, fat, hard cock against my tingling, wet pussy. Ooh yeah,' she sighed, as she ran her fingers up and down her labia.

Unable to suppress my sexual arousal any longer, my erection instantly blasted up to full length.

'Telling you about Dave clearly excites you,' insisted my wife, as a self-satisfied smile grew across her face, 'and when I tell you about how I *fucked* Martin,' she added, before pausing for dramatic effect, 'you're gonna go wild!'

With my hard-on throbbing away expectantly, I realised my wife was controlling me by my emotional response, and she knew it. I mean, saying what she said really gave her game away. This type of emotional and sexual control over me, was a new phenomenon, which relied on her antagonising Black Dog.

'Oh wow!' she sighed, whilst smugly eyeing my hard-on, 'now *you're* making me all tingly and wet.'

'And does remembering Martin also make you tingly and wet?' I questioned.

'You know it does,' said Angie, before adding that we'd turned a negative into a massive positive!'

Incredibly aroused, jealous, and angry, I just looked at my wife. As I stared at her, I thought how amazing she was at turning things round to minimise her actions and my upset. I guess this was a kind of a win/win for us both.

Like a mind reader, she suddenly announced that I couldn't judge her because I was getting off on her and Martin.

'I'm not judging you about trying to get pregnant,' I replied. 'And I'm not judging you for having an affair with him in the first place. Like you said, that was before my time. The only thing I'm cross about, is that you lied to me.'

'Yeah well,' said Angie, 'I'm sorry about that. It was done with the best of intentions.'

As I nodded in acknowledgment of my wife's apology, she looked down at my now flaccid penis.

'Mr Floppy looks like he could use a little help,' she said, before asking me if I wanted to know exactly how Martin *fucked* her.

Just hearing my wife say that, immediately made me hard again. I wasn't sure why, but I guessed it was probably because her affair was illicit, and she'd been a very naughty girl.

'Yes,' I said barely audibly.

'Yes what?' questioned Angie.

'Yes, I want to know exactly how you did it,' I replied, having failed to overcome my desire to stop humiliating myself by asking gut-wrenching questions.

'Mmmhh,' moaned my wife, as she drew her tongue across her top lip. 'Martin! Oooh yeah, I remember him well. He fucked me on the back seat of his car.'

'Lying down?'

'Nooo,' sighed my wife, 'we always started with me on top. I wore a short skirt so he could get easy access to my wanton, wet pussy. Like this Rich,' she added, before widening her stance beyond her shoulders. 'This is how I slid onto his rock-solid cock!' she continued, as she bent her knees and slipped two fingers into herself to emphasise the point.

Keeping her eyes firmly fixed on me, my woman then eased up and down rhythmically whilst fingering herself. It was just a small leap of imagination to see her actually riding on top of her lover. I felt my face flush, as I sprang off the wall and took a couple of steps forward.

Standing there, reluctantly transfixed by my woman's every word and action, I stared at her expectantly. I wanted more, and I needed it to be graphic and disgusting, even though it felt wrong. I think my wife sensed my moral guilt and was exploiting my perverse, sick, and perverted need to know everything.

Now she could go in for the kill with impunity, whilst also seemingly enjoying the baseness of it all herself. With this new addition to her armoury, she'd cleverly turned the tables, and was making this whole thing about me; my irrational, insatiable and insane need to know every last dirty detail of her cheating sex. And it had to be cheating sex, to have the desired effect. And it had to be in my wife's sleazy porn-mag-style too. I just knew that Mills and Boon romance or Jilly Cooper erotica wouldn't do it for me.

With my two-second psychological analysis complete, I swallowed hard, and then unthinkingly asked Angie to describe the bit before penetration. I then sat on the desk chair to be closer to the action.

'Mmmhh,' she sighed, 'the bit before penetration? That was pretty dirty.'

'How dirty?' I asked, breathing hard with anxious excitement.

'As soon as Martin picked me up in his car,' said my wife, 'we would kiss long and hard and his hand would always find my breasts. And then,' she continued, 'he would drive us to a secluded spot. Whilst he was driving,

I'd push my backrest down and pull my skirt up round my tummy.'

'Did you have any knickers on?' I urgently questioned, as I began stroking my hard-on.

'Of course not Rich,' mocked Angie, before asking me if I liked the image of her with her legs wide open for her lover.

'Yes.'

'Then, once I'd teased him by playing with myself,' she continued, 'I would undo his zip and pull his cock out, so I could suck it.'

At this point, my wife stepped across to the desk and bent over from the waist with her legs straight and wide. She then slapped my hand off my penis and sucked me. My breathing instantly quickened, as my excitement levels went through the roof. A couple of minutes later, she suddenly straightened up, making a loud popping sound as she pulled off my erection.

'Ahhh,' she sighed smugly, before a taunting half grin spread across her lips, 'it seems we are two peas in a pod.'

Keen not to get side-tracked into a conversation about the rights and wrongs of my behaviour or that of my wife's, I instead just prompted her to continue by saying 'and then?'

'And then,' she replied, 'I would sit up and guide Martin's hand down to my pussy to feel how wet I was for him.'

With that said, my wife immediately took hold of my hand and pulled it to her vulva. I slipped two fingers inside her with ease. She was sopping wet from describing her illicit sex with another man. She then took a couple of steps backwards and watched intently as I pulled my erection back and forth, before then gleefully telling me that I clearly couldn't get enough of her dirty sex life.

Ignoring her observation, I instead just asked her what happened after she guided her lover's hand down to her pussy. She responded with a smile, and then described how he sucked his fingers and smiled.

'And then,' continued my wife, 'I'd lick his helmet like a lollipop, and savour his delicious pre cum. Mmmhh,' she sighed, whilst sucking her finger suggestively, as she looked down at me from her standing position.

I carried on staring at my wife intently, whilst continuing to stroke my rampant hard-on. She was right in front of me, but I didn't want to touch her for fear of not hearing the details I needed to hear.

'What other sex positions did you do?' I urgently demanded.

'That's a very well-considered question Rich,' replied my wife, like she was talking to a barrister colleague. 'Once we'd parked up, and I'd ridden my lover like a horse for a while, he would fuck me doggy.'

'Doggy how?' I stupidly asked.

'Oh darling, really,' goaded my wife, 'you know what doggy is, don't you?'

'Please get to the point, Angie.'

'Of course,' she said, before telling me that Martin fucked her really fast. Faster than anyone she'd ever been with.'

'And I assume you had multiple orgasms with Mr Speedy Bollocks,' I responded, as a sense of inadequacy washed over me.

'No,' replied Angie, 'Martin never made me cum, either with his fingers or with his small dick. That should make you feel better,' she added, with an exaggerated smile.

That did make me feel better, but I didn't know why.

'If he didn't make you come,' I responded, 'then why have sex at all?'

'It's not all about coming, silly,' replied my wife, before stepping forward and bending down to whisper in my ear. 'I was excited! I felt desired, and I wanted to feel my man's cock inside me. And telling you about it has gone straight to my pussy! That's what it was all about!'

Angie's dirty description sent a huge surge of adrenaline racing through my body, causing me to shake. Now, with Black Dog in a rage, my heart pounded even harder in my chest. With my breathing quickened, my eyes involuntarily locked onto my woman's hanging breasts; juicy ripe fruit ready to be plucked and consumed. Now stroking my cock with increased urgency, I reached out and wobbled my woman's tits from side to side with my free hand.

'What about these?' I demanded to know.

'Ooh yeah,' sighed my wife, before straightening up, 'my tits. Martin always got them out when I was on top of him, and sucked them until my nipples were huge,' she announced, now standing tall, legs wide apart, looking slutty and exciting as she kneaded her breasts. 'That always went straight to my pussy,' she added, licking her lips. 'Mmmhh.'

Despite her stomach-churning and taunting performance, I couldn't stop looking at my filthy, debauched wife. My chest now rose and fell with even greater urgency, as I filled with yet more testosterone-fuelled adrenaline. Without realising, I flew up out of the chair and stood in front of my wife; tall, proud, and completely naked.

We then stared at each other for a moment with a mix of loathing, love, and licentious lust. Angie's eyes dropped a little, bringing a knowing smile to her face. I looked down at my penis pointing out in all its glory. My heart skipped a beat as an all-consuming, passionate desire, fuelled by conflicting emotions, made me want my woman more than ever before.

Unable to get my head round my intense, perverse, sexual excitement, I simply gave in to my primal desire, and picked Angie up in a sweeping cradle lift. I stepped across to the bed and threw her down onto her back. She smiled a wicked smile, before hooking her arms behind her knees to hold herself wide open. With her hold-up stockings and high heels on, my woman was the very epitome of an irresistible, slutty temptress. I instantly jumped onto the bed. Then, taking my stiff cock in hand, I aimed it at her engorged, wet opening and unceremoniously penetrated her … hard! Gripping her thighs, I stretched her open wider still and then proceeded to pound her with all I had; my oily hips working back and forth in powerful rhythmical strokes.

'Arghhh … arghhh … arghhh … yes… fuck … yes …' sighed my wife, whilst pulling me into her with every thrust, her nails digging into my arse.

After several minutes of angrily pumping my rampant cock in and out of my woman's vagina, I suddenly felt the need to look at our base physical connection. Rising to my knees, I grabbed her ankles and pushed them over her head. Having re-entered her, I closely observed myself going in and out of my wife; confirmation that I was taking her, and that she was mine. Her legs were so far back that her tummy rolls gathered and connected with her breasts. This was my mate in her raw primal state; the very epitome of womanhood, her wanton body oozing dirty sex. That made me want her even more.

'You need fucking Angie!' I insisted gruffly, whilst

drilling my stare into her eyes.

'Yes!' she whispered breathlessly. 'Fuck me, fuck me, fuck me.'

With my arse powerfully tense, I continued to pound my woman, slap, slap, slapping into her – fucking her like a man possessed. I again looked down at our physical interbody connection and observed my woman's labia being stretched open by my erection. That, together with the sight of the curve of her mons pubis, created a beautifully disgusting picture for my pleasure.

'Arghhh God, yes … yes … yes …' panted Angie, as I kept hard at it, huffing, puffing, and grunting all the while.

A moment later, I suddenly felt the need to take my wife on all fours. I hurriedly withdrew my penis and slid my arm round her back. I then flipped her over onto her tummy and pulled her up onto her knees by her hips, causing her to emit a fanny fart from the air I'd pushed into her with my powerful thrusting.

'Now I'm gonna fuck you like Martin did,' I said authoritatively, 'but better!'

With that said, I drew my cock-head up and down my wife's labia a few times, before then plunging straight back up inside her.

'Arghhh,' she groaned, as I thrust deep, hard and fast, hitting her cervix. It was painful for her, but I wanted her to have that pain. Usually I was softer, but now I wanted to punish her.

'Fuck me, Rich, fuck me,' ordered my wife, 'I want your cum up me!'

'Yeah?!' I said gruffly through clenched teeth, before slapping her arse with an almighty whack of my hand, causing her to yelp.

I then settled into a sustainable rhythm and concentrated on the all-consuming feeling of sliding in and out of my wife. Each stroke made me wilder still for my mate, as the need to release my semen into her vagina began to build in me. I was driven to come deep inside her. Not on her bum, tum or tits, like I'd done so many times before. No, this was an animal need, the likes of which I'd never known, and way more disturbingly exciting than when she admitted to being wet for Ryan.

Dripping with sweat, I continued to pound my wife whilst savouring the smell of her intoxicating sex aroma, as it rose up from between her legs.

'Ahh fuck I'm coming,' she whispered, clawing her fingers into the duvet.

Having heard that, I picked up my speed. I needed to pump faster than Martin. I needed to satisfy my woman so she wouldn't stray. At the same time, the intensifying climactic sensations in my cock became all-consuming. My whole body was now taught and primed, as I teetered on the brink of exploding into my woman. At this point, I felt her pussy tighten. That pleased me. Then, fuelled by stamina I didn't think I had, I quickened my pace still further as I energised for orgasm.

'I'm gonna come for you,' I declared in a deep, rumbling voice.

As soon as I'd said that, my wife let out a huge 'arghhhhhh', and began wriggling in orgasm, her arse gyrating like a performing porn star. But I wanted her quiet whilst I ejaculated into her. So, with frenzied urgency, I gripped her hips super tight and forcibly held her still. At this point, my fully stretched crossbow finally released, shooting copious amounts of semen out of me, in orgasmic pulsating waves, deep inside my wife. With all my semen where I needed it to be, I collapsed on top of her, forcing her arms to give way.

Completely spent, I laid on top of Angie for a moment to catch my breath. I then rolled off her without saying a word. She didn't speak either. This wasn't normal for us. Usually, we would cuddle before drifting off to sleep together. But this time, we turned our backs on each other, leaving a big space between us, both physically and emotionally.

Having flipped the lights off from my bedside, I stared into the darkness and tried to work out why I now felt so cold towards Angie, and why she quite obviously felt cold towards me. Why did I feel detached from her and emotionally unfulfilled, when we'd just shared such an exciting intimacy? That question remained unanswered though, as I reluctantly drifted off to sleep, having succumbed to the physical and mental ravages of a long, emotional day.

CHAPTER 9

My alarm went off at 7.30. Angie and I were both subdued.

Breakfast was painful. We hardly spoke, and what we did say was perfunctory and business-like.

At nine in the morning, we checked out of the Downs View Hotel, made our way to the VW in silence, and set off for home.

With our usual bonhomie chit-chat conspicuous by its absence, my thoughts went to the events of the night before. The first thing that came to mind, was how I thought about sex during my Black Dog episode. It was disgustingly base and graphic and was about me fucking my woman hard. She was there to be penetrated by my erection, not to connect with her, but to dominate her, to take her and to own her – both physically and sexually. And for her part, my wife enjoyed goading and belittling me to aggravate Black Dog to elicit my perverted hardcore sex response. We'd both articulated ourselves in a horrid, base way, like something out of a porn movie, yet we were both incredibly excited. I wasn't even sure if we fully respected one another. This debauched sex was the complete opposite of anything I'd ever known.

Then, a load of questions appeared in my head, like …

how could a loving wife cheat on her husband when she supposedly loved him so much? Why did I react so badly to something before my time? The answer to that question hit me straight away. I figured my wife's actions before my time, reflected who she was, and therefore the person she could possibly be. The one thing I knew for sure though, was that I needed the skeleton from her cupboard gone, so we could park the past and move on.

As soon as that thought had come and gone, a whole series of other questions came to mind, like …

Why did I want to hear about every last naughtyexplicit detail of my wife's illicitsecret affair?

Why did Black Dog elicit such incredible sexual excitement in amongst the angst of it all?

Did my want to know all my wife's personal details legitimise her affair in her own mind?

Did my want to know all my wife's personal details legitimise her actions and give her the perfect excuse to goad, humiliate, and belittle me as a way of getting back at me for judging her?

Or was she genuinely turning a negative into a positive?

And, is my wife's apparent delight in being a graphic teaser and wanton hussy, part of her *forgotten me?*

Unable to answer any of my own questions, I then began to wonder what was going on in Angie's head.

Before I knew it, over two hours had passed without my wife and I uttering a single word to each other. At breakfast, she looked concerned, but now she looked as if she didn't care. Past caring, because to care cost emotional energy, and she was out of that. I guess I wanted her to be contrite. It wasn't about making her feel bad, I just needed her to accept she'd done wrong, then I'd know she wouldn't do the same thing to me.

I was also cross with her because she lied to me from the outset. I felt betrayed, even though she hadn't cheated on me. Most of all, I felt my marriage was based on a lie – albeit a lie to keep me from ending things before they even got started. Angie was right, the truth would definitely have been a deal breaker at that time.

With three hours of silent driving under my belt, my mind drifted away from my marital woes as I contemplated the changing scenery. I'd driven past beautiful countryside, boring industrial structures, and ugly towns with high-rise boxes housing less fortunate people than ourselves. Those comparisons made me realise that life is made up of the good, the bad and the ugly.

If I could only eliminate the bad and the ugly in my life, that would enable me to concentrate on the good. With that in mind, I turned my frown upside down, on the basis that, whilst my Angie's wrongdoing upset and unsettled me on the one hand, it made me crazy to have her on the other. Although that was unfathomable and bizarre, perhaps I could reframe it to be a positive. I then asked myself if it was time to swallow my pride, but as usual, reason was side-lined as a battle of wills raged between Angie and me to see who would break first.

How the hell had we come to this, I wondered.

This is residual fallout from your wife's revelations, said demon voice. Now there's a massive trust issue which you ain't never gonna resolve.

As I drove through the village of Bancroft, my eye was drawn to a playground full of schoolchildren running around without a care in the world. They were completely focused on the here and now. I nodded in thoughtful contemplation, as I considered the value of not being distracted by the past or the future. Then, the thought of seeing the children, made me smile. And even though they always had lots of fun with their aunt Tracy, I knew they really loved it when Mummy and Daddy got home.

With under half an hour to go, I decided to extend an olive branch. As I drew a breath to say let's forget about the past and move forward, I was delighted to hear Angie clear her throat ready to speak. I wouldn't have to swallow my pride after all.

'I want a divorce, Rich,' she announced haughtily, without looking at me.

'Divorce?' I repeated in utter disbelief, having expected her to say sorry. 'Jesus, where the hell did that come from?'

'We're finished Rich. Got it?' my wife insisted firmly.

'You based our marriage on lies Angie, and now *you* want out?'

'Damn right! You sanctimonious arsehole!' she replied aggressively, whilst forcibly pulling my head down towards her lap by my ear.

'Get off me, you silly bitch!' I demanded, as I tried to keep my eyes on the road.

'I made a mistake you bastard!' said Angie, pushing my head away with a flick of her hand, her pent-up anger having finally boiled over.

'How would you like it if I made a mistake with Charlotte?' I demanded to know.

'What do you think? I couldn't trust you. I'd leave.'

'Exactly! So why can't you accept that your extramarital fucking makes me feel insecure?'

'I already told you,' replied Angie, in her awful goading tone, 'I didn't *fuck* him. *He* fucked me. Which bit of that are you struggling with?'

Hearing that really made my blood boil, causing me to change down from forth to third for no reason whatsoever.

'Why do you keep saying that?' I asked anxiously, as my stomach knotted. 'What does it mean?'

'You know what a *fuck* is Rich, surely?' replied my wife. 'Oh my,' she added calmly, wearing a smug, callous smile, 'you've gone puce!'

'Why are you taunting me Angie?' I shouted, gripping the steering wheel so tight that my knuckles turned white.

'Because I'm immoral Rich,' she replied in a matter-of-fact voice, 'and now I'm gonna divorce you.'

"No, that's wrong Angie! Say it's wrong!'

'Certainly not!' she replied, whilst nonchalantly looking out of the window.

'It *is* wrong!' I countered in a raised voice.

'It isn't!' retorted my wife, before turning to thrust her face in mine whilst looking directly at me. 'Divorce isn't wrong, and Dom would have approved of my affair! Probably enjoyed it like you. Go on, admit it – you love hearing about it.'

'I don't wanna know, Angie.'

'I'm gonna tell you every last detail again and again,' she insisted through clenched teeth.

'No!' I shouted.

'I'm gonna tell you how I moaned as he *fucked* me. You like hearing it, so you can't say it's wrong, can you?'

'No! It's wrong!' I protested, as I went erect and accelerated to eighty miles an hour. 'It's all wrong!'

'I won't be judged by you or anyone else,' declared Angie like a mighty orator. 'Got it? You won't make me feel worthless. I'm gonna divorce you, and that's that!'

'Divorce?' I questioned angrily, 'why are you …'

'I'm not talking anymore!' interrupted my wife, as she closed her eyes, covered her ears with her hands and sang 'divorce, divorce, divorce, divorce …'

'No! No! No!' I screamed, as I released the steering wheel, and bashed the sides of my head with my clenched fists in unimaginable frustration. 'Why are you being so nasty? Why? Why? WHYYYYY?' I demanded, as I suddenly stamped on the brakes in anger.

A moment later, I instinctively retook the wheel as the car skidded and fish-tailed from side to side. As I fought to regain control, it slewed onto the grass verge and bounced violently over the bumps, until the back end swung round and we came to a stop facing in the opposite direction.

'Why are you being so heartless?' I demanded, as I bashed the steering wheel repeatedly with my fists. 'Tell me why you're being like this, when what I need is your love?'

Angie looked concerned now. The realisation that I'd put her in harm's way had clearly shaken her.

'I don't know why I get like this,' she replied softly. 'I'm angry, I think. Angry at myself. I'm sorry.'

'Sorry?' I repeated as I shook my head. 'Huh, that's a laugh. Why be sorry only when I'm wound up like a spinning top and driving like a mad man?'

'I know, and I really am sorry. I don't like what I did to Dom, but I can't bring myself to admit it.'

'Can you not see how that makes me feel insecure?' I asked.

'It's not just about you, Rich,' came my wife's whispered reply.

I rested my forearms on the steering wheel and let my head slump into my hands.

'No, it's not just about me,' I said softly, 'it's about saving our marriage. It's about us and our beautiful babies.'

Angie looked at me through teary eyes and stroked my face.

'I'm sorry my big man,' she said through her sobs.

Shaking my head in utter disbelief, I picked up my phone and stepped out onto the grass verge. I turned to look at Angie through the window with vacant, blotchy, red eyes. She returned the same look. We were both completely emotionally drained.

With my shoulders rounded and my head hung low, I slowly walked away from the car without even thinking about where I was going.

* * *

My subliminal autopilot took me to the coast; the place where I could calm my mind and gather my thoughts. I walked for miles and miles, but the emotionally restorative power of the seaside failed to work its magic. I wasn't able to find a solution to my problems.

Exhausted and cold with just my polo shirt and jeans on, I dropped to my knees on the damp sand of a secluded cove. I was still reeling from Angie's revelations, her lack of remorse, and her decision to divorce me.

Just when I thought life had turned a corner and we were set to go from strength to strength, yet another major trauma knocked me sideways and brought me to my knees. It appeared that the good Lord thought I needed yet another difficulty to test my faith. To me though, it felt like vultures were circling my weakened being, waiting to eat me alive, once I succumbed to the weight of life's torturous trials.

From my kneeling position, I leaned back onto my bum, gazed across the never-ending ocean, and sighed deeply as I searched for answers. After a while, I reached into my pocket and pulled out my Post-it pad and betting shop pen. Ever since the recession hit me, I always carried my emergency cathartic kit; committing my thoughts to paper seemed to help me.

Shivering, I began scribbling to clear my head.

You think you know someone but suddenly you don't
You walk hand in hand along your expected path
To keep each other happy till death do you part

But now from nowhere new emotions tear at your soul
Churning your insides, imposing doubts and fears
Knocking you sideways like a demolition ball

How can our marriage come back from the brink?
How can we save our beautiful world from ourselves?
How can we save our innocent children heartache and
pain?

What will …

Unable to compose another verse, I suddenly stopped writing.

'How the hell can you fix this?' I asked out loud.

This can work! I told myself. I love my wife. It has to work, otherwise she's gonna leave me and take the kids.

As I scanned the horizon, the conversation I had with Charlotte at her dinner party suddenly came to mind.

Perhaps her therapist might be able to help.

With nothing to lose and everything to gain, I jumped to my feet and rang for an appointment. After ascertaining a few facts, Julia offered 10 a.m. on Friday, and I took it.

CHAPTER 10

A couple of days had passed since my horrid argument in the car with Angie. Thankfully, she hadn't said anymore about wanting to divorce me. I assumed it wasn't really meant and was said in the heat of the moment to get at me – which it did! Now that things had calmed down between us, I needed to tell her that I was going to see Julia on Friday. Choosing the right time to do this was crucial.

* * *

With my hands on my knees, I paused on the driveway to catch my breath after returning from my morning run. As I straightened up, I began contemplating the best way to approach Angie. After a couple of minutes, I had a rough idea of what I was going to say. Looking up at the sunny, blue, spring sky, I took a deep breath and blew it out slowly before walking into the house with a smile on my face. My wife was sitting at the kitchen table drinking a cup of tea whilst reading *The Daily Mail*.

'Hey,' I said softly as I leaned against the wall. 'Did the children get off to school alright?'

'Yes, but Connor forgot his book bag with his homework in.'

'Shall I run it up to school for him?' I asked.

'No,' replied my wife, glancing up at me momentarily. 'I told him he'd have to remember in future. He's gotta learn.'

I nodded and then cleared my throat to speak.

'I've been thinking about things,' I said. 'I've got a plan.'

'One that doesn't involve you thinking badly of me?' retorted my wife, without looking up from her paper.

'I don't think badly of you, it's just that with all this stuff from the past and talk of divorce and everything I …'

'You what, Rich?'

'I erm … I sometimes don't feel like you really love me.'

'At the heart of all great love is a great friendship,' replied my wife. 'And I don't feel we're friends anymore.'

'So you don't love me then, Angie? Is that what you're saying?'

'I do love you,' she insisted, looking directly at me. 'But I need you to be my friend and stop all this nonsense.'

'And I need you to acknowledge your misdeeds,' I retorted. 'So we can move on.'

'I'm not apologising to you!' said Angie. 'I didn't cheat on you.'

'But you did *lie* to me right from the start! Plus it feels like you cheated on me because I kinda felt like I'd taken the baton from Dom.'

'Taken the baton from Dom!' repeated Angie, whilst making air quotes with her fingers. 'What utter bollocks you talk!'

Having taken a deep breath to keep calm, I told Angie that I was just sharing my feelings, like all the experts say we're supposed to do. Appearing frustrated with the whole thing, she thought no harm was done as Dom never knew anything about Martin. She added that Dom was a good lawyer, but that he had confidence issues. I asked what that had to do with anything.

'You don't get it, Rich,' replied Angie in a softer tone. 'I told you before, and no disrespect to Dom, but he was boring! Martin was exciting, but a rubbish lover.'

'And what happens if you get bored with me?' I asked, screwing my face up in disgust.

'I won't,' she replied with unexpected warmth. 'You're extraordinary. Completely different from anyone I've ever known. You make me laugh; you're clever, determined, tenacious, strong, interesting, loving and kind. You're a larger-than-life character – no one could match that.'

I stared at Angie across the table with doubtful eyes.

Do I believe her? Sure, I *was* confident, but I'm struggling a bit now. But I still make her laugh, I insisted to myself. I'm a great dad, I'm a great problem solver, I'm nearly there with my trading, I care for her, I love her – I would give my life for her in an instant for Christ's sake.

My internal good cop/bad cop routine continued. Don't be stupid, Richie; you've served your purpose mate. She's had her kids and so it's just a matter of time till she fucks off with another bloke when the opportunity arises.

'Say something Rich!' said Angie anxiously, crashing through my thoughts.

'You're just saying all these nice things,' I replied softly, my face full of doubt, 'but you don't really mean them.'

'But I do. I …'

'You'll get bored,' I interrupted, 'and leave me for someone else. You're good at lies.'

Angie went quiet for a moment. She then stood up straight and inhaled deeply as if she was about to begin a great oration.

'Just to be clear, Rich,' she declared assertively. 'I wanted company too – not just sex.'

'Oh right. I'm sorry. How silly of me, Angie! I should have known that it's quite usual for a woman to have sex when she just wants company.'

'It wasn't like that, we did talk,' she insisted.

'Whatever … talking, walking, shagging. It's still cheating on a man you say you loved.'

At this point I realised I couldn't keep a lid on things and that it didn't take much for me to throw my wife's past in her face, but I couldn't stop myself. I realised that was a massive failure on my part which needed to be rectified.

Incensed, Angie marched round the table and shoved her face in mine. I tipped my chair back and turned my head away from her.

'We were fucking in his car!' she said angrily, screwing her face up. 'That's part of cheating, for Christ's sake. What did you think we were gonna do? Hold hands and discuss poetry the whole time?'

Having said her piece, my wife marched away again with a face like thunder. I felt myself hyperventilating and looked down at my chest rising and falling heavily. I didn't want this. My stomach was churning like a washing machine and saliva gathered in my mouth. After a long pause I demanded to know why Angie was being so cruel.

'Because I'm a whore and that's what whores do,' she replied emphatically, before folding her arms angrily and leaning against the work surface.

'Do they?'

'Yes! And you're quite right; I'll do the same to you. I need excitement. This whole thing and you are boring me rigid.'

'Why don't you think what you did was wrong?' I said. 'That's what I don't get!'

'I'm not gonna beat myself up over something from eighteen years ago, and before your time. People have pasts. If you can't handle it, let's get divorced.'

'You keep saying that Angie,' I replied softly, forcing myself to keep a lid on things.

'I'm not going to be judged by you!' she insisted haughtily. 'You shouldn't have married me.'

'That's a stupid thing to say!' I retorted, with a look of incredulity. 'How could I have made the decision not to marry you when I didn't know all the facts?'

'We can split next month on the rent anniversary,' announced my wife casually. 'I'll issue divorce proceedings.'

'Divorce proceedings?'

'Yes!'

'No!' I shouted. 'It's not fair – you can't do that!'

'Just fucking watch me.'

'Is it fair on me and the children when you didn't tell me what I was getting into?' I demanded to know. 'There's no justice in that!'

'I'm a barrister and I'm issuing justice,' declared my wife. 'Have you got that, you bastard?'

My blood boiled at the unfairness of Angie's attack. Heat gathered in my face and my breathing quickened even more as my heart pounded in my chest. Then suddenly, without realising, I stood up sharply and flipped the breakfast table into the air, causing chairs to go flying and Angie's cup of tea to crash to the floor.

'You don't frighten me, you arsehole!' she growled, strutting over to me purposefully. 'What you gonna do?' she demanded, pulling me down by my collar and thrusting her face into mine. 'Hit me? Go on then, hit me you bastard! Go on, hit me! I want you to.'

'Why are you being so nasty?' I retorted angrily, grabbing hold of her arms, and shaking her. 'You're gonna divorce me for the wrong *you* did. That's not fair!'

Angry and outraged, my wife pushed me away forcefully. I had hold of her dress; it tore. I stepped back. She dropped to her knees and began sobbing, her head in her hands.

Hanging my head in shame and regret, I stared expressionless at my Angie in a heap on the floor. What had I just done? All this anger, hatred and contempt born of a desire to love my wife. Jesus, how fucking ironic is that?

'I'm scum Angie,' I said softly. 'I'm sorry.'

She looked up at me with sad, tear-sodden eyes. My heart sank to my boots at the pathetic sight I'd created.

'I can't seem to let it go,' I added in a whisper, shaking my head slowly. 'I wish it was all meaningless to me, but it isn't. I'm sorry.'

'I wish it was all meaningless to you too,' said Angie, in a low voice. 'I don't really want us to split up, but I can't deal with your moral judgements. You make me feel worthless.'

'I know,' I replied, 'that's why I was trying to tell you my plan going forward, but you didn't even listen to it. You just kept coming at me, Angie.'

'I know I goaded you,' she said, looking sad.

'Why would you do that?' I asked softly.

'After you went mad in the car, I wanted to see if you would do it again; see if you loved me enough not to react and not judge me on my past.'

'Christ Angie,' I replied. 'That's just crazy!'

'I know,' she whispered. 'And I'm sorry.'

I felt numb as I quietly let myself out of the back door. Having walked a few paces, I puked up in a flower bed without warning. I looked down at the foul-smelling vomit splattered over the flowers, their beauty destroyed. I had just done the very same thing to our marriage. I couldn't look anymore. I just wiped my mouth with the back of my hand and walked on. I had no more emotion in me save for feeling that I was a piece of shit; scum of the first order.

'You fucking arsehole, Rich!' I said out loud. 'You're so not a gentle giant anymore; you're a bully. How big of you to tower a foot over your wife and shake her. You're supposed to be her protector.'

As I walked on, tears streamed down my face. Then, after what seemed like an age, I was all cried out.

Emotionally unable to return home, I headed for the beach. Maybe my old friend and confidant, Mr Blue, could help me figure out why I'd suddenly turned into such an ugly, angry monster, wreaking havoc in my own marriage.

* * *

I found myself at the end of a secluded cove, which I'd reached via a precipitous footpath from the clifftop. Here, a substantial rocky finger jutted straight out into the sea some seventy metres. At its high points, it towered fifty feet above the sea. I'd been here before in happier times, and had been inspired by its seclusion and spirituality. As

I scrambled along its length to the very end, I wondered if Inspiration Point, as I called it, would deliver this time.

Having reached the end, I pulled myself up onto the farthest rock and took my seat of contemplation. Completely alone, I was surrounded on three sides by tuneful splashing brine whose salty smell pervaded the air in fine droplets. Whilst I surveyed the horizon, the pitiful image of Angie on the kitchen floor appeared in my mind's eye.

Christ! Where has this angry, aggressive behaviour come from after sixteen years of marriage? First the car and now this. Before now we argued, but not on this scale. Not like some Hispanic shouting couple from the ghettos of Harlem. That's their culture. But me, an English gentleman I thought, and Angie an upstanding barrister – how does that work? I guess love that means so much begets powerful negative emotion. Now that's a paradox of gargantuan proportions – two people attacking each other in the name of love.

'So what am I going to do?' I said slowly, addressing my question to Mr Blue.

He completely ignored me and kept splashing and churning below. Round shouldered and emotionally exhausted, I looked up to the heavens.

'Are you gonna help me God, send me a guardian angel?' I asked softly. 'What on earth have I come to? Why am I so out of control; so tortured and pained? Why am I so upset with my Angie?'

Still gazing skyward, I remained quiet and waited for answers. When none came, I sighed heavily with disappointment and lowered my gaze to the sea.

'Please send me some help God,' I whispered. 'Send me some help,' I repeated firmly, lifting my head. 'Send me some fucking help!' I shouted, whilst shaking my clenched fists at the sky.

Mr Blue swallowed my words.

'Why do you test me God?' I asked. 'Why send me trials? I love my Angie! Can't you just let me love her in peace? Isn't that what you're about? LOVE?! Why make me judge her with values which conflict with my love for her. How can a man deal with that? Why do you ...'

Having suddenly stopped mid-sentence, I realised that there was no point to my questions, because there were no answers. With a big sigh, I cupped my face in my hands, and peered between my fingers at the flotsam bobbing and weaving around below me. Some bits were trapped between the rocks and were looking for a way out with each receding wave. What was my way out I wondered? I waited yet again for an answer from my God. Nothing came. I took another deep breath, exhaled slowly, and reached for my Post-it pad ...

What happens to love to turn it so cruel?
Destroying those it once did fuel

'Huh, if I knew that,' I muttered, 'I wouldn't be in this mess.'

Trying desperately to make things right
Wishing good to happen to make delight

Injustice begets anger when the mind is weak
And opens the door for violent rage to speak

You turned your protecting hand on your wife
Now you must endure your own ruined life ...

I looked up from my puerile rhyming couplets and surveyed the sky.

'Huh, still no sign from God,' I muttered.

In the absence of a flash of inspiration, I stood up, shoved my Post-it pad and pen back in my pocket, and carelessly made my way back over the jagged rocks to the shore. I didn't care if I fell and hurt myself, or even drowned. I felt worthless.

Despondent, I dragged my heels in the sand as I contemplated my situation. My old dad's words came to mind. Falling over doesn't define you, we all do that, it's how you get up. That sentiment gave me hope that all may not be lost.

My musings were starkly interrupted by a text alert. Angie, I thought to myself, she needs me. With that in mind, I wrenched my phone from my arm band and opened the message with all haste. It was Julia.

'What does she want?' I muttered, annoyed that it wasn't Angie.

"Hi Richard, can you come 12 noon on Friday instead of 10 am? Thanks. Julia."

'Hmmm, do I really want to see her after all?' I asked myself thoughtfully.

After a bit more thought, I decided that, even though she sounded very nice on the phone, she probably wasn't what was needed.

I typed my reply. "Really sorry no can do. Can we please cancel the appointment as I am very busy atm. Thank you."

I was just about to hit send, when it suddenly occurred to me that I'd received Julia's text for a reason.

'Oh, my, God,' I whispered slowly, as I stared at the phone, riveted to the spot. 'This is no coincidence. This is

God sending me my guardian angel.'

I called Julia straight away and briefly explained what had happened. She told me she had a cancellation and could see me within the hour if that suited me.

Buoyed by my epiphany, and in the certain knowledge that Julia had the answers I needed, I ran full pelt along the compacted sand of the shoreline to catch the next bus to Plymouth.

CHAPTER 11

Fixed to the wall of a substantial Victorian semi in Plymouth, was a white ceramic name plate edged with brightly coloured birds in flight. It read:

JULIA PHILLIPS MBACP NCH LPC
PSYCHOSYNTHESIS AND SEX THERAPY
FOR ENLIGHTENED LIFE JOURNEYS

'Hmmm,' I sighed, as I hovered my finger over the doorbell. 'That's a bit namby-pamby.'

Then, after an anxious moment where I contemplated walking away, I remembered Charlotte saying that Julia was really good, but somewhat alternative. I then inhaled deeply before finally pressing the buzzer on the exhale. A moment later, the big half-glazed front door swung open.

'Hello, you must be Richard,' said a smiling grey-haired, pony-tailed, fifty-something woman.

'Yes, hi,' I replied hurriedly.

'Julia,' she said, extending her hand. 'Do come in.'

After a warm handshake, Julia led the way to a big bay-windowed consulting room. A handsome white marble fireplace with a huge ornate gilt framed mirror above, lifted the understated decor. The sunshine brightened the room, but not my spirits.

Julia gestured to me to sit on a two-seater burgundy leather sofa. She sat on its twin opposite. Between us was a light oak coffee table on which sat a jug of water, two glasses and a box of tissues. The room was scented with diffusers and fragrant candles. It looked like it had been haphazardly furnished some thirty years back, without ever being updated.

With a floral print dress draped over her tall, well-proportioned figure, Julia looked like she was teleported from the 1960s. She was an attractive size twelve with a round freckled face, punctuated by pretty pale blue eyes. She didn't look at all professional. That undermined what remained of my confidence in her; until that is, I remembered that she was part of God's plan.

Julia cleared her throat.

'What do you like to be known as?' she asked softly.

'My friends call me Rich,' I answered quickly, willing her to speed things up.

'Rich it is then,' said Julia, before adding that I needed to sign a counselling contract before we got started.

I nodded in response.

'If you could read this and then sign by the pencil cross,' she said, placing a single page document in front of me. 'That would be great.'

'Sure,' I said, before signing on the dotted line.

'Just so you know, Rich,' continued Julia, before sitting down, 'I have my notes from when we chatted on the phone, and I'll be taking more notes as we go.'

Having replied with an affirmative nod, I slid the counselling contract across the coffee table. I then waited for Julia to speak. She asked me why I'd come to see her.

I drew in a super-sized breath and tried to compose

myself, but it didn't work. I started to tremble, so thrusted my hands between my knees to stop the shaking. I then asked Julia if she remembered why I rang for an appointment in the first place.

'Yes,' she replied, looking at her notes. 'You and your wife had a big argument in the car the other day, and another upset this morning.'

'Yes,' I said. 'I wanted to tell Angie that I was getting help from you with my issues, but she just chopped me down.'

'Okay,' said Julia. 'And then?'

'And then I went berserk,' I replied. 'I flipped the dining table over. Angie got in my face and pulled me down by my collar and told me to hit her. I lost it and shook her whilst demanding to know why she was being so nasty and divorcing me for her wrongdoing. I didn't realise what I'd done, until after I'd done it!'

The emotional release of talking to someone overwhelmed me, causing me to break down and cry. With tears streaming down my face, my head involuntarily dropped into my hands.

Sitting forward, Julia pushed the box of tissues across the coffee table. Having wiped my eyes and nose, I met Julia's gaze. She looked very concerned and asked me if Angie was alright.

'Yes,' I replied. 'She's fine, but we're both emotionally wrecked, and I haven't seen her like this before.'

'Like what before?'

'Her mood has changed, and she's a lot more attacking and aggressive than I've ever known her to be. And she has this way of pressing my buttons. Then I become anxious, and my response soon escalates to frustration and anger.

We've never been like this with each other before, and I don't know how to deal with it.'

'May I ask how old your wife is?'

'Forty-six.'

'Okay,' said Julia. 'She is more than likely perimenopausal.'

'What does that mean?' I asked.

'It can mean significant changes for a woman. Ranging from mood swings, irritability, anger, aggression, self-esteem issues, questioning life, hot flushes, increased or decreased libido, and other physical symptoms.'

'Ahhh,' I sighed. 'That's good to know.'

'It's not a reason though, Rich,' said Julia, 'to blame everything on women when they go through hormonal changes.'

'I'm not blaming my wife,' I instantly replied. 'I'm a dogmatic arsehole sometimes, but if I can better understand her, I can stop arguments from escalating.'

'That's a good thing,' said Julia.

Then, after a short pause, she sat up straight and appeared more business-like. She cleared her throat and told me that when she talks to clients about domestic abuse, her code of practice sometimes requires her to inform the police in the event she feels something catastrophic may come to pass.

Christ, I never thought the words "domestic abuse" would ever be related to me. I only thought you read about that sort of thing in the papers.

Having dropped my head in shame, I then listened as Julia told me that she didn't think anything catastrophic was about to happen in relation to my marriage. I lifted my head to look at her as she told me that both Angie and I were responsible for our actions, and that blaming circumstances or other persons was no excuse, either morally or in law.

I was taken aback by the directness of Julia's comment, but accepted that it needed to be said. As I nodded in response, she went on to tell me that a simple coping strategy would be to physically walk away from arguments.

'From what you've said,' she continued, 'both your wife and you are very vociferous and volatile. How you react to each other, needs to be managed.'

I again nodded in response, and was all ears as Julia explained that Angie pulling me down by my ear in the car, and by my collar in the kitchen was domestic abuse, as was tipping the dining table over and shaking Angie.

'I make this point very clear,' she added, 'because behaviours like this can appear in a relationship after a significant emotional event, and then become normalised.'

Feeling like I'd been admonished by a fearsome headmistress, I told Julia I recognised the gravity of what she was saying, and that I was grateful for her candour. I then asked her what Angie and I should do going forward.

'It's clear that each party can elicit an angry response from the other,' she replied. 'And that's down to personalities.'

'But it wasn't like this before,' I said.

Having nodded in response, Julia asked me to give her some more background detail. I went through the whole thing with her.

How Angie had told me, on our very first date, that she'd slept with a married man just days *after* her husband Dom had died, and how I felt that disrespected him.

How she then recently told me the truth … that she'd been having an affair for over a year with the man, even whilst her husband was dying. On top of that, she was trying for a baby with both her husband and her lover, in order to give her husband a child.

I also explained about Angie's confidence and self-esteem issues, which I thought was caused by me losing the family's money.

As Julia made notes, I told her about Angie's *forgotten me,* and her need to find herself and her desire not to be invisible. I also mentioned our *Indecent Proposal* conversation and what happened with salsa Dave and Ryan, and my heightened angry sexual reaction.

I then asked Julia if she thought Angie and I were finished as a couple.

'Not at all Rich,' she replied. 'The issues at play here are incredibly emotive for both of you. But once there's closure,' she added, 'those extreme emotions will no longer be relevant.'

'So are you saying that we can sort this out?' I questioned anxiously.

'Sure,' said Julia, sounding warmer and much less business-like. 'With a little management, I'm sure loving relations between both of you can be completely restored.'

Pleased to hear that, I told Julia that I wanted that more than anything in the world. I then went on to explain that I loved Angie with all my heart, and that I felt the root cause of our upset, was my judgement of her.

'That's definitely one of the issues at play here,' commented Julia.

'As a Catholic,' I said, 'I was sort of brought up to morally judge people.'

'That's as maybe,' responded Julia. 'But the important thing is that there are appropriate therapies for both you and Angie.'

'So are you saying that my wife needs to see you too?' I asked.

'Yes,' replied Julia. 'Couples counselling is clearly what's needed here.'

Having nodded in thoughtful response, I said that I would speak to Angie about that. Julia was pleased, because conflict resolution needed both parties to buy into it for it to work.

After a short pause, Julia sat up a little straighter and cleared her throat. She then asked me where I thought my anger came from. I said it stemmed from the fact that Angie lied to me from the very start of our relationship, and had I known the truth about her lover, I wouldn't have married her.

'It's the unfairness of her calls for divorce that really make me angry,' I added, 'when she's the one that's put us in this position by lying.'

With that said, I paused for a moment and waited for Julia to finish taking her notes. When she was done, she looked up at me expectantly.

'Not wishing to play the blame game,' I continued, 'but I can't help feeling that my wife's cheating was wrong. That makes her really angry.'

'That's because she feels judged!' retorted Julia quickly, as if defending Angie without thinking.

'But the problem is,' I responded, 'those lies have brought toxicity to our relationship. They have made me insecure about Angie's love for me, and I don't trust her, especially as she blames her late husband for her own failings.'

'And how does that make you feel?' asked Julia.

'Well, that a leopard never changes its spots, and that

Angie will cheat on me,' I replied, before then easing back onto the sofa. 'Plus,' I added, 'as much as I'd like to see the good in her trying to get pregnant by her lover for the benefit of her husband, I struggle with the morality of that. I kind of see it as a convenient excuse to continue to cheat on her husband when he became sick.'

I felt better for sharing all that with Julia, but then, as I gazed at her expectantly, my eyes suddenly filled with tears. She looked back at me completely unfazed and waited for me to continue. Having dried my eyes, I told her that there was more stuff, and asked her if she wanted me to tell her about it.

'Yes of course,' she replied. 'If you want to.'

'Well,' I began, 'like I said on the phone, I wanted to know every last sexual detail about my wife's affair.'

Hearing myself say that embarrassed me, and made me think twice about sharing any further details. Sensing my discomfort, Julia reassured me that there was very little she hadn't heard in her consulting room, and that she was a qualified sex therapist. She then prompted me to continue with a wide-eyed expectant nod.

'My wife's intimate sex details totally destroyed me,' I continued, 'but also aroused me like never before. Does that make me weird?'

'Not at all,' replied Julia. 'Some people don't want to know anything about a partner's affair at all, and an equal number literally need to know every last *painful* detail. You're not weird.'

'And why did I get so turned on?' I asked anxiously.

'You experienced a competitive cuckold response,' replied Julia. 'And recreational cuckolding,' she added, 'is surprisingly common amongst more liberated couples.'

'But I'm not liberated,' I responded. 'And it wasn't something I'd agreed to.'

'I appreciate that Rich,' said Julia. 'I was just explaining that your sexual arousal wasn't unusual, and that cuckolding is a desire many men have within a committed, loving relationship.'

I was extremely pleased to hear that, because I felt rather pathetic for deriving pleasure from my wife's sex with another man. Somewhat relieved, I smiled and then wanted to know whether women thought their men weak for being a cuckold.

'Not really,' replied Julia. 'They tend to see them as liberated and supportive.'

Feeling better about myself, I then asked my counsellor if women in general liked the idea of being the cuckolder.

'Cuckoldress!' stressed Julia. 'But yes, generally, once a woman has grasped the concept, they love it. It's confidence-boosting, guilt-free, naughty fun. Plus, because their man doesn't have sex with anyone else, the woman doesn't have to deal with jealousy, and is made to feel special by their partner who is proud of their sexiness.'

'It's very loving of them to do that for their husband's benefit,' I said.

'There's an element of that,' said Julia. 'But research has shown that women who are lovingly encouraged and feel morally free to have extramarital sex, do so largely for their own excitement and pleasure. But she is also extra turned on because she's exciting her partner all the more.'

'Wow! So she's not taking one for the team then?'

'Absolutely not,' said Julia. 'And if she felt pressured like she was taking one for the team, then that is coercive behaviour and is totally unacceptable.'

Nodding in acknowledgement, I then listened as Julia told me that the women find it sexually empowering to cuckold their partner as well as partaking of very erotic forbidden fruit.

'So do women fantasise about sleeping with other men then?' I asked.

'Yes,' said Julia. 'It's up there with a two-men one-woman threesome fantasy.'

'And what happens when a husband shares his cuckold desire with his wife?' I asked, 'and she hasn't fantasised about another man?'

'Women can get turned on to the idea,' said Julia, 'but in most cases, the woman nearly always immediately rejects the concept at first, because she sees it as cheating and expects to be judged.'

'Oh, okay,' I said.

'But as I said earlier,' continued Julia, 'once they grasp the concept of having sex with another man just for the fun of it, they generally become enthusiastic converts, but only on the basis that it's something they do as part of being a couple. And it often strengthens a relationship,' she added. 'As does swinging.'

Having acknowledged Julia's explanation with a nod, I then told her that I'd had two more cuckold-type responses. One when Angie described how her salsa partner, who she fancied, rubbed his erection against her nether regions. And the second, when she flirted with a guy called Ryan and he squeezed her breasts.

'But the thing is,' I continued, 'even though the sex was incredibly exciting after hearing all the juicy details, I got angry and felt detached from my wife. At the same time,' I added, 'I got very possessive, and had this unstoppable need to shag her to within an inch of her life.'

Having realised what I'd just said, I felt my face redden and then apologised for my language. Julia smiled and then told me that she'd heard a lot worse, and that I wasn't to worry.

Then, looking a little more serious, she went on to explain that being cuckolded produced many types of emotional and sexual responses. Apparently, my excessively angry response was down to the fact that I wasn't aware of my latent cuckold desires. Because I wasn't conscious of that, it was somewhat against my emotional and moral grain. That, however, was countered by my heightened sexual excitement.

Having again nodded in acknowledgement, I then asked Julia if a man could discover a cuckold tendency by chance. She told me that many men reported discovering such a desire when they learned about their partner's infidelity.

'And did that sort of save the relationship?' I asked.

'Once the trust issues were resolved, yes.'

'Hmmm,' I sighed, nodding thoughtfully.

'But getting back to you though,' said Julia resolutely, 'by asking questions and becoming aroused, you are, at a subconscious level, encouraging your wife in her cuckoldress role.'

Not really knowing how to respond to that, I asked Julia why Angie was sometimes so graphic, and almost vengeful, when she told me the specifics of her sex with Martin.

'There's a mix of emotional drivers here,' replied Julia. 'Again, your wife probably felt judged, and so pushed back. That assertiveness made her feel good. I would also say that your arousal mitigated her historic actions.'

Having acknowledged Julia's point with a thoughtful

nod, I told her how Angie used to be so judgemental about other women. Women who cheated that is.

'That's known as sexual hypocrisy,' replied Julia. 'Where someone judges others more harshly than themselves, for the same wrongdoing. I don't like to comment on specific individuals, but in general terms people often get cross with themselves for failing to meet their own standards. When people find it hard to admit to their own shortcomings, they often subliminally justify or minimise their actions.'

Julia then went on to tell me that the root of hypocrisy is fear. It typically stems from a sincere belief that they should not be held to the same standards as others because they have better intentions. Plus, to them, it feels good to be morally superior to someone else and helps them avoid painful emotions.

Somewhat gobsmacked by the depth of Julia's psychoanalysis of my wife, I stared at her wide-eyed for a moment, before asking her how I should deal with this.

'You don't "deal with it" per se,' said Julia, making air quotes. 'You simply accept your wife the way she is, instead of trying to change her thinking to match yours. Remember,' she added, 'you can't change other people's behaviour and thinking, you can only change your own!'

Having nodded in thoughtful response, I then turned to the subject of Angie's *forgotten me*. I reiterated that she felt invisible to men, and that she needed male attention to boost her self-esteem and confidence. I went on to say that she suffered badly when I lost my business. Julia wanted to know more about that, so I elucidated. She then told me that losing everything would definitely have impacted Angie's self-esteem and confidence.

'That's down to me,' I whispered, grimacing with regret.

'Life's not about blame, Rich,' countered Julia. 'And your wife's current frame of mind is not all down to the loss of your business.'

'So what other elements do you think are at play then, Julia,' I asked.

'That's what I need to work out,' she replied. 'You've identified your wife's feeling of being invisible to men, and that's certainly a factor here, as is the likelihood that she is perimenopausal and questioning her life. Women have usually sacrificed themselves for the family, so they've got some "me time" to catch up on.'

'So she's not depressed then?' I said.

'From what you've said,' replied Julia, 'I don't think your wife is depressed. The perimenopause sounds like the culprit. HRT should be the first line of defence. NOT antidepressants, which is sadly what most GPs will prescribe.'

I was pleased that Julia had ruled out depression. I then questioned why Angie wanted to sleep with another man, as a way for me to prove my love. I then asked Julia if that meant that Angie was intrinsically unhappy in our marriage.

'I would say,' she began, 'that HRT will help your wife enormously. That aside though, I also believe she has unresolved issues to do with her past, and her self-esteem and confidence around being a woman.'

At this point, rather than prompt me to say something more, Julia pursed her lips in thought. She then asked me to tell her a little bit about Angie's parents and their marriage.

'Sure,' I said, before giving her a quick potted history.

After that there was a short pause. Julia cleared her throat. Then, having allowed her knees to lean to one side, she regarded me thoughtfully with her hands on her lap.

'As I mentioned earlier,' she said, 'I try not to talk specifically about personalities, but I will in this instance, because it will greatly assist your therapeutic care.'

'Thank you.'

'There's a pattern here, Rich,' said Julia.

'A pattern?' I repeated, widening my eyes.

'A pattern of your wife having affairs,' replied Julia, 'and I'm not judging her when I say that,' she added, 'I'm just making an observation.'

'Does that mean she's going to cheat on me too then?' I asked fretfully.

'With proper therapy and understanding,' replied Julia, 'no.'

She then went on to talk about the emotional drivers at play in Angie's past, which gave her a frame of reference for her subsequent behaviours. Apparently, her father was a big influence on her; she took "modelling" from him, when he left her mum for his mistress.

Julia also told me that, from what I'd told her, it appeared that Angie was deprived of proper attention from her father. That forced her to seek it from other men. My counsellor then explained that a woman often best achieves this by using her sexuality, which would go part way to explaining why Angie took extramarital lovers. At this point, Julia paused for a moment to look at her notes.

'Turning to your wife's previous marriages,' she said, 'and their impact on her behaviour, it's plain to see that Dom didn't provide her with everything she needed.'

Julia then unpacked that by explaining that, on the one hand, Angie craved the security, reliability, and dependability which Dom provided. On the other hand, she wanted the extra male attention, approval, and danger which her lover provided.

'And there's something about transgression,' she added, 'which makes the desire really potent. Plus there's a big attraction to the forbidden, which makes it very erotic.'

'Hmmm,' I sighed. 'I'm not sure Angie would come for counselling, especially if she knew she'd be discussing her infidelities.'

'Well,' said Julia, 'that element will definitely need to be addressed to ensure the best possible outcome.'

So with the question of Angie's attendance at therapy in the lap of the gods, I then went on to discuss her *Indecent Proposal* scenario. Julia agreed that my wife's so-called jest was indeed a way for me to prove I loved her by not judging her.

'But I'd go crazy with jealousy,' I said.

Then, in a throwaway comment, Julia remarked on how interesting it was that jealousy is greatly reduced in swinging and polyamorous couples. She then quickly added that Angie's cuckold scenario was more than likely driven by a desire to not be judged by me.

'But bearing everything in mind,' she added, 'your wife's proposal may also be a fantasy that interests her. I think it would be helpful for you to discuss that possibility with her.'

I responded by saying that I didn't think I could ever support Angie in that way. And then, just the prospect of being cuckolded made my penis go hard. Red-faced, I pushed my bum back into the sofa to make my erection less obvious.

Clearly distracted by my sudden and awkward movement, Julia's eyes dropped momentarily. Then, having looked back up at me, she held my gaze and waited for me to say something. It was like she knew that I wanted to know more about my cuckold response. Having swallowed hard, I then reluctantly asked her to explain it to me in more detail.

'Not that it's my sort of thing,' I added, through an awkward chuckle. 'And even if it was, I'd be way too jealous.'

Both troubled and interested in equal measure by my sudden fascination with cuckolding, I listened intently to Julia explain that "cuckold" is an historic, derogatory term for a husband whose wife is cheating on him.

'The word is derived from the cuckoo,' she continued, 'who lays its eggs in another bird's nest.'

'Yes,' I said, pleased that my penis had now gone flaccid, 'that's how I've always interpreted the word.'

'But now,' continued Julia, 'it's a modern-day term for an increasingly popular couples sexual activity, where a wife has sex with another man with the husband's encouragement.'

Julia went on to say that being cuckolded is no longer regarded as derogatory. She then explained that there were two types of cuckolding. One is where there is an element of male submission and humiliation. The other is called hot-wifing, where husband and wife are equal partners, and there's no humiliation involved. In both cases the husband can be present and watch his wife, or she can be somewhere else and tell him all about it when she gets home.

'The husband and wife usually have lots of passionate sex after the event,' added Julia, 'partly driven by the husband's competitiveness.'

'And the husband just watches and doesn't get involved

when he's cuckolded?' I questioned.

'Exactly right,' said Julia, 'otherwise it would be a threesome. Unfortunately,' she added, 'there isn't enough time for me to elucidate any further on the subject.'

Smiling, I thanked Julia for her explanation, and then asked her how people dealt with jealousy.

'Jealousy does tend to reduce with exposure,' she replied, 'but couples do need to be very secure in their relationship to even consider cuckolding.'

'But how can people who do that possibly love each other?' I asked, grimacing with incredulity.

'We've gone a bit off topic here, Rich,' replied Julia, looking a bit sheepish.

'Sure,' I said, 'but just briefly.'

'Just briefly then,' repeated Julia, before quickly explaining that jealousy in polyamorous and swinging couples changes over time, such that they enjoy "gifting" the pleasure of another person to their partner.

'Gifting sex do you mean?' I asked, wide-eyed.

'Well, no-strings sex in the case of swingers,' replied Julia, 'yes, but in the case of polyamorous couples, gifting their partner an additional loving relationship, which includes sex.'

'How? I mean, why?' I questioned, stumbling over what to ask first.

'Liberation from misplaced familial and societal morality,' replied Julia, 'is the answer to that question.'

Not really able to fully grasp that thinking, I simply smiled at Julia and then asked her if wife swapping was more common than polyamory. She immediately reprimanded me for saying wife swapping. She explained that "wife swapping" was a pejorative term, which implied that the wife was an object owned by the husband, to be swapped at his will.

'Swinging,' she continued, 'usually involves swapping partners, not just wives.'

'But that goes against every basic human instinct,' I said, screwing my face up in disbelief.

'It does indeed, Rich,' replied Julia, 'but once the shackles of conventional judgemental morality have been cast off, the freedom of emotion and depth of spiritual connection with one's partner is incredible beyond belief.'

'Is it really?'

'Yes,' said Julia. 'And for men, swinging is often seen as a variation of Freud's Madonna-whore complex.'

'Madonna-whore complex?' I repeated, wrinkling my nose. 'What's that?'

Julia explained that Freud posited the idea that men wanted virtuous women to marry and be mum to their children, but could only get aroused by sexually promiscuous women. With swinging, their appetite for sex with their wife is reignited as they see the "whore" in her, to use Freud's terminology, when she desires and allows other males to have sex with her.

'I was just giving you an example of alternative thinking,' added Julia. 'As the sayings go … change your thinking – change the outcome. Or, do what you've always done and get what you always got!'

With that said, Julia smiled and then quickly talked me through some anger management strategies. Once that was out of the way, I settled up and was gone.

Having stepped into the afternoon sunshine, I was pleased that I had a better understanding of my wife. That would help me to consign the past to history, where it belonged, and allow me to concentrate on making my marriage beautiful once again. Despite Julia's bizarre thinking on polyamory and wife swapping, or should I say "partner" swapping, she had helped me to untangle the mass of spaghetti in my head. Additionally, she had explained my cuckoldesque response, so I at least knew that I wasn't weird. But more importantly than that, she had given me simple strategies to manage my upset, thus giving me the confidence to know that I would never lose control with my Angie ever again.

CHAPTER 12

As I sat on the bus back to Hope Harbour, I dissected my therapy session with Julia. Within minutes, the mass of tangled spaghetti slowly reappeared in my head, just when I thought I'd got it all sussed. Unable to make sense of everything Julia had said, I got off the bus a couple of miles from home to get some fresh air and to clear my head.

Just a few paces away from where I alighted was a riverside trail which led all the way to the sea. As I sauntered thoughtfully along the path towards the beach, I stopped on the brow of a small, humpback bridge, which straddled the River Hope. Here, I rested my elbows on the coping stones which sat atop the bulbous balustrades. Looking down at the water, my gaze was drawn to a boulder which interfered with the water's flow and gave rise to that soulful, babbling brook sound. As I observed the mesmeric eddy currents swirling round below, I began contemplating Julia's bizarre comment about the mindset of poly people, or whatever they're called, and swingers. Although I knew she was just giving me an example of different thinking, I started to wonder if ditching my jealousy could actually save my marriage from disaster.

'There's no doubt about it,' I muttered in a light bulb moment. 'A different mindset would accommodate Angie's *forgotten me* and all that entails.'

And then, a moment later, I remembered Julia's mantras – change your thinking, change the outcome! And, do what you've always done, and get what you've always got!

The more I thought about changing my mindset, the more sense it made to me. And, if Angie was serious about sleeping with another man as a way for me to prove my love for her, my revised thinking would accommodate that as well. That would tick her "unconditional love without judging" box, then she'd have no reason to leave and take the kids . Plus, looking on the bright side, perhaps like Julia said, the jealousy thing would wear off and it would be exciting for me, rather than emotionally traumatic. Like they say, love is giving when it hurts. That definitely made sense to me, because I've always thought that with true love comes real happiness, even though, as Shakespeare put it, the course of true love never did run smooth.

Having processed that thought, I began laughing out loud whilst shaking my head.

Am I seriously gonna get sucked in by Julia's namby-pamby thinking? Psychosynthesis and Sex Therapy, for God's sake, what a load of old airy-fairy bollocks.

Still and quiet, I gazed vacantly over the river and sighed heavily. I then wondered whether Angie would someday cheat on me, based on the pattern thing Julia referred to. I also contemplated what would happen if Angie refused to see Julia. Would her stupid *forgotten me* need to have its own way? Could I really allow her to shag another guy without judging and moralising? Could I suppress my jealousy, anger, and protective instinct?

'Arghhh!' I sighed crossly. 'So many ifs, buts and maybes! God give me strength!'

Yes, give me strength God, I thought to myself. Help me out here. Let me help Angie blossom into who she really is, not just to save my marriage, but also to prove my love for her. After that thought came and went, I fixed my stare on a tiny fish darting about in search of food.

'Ahhh, such a simple life being a fish in a river,' I whispered.

Perhaps your life could be simple too, Richie? I thought to myself, perhaps God has sent you Julia to make you think like a swinger?

'Are you mad?' I countered out loud. 'Would God really send you a therapist who puts you on to swinging to save your marriage? You'll be excommunicated, for heaven's sake!'

After half an hour of quiet reflection on the bridge, I gradually straightened up as a tangible plan grew in my head. A knowing grin slowly spread across my face as it dawned on me that God really does work in mysterious ways. With that thought foremost in my mind, I set off for the beach with all haste to fine-tune my strategy.

* * *

I soon arrived at Eddie's Coffee Shack, my second most favourite place by the sea, after Inspiration Point, which you could actually see in the next cove along. Beyond that, was Hope Harbour.

Having purchased a coffee and a cheese sandwich at the counter, I took my seat on the wooden terrace just a few feet from the sea. I loved the beach. If I was happy, it would amplify that and lift me higher still. If I was sad, it was the place to clear my mind and make sense of things.

Angling my phone away from the other tables, I

Googled "swinger's mindset". After a bit of trawling, I came across a downloadable booklet called *Sex For Us – A Guide to Swinging For Beginners.* I became instantly absorbed. It explained the psychology of swinging and how wonderful it was to be unshackled from destructive feelings of jealousy and insecurity. It discussed how trust between partners took on a new dimension, and actually became stronger, presumably because infidelity wasn't an issue for them. Also, a couple's love for each other often became deeper and more meaningful.

Having read *Sex For Us* from cover to cover, I sighed thoughtfully as I recalled Angie saying that I was extraordinary. That made me wonder whether allowing her to sleep with another man (presumably Dave) as a one-off without judging her, would stop her straying, whilst proving my unconditional love for her at the same time.

Sitting back, I nodded thoughtfully at that sentiment. I then began contemplating another book I'd read on how to restore your marriage, by letting your love flow. Even though the author, Don Lewis, was criticised by some for his unusual approach to relationship management, I found him really helpful and enlightening. He, *Sex For Us* and Julia's "change your thinking, change the outcome" mantra, made me realise that radical action was called for, so that Angie, the children, and I could all live happily ever after.

Buoyed by my more enlightened thinking, I turned my attention to the revealing light Julia had shone on Angie. It was clear that she needed to cast aside the veil of virtuosity she'd reluctantly worn for so many years. And I agreed that she would undoubtedly feel liberated and empowered if she could only be herself. I wanted that for her, and above all I wanted our lovely happy family to stay together. This was assured if Angie blossomed into her *forgotten me.* Even though I knew it was utterly bizarre to suppose that thinking outside the box could strengthen my marriage, I knew I had to give it a chance.

For once I was in a win-win situation. If this wasn't actually God's plan, then Julia had got Angie all wrong, and she would simply reject *Sex For Us,* and that would be that. I wouldn't have to be a cuckold or swinger, and no harm done.

Armed with my insight into what drove swingers, I decided to see what they actually did. I called up a couple of sites to look at some profiles. I was amazed to see that married women wanted another woman to join them. Even more couples pursued another man, or even men, to join them in their bedroom. Most common (but not by a significant margin) were couples seeking other couples for swapping or group sex.

Even though I didn't consciously want to be a swinger, I was intrigued by the thought of how it could pan out for me and Angie. The first thing I realised was that I didn't want another woman to join us in our bedroom.

'What's wrong with you man?' I whispered to myself. 'Isn't that every guy's fantasy?'

Having stopped to think for a moment, I asked myself if I wanted to swap partners with another couple. Me shagging some guy's wife whilst he shagged mine, and we all watched each other. That thought made me feel sick, and I suddenly felt my heart beating faster in my chest as my breathing quickened.

What the hell are you thinking? Just the thought of Angie with another man has got you into a tailspin.

At this point, I suddenly became aware of a full erection

throbbing away in my jeans.

Shaking my head in disbelief at my bizarre hard-on, I once again stared out to sea in search of answers. None came, so I quickly ate my sandwich before washing it down with my cold coffee.

Having stepped straight off the terrace onto the sandy beach, I ambled along the water's edge, deep in thought. As I went, I watched the waves crashing into the rocks, creating a dramatic mass of white sea spray, which the stiff breeze carried to my face so that I could taste the salt. The bright sun and blue sky made the sea look deceptively inviting. Whilst on holiday here three years back, I'd plunged straight into it, only to run out at speed to catch my breath. It reminded me that what you see isn't always what you get. I wondered if that was perhaps the case with Angie. That thought stopped me in my tracks. I looked down at my feet and spotted a pretty shell right beside me. I picked it up and popped it into my pocket for my little Phoebe. I then, once again, stared out to sea for inspiration.

What should I do? I wondered. One second I'm convinced a radical solution is the answer, and the next I can't see it working at all. And if I did something so radical, my marriage would never be the same.

But then again, I thought to myself, sometimes moving forward requires new thinking. And if you want a rainbow, you've got to put up with the rain!

Having drawn in a super-sized breath I then let it out slowly and deliberately.

'Jesus!' I said, 'I can't believe I'm so totally consumed by all this cuckolding and swinging stuff.'

A moment later, I concluded that it's not at all normal for a man to contemplate such matters. And because the whole concept is so marginal and radical, I guess a lot of thought must go into it before deciding what to do.

Walking on, I thoughtfully watched the breaking waves and realised the truth in the ancient phrase that time and tide wait for no man. Even though it's something of a cliché, it did make me profoundly aware that I only had so many breaking waves left, and that I mustn't waste them. With that in mind, I knew that I had to save my marriage, so that Angie and I could raise our wonderful children together, in a proper family home. That thought stopped me in my tracks. Then, having turned to face Mr Blue square-on, I told him that a faint heart never won a fair maiden, and that I had to come up with a bold plan to let Angie be herself. A plan to let her *forgotten me* blossom.

'And if that means becoming a swinger, Mr Blue,' I added emphatically, 'then so be it!'

CHAPTER 13

Once home, I went straight to the outhouse office. Having placed my Phoebe's shell on the windowsill ready to give to her when she got home from school, I printed off a copy of *Sex For Us.* I then rolled it into a tube and shoved it into the big side pocket of my tracksuit bottoms. Keen to know whether or not Angie actually wanted extramarital sex, I made my way over to the house with all haste. I then gingerly entered the sitting room, where she was ironing in front of her beloved Jeremy Kyle show.

'Sweetheart,' I said in a low voice as I leant against the wall, 'I'm really sorry for shaking you. I'm scum for doing that.'

'You didn't hurt me. I was just worried you'd have a heart attack because you were so red in the face.'

'So why did you keep on pressing my buttons then, Angie?' I enquired softly.

'Because it's my right,' she retorted. 'And I shouldn't have to stand down. And I won't stand down. Why should I?'

'To spare me?' I suggested gingerly.

'Spare you?' repeated my wife, slamming the iron down. 'Have you any idea what you look like when you get into a rage like that? A huge man towering over me with such hateful eyes. I knew you were gonna snap the moment you went like it.'

'I'm sorry,' I said warmly. 'Sorry I couldn't control my temper. I'm not a bully,' I added, 'I just snapped. I didn't know what I was doing, until I'd done it.'

'You let me down,' insisted Angie, glaring at me.

Bowing my head in shame, I studied my shoes whilst contemplating my despicable actions.

'You're right,' I whispered. 'I did let you down.'

With my gaze still downcast, I could feel Angie's reproachful eyes burning into me. I had to man up and face the music, and so eventually looked up to speak.

'I've got anger management strategies,' I said, 'to control my emotions.'

'Yeah right,' scoffed Angie.

'I have,' I insisted. 'And I *am* your protector, my love,' I added, 'and would give my life for you in an instant.'

With that said, I slowly walked across the room and wrapped my arms round my lovely wife. She responded warmly and then held me at arm's length.

'You need to support me,' she whispered, 'otherwise you'll lose me.'

'I *will* support you,' I insisted, 'and we'll let your *forgotten me* blossom together.'

At this point, we stood facing one another in silence for a moment. My hands on my wife's hips, her hands on my biceps. Holding me still, she studied my eyes.

'Ahhh Rich,' she eventually sighed, before relaxing into a loving smile. 'Letting my *forgotten me* blossom, sounds wonderful.'

'So you don't really want a divorce then Angie?' I asked, looking for reassurance.

'No,' she said softly. 'To be honest, I wanted you to beg

me not to divorce you so I knew you loved me.'

'You know I love you, Angie.'

'Not always,' she whispered. 'I sometimes wonder how a morally sound man like you could love a woman with a past like mine.'

'Don't be silly,' I said. 'You're amazing Angie.'

'But I am silly,' she insisted, 'because I wanted you to keep showing me your love no matter what. I'm not sure what's wrong with me.'

With that said, my wife proceeded to trace her fingers down my arms and take hold of my hands. She then squeezed them tight, whilst giving them a warm shake of hope. Having returned my hands to me, she unmuted the TV and resumed her ironing.

I sat on the sofa and breathed a quiet sigh of relief. Relief, because I'd just been given the chance to redeem myself, by proving I loved my amazing wife beyond any doubt. I couldn't mess that up, otherwise the marriage would fail, and the children would miss out on a proper full-time dad. A double kick in the bollocks for me!

Having gathered my thoughts, I concluded that, to give my relationship the best possible chance of success, I needed to man up and put my cards on the table. With that in mind, I waited for the adverts to come on before speaking.

'Hu hum,' I began gingerly, 'I went to see a counsellor called Julia earlier today, and she …'

'Oh yeah!' interrupted Angie sharply. 'What for?'

In light of my wife's sudden change of mood, I was reluctant to say anything at all. But then, spurred on by Julia's "do what you've always done, get what you always got" mantra, I decided to speak up.

'I'm trying to get this affair thing sorted in my head,' I said evenly, 'so I can feel secure.'

'Oh not this crap again,' snapped Angie, sounding utterly exasperated. 'You know what happened. I'm not talking about it anymore. Got it?'

'Please hear me out sweetheart,' I pleaded. 'It's important.'

'So long as I can watch *Doctors* uninterrupted,' she replied sharply. 'It's about to start, and then I have to do the school run,' she added, 'so you'd better be quick!'

My wife's dismissive attitude towards such an important conversation made me angry. I wanted to shout, "are you fucking mad? Can you seriously *fit in* a conversation to save our marriage around a stupid bloody soap opera?" Thankfully though, I remembered one of Julia's coping mechanisms and took a deep breath. I held it for a short while, before then letting it out slowly whilst repeating 'replace anger with kindness' in my head. That was difficult to do when my heart was beating hard with outrage.

'Angie,' I said softly. 'This is serious. Can we please turn the TV off?'

My wife shot me a contemptuous glance before picking up the remote and muting the TV. She didn't want to talk, that was obvious. But we had to. How else could we resolve our issues going forward? At this point in the proceedings, she chose not to look at me, and instead continued ironing as she watched the muted television.

Hmmm, I thought to myself. I remember reading about this sort of response in Don Lewis's book. It's intimidation to pressure me into not talking. Despite being cross, I knew I had to defuse the tension with love. Knowing Angie's mantra was "the best form of defence is attack", I decided to present a loving front she would find difficult to chop down.

'Angie darling,' I said warmly. 'There were lots of factors at play in your life which shaped what happened.'

'Being a whore do you mean?' she said, screwing her face up in disgust.

'No sweetheart, you're not a whore.'

'Okay, so I'm not a whore,' said Angie, in an exaggerated matter-of-fact voice. 'I'm a slut!'

'Darling, I beg you, please don't slut-shame yourself. This is utter madness. If we follow Don Lewis's guidance, love will prevail!'

'I read him too,' snapped Angie, 'but what you don't get is the *unconditional* love bit. Loving me for who I am!'

'I do get that!' I responded. 'But it's just ...'

'So why all these stupid fucking discussions?' interrupted my wife, as she slammed the iron down on its rest. 'This isn't unconditional love, is it?'

I didn't reply to my wife's question. I really didn't know what to say, so I just kept schtum. She soon broke our awkward silence though, by demanding to know what Julia had said.

'Go on, spit it out,' she added, thrusting her head forward.

'STOP! OKAY! Just STOP!' I insisted in a raised voice. I then told my wife to let me speak without interruption, so she could be in command of all the facts.

At this point I explained what I learned from Julia. How I had a cuckold predisposition. The impact of the perimenopause. How we were abusive to each other and how things aren't always black and white, and that she had modelling from her father.

'Modelling?' questioned Angie. 'What the fuck's modelling?'

In response, I carefully shared Julia's thoughts with Angie about how she copied her father, who cheated on her mother. I was pleasantly surprised by her apparent interest in what Julia had said, and took that as a good sign. Next, I explained that Angie's previous husbands didn't allow her to be herself, and didn't give her what she needed, which is why she strayed.

'That's probably all true,' she said, looking at me with sad, soft eyes. 'They were both really horrible to me sometimes.'

I nodded in agreement with my wife and then, sensing she had more to say, waited for her to speak.

'Dom never told me he loved me unsolicited,' she continued. 'I would always say "I love you" and he would just say "and I you too".'

Having gotten that off her chest, my Angie closed her eyes, causing the tears that had gathered there to cascade down her cheeks. The protector response in me immediately kicked in. I sprang over to her and wrapped my arms round her middle. As I held her close, she lifted my hoodie and untucked my polo shirt so she could feel my skin. I again felt a sense of relief at making progress.

'I love you Angie,' I whispered.

'I love you too,' she replied, wiping her eyes on my hoodie. 'You always face difficulties head on,' she added, 'and I admire and respect you for that.'

After a moment of quiet closeness, my Angie drew in a big sniffy breath.

'I love your smell, Rich,' she declared warmly. 'It comforts and reassures me.'

Having nodded in acknowledgement of my wife's kind words, I kissed the top of her head. Then, feeling like I was on something of a roll, I inhaled deeply in readiness to share Julia's home truths about our marriage, starting with my cuckold response.

'I was right,' said a smug-looking Angie, holding me at arm's length. 'You got off on me telling you about Martin, Dave and Ryan.'

'Yes that's true,' I replied. 'And I'm trying to get my head round that.'

Although my wife wanted to get into that some more, I didn't want to get bogged down with it at this time, so quickly mentioned Julia's thoughts on the perimenopause.

Angie became indignant and said that was an old woman's problem.

'They get dry vaginas,' she added, 'and I certainly don't have that problem.'

Bearing my wife's response in mind, I parked that conversation for another day. I then told her that Julia had said, in a roundabout way, that there was a pattern of infidelity because Angie felt let down.

She immediately stepped away from me like she'd received an electric shock.

'Oh I get it,' she said, with contempt etched on her now blotchy red face. 'Your stupid fucking therapist thinks I'm easy. Go on,' growled my wife, 'make me feel dirty and cheap why don't you?'

'Angie darling,' I said warmly. 'This isn't easy for me when I see how upset it makes you.'

'Oh yeah,' she scoffed. 'Let's make this all about you, shall we?'

'It's not about *me!*' I insisted. 'It's about *us!*'

Feeling that boldness was called for, I took hold of my wife's hand and towed her to the sofa. She resisted like a five-year-old in a strop. We sat down. I then lovingly reiterated what Julia had told me about how things weren't always black and white, and that Angie's relationships obviously didn't satisfy her, which is why she looked elsewhere.

Tucking her feet under her thighs so she could face me squarely, Angie cupped my face in her hands and kissed me tenderly on my lips. She then thanked me for trying so hard to work things out. I smiled and nodded in response, and then listened as she told me that she knew she'd lied to me from the start.

'But I had to,' she added, 'otherwise you wouldn't have married me.'

'It's okay my love,' I responded warmly. 'No need to …'

'I loved you the moment I met you,' interrupted my wife. 'And I couldn't bear the thought of not being with you.'

'Aww, my love,' I whispered, 'that's so beautiful.'

Smiling in response, my wonderful wife searched my face with loving eyes. She then stroked the side of my cheek tenderly, and even though her face was blotchy and streaked with mascara, she looked more beautiful than an angel to me.

After being lost in the moment for a wee while, my Angie again kissed my lips before then hugging me with all her might. It was so lovely to absorb the warmth of her embrace. Alas, that loveliness was soon disturbed when I began to wonder how I was going to broach another of Julia's difficult considerations. I knew I had to put it out there, to give Angie the opportunity to be whoever and whatever she wanted to be. Plus I needed to know who she really was. With boldness in my heart, I eased away from my wife and then took hold of her hands.

'Sweetheart,' I said through an awkward smile, 'Julia also mentioned something else which might be worth considering. Couples counselling.'

'What, so she can pass judgement on me?' snapped Angie. 'No chance! I'm not going anywhere near that silly bitch.'

'That's okay,' I said, disinclined to counter such a vitriolic attack. 'We don't need that really. But there's another thing.'

'Oh yeah,' said a cautious-sounding Angie.

'Now please don't think this is mad,' I continued, 'but Julia did mention the possibility of us adopting a swinger's mindset. That way you could …'

Before I could even finish my sentence, my wife withdrew her hands from mine at lightning speed. A look of utter disdain then slowly grew on her face.

'Where's this going?' she demanded aggressively. 'Why did you even bother seeing this stupid woman?'

'I'll tell you if you'll give me a chance!'

'Go on then, spit it out!' insisted Angie. '*Doctors* is just about to start.'

Although outraged by my wife's attacking response, I remained calm and reminded her of our conversation in the car, where she wanted me to prove my unconditional love for her, by doing the *Indecent Proposal* thing.

'My proposal was about you not judging me,' she responded. 'Not about sex!'

'Well Julia didn't think so,' I retorted.

'Oh, and that silly bitch thinks she knows me?' countered an angry Angie.

'But you did say you liked a bit of attention from men to

make you feel attractive and like you've still got it.'

My wife reluctantly nodded in agreement and relaxed a bit. She then told me that her flirting was innocent, and pointed to Ryan as an example.

'I didn't do anything behind your back then,' she added. 'Did I?'

'No,' I replied. 'And that's how it should be.'

'True,' said Angie. 'But you loved your cuckold response, didn't you?'

I told her that I did, but that it was also emotionally upsetting for me. I then added that now wasn't the time to get into the whys and wherefores of that. She told me that her indecent proposal thing was a throwaway comment and that she didn't want it to be a reality.

'But if you did need me to prove my unconditional love to you in that way,' I said, 'then I would try to make it happen.'

'I'm not sleeping with another man so you can watch me being fucked for your own perverted needs,' declared my wife. 'You're not coercing me into doing that. It's abuse.'

'I don't have to watch,' I replied. 'You could do it in private. I'm just trying to prove my love so you can get it out of your system if you feel you want to.'

'And this is what that stupid bitch Julia recommended?' scoffed my wife, shaking her head in disbelief.

'Not a recommendation, just a possibility,' I replied. 'And it wouldn't be easy for me,' I added. 'Julia says I would have to change my mindset to limit my jealousy and turn the whole thing into a positive. It all depends on whether it's something you need for your *forgotten me.*'

'Where's this therapist arsehole coming from?' demanded Angie crossly, her face contorted with contempt.

'She doesn't even know me! She's just some stupid do-good counsellor who's done a week's course. Passing judgement on me like some paragon of virtue. Who the fuck does she think she is?'

With that said, my wife stood up and returned to the ironing board. As I watched her ironing angrily, I wondered if her outrage was genuine, or whether "the lady protesteth too much". Before I could formulate an answer in my head, she looked up and glared at me.

'And you, you stupid bastard,' she announced, 'are being led by the nose with all this therapist bullshit!'

Indignant, I told my wife it was she who wanted to be herself and for me to prove my unconditional love.

'I was just trying to make that happen so we could live happily ever after,' I added.

Angie responded by telling me that I'd made this whole therapist thing about me.

'No, I haven't,' I insisted. 'We both have to be completely open and honest if we're gonna make things work.'

With that said, I stood up and waved the *Sex For Us* booklet in front of my wife's face.

'Read this,' I insisted. 'It might be of interest.'

Angie snatched it from my hand at lightning speed, read the title and then flung it across the room contemptuously. Undaunted, I told her that it just explained the concept of swinging, because Julia thought Angie appeared to need to explore her latent sexuality as part of her *forgotten me.*

'Me!' she proclaimed, in a mighty orator's voice, like the Wizard of Oz. 'A swinger?! You mean letting strange blokes have sex with me? They're dirty sluts that do that,' she added, screwing her face up in disgust so much that I hardly recognised her.

Frozen like a statue with her face still distorted and angry, my wife just stared at me expectantly. I assumed she wanted me to apologise for calling her morality and integrity into question. But as it was done with the best of intentions, I didn't feel an apology was due. So, with nothing more to be said, I thought it best to leave. Having turned on my heel, I headed for the door.

'Oh I get it,' declared my wife, 'this is all a ruse for you to fuck other women and pretend it's all about me.'

I turned round to speak, but before I could say anything, Angie continued.

'Am I not enough for you?' she demanded angrily. 'Who do you want to fuck?' That sanctimonious posh bitch Charlotte?'

I shook my head, thinking it best to let the matter drop, but Angie wasn't having any of it. As usual, when she started, she had to finish. The heated exchange continued as she proceeded to deride Charlotte, telling me she was a whore, because she'd slept with half the boys in her sixth form.

Ignoring her vitriolic attack, I suggested that *Sex For Us* was something we should explore together in case it allowed her to be the person she wanted to be.

'This is about your sick fantasies,' retorted Angie. 'And Julia's confirmed that you're a pervert, so stop putting your inadequacies onto me.'

'I'm not a pervert,' I protested,

'You have a deep seated perverted sexual side of you that I never knew existed,' said Angie. 'And Julia's just making you worse!'

'That's not true,' I responded. 'And if you read that,' I added, nodding at the discarded booklet, 'you would see that swingers are committed, loving couples.'

'This whole thing is fucking ridiculous,' exclaimed my wife, before un-muting the TV.

She then immediately resumed her irate ironing. I stood still and surveyed her red, hostile face. Then, having suddenly met my gaze, she tossed her head back in dramatic style to make a point of ignoring me.

Without saying another word, I quietly left the sitting room to get on with my work.

Whilst making my way to the office, I pondered the totally bizarre conversation I'd just had with my wife. I mean, I was actively suggesting that she sleep with another man, so I could prove that I wouldn't judge her. But if I stifled her true self, and/or her *forgotten me*, by not putting that possibility out there, she would either end the marriage, or cheat. And although I'd clearly articulated that consideration in my mind, and in line with Julia's thinking, part of me wondered if I subconsciously wanted my wife to have sex with another man. And then, a moment later, I completely dismissed that thought as ridiculous, because, deep down, what I really wanted was to keep my wife all to myself.

As I approached the office, a smile gradually appeared on my face as I realised that my wife's vehement and aggressive rejection of swinging was actually a really good thing. It proved that, all said and done, my Angie liked a bit of male attention, but really only wanted me. And now, despite her horrible bedside manner, I felt both loved and secure.

Having reached the office, I flopped into my desk chair with a huge sigh of contentment. I then opened my charts in readiness to trade with the clearest head I'd had in a very long time.

❖

CHAPTER 14

A few days had passed since Angie and I had our heated exchange in the sitting room. We had both calmed down, and everything was back to normal. My lovely wife had been doing a wonderful job of keeping up with homework assignments and helping with school trips etc. I had been painstakingly making a shell necklace with Phoebe, and a kite with Archie. The two big ones largely did their own thing, but always joined me at the driving range for golf practice. Life was sweet. And then, for no apparent reason, I suddenly felt uneasy about the veracity of my wife's vehement rejection of swinging. I couldn't quite put my finger on what actually troubled me. I had nothing tangible to go on. Just one of those feelings you get when something doesn't sit a hundred per cent right.

* * *

Sitting in the morning sun on the raised decked terrace at Eddie's, I eagerly awaited John's arrival. I was in desperate need of a man-chat. As I waited for him, I observed the spring sun shining on the sea, which rolled in and out, playing its calming mellifluous melody as it went. I was trying hard to count my blessings and be in the moment, without contemplating problems past, present or future. I'd recently been introduced to the concept of mindfulness, but it was proving quite difficult to master.

John and I were good social buddies; we played golf together and occasionally chatted about man stuff over a few beers. He had confided in me in the past, so I now felt able to confide in him. He soon arrived.

'How are you, John?'

'Yeah, mustn't grumble,' he said, as he sat opposite me. 'More to the point, how are you?'

'Well, to be honest, I don't think all is completely rosy in my marriage garden right now.'

Just then, Lucy, our forty-something waitress, suddenly appeared and stood by our table smiling. I watched her as she took the coffee orders from John. I contemplated the stark difference between her life now, and this time last year, when she and hubby were happily working away saving money for their world travels. Now everything had changed. Her husband suddenly died only three months ago, yet she always smiled for the customers. I really admired her for that. Her fortitude inspired me. And even though I knew I had no right to whinge and moan by comparison, I sometimes found it hard not to. My own pathetic troubles dominated my thoughts and were the centre of my own little universe.

I knew Lucy couldn't redeem her situation, but I could redeem mine. That's why I owed it to myself to make sure I lived the best life possible, and that meant making my marriage the best it could be.

As I watched Lucy take the order, a sense of outrageous unfairness at the loss of her husband came over me. I wondered why fate often kicked nice people in the teeth, whilst real bastards somehow sailed through life, often at the expense of others, never getting their comeuppance.

'So,' said John, as Lucy turned on her heel, 'you were saying all is not completely rosy in your marriage garden right now.'

'It's complicated,' I replied, having snapped out of my maudlin musings.

Leaning in towards John with my elbows on the table, I quietly began sharing my story with him. He leant forward and listened intently.

When I'd finished explaining everything, John just sat there looking at me wide-eyed. Feeling like I ought to say something more to fill the silence, I told him I was really looking for a sanity check from him on what was going on in my marriage.

'Sure,' he said, before explaining that he thought all Angie's stuff from the past had come home to roost. 'But you have to forget what's happened in the past,' he added. 'She's been a good wife for sixteen years, and whilst swinging sex with other people sounds fun, I think it will create more problems than it solves.'

Having nodded in thoughtful response, I then listened as John told me that he really rated Julia.

'And as you say,' he continued, 'she was only using swinging as an example of different thinking. NOT as a solution to the difficulties in your marriage. And anyway Rich,' he added, 'Angie's already slammed swinging, so it's a non-starter. So no new pussy for you then!'

Having chuckled politely at John's funny, I then told him that my judgemental outlook sort of made Angie model herself around my values and expectations.

'She hasn't been her true self,' I added. 'And that's the problem!'

'But everybody sacrifices a bit of who they are in a marriage,' replied John.

'They shouldn't have to though,' I said, before mentioning that Julia thought that Angie felt constrained by familial and societal moral pressures, which could leave her frustrated and disillusioned with our marriage. 'She needs to *feel* free to be herself,' I added.

'Flirting is one thing,' said John, 'but I don't think Angie wants to sleep with other men. She loves you.'

'You say that,' I replied, 'but I actually think she meant her *Indecent Proposal* thing, on the basis that it was about judgement and not sex. Also,' I added, 'I can kind of see how sleeping with someone else could be a mechanism to undo all the judgement I passed on her over the years.'

'Blimey,' said John, 'that's a big ask. So in a way, Angie will be taking one for the team as a kind of therapy to neutralise your judgement of her?'

'Not taking one for the team John,' I replied, 'because she would need to desire it for it to work therapeutically. I would have nothing to judge if she did it for me. If you see what I mean?'

'I think this is all crazy,' said John. 'But just hypothetically speaking, is there any benefit to you in terms of your sexual competitive response?'

'No, is the short answer,' I responded, 'because it would be too emotionally painful. But since I spoke to Julia, I think I can handle, and even enjoy, a competitive response if Angie gets a bit flirty with some random guy.'

'I get that,' said John, 'because I've been a bit like that with Charlotte and vice versa.'

'Well there you are then,' I said.

'But with respect,' said John, 'I think you overanalyse

everything. To me, this *Indecent Proposal* thing and swinging is all a bit bonkers, especially as Angie's made it clear that she's not interested.'

'I can see why you'd say that,' I replied, 'but I believe that the best marriages are those where each partner wants to support the other for who they are. I read that in a book on relationships.'

At this point the coffees arrived. When Lucy left, I went on to explain how the author's philosophy is about the joy of giving love, rather than taking it selfishly. John immediately countered by saying he thought it was a bit too idealistic, and not something that would work in practice.

'I mean I love Charlotte,' he added, 'but sometimes I really don't like her.'

'I see what you mean,' I said, 'but what I'm saying is that I'm "changing my thinking to change the outcome", in line with Julia's rationale.'

John nodded in response, but made no specific comment. Instead, he told me that the menopause is something that could have a big bearing on everything.

'It really affected Charlotte badly,' he continued, 'and she had to have HRT because things got so bad.'

'What were her symptoms?' I asked, to compare notes with Angie.

'Moodiness and irritability,' replied John, 'incredible hot flushes and massive sweating.'

'Wow! And HRT sorted all that out overnight?'

'I wish,' chuckled John. 'No, it took a few weeks to kick in and a couple of months to reach full strength.'

'So not instant then?'

'No, but incredibly effective,' replied John. 'I really think Angie should see the doctor.'

'I agree,' I said, before adding that I didn't think HRT would change her outlook on me.

'No?' questioned John.

'No,' I said. 'And it won't stop her feeling invisible to men,' I continued, 'or fix her shattered self-confidence, which is down to me.'

'It might do,' said John.

'I haven't always loved her as I should have,' I said. 'I was a real bastard to her sometimes. And like I said, I shook her the other day.'

'All partners are sometimes horrid to each other, Rich,' insisted John. 'I mean I haven't always been a saint with Charlotte and vice versa,' he added.

I nodded in agreement, and then eased back in my seat to gather my thoughts. John glanced at his watch and instantly widened his eyes.

'Jesus!' he blurted out. 'Look at the time!'

With that said, he jumped up from the table and gulped down the rest of his coffee in one. He then extended his hand to me whilst picking up his rucksack from the chair next to him.

I immediately stood up to shake my friend's hand and said goodbye.

Remember Rich,' he quickly said, 'marriages take a bit of work sometimes. And, no disrespect to Angie, the menopause thing is having a big impact on your situation.'

'Thanks for that, John,' I said, 'you've been a great help.'

'Pleasure,' he said as he turned on his heel and dashed across the terrace towards the car park.

❖

CHAPTER 15

It was barely twenty minutes since I saw John. After our chat, I thought I'd sorted my head out, but now, given time to reflect on things on the walk home, I was decidedly more confused than I was before. The one thing I knew for sure though, was that I loved my Angie, and I loved our family ensemble. That conclusion inspired me to make things work. For that, I would need God's continued help and guidance.

As I stepped onto the bumpy farm track leading to Hope House, I stopped for a moment and looked up to the heavens. Having clasped my hands together, I asked the good Lord to save my marriage …

'And please give me the strength to do what I have to do,' I continued, 'to make it work.'

My simple prayer lightened my heavy heart in the knowledge that God Almighty himself was on the case. With my trust placed in the good Lord, I walked on with a spring in my step, even though I knew he probably wouldn't make things easy for me. There would doubtless be a tough and meaningful lesson to be learned along the way. But hey, forewarned, as they say, is forearmed!

* * *

When I got home, I walked into the sitting room. There was Angie with her legs stretched out on the sofa, sipping a glass of red wine. Her eyes were glued to her laptop. Soft music played in the background, and a copy of *Sex For Us* was on the occasional table beside her. She looked both serious and thoughtful.

Surprised to see my wife drinking at this time of the afternoon, along with a copy of a swingers handbook in plain sight, I immediately asked her where the children were.

'Don't panic Daddy,' she replied, lifting her head to look at me, 'Connor is sleeping over at Dylan's, and Livy's at her boyfriend's.'

'And the little ones?'

'They've gone to Della and Tom's to have a go on their new trampoline.'

'Oh, okay,' I said. 'So I guess I'll have to pick them up at some point then?'

'Actually no,' replied Angie. 'Jane said she'd run them back en route to pick her sister up from the station.'

Having nodded in reply, I then immediately concluded that I must be in for a bollocking, because my wife was reading *Sex For Us*, in order to hang me with it, despite her outwardly relaxed demeanour. Thinking on my feet, I quickly formulated a pre-emptive apology.

'Angie darling,' I began in a soft voice, as I leant against the wall, 'I was an idiot for thinking swinging was a way to put us back on track, and I'm really sorry. I didn't mean to cast aspersions.'

In response, my wife looked up at me and held my gaze. Her face was still serious and thoughtful. I braced myself for another tongue-lashing about how she could never be a swinger, and that women who did that were whores. To my amazement though, she returned her attention to her computer without saying a word. She then sniffed, before pursing her lips in concentration.

'Actually Rich,' she said warmly, 'I don't think you're an idiot at all. And having read your swinging booklet, I now completely get the concept.'

'You do?'

'Yes,' replied Angie, before nervously adding that she found the prospect of having sex with another man really exciting.

Hearing that sent my heart crashing to the floor. And, despite her flirting, I'd always assumed I was my wife's one and only man. Completely lost for words, I simply looked at her and waited for her to say something. Without returning my gaze, she reached across to the side table and picked up her bottle of wine.

'I see what they mean,' she eventually said, filling her glass.

'You do?'

'Yes,' she replied, replacing the now empty bottle on the side table. 'There's a *huge* difference between loving sex, and no-strings sex,' she explained, having finally lifted her gaze to meet mine.

'What do you mean exactly?' I asked.

Having taken a big swig of wine, Angie told me that most people in committed relationships fancy other people, but resist temptation because of their moral commitment.

'But with swinging sex,' she added, 'loving couples get to have honest fun, and be their authentic selves. And that's what's so amazing about swinging!'

Completely taken aback by my wife's dramatic U-turn, I

just looked at her in disbelief. She must have picked up on my surprise, and so rather than waiting for me to say something, she continued speaking to fill the awkward silence.

'There are no emotions involved in swinging sex,' she said, 'it's just about trying more than one pudding on the menu, and having some naughty adult fun.'

At this point, my wife's high-handed, self-righteous rejection of swinging suddenly came to mind. Indignant, I demanded to know why she went into one when I brought the subject up a few days ago.

'Because I hated that you thought I could do such a thing,' she replied.

Somewhat disarmed by my wife's response, I just nodded in reply. I then told her I kind of got where she was coming from.

In the ensuing momentary silence, I suddenly began to struggle with the position I'd put myself in. It now appeared to me that there was no backing out. But when swinging was just a concept in my head, I thought I could do it. The impending reality of it though, was quite different. It's a bit like saying yeah, I'm good with a parachute jump, but when you actually come to do it, you're shit scared. Afterwards though, you're buzzing and want to do it again. That thought prompted me to wonder if it would be the same with swinging.

Breaking the short silence, my wife told me that she'd always had naughty fantasies, but they remained just that, fantasies in her head.

'But when you asked me about swinging,' she continued, 'where fantasies become reality, I felt cheap, so I attacked it.'

'And me as well, Angie,' I said.

'Yes, I attacked you as well,' she agreed, 'because I

wanted to appear virtuous to you.'

'But I don't want to judge you, Angie,' I insisted firmly.

'But you have judged me in the past,' she retorted. 'And I've also judged myself.'

Not quite sure what to say to that, I simply nodded in reply. I then withdrew my hands from my pockets and ran them over my head. As I was gathering my thoughts, Angie told me that she didn't feel able to share her feelings with me until now. She then explained that she was ashamed of herself for wanting to try swinging.

'Please don't be ashamed of who you are, my love,' I responded warmly.

'But *you're* ashamed of me though Rich, aren't you?'

'Not at all sweetheart.'

'Well anyway,' continued my wife, as the round of her chin began to quiver, 'it's been hard for me to admit that I wanted to do this. Probably because I thought you were going to judge me.'

I looked on as tears formed in my wife's sad eyes. I so wanted to reach out to her, but my legs froze and refused to carry me to the sofa. Smiling sympathetically, I told her that I was both impressed and grateful for her honesty.

'You're helping me to be me,' she said, as she began crying in earnest. 'And I love you for that.'

Still stuck to the spot, I told Angie that a good husband should always support his wife.

'And vice versa,' she replied, before placing her wine down on the side table.

She then spun round on her bum to put her feet on the floor, whilst deftly holding her laptop in place. Having clearly snapped out of her momentary malaise, she smiled brightly, whilst looking directly at me with her beguiling, tear-filled eyes. Wiping her tears away with her sleeve, she patted the space beside her. My legs finally unfroze, allowing me to walk across to the sofa. I took my seat beside my wife and watched her reach across for her wine, which she knocked back in one, before placing the glass back on the table. She had literally polished off a whole bottle of wine. I thought this was a good thing because it had loosened her tongue.

After a short thoughtful pause, my wife announced that she'd been thinking of swinging possibilities.

'Have you?' I asked, trying to mask my surprise.

'Absolutely!' she replied, sounding proud of herself. 'And we need to figure out what we fancy as a couple,' she added excitedly.

At this point, a million questions came to mind, as my need to know who my wife actually was, overwhelmed me. The first thing I wanted to know was what prompted her to "come out" so to speak. She told me there was already a subconscious interest in swinging within her, which I'd ignited by giving her the booklet. She then went on to explain that, having read *Sex For Us*, she felt able to pursue swinging because it didn't breach her marriage vows.

'And as you proposed it,' she continued, 'I knew it wasn't immoral. And on top of that,' she added, 'I was pleased to note that swinging often brings couples closer together.'

Grateful for my wife's explanation, I nodded in response. Then, keen to deal with one question at a time, I angled myself towards her and asked her what possibilities she'd been thinking of.

'Just thoughts of how it might work for me,' replied my wife. 'That made me really horny.'

'Did it?'

'Yes. And even though I think swinging is just an excuse to be a bit of a slut, I know I'm gonna love it.'

'And does that trouble you, Angie?' I asked.

'No, because I've grasped the concept,' she replied. 'And anyway,' she added, 'most girls have a slutty side that needs to get out, but they just can't admit it.'

Having again nodded in response, I then asked my wife what her *Indecent Proposal* scenario was actually about.

'That was a truth said in jest,' she replied, 'and was about proving you wouldn't judge me. I didn't want to cuckold you per se. I didn't even know what that was back then.'

'Neither did I.'

'And I would still do that for you,' continued my wife, 'to give you the chance to free yourself after all the judgement you've passed on me.'

'Do it for me?' I questioned wide-eyed.

'Yes.'

Christ, she's framing an extramarital shag as a way for me to put right a perceived historical wrong, and to liberate myself from guilt. That's fucking clever!

With the passing of that thought, I drew a breath to speak, but was beaten to the punch when Angie told me her *Indecent Proposal* scenario was also about making her feel properly loved.

'Do you mean unconditional love?' I asked.

'Yes,' replied Angie. 'Plus it's flattering and empowering. And, as you've already admitted to having cuckold tendencies,' she added, 'me going with another man won't be a hardship for you. Quite the contrary.'

Not sure what to say to that, I instead explained that there were two different types of cuckolding.

'One where the husband is willingly humiliated,' I continued, 'and the other is a hotwife, where husband and wife are equal partners. In both scenarios, the husband can either enjoy watching his wife having sex with another man, or she can tell him all about it after the event.'

'Hotwife,' said Angie. 'I like the sound of that. And I think that's more us.'

'Even though that prospect gives me a hard-on,' I said, 'I'm not sure I could handle watching you shag some random bloke.'

'Oh no,' scoffed Angie, 'I wouldn't want you to watch. To be honest, I'd be self-conscious, and I think you'd cramp my style.'

'Sure,' I said, as the genuineness of her desire sent me hard.

'But you know you're gonna love me telling you all the juicy details afterwards,' insisted my wife. 'Don't you?'

'I get competitive for you,' I said.

'I like that,' said Angie. 'I adore you vying for me. Makes me feel valued, desired, loved and sexy.'

'That's a good thing,' I responded. 'But like I said, I'm not sure how I'd feel.'

'But if we did this swinging thing,' continued Angie, completely ignoring my comment, 'in whatever guise, then you couldn't judge me because you would have done it too.'

'Angie,' I sighed, 'I don't want to judge you. I just want your *forgotten me* to blossom, and I want you to be you.'

With that said, I inhaled deeply, and then ran my hands over my head as I exhaled long and hard. With my erection subsided, I took hold of my wife's hands and told her that I wanted her to be fulfilled, because then the whole family would be happy. She told me she wanted the family's happiness too. Then, after a pregnant pause, she released my hands back to me and asked me if my so-called "counsellor" had labelled her a slut, who should practise her sluttery in the open.

Shocked and surprised by my wife's totally bizarre question, I simply responded by saying that Julia hadn't said anything like that.

'And what about you, Rich?' asked barrister Angie.

'Erm?' I replied, stumbling over my response.

'I put it to you,' she said, 'that you like the idea of me sleeping with another man, under the guise of proving your love, when in fact it is just a ruse for you to get your latent cuckold rocks off with impunity.'

'No Angie,' I protested. 'That's not true.'

'And then,' she continued haughtily, 'you would have pretended you did it for me, and still secretly judged me whilst not judging yourself. Typical Catholic,' she added through a teasing laugh. 'Guilt-free sinning!'

'No,' I said.

'Yes,' insisted my wife, before telling me that my cuckold desire was why we were actually discussing swinging, even if I didn't know that myself.

'I just wanted to make all that clear,' she added, 'so you know you're not in a position to judge.'

With that said, my wife smiled and told me she was pleased she'd got that off her chest. She then asked me what I wanted from swinging.

Still somewhat taken aback by the courtroom-style cross-examination and admonishment by the prosecution, I said I wasn't sure if I wanted anything at all. Angie laughed and told me she knew I wanted to be cuckolded, before adding that objectively speaking, it would be fairer on me if I went with somebody else as well.

'Like I said,' I replied, 'I'm not really sure.'

'I want you to have some naughty adult fun in your own right,' said Angie. 'Even though I'd be jealous, I'd need it to be quid pro quo to keep the whole thing equally balanced.'

Despite being pleased to learn that my wife would be jealous, I didn't know quite what to say in response, and so just remained silent.

As the cogs went round in my head, I realised that, with all this talk of dirty sex, augmented by wine, my wife was clearly very horny. And, despite the upset and confusion that came with our discussions, I was pretty horny too. I was just thinking of how to share this with Angie, when she suddenly announced that she'd checked out some swinger's profiles.

'The women are confident and sexy,' she added, 'and they know exactly what they want.'

'Do they?' I asked.

'Definitely!' replied Angie. 'And there are a few blokes on there I wouldn't say no to either,' she added enthusiastically, before immediately turning her laptop screen to me.

I was confronted with a profile of a late-thirties single guy who was into older women. "Here To Please" was his profile name. He was standing tall and naked holding his big erection at its base. He was well toned and good-looking.

My wife's genuine desire for this guy really aggravated Black Dog, whilst sending me hard, yet again. But knowing I had no right to be outraged, because it was me who suggested this whole thing, I forced myself to calm down. Then with my wife looking at me expectantly, I widened my eyes and nodded in approval. Clearly pleased with my non-judgemental, positive response, she spun her laptop back to face her and sighed contentedly.

Sensing her obvious excitement, I asked Angie if she specifically liked looking at the guy's big cock.

'Would it make a difference if it wasn't erect?' I asked.

Angie explained that we were looking for sex and that a good body and a decent cock were prerequisites for her.

'And it's way more exciting to see a big, hard cock,' she added, 'than a flaccid one. It's a bit like you wanting to see a woman's sexy bits.'

'I suppose so,' I replied, still feeling a bit insecure about Mr Big Cock.

After a short pause, I suddenly felt the need to talk about swinging in terms of "us" as a couple, rather than just Angie by herself and me by myself.

'I read that swinging is about loving couples exploring their *joint* sexuality,' I said. 'Is that how you see it, Angie?'

'Absolutely,' she replied, before placing her laptop under the sofa.

Despite my initial shock at my wife's deviant desires, I was pleased she could think about swinging in terms of us as a couple. Plus I was strangely happy because she was happy. I had facilitated that in my own way by embracing her for who she is. She was being herself and honest with it. I was grateful for that and relieved to know that I wasn't being deceived. Remembering that "God works in mysterious ways", I realised I had to challenge my debilitating values, so that Angie, me, and the children could live happily ever after.

With her computer safely stowed under the sofa, my wife hoicked her dress up round her thighs, and crossed her legs in a semi lotus position so she was facing me.

'So,' she said excitedly, 'let's talk about the various possibilities.'

'What sort of possibilities?'

'Well,' sighed my wife, 'there's a soft swap, full swap and cuckolding for starters.'

'Just for starters?' I questioned, raising an eyebrow.

'God yeah,' replied my wife. 'And there's plenty more,' she added enthusiastically, 'including double-teaming, gang-bangs and bukkake.'

'Christ!' I exclaimed, wide-eyed, 'you're much more clued up on all this stuff than I am.'

'I'm a barrister, Rich,' said Angie, 'and I take everything in. It's pretty diverse though, isn't it?' she added, before holding my gaze, wearing a cheeky half smile, her eyes sparkling and full of mischief.

'Erm, so what do you fancy then?' I asked gingerly, not really wanting to know, but yet needing to.

'Cuckolding or a full swap is what a lot of couples have on their profiles,' responded my wife.

'Really?'

'Yes! And I know I'll need to let you have sex with other women,' she continued, 'so I can have sex with other men!'

Countering my wife's gung-ho attitude, I mentioned that *Sex For Us* said that individuals are supposed to work within their emotions, as opposed to making everything quid pro quo.

'So what does that actually mean in reality?' asked my wife.

'Well, imagine a wife couldn't handle her husband shagging another woman,' I replied, 'but she wanted to go with other guys and hubby was cool with that, then …'

'Then it's a non-starter,' interrupted Angie, 'because it's not fair on the husband.'

'Swinging has a selfless element to it,' I said, before explaining that each partner had to accommodate the other as far as their emotions would allow. I then went on to fully explain the example I used about the wife who couldn't handle her husband going with another woman, but he was emotionally able to cope with her going with another man.

'Even if he's only neutral to it,' I continued, 'then he still supports his wife's desires, because he wants her to have what she wants. Her happiness is his happiness.'

'Oh, okay,' said Angie, before asking me how I would feel if she was the woman in my example.

'But you originally said I should have some naughty adult fun to make everything balanced,' I responded.

'I know,' replied Angie, 'but if I'm honest, I'd be jealous of you and another woman. And unlike you, who would get really excited with me shagging another guy, I wouldn't get anything out of you shagging another woman. If that makes sense?'

'So you'd basically cuckold me then,' I replied. 'I don't know how I'd feel. But what I do know,' I added, 'is that I love you with all my heart.'

'I know you do,' replied my wife, taking hold of my hands, 'and I never want to take advantage of that. But like I said,' she continued, 'I would get jealous if you went with another woman; so, if you not going with another woman was an option, well, I would happily be your cuckoldress.'

Wow, talk about having your cake and eating it, I exclaimed in my head, before then immediately reminding myself that each partner is supposed to accommodate the other, as far as their emotions will allow.

With my Angie holding my gaze expectantly, I again told her that I wasn't entirely sure I could handle her going with someone else. She then playfully turned her mouth down in disappointment for a moment, but then smiled a cheeky smile.

'Knowing you as I do,' she said, 'I kind of know how things will pan out.'

With that said, my wife's expression suddenly became quite serious. She then reiterated that part of her wanted me to go with another woman, despite her jealousy, so that I couldn't judge her.

'You'd be equally culpable then,' she added, before returning my hands to me.

Still not really sure why Angie kept going on about this judging thing, I again said that I didn't want to judge her anymore. I then went on to say that swinging is complicated and dangerous, before adding that some people were put off just by the thought of it.

'I'm not put off!' declared Angie. 'I totally get the concept. So what exactly do you fancy then?' she asked in a light tone, before waiting for my response with a smile.

As I gathered my thoughts, I spun round on my bum to completely face my wife. Having taken hold of her hands, I looked deep into her bright, expectant eyes, and held her gaze for a second. I then suggested she could have sexy chats online, and that we could then perhaps progress to a soft swap. She instantly countered by saying that wasn't really doing *anything*. I insisted that a soft swap *was* proper swinging, because couples swap partners for foreplay but not penetration.

'But the point is to actually *try* different puddings on the menu,' said a slightly disappointed Angie.

'You mean you'd like to get it on with "Here To Please Big Cock",' I said sharply, as I went erect and let go of her hands.

In response, she quickly took hold of my wrists and held my hands to her chest. I think she was secretly pleased that I was jealous. Smiling broadly, she then told me that she fully appreciated that single guys might be off the menu.

'But maybe a full swap in separate rooms could be a plan?' she suggested, before explaining that if I was out of sight and didn't tell her what went on, then she wouldn't get jealous.

Before I had a chance to consider my response, Angie told me she was only exploring possibilities, and that we could do a recce of a swingers club she'd found in Plymouth. She then returned my hands to me, cocked her head to one side, and waited wide-eyed for my reply. Momentarily lost for words, all I could do was return her gaze, whilst processing her suggestions. I mean she knew *exactly* what she wanted, and I had no idea it was so extreme. "Separate rooms" went straight to the heart of Black Dog. That made my heart race and my cock throb even harder. I countered with slow, deliberate breathing.

With the silence now awkward, Angie's happy, expectant expression slowly morphed into a concerned look. Having turned my gaze to the ceiling, I wondered if this swinging stuff was really part of God's plan to save my marriage after all. I then concluded that he was indeed saving my marriage, and that swinging was him "working in mysterious ways". I also concluded that he wasn't going to make it easy for me to support my wife, because he always gives us trials and tribulations, so that good can prevail. Without the relative comparison, we cannot appreciate the good in our lives.

Having finally quietened my racing heart, I told my wife that a full swap in separate rooms was probably a bit too much to begin with, and that we'd need to have rules.

'But I don't want you to impose rules on me, Rich!' she insisted, looking me square in the eye. 'I'm not a commodity you own. We're in the twenty-first century now, and I just want to be free to be me.'

Unable to formulate a reply, I just nodded and remained silent. Angie continued to look at me. She looked like she was collecting her thoughts. She then said that if a full swap in separate rooms was too much for me to begin with, then I might prefer it if she cuckolded me and told me about it later.

'And if you *wanted* me to do that,' she continued, 'as something we're doing as a couple, I would happily oblige.'

'I don't think I want that,' I replied, before withdrawing my hands from Angies to adjust my unwelcome hard-on through my jeans.

Angie's eyes followed my hands. She then smiled smugly and told me that she would do a great job of being a complete slut for me.

'No,' I said, 'you keep saying I'm a cuckold, but I don't think I am.'

'But remember how rampant you became at the golf hotel,' she countered, 'you know, when you demanded to know about my sex with Martin?'

'Yes, but that was …'

'Well just imagine how excited you'll be when I have sex with other men? Off the scale!' She enthused, holding my gaze with wide, affirming eyes.

At this point, a mass of thoughts immediately burst forth into my head, accompanied by one angry Black Dog.

Having forced him back into his kennel, my first clear thought was that Angie's affair with Martin wasn't the same as her having extramarital sex whilst married to me. My second clear thought was, when she said *men*, is she talking singular or plural? I had to know.

'Do you want to have sex with two guys at once then Angie?' I demanded a little sharply.

'Oh God yeah,' she instantly replied, causing my erection to throb away even more. 'Two blokes at once is women's number two fantasy come true.'

'Why?' I asked, as I felt my face flush from anxiety.

'A survey said it was sensory overload,' replied my wife.

'Sensory overload Angie?'

'Yes, you know,' she said, 'the touch of four hands, lots of kissing and being penetrated repeatedly.'

'That's probably made up by *Cosmo*,' I scoffed, keen to show that it wasn't at all normal.

With my insecurities now at full tilt, I found myself inwardly backtracking on my gung-ho thinking that I could become a swinger if I needed to. Just talking about it made me jealous and anxious. I wanted to rein all this debauched nonsense in, but I knew it was way too late for that. The horse was out of the starting gate and well and truly into its stride, jumping hurdles with relish as it went. All I could do now was hang on for dear life, until it had run its course.

Like a dog with a bone, Angie immediately challenged my dismissive suggestion that her assertion had no basis in truth. She then backed that up by pointing to research published in the *Psychologists Review*, about women's sexual experiences with multiple men at once.

'It's way more common than you'd think,' she added, 'because women are increasingly overcoming the ingrained conditioning and judgement of men!'

I graciously conceded my wife's point with a smile, and then listened as she told me that she wasn't that bad or unusual.

'Most women have secret desires,' she continued, 'they just don't tell their partners.'

'They're being deceitful,' I suggested.

'No Rich!' snapped Angie. 'Lots of women can't be themselves because they feel judged.'

'Judged?' I repeated, my erection instantly subsiding with the weight of intellectual argument.

'Yes, because blokes want their wives to be virtuous,' countered Angie, 'and they expect them to meet their standards and values. It's a form of control.'

'A form of control?' I questioned. 'I don't think so.'

'Yes, a form of control,' retorted Angie, 'because it undermines their wife's confidence.'

'Is that right?' I asked, barely veiling my cynicism.

'Yes,' responded Angie, 'I had it with my previous husbands, and with you as well.'

'And now?' I asked.

'And now,' sighed my wife, having suddenly come down off her high horse, 'I feel completely free to be me!'

'I'm glad sweetheart,' I replied warmly, keen to move on from our heated debate.

During the short silence which followed, my irrational insecurity got the better of me. I couldn't stop myself asking my wife if I was boring, and wanted to know if that was the reason she wanted to be a swinger.

'Don't be silly,' she replied warmly, 'we have amazing sex. Swinging is just a way to take our sex life to the next level.'

Even though I wasn't able to get behind my wife's

thinking, I felt reassured. A second later though, I wondered why Black Dog had become angrier at her two-man fantasy, compared to her one-man fantasy. Keen to work this out, I asked her to tell me more about her threesome scenario. The first thing she told me was that it's actually called double-teaming. She then told me that she'd also fantasised about a third guy who would lick her down below, whilst the other two were massaging and sucking her breasts.

Completely taken aback by this whole new insight into my wife's mind, I just stared at her with wide, disbelieving eyes.

'You look shocked,' she said, as her face turned red, 'but you shouldn't be. All I'm doing is articulating the physicality of a sexy fancy.'

She then went on to tell me about Nancy Friday's book on women's fantasies, and how it sold millions of copies.

'There's a reason for that,' she added, 'it's because wanting fantasies to come true is perfectly normal.'

'Having sex with multiple men at once isn't normal, Angie,' I responded.

'It is what it is,' came her matter-of-fact reply. 'The trouble is that people want to be *disgusted* from Tunbridge Wells. But what they don't realise,' she continued, 'is that they'd have much more fun if they were *disgusting* from Tunbridge Wells!'

With that said, my wife laughed at her own funny. I laughed as well. And then, having lightened up, I asked her what the top fantasy come true for women was. She told me it was meeting a tall, dark, handsome stranger, and having a night of dirty unbridled sex with him.

'It's something I've actually fantasised about too,' she continued. 'I can be as dirty as I like because I won't see him again.'

'Is that right?'

'Yes,' said Angie. 'And he can dominate me and use me.'

'But you said it was the twenty-first century. You shouldn't be dominated by men.'

'Oh Rich,' said Angie, sounding exasperated, 'satisfying my sexual desires is me being in control and getting what I want. Outside the bedroom,' she added, 'there's no question of any man dominating me.'

'But doesn't sexually dominating you actually represent objectification of women?' I countered.

'Idiot feminazis espouse that sort of crap,' retorted Angie, 'yet we all know that casual sex is about sexual attraction. And sexual attraction,' she added, 'involves both parties being sexual objects to each other.'

'Sexual objects to each other?' I questioned.

'Yes, it's perfectly natural,' responded Angie. 'I mean most girls lusted after the guy in the Diet Coke ad when he took his T-shirt off.'

'And that's not objectification?' I said, somehow feeling the need to be contrary.

'Like I said, the feminazi's call that objectification,' retorted Angie. 'Normal women call it sexy!'

Unable to counter my wife's argument, I just nodded and smiled. She instantly seized the silence, doubtless driven by the bottle of red she'd consumed, and continued with fervour.

'And when random guys check me out,' she said, 'I like it. And make no mistake Rich,' she added, 'us women like to be noticed and fancied. We may not fancy the guy back, but that's not the point. Women don't want to be invisible,' she continued, before pointing out that it must be true, because they said it on *Woman's Hour*.

Still being contrary, I told Angie that she didn't like it when men talked to her tits, to use her terminology.

'I definitely don't like it if he's creepy and pervy,' she replied. 'But if he's good-looking and I fancy him, then I must admit, I quite like him talking to my tits. I'm being honest,' she added, 'unlike a lot of women.'

With that said, my wife suddenly jumped up onto her knees. She then hoicked her dress up and straddled me so that her crotch was against my tummy. Then, taking hold of both my hands, she raised them to her lips and kissed them.

'You know there can never be anyone else for me, Rich,' she said emphatically, whilst surveying my face with her big, adoring eyes. 'Don't you?'

I nodded and smiled.

'You've always been my hero,' continued my wife. 'So capable, so resourceful, so loving. My big protector with your strong arms and kind eyes. You physically envelop me, and I love that.'

'Wow!' I sighed, beaming with delight. 'I feel so secure when you say such lovely things to me, and I know I could do anything for you given time.'

Squeezing my hands in response, my Angie then asked me if I really could do *anything* for her.

'I mean, what if you don't like me for who I am?' she asked, searching my face for the right answer, looking like a little girl lost.

'Aww sweetheart,' I whispered, 'don't worry, I'm not judging you. You need to trust me, and be true to yourself.'

'Yes, that's the bit I took from Don Lewis's book,' said my wife, before adding that she needed me to help her blossom and feel special because of who she is.

'My darling Angie,' I whispered, 'I love you and I …'

'Warts and all?' she interrupted sharply, before throwing my hands back to me.

I knew my Angie wasn't really cross with me, and that her unexpected response was the work of her inner demon. I also knew that I was, slowly but surely, disarming her with love and understanding. Still looking deep into my wife's eyes, I told her that her inner demon was mischief making, and that I didn't love her "warts and all".

'I just love *you*,' I insisted, before delighting in the beautiful smile which gradually replaced the pain on my Angie's face.

Tipping her head to one side, she cupped my face in her hand and kissed me tenderly on my lips. Having dismounted, she repositioned herself so that her back rested against my side, before drawing my arms round her middle and holding them tight to her body.

With a contented sigh, my wife pulled her knees up to her chin, causing her dress to cascade down her shapely, milky-white thighs. I admired her beauty as I caressed the underside of her soft exposed legs. Moments later she flopped them open and placed my hand on her mons pubis. She then squeezed her thighs closed tight and hugged my forearm as hard as she could to her chest, before juddering to emphasise the closeness of our connection. With so much beauty in such a small act, I felt totally loved-up.

We were alone with our thoughts for a short while, until I suddenly blurted out, 'If we did swing, there would be no kissing playmates – that's a special intimacy for us.'

'You must be joking,' exclaimed Angie, half laughing as she craned her neck to look at me. 'So I can suck a guy off and let him fuck me every which way, but kissing's a *no-no*?'

'It's not that simple!' I replied in a serious voice. 'Soft, warm kisses are personal and intimate.'

'I say,' replied my wife, before un-craning her neck, 'if you're gonna fuck, then fuck! Anything goes!'

'Well I'm not sure I ...'

'Please don't worry, Rich!' interrupted Angie. 'I'm not gonna love these guys. Swinging is about pussy lust – emotionally dissociated sex, but kissing is part of it.'

At this juncture, I realised there wasn't much point in countering my wife. She was clearer than ever before about what she wanted, and that was that. Sensing my concerns, she lovingly reassured me that reservations were normal, and then said we should check out the swingers club.

'Let's suck it and see,' she quipped with a laugh, before adding that over seventy-two per cent of swingers said swinging actually *improved* their relationship.

'That's as maybe sweetheart,' I replied anxiously, 'but I'm not sure I could jump straight into separate rooms. I'd want us to be together.'

'I know,' said my wife, 'but like I said, I'm not sure I could handle watching you fuck another woman. Somehow, out of sight out of mind!'

Not entirely clear about what Angie was actually saying, I asked her what she meant. She said she would be comparing herself to the other woman.

'Are her tits bigger and firmer than mine?' she continued. 'Is she a stick insect? Are you having a better time with her? Etcetera, etcetera.'

Somehow equating my wife's position with being insecure, I asked her if she was secure in our relationship. She said she was totally secure because she knew I loved her. She then explained that being open and honest was the key to success, and asked me how many women could tell their husband they want multiple blokes to shag them senseless.

'And that she wants anal too,' she added.

'Anal too, Angie?' I repeated.

'Yes,' she replied, 'because I've never tried it before, because you don't like the idea of it.'

Even though my wife's directness caught me by surprise, I was really pleased to see her being herself and being so open and honest with me. I then realised there were a thousand and one emotional dynamics at play in swinging. This underscored the need to proceed with caution, so that neither of us was left emotionally upset. Once a deed is done, I thought to myself, it cannot be undone. Just as I was going to share that thought with Angie, she excitedly announced that she'd got an interesting fact to share.

'I read that lots of partners fantasise about other people when their partner is making love to them,' she said.

'Do they?' I asked, genuinely surprised.

'Yes,' replied Angie. 'And I was wondering if you've ever done that with me?'

Pausing for thought, I shook my head.

'No,' I said, 'I can't say I have. Have you then?'

'Yes,' replied Angie, wearing a cheeky smile, 'just recently.'

'Oh yeah,' I replied, smiling back at her, 'who was it then, Daniel Craig?'

'No. Try again.'

'It must be Tom Cruise then; you've always fancied him.'

'No silly,' said Angie with playful dismissiveness, 'it was Ryan.'

'Ryan?' I repeated, withdrawing my arm from around

her middle as my cock went hard in the blink of an eye.

Reacting to my reaction, my wife spun round on her bum to face me and then sat back on her calves. She looked surprised.

'What's wrong?' she asked.

'I don't think Ryan would be particularly flattered if he knew you were thinking of him,' I said spitefully, at the behest of Black Dog.

Angie looked crestfallen as she demanded to know why Ryan wouldn't be flattered. Spurred on by jealousy and insecurity, I told her it was because he has a sexy, slim wife who is ten years younger than her.

In response, Angie insisted, like a spoiled child, that Ryan did fancy her.

'He was pissed and you looked like mutton dressed as lamb,' I countered vengefully.

'He was *begging* for me, you bastard!' retorted my wife, leaning into me. 'And you can't deal with that!'

'It doesn't bother me, Angie,' I responded nonchalantly.

'It actually does! And FYI,' she added, 'he had a *massive* cock.'

'You're making that up,' I said.

'Well it felt pretty damn big to me when I squeezed it,' she announced.

'You never said you *actually* felt his hard-on?' I responded, somewhat shocked.

'Well I did,' replied Angie, 'when he pulled me to him to say goodbye. I had my hand in front of me and squeezed it. It was *big*. Bigger than yours. And very hard!'

'Bigger than mine and hard?' I questioned angrily.

'Yes,' replied Angie, through a taunting smile. 'And I wanted him deep inside my wet tingling pussy,' she added, having gotten right into my face.

Hearing those words from my wife immediately sent Black Dog mad, and awoke the unwelcome lion response in me. Now it wasn't just about taking my wife to soothe my jealousy. Now I was driven to see off my competitor. I had to penetrate *my* woman and leave *my* semen deep inside her to mark my territory. With that in mind, I immediately sprung off the sofa and man-handled her onto her back. Totally obsessed with having my woman, I hastily dropped my jeans and allowed my full hard-on to spring out ready for action.

'I'm gonna fuck you Angie,' I declared gruffly, as I lifted her dress over her tummy.

'Let's see what you can do with that inferior cock of yours,' she goaded.

I responded by pushing her legs apart. She hooked her left calf over the arm of the sofa and rested her right foot on the floor. I had never seen her open that wide before. I tugged her sodden knickers aside, parted her labia with my fingers and then unceremoniously penetrated her from my kneeling position on the floor.

'So you've been thinking about Ryan whilst I've been making love to you?'

Angie didn't reply.

'Well?' I demanded, in time to a hard thrust.

'Yes,' she whispered. 'I already told you that.'

'You don't think of him now,' I ordered. 'You got that?'

'Yes.'

'And am *I* big and hard for you Angie?' I insisted on knowing.

'Yes,' came her breathless reply.

Whilst angrily pounding my wife, I unbuttoned her dress and hoicked her breasts out of her bra. I then divided my gaze between her bouncing tits, and my rock-solid cock thrusting in and out of her stretched-open pussy. This was the very epitome of a dirty, detached, primal lust-fuck.

After a few frenzied minutes of wanton penetrative sex, Angie suddenly fixed her gaze on my eyes.

'Yes, oh yes!' she whispered. 'Yes, fuck me, I'm coming.'

At that moment, she dug her nails into my arms and then dragged them down, leaving bleeding scratches in their wake. My woman's moans then turned to panting until she went rigid and quiet. Her grip tightened round my cock as she neared orgasm. She then suddenly let out an involuntary 'arghhh', whilst writhing and wriggling as she climaxed.

With the fading of my wife's panting, I stood up and lifted her big, round arse up onto the arm of the sofa so that she was sitting up facing me. My angry eyes locked onto her anxious, yet expectant stare. We froze for an intense moment.

'Fuck me then!' she ordered.

In response, I purposefully pushed her top half back onto the sofa seat with the flat of my hand on her chest. She grunted with surprise at my forceful manhandling of her. I then grabbed her delicate lacy knickers with both hands and ripped them apart to make an opening. Having taken hold of her ankles, I held them up by my face before drawing my cockhead up and down her wet opening a few times to mark her. I then plunged deep inside her, hitting the buffers in the process.

'My turn now,' I announced gruffly.

Whilst slap, slap, slapping into my woman, I suddenly remembered her want for anal because she'd never had it before. I needed to be the one that gave that to her first. With that thought overwhelming me, I pulled out of my wife's vagina with some urgency, and then pushed her knees back towards her face to open her wide. With her open arse balanced on the armrest and her head resting on the sofa seat, I rubbed our combined lube in circles round her anus and then pushed into her.

'Arghhh,' she moaned gruffly.

'Are you thinking of him giving you anal now, Angie?' I demanded to know as I rammed home.

'Who?' she goaded.

'Ryan!' I roared.

'Yes,' replied Angie, through clenched teeth. 'What you gonna do about it?'

'I'm fucking your arse,' I insisted angrily, 'that's what I'm doing about it!'

With that said, I suddenly felt the need to see myself penetrating my woman. I held her open by her thighs and watched my rampant, throbbing cock going in and out of her. Her sphincter gripped me tighter than her pussy, but not the whole length, just at the point of entry.

I felt my crescendo building fast. One last hard thrust, the hardest and deepest of them all, was accompanied by a guttural roar, as the intense physical and emotional pleasure of my pulsating penis overwhelmed me. Whilst I fired hot semen into *my* woman, my orgasm raced through my body, making me judder from head to toe. With all my semen completely discharged into Angie's anus, I released my vice-like grip on her thighs, leaving red handprints in their wake.

With my hands on my hips, I stood tall and dominant as I watched my mate slide her bum off the arm of the sofa. She then straightened herself up, before tossing the backrest cushions onto the floor to make room for me.

Still standing tall, I continued to look down at my wife in

silence, my chest heaving and my expression emotionless. She looked up at me with pensive eyes without saying a word.

Having caught my breath, I began to come down from the primal, angry emotions that had visited me without my permission. I don't even like anal sex, yet I felt compelled to do it. What in God's name was that all about?

As my loving persona returned, I felt the need to hold my Angie close, and went to lie with her. She rested her head on my chest and slid her arm round my middle, before resting her bent leg across my nether regions. We were connected like we were one. The quiet of our beautiful post-coital cuddle, ushered the soft background music into focus. In that moment it felt like the incredibly soulful songwriter, John Legend, had picked up my thoughts and turned them into lyrics.

Deeply moved by the beautifully delivered, wonderfully profound words to *All Of Me*, I began to cry. And then, whilst I slowly traced the fingers of one hand up and down Angie's side, I sighed with relief. Relief that I now knew her better than ever before. This meant I could manage my marriage going forward, to make sure we all lived happily ever after. My heart, soul and body smiled with the warmth of that thought, as more tears of joy tumbled out of me.

As we held each other close, we both drifted into that wondrous, surreal state, betwixt awake and asleep. After a few dreamy minutes, Angie suddenly pushed herself up onto one elbow and looked at me.

'Love you, my rampant wild man,' she whispered.

'Love you too,' I whispered back, smiling.

'We're stupid aren't we,' she said, 'we go from being totally relaxed and loving one minute, to vindictive and angry the next.'

'I know,' I said, nodding in agreement.

'And you go mad like a wild silverback,' added my wife, 'and fuck me to within an inch of my life.'

'I know,' I said, 'but I just can't seem to …'

'Don't get me wrong,' she interrupted, 'I *really* love being your hotwife, but I think you also like a bit of humiliation thrown in to really get you going.'

'Yeah?' I questioned.

'Yeah,' she said, before recounting how she loved me balancing her arse on the armrest to penetrate her. 'Oh my god,' she exclaimed, 'that was so wickedly wonderful. And that you were my first,' she added through a smile, 'is so lovely.'

Feeling totally loved by my amazing wife, I smiled from ear to ear as I explored her beautiful face with my slightly watery eyes.

'And you were all competitive and jealous,' she continued. 'It's like you were Jekyll and Hyde, and when you'd come, it was as if the good doctor had returned.'

Not knowing quite how to reply to that, I said nothing. I just drew Angie back to my chest and hugged her tight. She slipped her arm round my middle and squeezed me with all she had.

After a few more minutes of savouring my wife's heart beating next to mine, I suddenly felt inadequate compared to Ryan. That he was tall, good-looking and younger, didn't bother me at all. No, it was my inability to compete with his giant schlong that got to me. Knowing I was being stupid, I refrained from saying anything and tried to relax, but then, after a few more minutes, I succumbed to my feelings of inadequacy.

'Erm, Angie,' I whispered gingerly, 'so was Ryan's you

know, erm really big?'

'No silly,' she interrupted through a dismissive laugh. 'I just said that because you said I was mutton.'

'I didn't mean it, sweetheart,' I said, before adding that she looked stunning at Charlotte's dinner party.

'Aww, thanks Richie,' she responded. 'And just so you know, Ryan's cock really wasn't very big at all.'

With a contented sigh, I relaxed back into our cuddle. Before long though, I sensed a presence and opened my eyes a little. There was a thirty-something guy gawping at us through the window holding a box. With Angie's thigh pulled up over my tummy and her dress round her waist, *everything* was on show!

'Angie,' I whispered, still keeping my eyes mostly shut, 'the postie's here with a parcel.'

'What? Where?' she whispered back, pretending to be asleep.

'At the front window, checking your arse out,' I said.

'Oooh, what's he doing there?' she said urgently, as she pulled her dress down, before then jumping up and straightening her hair.

As the postie headed for the doorbell, he paused at the side window and stared at my wife's breasts, which were beautifully displayed on top of her bra cups. I watched her smile at him, before then looking down at her chest. He widened his eyes and smiled back. I thought I'd be okay, but I was jealous.

'Rich,' whispered Angie excitedly, whilst hurriedly slipping her bra off and magically pulling it out of her dress sleeve, 'he couldn't take his eyes off me!'

'I know,' I replied flatly, as I quickly pulled my jeans on.

'Shall I be a bit naughty and sign for the parcel like

this?' she asked eagerly.

'I'll go,' I insisted sharply, as my cock went hard with jealousy. 'You stay right here,' I ordered, 'and put those away!'

CHAPTER 16

As it was half term, Angie and the children were having a lie-in. Tiptoeing around, I got dressed and downed a quick cuppa. I then quietly slipped out of the back door and set off for Plymouth to keep my follow-up appointment with Julia. I thought it best not to tell Angie, because she didn't rate Julia and was convinced she had judged her badly. So as far as my wife was concerned, I was nipping out for an early morning round of golf. I took my golf clubs to complete the charade.

At just before eight on a sunny Tuesday morning, I parked up outside Julia's house. I felt great as I bounded up the steps and rang the doorbell. The big half-glazed front door soon swung open, revealing Julia's smiling freckled face.

'Good morning,' she said.

'Good morning!' I replied with a smile.

'How's things?'

'Great thanks, Julia,' I responded cheerily. 'I've had an epiphany!'

'Sounds very positive,' said Julia, shutting the front door behind her.

She then gestured to the consulting room and asked me if I wanted a coffee. I nodded and said white with one.

Julia then trundled off down the hall. I stepped into her huge consulting room and headed straight for the big bay window. Grinning like a Cheshire cat in anticipation of sharing my epiphany with Julia, I tipped my head back and stared up at the blue sky. I then absorbed the warmth which rained down on me. Such a contrast in my mood compared to the last time I was here.

After a few minutes, Julia breezed in with a tray of coffee and biscuits.

'Bickies too!' I exclaimed, as I headed to the sofas.

Julia smiled and then set the tray down on the low coffee table which separated her sofa from mine. I sat down, reached for my mug, and took a jammy dodger off the plate. I then popped it into my mouth, before washing it down with a big swig of coffee. Julia sat opposite me and picked her notepad up off the coffee table. She then opened it at the page marked by her pen, and placed it on her lap.

'You mentioned an epiphany, Rich,' said Julia, getting down to business. 'Can you expand on that?'

'I can indeed,' I replied, sitting up straight. 'I now have a better understanding of Angie and have a plan going forward.'

'That's great news,' replied Julia. 'And how have you been coping?'

'Very well, and I've been using your coping strategies to great effect.'

'That's good to hear.'

'Unfortunately,' I continued, 'I didn't make any headway with Angie coming to see you for couples counselling, and she was none too pleased about being classed as perimenopausal.'

'Oh,' said Julia, 'that's a shame. What happened?'

I explained that Angie refused to believe she was perimenopausal because she was way too young and said it was an old woman's problem. Looking disappointed, Julia nodded with reluctant acceptance and then asked me what brought me to see her.

'I wanted to get your take on things,' I replied. 'You know, get your view on what I'm doing.'

Julia said she was happy to listen to me, but didn't advise per se. I nodded in response and went on to explain that I'd asked God to support my love for Angie, and not to limit it with Christian morals. Julia thought that was fair and reasonable. I then told her that I'd been reading a book on how to manage relationships. She asked me what I'd taken from it.

'Loving your partner for who they are is a priority in any relationship,' I replied.

'Supporting personal development and freedom,' remarked Julia, 'that's a good thing. So how does that work in your marriage then, Rich?' she asked.

'Angie says she's been wife, mum and career woman,' I responded, 'but now wants to find herself. Her *forgotten me* as she calls it.'

Julia smiled and nodded in response. Her usual trick to get me to speak. I smiled back and explained that Angie wanted my love and support going forward, rather than my old Catholic moral judgements.

'So Angie doesn't feel judged by you anymore then, Rich?' said Julia.

'No, not now,' I replied.

'What changed do you think?'

I told Julia that her "change your mindset, change the outcome" mantra made perfect sense to me, and that I wasn't going to "do what I'd always done, and get what I'd always got".

'That would be the death knell for my marriage,' I added emphatically.

Julia nodded in approval, and then asked what practical changes I'd made. I explained that helping Angie blossom into her true self, made me both proud and happy.

'The same sort of feeling I get,' I added, 'when I nurture my children.'

'That's really good, Rich,' said Julia. 'And how did you get to this place?'

'I used a technique from my relationship book,' I replied.

'What technique?'

I paused to gather my thoughts. Julia caught herself slouching and sat up straight. She then waited expectantly.

'I think of my new belief,' I began slowly, 'and then repeat it to myself in my head, especially when I'm running. I then accept it in my mind as my new value.'

'I also prescribe that technique to my patients,' said Julia. 'It's very effective when applied to misplaced values. So what are you working on at the moment then?' she enquired.

'Shall I repeat my mantra to you?' I asked.

Julia nodded in reply. She then looked down at her pad and made a quick note, before lifting her head and prompting me to begin with her eyes.

'It's quite explicit,' I said, 'because I need my subconscious to be sure about what I'm telling it.'

'No problem at all, Rich,' said Julia, 'you won't shock me.'

With that said, she relaxed into her seat as if waiting for a recital to begin. I took a deep breath and then repeated my mantra.

'I am a swinger and fully support Angie's want to have sex with other men. This pleases me because her happiness is my happiness. I can do this because I am not jealous or insecure. I will enjoy being cuckolded by my hotwife and I can have sex with other women.'

Having concluded my mantra, I looked at Julia expectantly. She sat forward looking both serious and pensive.

'That's it,' I added boldly, filling the embarrassing silence.

'Thanks Rich,' said Julia quietly, before falling silent again.

I could hear the cogs going round in her head. The silence became quite deafening, and I began to feel uneasy and a little foolish. I felt the need to say something to escape the awkwardness, but before I could open my mouth to speak, Julia referred to my mantra and asked …

'Do you actually want to have sex with another woman then, Rich?'

'It's not a burning desire,' I replied. 'I'm happy with just Angie.'

I then went on to say that Angie wanted me to have sex with another woman, even though she'd be jealous. Julia asked me why. I told her that meant Angie could have guilt-free sex with another man, because I would be just as culpable as her.

'In other words,' I added, 'I wouldn't be in a position to judge her.'

Julia nodded in reply, and then asked if there was anyone in particular I would "play" with if Angie insisted.

'My wife's sister Paulette,' I answered. 'But that would only be if she was single and wanted to of course.'

'What did Angie say to that?' enquired Julia.

'She said I liked Paulette because she was a virtuous version of her, but without the tits, looks and brains! She jokingly said I'd soon get tired of her taking to bed with migraines.'

'Hmmm,' sighed Julia. 'So why Paulette then, Rich?'

'She's dead sexy! Great arse and legs. And although people aren't kind about her smaller breasts, I think they're gorgeous – pert as anything with huge nips – and she's pushing fifty!'

Bloody hell Rich, I exclaimed in my head, where the hell did all that come from?

'I can tell you really like her,' said a smiling Julia, before asking questions about Paulette's relationships.

I told Julia that Paulette had an extramarital encounter, because she needed to feel special as Brian, her husband, was too wrapped up in work.

Julia said Angie appeared to be jealous of her sister. She also placed a lot of emphasis on Paulette's affair being based on the same modelling Angie had from their father, i.e. when he had an affair and left their mother.

'But Paulette and Brian got through the affair,' I said, 'and are now stronger than ever!'

'So how do you feel about Paulette's affair?' asked Julia.

'These things happen,' I replied, shrugging my shoulders. 'She's a good girl. Very active in her church. She taught Sunday school, as did Angie.'

During the short silence which followed, Julia sat forward and placed her notepad on the table. She then let her knees fall to one side, before clasping her hands together and placing them on her lap.

'Rich,' she began softly, 'I'm glad to see that you don't

judge Paulette, and that you have clearly changed your mindset for the better.'

Pleased with my therapist's praise, I smiled like a schoolboy receiving a commendation at assembly. That soon changed though, when she told me, in a very grave tone indeed, that I must proceed with caution.

'Really?' I questioned, looking at her with a face full of surprise and incredulity.

'I'm not supposed to advise as such, Rich,' continued Julia, 'but I think I'd be failing you if I didn't say something on this occasion.'

'Failing me,' I repeated. 'Why?'

'Because, from what you've said,' replied Julia, 'you haven't fully adopted the swingers' mindset.'

'No?'

'No, but you clearly understand the concept.'

In the absence of a reply from me, she went on to say that it appeared that Angie was emotionally ready for swinging.

'From what you've said,' she continued, 'she is clearly ready to pursue her personal journey of self-discovery and expression.'

I said I was ready to support my wife on that journey. I then asked Julia what was wrong with my desire to do that, especially as there was something in it for me because of my competitive cuckold tendencies.

'It's great that you want to support your wife,' replied Julia, 'but your mantra needs to support something you're a hundred per cent committed to.'

'But you counsel couples to support each other,' I retorted.

'I only suggest redefining an intrinsic value,' replied Julia, 'in response to a genuine conscious and subconscious preference.'

I looked away from my so-called therapist, and stared out of the big bay window to collect my thoughts. I was taken aback by her complete U-turn compared to our last session.

After a short silence though, I admitted that I got aroused, angry and jealous when Angie expressed an interest in having scx with other men. Julia referred to our previous session. She then reminded me that my angry cuckold response was brought about by sexual competitiveness.

'That sort of response does have its place in swinging,' she continued, 'provided the husband has bought into it for his pleasure as well as his wife's.'

'I think I have bought into it,' I replied.

'You need to be sure,' said Julia, 'otherwise being cuckolded can be very destructive.'

'In what way?' I asked.

'It generates insecurity which can make it difficult for you to believe you are worthy of love,' responded Julia. 'And it can make it hard for you to function in a relationship. A lack of trust can cause you to engage in unhealthy behaviours that could cost you your relationship.'

'Oh,' I sighed.

'I shouldn't really comment like this Rich,' said a serious looking Julia, 'but I get a sense that your wife is promoting her agenda over and above your emotional wellbeing.'

'Do you think so?' I questioned.

'Yes, but not wittingly,' replied Julia. 'I also think being cuckolded goes against your deeply ingrained moral code.'

'So why am I so passionate for my wife?' I asked.

'Your passion is inflamed by jealousy, insecurity and possessiveness,' said Julia. 'And there's something called cognitive dissonance,' she added, 'where a person, without realising, supports a flawed position they are biased toward for their own reasons.'

Looking at my therapist slightly aghast, I asked her if she meant I was subconsciously supporting Angie to stop my marriage failing. She suggested that could very well play a part in my thought processes and decision making.

Feeling a bit foolish, I leant back on the sofa and rubbed my face hard with my hands.

This is all too complicated Richie boy, insisted my demon voice. You didn't come here for this bloody U-turn. You wanted reassurance on your plan, he added, not all this mumbo-jumbo psychobabble bullshit!

Having gone quiet, I forced myself to wait for Julia to say something, instead of being pressured into speaking first. She duly obliged by telling me she was a qualified sex therapist who had worked with swinging couples. She explained that swinging was all about working within one's emotional capabilities, and that there were often disparities between partners as to how far they could go.

'Bearing that in mind,' she continued, 'you must not reprogram the mind to do something it doesn't want to.'

'Sure,' I said, 'but you say that true love is giving even though it hurts sometimes.'

'I agree,' replied Julia, 'but it has to be properly structured and managed.'

Having nodded in reply, I turned my gaze to the bay window to avoid eye contact. At this point, I felt like I'd been seriously told off by Julia, and wondered why she was shooting me down in flames. I knew I had to let my wife blossom, otherwise she'd divorce me for sure. Plus I loved her, and wanted her happiness, even at the cost of my own. With all this in mind, I thought it unprofessional of my therapist to disrespect my input and contradict her own teaching.

With my faith in Julia now severely diminished, I decided to call it a day and politely told her that I needed to reflect on all that she had said. I brought our session to an end and settled up.

Having said goodbye at the front door, I rushed down the steps to the pavement, to get away from the confusion that was Julia. I then literally bumped straight into Charlotte and John. Oh God, I thought to myself, as I smiled and said hello, here comes the Spanish Inquisition!

CHAPTER 17

'Don't let me forget my fuck-me heels, Rich,' said Angie excitedly, as she smoothed her cocktail dress down with her hands.

'Sure,' I replied, coming out of my anxious musings.

'I'll wear flats till we get there,' she added, whilst scrutinising her look in the mirror. 'So, what do you think then, my big man?' she asked, having spun round to face me.

'I can see your panty line,' I replied flatly, 'where it cuts into your mummy tummy. But yeah, alright.'

'Not sexy?' said Angie, looking seriously crestfallen.

'Oh my God!' I replied, way over the top. 'Sexy doesn't even begin to describe it!'

'Stop this snide bollocks,' snapped Angie, 'okay? I'm already worried enough as it is without you adding to it. I mean, what if no one likes me?' she added anxiously.

'I'm sorry sweetheart,' I said contritely. 'I was being horrid, and I don't know why.'

'We're both nervous, Richie,' came Angie's warm reply. 'Let's try and relax and enjoy our fun night out.'

Keen to calm down, I sat up straight and inhaled deeply. I then let my breath out slowly, relaxing my shoulders as I went. Angie turned back to the mirror and began applying her lipstick.

I picked up my favourite silver cufflinks from my bedside table and set about putting them on. As I admired them thoughtfully, I smiled at the memory of Angie giving them to me by the open fire in her sitting room. That was our very first Christmas together. I even remembered that she'd got them from Selfridges. The Rolex she'd bought me was my other treasured accessory. I literally never took it off.

Reminded of the wonderful love Angie had always shown me, I came out of my reverie feeling less anxious about the evening ahead. I rose from the edge of the bed, straightened my beige linen trousers, eased into my brown brogues, and then ventured downstairs.

'Hey,' I said, as I walked into the sitting room, 'Mum and I are off out now, so remember, don't open the door to anyone and call me if you get worried at all.'

'Sure Dadda,' replied Connor, keen to get back to *The Simpsons Movie.*

'Charlotte and John can be here in seconds,' I added in an official tone, disturbing their viewing still further, 'and the landline has my number ready on redial and John's number is stored.'

Just as I finished my safety announcement, Angie popped her head round the door.

'Ready Rich?' she asked.

'Yes,' I replied,

'Okay you two,' said Angie, smiling her mummy smile, 'the two little ones are sound asleep, so please keep the noise down and don't stay up too late, okay?'

'We won't,' replied Livy.

'Bye,' said Angie.

'Bye,' said Connor and Livy in unison.

'Enjoy your romantic night out!' added Livy, waving enthusiastically with both hands as we headed for the door.

CHAPTER 18

'There it is!' announced Angie in an excited whisper, as I slowly eased the VW down a narrow street. 'Oh, and there's a parking space just waiting for us,' she added, smiling with relief, almost as if the parking space was a sign that all was going to be well.

Once I'd parked up, Angie slipped her red stilettos on and we alighted from the motor. It was still warm, even though it was past 9 p.m.

'You can't see my stocking tops can you Rich?' whispered an anxious Angie, as we walked towards the venue. 'I don't want to look tarty.'

'You look just fine sweetheart,' I insisted.

'Oh good,' she replied, taking hold of my hand and swinging it back and forth like an excited five-year-old off to the circus. 'Thanks for this by the way,' she added warmly.

I squeezed my wife's hand in acknowledgement, and then walked on in silence, all the while wondering what the hell I was doing here. When we arrived at the gates to the venue, Angie suddenly pulled me to a halt.

'You will stick close to me Rich, won't you?' she whispered urgently.

'Sure, but you'll be alright,' I replied, 'you're very sociable.'

'I am, but I still like you to take the lead,' insisted my wife, 'be the man and take care of me.'

'I always do my love,' I replied warmly, before sliding my arms round her middle, and drawing her to my chest.

With our profoundly loving hug completed, we passed, hand in hand, through a substantial pair of wrought iron gates. As we proceeded along the drive towards an imposing Georgian house, Angie appeared at once nervous and excited. Having climbed the steps to a palatial Corinthian-columned entrance portico, I took a deep breath and let it out slowly. Once through the double front doors, Angie and I were greeted by a curvy forty-something woman, with her ample décolletage well on show.

'Hey!' I said smiling. 'I'm Rich and this is my wife, Angie.'

'Lovely to meet you,' she said, tiptoeing to plant a kiss on my cheek.

'You must be Lydia,' said Angie.

'I am indeed,' replied our curvy hostess, before hugging and kissing my wife like a long-lost friend.

'We spoke on the phone,' continued Angie.

'I remember,' said Lydia with a smile. 'Do please come in,' she added warmly, 'and I'll introduce you to a lovely couple who will show you around and answer any questions.'

With that said, Lydia led us along a spacious and softly lit entrance hall, into a pleasant lounge. She introduced us to Marcus and Natalie, who were propping up the bar. With the introductions completed, Lydia said her farewells and was gone. And this is where my story began.

Looking around, all the ladies were dressed in sexy attire. Many wore negligees so loosely tied that their breasts and nether regions were on show. Angie and I, and Marcus and Natalie were cozied up chatting and flirting away on our sofas. Angie loved feeling desired and was really smug at making Marcus erect. I was struggling with my emotions and debauched demons.

The girls suddenly decided they needed the loo and took off together arm in arm like they were old school friends. Still seated side by side on our sofa, Marcus and I began chatting. He was easy company, and I was pleased his erection was fading because, as much as I tried, I couldn't stop dropping my gaze.

Was this some sort of homoerotic thing? I mean I didn't want to touch Marcus's hard-on or suck him. I just liked looking and wanted to see him fuck someone. That's not gay. All blokes like watching men and women shagging.

Feeling less uncomfortable about the erection that was throbbing away in my boxers, I got back into the moment with Marcus. He was telling me that he was an architect, and that Natalie was a ward manager.

Having nodded in acknowledgement, I asked about the four huge plasma screens on the wall.

'That's a great feature of this place, Rich,' replied Marcus.

'They don't mind people watching remotely?' I said, raising the pitch of my voice.

'No, they love it! I mean I often watch Natalie,' continued Marcus. 'She points out prospects, and I make it happen.'

Having nodded in thoughtful response, I then asked Marcus what happened next.

'I watch whilst I have a drink,' he replied, 'and sometimes,' he added, 'Natalie teams up with Lydia, whilst her husband Stu and I watch together.'

His comment made me swallow nervously. No matter how hard I tried, I just couldn't get my head round his thinking at all.

'Ermm, what's in it for you then?' I asked gingerly.

'Well, not to put too fine a point on it,' replied Marcus, in his confident, well-spoken voice, 'I love watching my wife being fucked!'

'Why?'

'Because her pleasure is my pleasure, and it turns me on.'

Marcus then told me that his wife could only play if he enjoyed it.

'I guess that's the nature of true love,' I said.

'It is indeed Rich,' he replied, before explaining that "playing" really built his wife's confidence up and made her feel good about herself. 'Plus, she attracts men considerably younger than herself,' he added, 'and I'm really proud of that.'

Having told Marcus I was also proud of my wife for being sexy, I then asked him if he thought that younger guys were about getting easy sex from grateful older women. He told me that things had changed.

'Older women want younger men who can keep going,' he said, 'and younger guys really love the more experienced woman who can let go and express themselves.'

As I nodded in thoughtful response, I realised this was the case with my Angie. She wanted to be herself without being judged, and that's why she needed me to prove my love by letting her sleep with another man. But, as much as I wanted to, and despite my mantra, I just couldn't see myself supporting that at this time. I was about to say as much to Marcus when he told me that Natalie and Lydia love performing for him and Stu.

'Gives them an extra thrill,' he added.

'Why?'

'Because they know it excites us, which means they can be as naughty and as sexy as they like without feeling inhibited.'

'You're their biggest cheerleader?' I suggested.

'Absolutely. And that makes us feel really close to each other.'

Marcus then went on to explain that he likes Natalie to cuckold him, either where she has sex with another man in front of him, or where she comes back to him and tells him about her night of naughtiness.

'And I go crazy for her afterwards!'

'Wow!' I responded, as I instantly went hard at the prospect of being cuckolded by my Angie.

'Passionate!' added Marcus, 'doesn't even begin to describe it.'

'And do you ever have sex with Natalie and another guy?' I asked.

'God yeah. That's called double-teaming.'

Then, as Marcus told me how emotionally close he and Natalie were after her liaisons, I asked him what his favourite thing was.

After a thoughtful pause, he told me he liked playing as a couple, but his favourite thing was watching Natalie get shagged repeatedly by different guys.

'Repeatedly?'

'Yes, repeatedly,' replied Marcus, before gleefully telling me how Natalie sometimes just liked to be taken *continuously* by her playmates.

'And you watch?'

'When it's multiple guys, yes. And I love to facilitate that as well. And when one guy withdraws,' he added, 'another guy takes over, leaving the remaining two to suck her breasts and caress her so the rotation keeps going.'

'Wow, intense,' I commented. 'But doesn't she feel used?' I asked, before grimacing at such an awkward question.

'No,' replied Marcus. 'Natalie actually likes the feeling of being used. It's detached, transactional sex for mutual excitement and pleasure. Men have known about transactional sex for a long time. Now women can do it too.'

'So, you enjoy watching them fuck your wife and you're not insecure?' I asked.

'Not at all. Natalie doesn't want to cuddle up on the sofa with them. I know my wife loves me and that I am her man, and she is my woman.'

I told Marcus that actually made sense to me. He smiled and then told me he'd make a swinger out of me yet, before laughing at his own joke. He then explained that it's like watching a live porn movie and that Natalie was the most beautiful porn star on the planet because he loved her.

'That's mind-blowingly amazing,' he added. 'Plus, I get a thrill out of indulging her and I feel so privileged that she's so honest that she shares her innermost thoughts and secrets with me.'

Nodding at Marcus, I told him that I also felt close to Angie when she shared her secret feelings with me. I then asked him if Natalie had sex with other guys to indulge him.

'Part of her likes it because she knows I like it,' replied Marcus, 'but make no mistake, she is totally in the moment getting shagged senseless, and that's very much about her enjoying herself for herself. I love that.'

At this point, Angie's fantasy of having three men at once came to mind. That sent my heart racing and re-stiffened my fading erection, even though I was never going to allow such a thing. Despite wanting to be like Marcus, I just wasn't that liberal-minded or confident.

'And there's a big mental side as well,' he continued, filling the momentary silence. 'Natalie's flattered and feels desired. She also likes to know she's excited her men and loves to see them come for her.'

Even though I was impressed with Marcus's in-depth knowledge of his wife's sexual drivers, I ignored his specific comment, and asked him if swinging initially went against all his natural instincts.

'*Initially,*' he replied, 'yes. But once you get past that,' he added, 'it actually makes perfect sense.'

'Perfect sense?' I repeated. 'How?'

'Well, take the animal kingdom,' began Marcus, 'a male can only service one female, and then he's spent for a while, but the female can be serviced repeatedly, and often wants to be.'

'Yeah, I guess so,' I replied, feeling obliged to agree.

'In the wild,' continued Marcus, 'males fight to penetrate the females, but we're a bit more sophisticated here!' he quipped.

Having completely failed to comprehend Marcus's humour, I forced a polite laugh. I then asked him if swinging took a lot of getting used to. He responded by saying that you had to be broad-minded, and that it wasn't something a Vanilla would contemplate. When I screwed my face up quizzically, he explained that Vanilla's were people who would never consider swinging. At this point, I asked Marcus if that meant ordinary people.

'We're ordinary people too,' he replied, 'except we have an enlightened outlook. That's all.'

'Sure,' I said, even though I didn't really get where he was coming from.

'Mind you,' continued Marcus, 'you have to have a really solid relationship. Swinging won't fix a broken marriage,' he added, looking serious.

Am I trying to fix a broken marriage? I asked myself before being distracted by the return of the girls.

With our drinks finished, we were ready for the tour. Marcus and I stood up and then he led the way out of the bar, into a capacious dimly lit entrance hall. As we walked across the hall, Marcus told us in his rich, posh voice that the main thing was to always ask before you touch. And that no, means absolutely no.

'The ladies,' he added, 'control everything.'

Acknowledging the importance of Marcus's statement, Angie and I both nodded vigorously.

Having arrived at a huge six-panelled door, Marcus gestured to us to take a seat on the adjacent leather sofa, which was tucked away in a cosy recess. He apologised for needing the loo and left. Natalie and Angie sat down, and I leant against the wall. I then asked Natalie what got her into swinging.

'Marcus and I wanted to spice up our sex life and play out our fantasies,' replied Natalie. 'How about you guys?'

'Similar thing really,' responded Angie.

'Well you've come to the right place,' said a smiling Natalie, before adding that she was here to help if we needed anything.

As Angie continued to chat with Natalie, it became clear to me that she and I had been inexorably sucked into a bizarre sexual vortex. But, because we'd only agreed to a recce, I felt safe and in control. Permission was needed for touching, and despite everything, I wasn't comfortable giving that permission. Having tuned back into the girl's conversation, I asked Natalie if she preferred it when Marcus and she played together with couples, or if she preferred multiple men.

'I'm a greedy girl if I'm honest,' chuckled Natalie. 'Plus I have the most amazing one-to-one sex with Marcus, so I like my swinging experiences to be different.'

'Because?' questioned Angie.

'Because with multiple guys,' said Natalie, 'I'm the centre of attention, and they're arousing me everywhere all at once. And,' she added, 'I alone have excited them, and that excites me.'

After a short pause, Natalie went on to explain that playing as a couple is different again because it's more sensual and erotic.

'There's a different dynamic with couples,' continued Natalie, 'and it's especially lovely when the woman is bi. You can't beat the sensual touch of a woman,' she added, 'when combined with the passion of a man!'

Angie smiled gleefully in response, whilst I asked Natalie if she had any regrets, almost as if I was cross-examining the witness for the defence. Natalie said her friend Sue judged her badly and made her feel cheap. Angie said it was strange how women often judged other women really harshly, instead of showing solidarity. Natalie agreed, and said Marcus thought that Sue was one of those repressed women who protesteth too much.

'She was probably virtue signalling,' suggested Angie.

Natalie nodded in agreement, and then said that she and Marcus felt super close when they made love afterwards. Said it was incredibly loving, exciting, and emotionally fulfilling.

At this point, Angie suddenly announced that she needed the loo again. Both girls then stood up and wandered off down the hall arm in arm, chatting like best school mates again.

I sat down on the sofa and began to wonder why Black Dog was so quiet. I mean, he was definitely there in the background, but by no means as bad as I thought he'd be. I figured that was because I too was turned on by someone else. Perhaps that seemed fair to Black Dog. That thought prompted me to think that maybe I could be like Marcus after all, then Angie would blossom into her true self, and we'd all live happily ever after. It took me exactly one second to dismiss that idea though, because I knew I wasn't even close to being like Marcus. I also knew that Angie was exactly like Natalie. I then wondered how I was going to support her, when I didn't have Marcus's emotional maturity. As I was contemplating the answer to that question, I was suddenly distracted by people moving around the hall. I lifted my gaze to observe them for a while, until I heard hurried high-heeled steps coming across the oak floor. I then looked to my left, and observed my beautiful wife trotting towards me, like an excited teenager at a prom.

'Rich!' she whispered excitedly, before dropping onto the sofa beside me. 'What do you think of it all then?'

'I think you should pull your dress down!' I replied flatly, as Black Dog quite suddenly and unexpectedly reared his ugly head without my permission, 'because your thigh fat is hanging over your hold-ups.'

'Why are you being so nasty?' demanded my wife, her face scrunched up in disbelief, 'when I've done nothing wrong.'

'I'm not being nasty Angie,' I protested weakly.

'Oh but you are,' she insisted, before telling me that I couldn't see her visible panty line anymore. 'And shall I tell you why?' she asked, cocking her head to one side.

'Yes, tell me why Angie?' I said flatly.

'Because I took my knickers off and threw them away,' she replied in an angry gruff whisper, 'because Marcus got fireworks exploding between my legs, and I'm sopping wet for him!'

'Oh yeah?' I scoffed.

'Absolutely oh yeah,' replied my wife. 'He couldn't take his eyes off me, thigh fat and all Rich,' she insisted. 'Okay? So you can stop putting me down and support me like Marcus does Natalie!'

Somewhat taken aback by my wife's no-nonsense response, I just looked at her and grimaced with regret.

'Sorry,' I eventually said, 'I don't know where all that came from.'

'If you want,' said my wife, completely ignoring my apology, 'we can leave right now. What do you want to do?'

'Well erm, we might as well stay,' I replied hesitantly, having suddenly realised that I had a perverted interest in finishing the tour.

'I thought so,' said Angie, 'because you love watching me arousing Marcus, even though you're jealous. And you wanna see him *fuck me!*' she added with a glint in her eye, 'don't you? Because it's turning you on, isn't it?'

'No!' came my indignant reply.

'*And* you wanna fuck Natalie!' insisted my wife, before telling me that I shouldn't judge her, because she wasn't judging me.

With that said, my wife then turned her back on me and folded her arms. My heart raced furiously as Black Dog went barking mad at the prospect of Marcus fucking *my* wife.

Staring at Angie's back, I contemplated my behaviour. Being honest, I had to admit that there was some truth in what she'd said. Yes, I did want to have sex with Natalie, but denied it to myself earlier. But was Angie right in saying that I actually wanted to watch Marcus have sex with her? Something momentarily made that prospect both totally abhorrent, and yet disturbingly exciting to me at the same time.

Maybe *I* needed to blossom? Maybe this whole thing was actually about *me, my* desires, *my* demons? Either way, I couldn't leave. This had to play out if I was to trust in God's plan to let my wife be herself, and not judge her. But is this God's plan? Or some sort of convenient excuse?

Dismissing that thought as too much to contemplate, I took a deep breath and slowly blew it out.

'I'm sorry Angie,' I whispered, having tugged her arm to face me, 'this whole evening has been emotionally challenging for me.'

'And for me too, my big man,' she replied sympathetically, 'but why don't we just relax and see what's what?' she added. 'After all, we're just here for a recce.'

My wife's reassuring words instantly quietened Black Dog. Feeling back in control, I nodded and smiled. I then concluded that a new and potentially dangerous emotional dynamic was at play here. That made me realise that I must proceed with all caution in this surreal, yet very real-life drama.

Smiling warmly at me, Angie took hold of my hands and asked me what I thought of Natalie.

'To be honest,' I whispered, 'she's turning me on. Big time!'

'I could tell,' said Angie.

'So what do *you* think of it all then?' I asked, widening my eyes.

'I like that most women here have a bit of a mummy tummy like me,' said Angie.

Unable to think of a suitable response to my wife's comment, and despite feeling back in control, I suddenly got jealous of the "fireworks" Marcus got exploding between her legs. With that thought in mind, I withdrew my right hand from my wife's grip, and slipped it up her dress.

'So Marcus got fireworks exploding in here?' I whispered gruffly, as Black Dog barked in my head.

'You tell me,' teased my wife, 'you're the one examining the crime scene.'

'You're sopping,' I retorted sharply.

'Well, with Marcus's hard cock and gorgeous body beckoning,' teased my wife, 'what woman wouldn't be?'

'Yeah,' I said, 'but he didn't touch you, and yet you're dripping!'

'There doesn't have to be contact, silly,' said my wife, 'it's all about anticipation.'

'Anticipation!' I replied anxiously, 'but nothing's going to happen!'

'I know, but it's still exciting,' responded my wife. 'And if I'm honest,' she added, 'all I wanted to do was drop to my knees to suck Marcus's cock.'

Even though I thought I was back in control, Black Dog responded badly to my wife's desire. And despite my throbbing hard-on I told her that she wasn't to touch Marcus.

'I know you're jealous,' retorted my wife, 'but I'm jealous too. I mean it's not easy seeing you drooling over Natalie,' she added, 'but jealousy's part of it.'

At that moment, Marcus and Natalie appeared in the hall and walked towards us. My feelings of jealousy subsided to some extent, as I looked Natalie up and down. Now my jealous hard-on was mostly replaced by a lustful one. At this point, I realised my jealousy was somewhat tempered when Angie and I were both being turned on by other people. I put that down to the tit for tat nature of our mental infidelity.

'Hey!' said Angie, as we both stood up.

'Hey!' replied Natalie with a big smile as she and Marcus drew to a halt in front of us.

Marcus then turned on his heel to face the big, panelled door.

'This is the biggest playroom,' he announced pointing to the door. 'We have four others,' he added, 'one of which is the dark room where …'

'That's amazing!' interrupted Natalie. 'You just feel around and play with whoever you fancy the feel of.'

'And I can't show you that unless you get naked,' quipped Marcus, looking directly at my wife with a glint in his eye.

'And then there are the dungeons and bondage rooms,' said Natalie, continuing with the breakfast TV double act. 'We'll hopefully get to those later.'

'Wonderful,' whispered a smiling Angie.

'So,' said Marcus, 'ready for the tour?'

Angie widened her eyes and nodded.

'Yes,' I replied, filled with a mix of moral apprehension and a downright desire for filth.

Marcus then slowly swung the big, panelled door to the playroom open. My heartbeat quickened in anticipation of the debauchery which lay ahead. Whilst following on behind the girls, a sinking feeling then suddenly came over me. As I neared the threshold to the unknown, I wondered if the heady mix of sexual desire and alcohol could lead to regret. I swallowed hard in trepidation, but then also delighted in my perverse, throbbing hard-on at the same time.

Upon walking into the room, my gaze was immediately drawn to the noise of a couple shagging deep stick on a square, padded waist-high platform. The woman moaned and sighed with pleasure. I was surprised that I liked the way her ample breasts bounced and wobbled around – it was exciting. Lying down at the other end of the platform, a couple looked on as they caressed each other. Standing up with a wide masculine stance, next to the fornicating couple, was a tall muscle-bound man stroking his huge erection. I assumed he was getting ready to penetrate the woman, when her other lover withdrew from her.

As we walked past that scene, I looked up at the ceiling. The lights were like little stars twinkling from above; enough to see people by, but not so bright as to make the room clinical. As I lowered my gaze, I noticed that all communications were being carried out in a whisper, alongside the erotic sighs and moans which filled the room like a stirring sexual symphony.

Still trailing a few paces behind the group, I observed

Angie and Natalie cuddling each other's arms like teenage girls, and wondered where that might lead. Then, the prospect of Natalie and my wife kissing, caressing, and licking each other flashed through my mind. Black Dog was cool with that. He was also cool with the prospect that Marcus would see my wife naked if she got down and dirty with Natalie. That pleased me.

'This is very popular,' whispered Marcus, as he arrived at a swing and tapped its leather seat.

Hanging from the ceiling in a big alcove was a sex swing suspended by two substantial chains, which supported a half-reclined seat. There were two thick, leather, studded straps with loops, one attached to each chain, designed to hold the occupant's legs up and open.

'The girls love this!' enthused Natalie. 'It's so erotic being swung back and forth on your playmate.'

'I'll demonstrate,' said Marcus in a hushed tone, before slipping his wife's negligee off her shoulders, and discarding it onto the floor.

With just her short see-through babydoll on, Natalie extended both her arms out sideways. Then, with one hip dropped, she stood for a moment like a magician's assistant. She was clearly performing for us. She then wrapped an arm round Marcus's neck, before beckoning me with her eyes to assist. I immediately stepped forward and enjoyed the sensual way she slid her hand from halfway down my back, to up and over my shoulder.

Marcus and I then lifted Natalie onto the swing seat. Leaning back, she raised her right leg to allow Marcus to thread her foot through one of the leather loops. Angie then stepped forward and did the same with Natalie's left leg. Marcus raised his loop up high with the adjustable strap;

Angie followed suit. She then caressed Natalie's stockings all the way to the top of her thigh to smooth them out. My eyes, and Angie's come to mention it, were on stalks. There was Natalie, half reclined, legs hoisted up high and wide. She was raw, primal sexiness at its best, and I knew she fancied me. That stimulated a subconscious animal urge in me to plunge my raging hard-on straight into her open vagina. But for the fact that Marcus and Angie were present, I would have, without doubt, succumbed to the mind-blowing temptress that was Natalie.

'Thanks for smoothing my stockings,' said Natalie in a sultry voice, whilst beaming at Angie a little too long.

'My pleasure,' she replied through a coquettish grin, before taking half a step back to observe the proceedings.

Having noticed Marcus's erection holding his towel out in front of him, I then looked over at Angie who, like me, kept glancing between Natalie and Marcus.

'Do lots of girls play together?' I asked softly, subconsciously wanting Natalie and Angie to get it on.

'Absolutely,' said Marcus. 'Something like sixty per cent of straight women swingers will have a soft interaction with another woman.'

'Soft interaction?' I enquired, raising an eyebrow.

'Not one-on-one with another girl,' replied Marcus, 'but as part of a play group which includes a man or men.'

'Oh okay,' I said.

'Usually kissing and caressing to begin with,' continued Marcus. 'Oh, and for some reason,' he added with a smile, 'they're always keen to go down on each other.'

With that said, Marcus then unhooked his towel. It momentarily balanced on his erection, before falling to the floor, leaving his hard-on to ping-up in style.

Angie's eyes widened in response. My heart skipped a beat at her unashamed interest, even though I was doing the same with Natalie, and was excited to the point of exploding in my boxers.

'As you know,' said Natalie, 'I often like playing with the woman as well as the man, when Marcus and I play as a couple.'

Then, holding Angie's gaze with a glint in her eye, Natalie explained that it was erotic without being lesbian. Angie nodded in response, before telling Natalie that she totally got that.

At this point we all fell silent, whilst Marcus ran the head of his penis up and down his wife's opening. I watched her outer lips hugging him with each up and down paint-brush-like stroke. A moment later, he slowly and deliberately pushed deep inside his wife. She then moaned and sighed as he swung her back and forth along his length. Angie and I watched intently. It felt surreal because of the matter-of-fact way sex was happening right in front of me, and because I'd never seen another man's hard-on in the flesh before this evening.

After observing the mesmeric back and forth swinging motion for a short while, Angie suddenly smiled a wicked smile.

'It does look like fun,' she said.

'Have a go if you fancy,' suggested Marcus.

My wife looked at me. I narrowed my eyes a little and shook my head.

'I won't just now, thanks Marcus,' responded Angie.

I was relieved. I wasn't ready for this. We were here for a recce. Not to jump in feet first. I just didn't want Angie looking dirty and inviting with her legs wide open lusting over Marcus, and him taking that as a sign to slip deep inside her right in front of me. There'd be a fight for sure!

Natalie spotted Angie's obvious interest in having a go on the swing, and smiled knowingly.

'It's all a bit obsessive to begin with,' she said, whilst Marcus continued to swing her back and forth on his cock, 'because it's all so wickedly exciting.'

With the demonstration complete, Marcus pulled out of his wife. My eyes met with hers. She smiled her sexy smile at me, before then raising her eyebrows suggestively. I smiled back at her, and then lowered my gaze to the delicate folds and wings of her engorged, inviting opening.

Marcus looked at me and tipped his head to the swing seat.

'The biggest fear amongst newbies,' he said, as we lifted Natalie out of the swing, 'is that their partner will run off with someone else. I need to reassure you,' he added firmly, 'that I've never known that happen.'

'Swinging,' continued Natalie, in breakfast duo TV mode, 'actually brings loving couples even closer together. It builds trust and security, based on honesty, respect and integrity.'

With the swingers pitch out of the way, Marcus picked his towel up and wrapped it around his waist, whilst Angie quickly swept Natalie's negligee off the floor, and draped it over her shoulders. We then slowly followed behind Marcus. The ever-present scent of sex wafted through the air, conjuring up one's appetite like the smell of grilled bacon the morning after a heavy night.

My eyes and ears were filled with the sights and sounds of hardcore sex, weirdly juxtaposed with hushed friendly chit-chat. Some people were going at it slow and easy, while others were fucking fast and furious. Arms, legs, tits, pussies, and cocks everywhere. Others carried on as if they were having a coffee at Costas.

As we continued the tour, a number of people checked us out, clearly hoping to engage with us. Angie made eye contact with them, and then strutted her sexy hip-swaying walk (one high-heeled foot *directly* in front of the other) and pretended not to notice them. Some couples, trios, and foursomes, quite obviously enjoyed performing for us. The place, as you would expect, oozed dirty, disgusting, exciting sex. It was the very essence of a den of iniquity, where debauched behaviour was not only expected, but encouraged.

Having reached the other end of the room, we came upon a recess where a big, round, waist-high platform was to be found. Sitting on top of the platform was a red-leather buttoned mattress.

'Why don't we chill here for a bit before continuing the tour?' suggested Natalie.

Angie and I nodded in agreement, and then watched as Marcus unhooked his towel and let it fall to the floor. I followed my wife's eyes straight to his dangling package. He and Natalie climbed onto the red-leather platform and got comfortable. Angie then climbed aboard and sat facing her bedfellows. I remained standing and quietly observed. With my wife exuding sex from every pore of her body, nothing she did escaped my attention.

At this point, I began to feel a little anxious. My emotions were up and down like a yo-yo. Tense then relaxed; insecure then okay; jealous and angry, yet excited and rampant. And so it all went round in my head and stomach. I kept reminding myself that we were just here for a recce, and that I had no right to be jealous, because I too was getting turned on by someone else.

'We were in this very spot last week,' said Natalie, as she nonchalantly stroked her husband's cock.

Marcus, who was resting on his elbows with his legs stretched out, told us that Natalie was amazing, and that she actually got sex drunk with Shauny and Spence.

'Sex drunk?' repeated Angie, furrowing her brow.

'Yes,' said Natalie, 'it's where you get light-headed when you're repeatedly taken to the brink of orgasm. But when you finally come,' she sighed, 'it's amazing, and you can hardly walk. I sometimes gush as well,' she added, seemingly proud of herself.

Angie nodded in acknowledgement, and then reached behind herself and pulled my hands to her chest. Still standing, I slid them down the front of her dress. As I gently massaged her breasts, I looked at Natalie. She was sitting cross-legged with her beautiful vulva on show.

'Isn't gushing actually wee?' I suddenly piped up, having finally lifted my gaze to Natalie's eyes.

Marcus chuckled, and then explained that gushing, or squirting as it's sometimes called, is actually an excess of lubrication fluid some women produce when they're super stimulated. Angie nodded, before then pulling her right knee up to her chin. With no knickers on, and her bent left leg resting on the bed, everything was on show.

From my standing position, and still with my hands down the front of my wife's dress, I wondered what Marcus found so amazing about seeing his wife shagged by Shauny and Spence. I then concluded that I had to think exactly like Marcus, in order to support Angie for who she really was. At this point I winced inside, because, even if that was possible, it wasn't going to be easy. But alongside the emotional pain of it all, there would undoubtedly be a great deal of X-rated pleasure.

I came out of my musings when Angie tipped her head back to speak to me.

'Get these off,' she whispered, tugging at my chinos, 'so we can have a play together.'

The prospect of shagging my wife in front of Natalie and Marcus really turned me on. I never thought that would excite me, and I never thought I'd enjoy watching another couple at it either. But I was loving it. And, quite amazingly, Black Dog was still cool with it, probably because I had Angie to myself. Following her instruction, I immediately slipped my chinos off, along with my shoes and socks, in one smooth operation. I then discarded them onto the floor with a flourish.

Marcus and Natalie watched as I knelt bolt-upright beside Angie. She then immediately pulled my boxers down at speed, allowing my hard-on to ping up, proud and bold. Marcus and Natalie smiled their wicked, knowing smiles of approval. Knowing, because I got the feeling they were seducing us for their own pleasure. Nevertheless, their attention made me feel good. Proud of my well-toned top half, and keen to show off to Natalie, I unbuttoned my shirt before taking it off like a showman, much to her delight. Marcus then removed Natalie's negligee and positioned her between his legs, so that her back rested against his chest. He then popped her breasts completely out of her babydoll, and began running the tips of his fingers over her big nipples.

'Natalie loves both breasts being sucked at the same time,' announced Marcus, in his rich, sexy voice, whilst looking at Angie and me expectantly.

With that said, Angie nimbly manoeuvred herself onto all fours and crawled into the space between Natalie's thighs, which rested on top of Marcus's stretched out open legs. My wife then poked her arse out like a wanton hussy. I moved forward and pulled her dress up and over the round of her bum to her waist. I then observed her slightly parted pouting pussy. It begged for attention, but instead of kissing her there, all I could do was watch her delicately kiss and caress Natalie's breasts. Natalie sighed appreciatively, whilst easing Angie's dress off her shoulders down to her waist. Only another woman would know to cover her lover's midriff, rather than to remove her dress completely. Natalie then unclipped my wife's bra and removed it with ease, leaving her breasts hanging down beautifully.

Meanwhile, Marcus smiled as he watched the show over the top of his wife's shoulder. At this point, I moved beside the girls to get a better view of things. As I looked on from my kneeling position, I willed Natalie to touch my wife's exquisite breasts, but instead, she just caressed her back lovingly. Moments later, to my delight, Angie rose up onto her knees so that she was face to face with Natalie. As they gazed into each other's eyes, Natalie traced her hands over the rounds of Angie's shoulders, and then down to her breasts. The unmitigated eroticism of watching another woman cup and caress my wife's breasts, made my heart skip a beat.

Totally transfixed, I continued to stare at these two beautiful women making out. Angie now began massaging Natalie's breasts in return. They continued with this mutual caressing for a wee while, whilst still looking deeply into one another's eyes. Natalie then took the lead as she slowly moved her head towards Angie's face. Angie moved forward to meet Natalie's lips. My heart skipped another beat as they kissed slowly, sensually, and erotically, like it was in time to an easy blues song. It was incredibly sexy watching their tongues dancing in and out of each other's mouths, occasionally stopping to gently bite each other's lips. Amazingly beautiful; loving even.

As the kissing continued, Marcus repositioned himself so that he was kneeling on the other side of the girls to me. Looking past them, I could see the intense desire in Marcus's eyes, and felt my body tense when I thought he was going to make a move. I then relaxed as I remembered his strict requirement to "ask before you touch". That meant he had to ask Angie, which effectively meant he had to ask me, and I wasn't going to agree to anything.

The scene now consisted of the two girls kneeling in the middle of the huge round platform, their bums on their calves. They were kissing one another passionately, whilst caressing each other's soft, sensual curves. I was kneeling up straight on one side of the girls stroking myself, whilst Marcus mirrored my actions on the other side.

Having been engrossed in the girl's erotic performance for a few minutes, I suddenly noticed Marcus rubbing his cock on Natalie's breast. Now, his erect penis was just inches away from my wife's mouth. I tensed up again. With my eyes wide and my heart pounding harder than ever, I once again thought that Marcus was going to make a move on my wife. A second later though, I relaxed, as I reminded myself that Angie and I hadn't agreed to anything.

After a short time, the girls stopped kissing and lowered their heads down to Marcus's erection. He instantly knelt up straight so that his cock protruded to its maximum. Natalie then took hold of her husband's hard-on and looked up at him with a knowing smile. I throbbed hard in anticipation of watching her take him into her mouth. But then, she waved it in front of Angie's face instead, whilst holding her gaze with wide, suggestive eyes. My wife smiled the wickedest smile imaginable. Then, to my surprise and horror, she latched onto Marcus's cock without a moment's hesitation. I watched my woman's mouth being stretched open as she sucked Marcus with fervour. She then slipped her fingers between his bum cheeks to massage his anus.

Still not sure if I could actually handle all this, I reluctantly accepted that I enjoyed my wife's overt prick teasing, and that I was proud of her sexiness (despite the angst it caused me). Still frozen with uncertainty, all I could do was watch my wife's porn movie play out before me. She was completely absorbed in her filthy fun, and paid me no attention at all.

Despite being turned on like never before, I was getting angrier and angrier by the second, and was on the brink of telling Angie to stop, because we hadn't agreed to this. But then, before I could react, Natalie gently turned my wife's face towards her own and kissed her, leaving Marcus's cock loitering with intent.

At this point, I wondered if Natalie had orchestrated things so as to gauge my response. A moment later, I realised that if I let Angie suck Marcus's cock again, it would be on a quid pro quo basis, because I would let Natalie suck me. So fair exchange – no robbery.

From my upright kneeling position, I continued to watch my live porn movie play out below me. The girls were still opposite one another, resting their bums on their calves, which accentuated the beautiful curves of their waist, hips, and bum. I watched them kissing each other, warmly, erotically, and tenderly all rolled into one. It was beautiful. Then, just as I'd settled into the moment, Angie turned her head away from Natalie and again looked up at Marcus with naughty girl eyes. He then eased his cock forward as she lowered her head. She then took him into her mouth for a second time. I once again froze in disbelief with a raging hard-on.

Now excited, jealous, and possessive beyond belief, my chest heaved hard as a surge of adrenaline coursed through me.

He should have asked before touching, I told myself, but then realised that Angie had actually touched him. Then, having finally found the ability to move, I took hold of Angie's shoulder and gently eased her off Marcus, despite thinking I wanted a soft swap. Angie then immediately grabbed my hand tight and, leaning away from Natalie and Marcus, pulled my face down to hers.

'Please don't get upset, Richie,' she whispered urgently. 'I thought you wanted to watch me with another man. You know, after making me tell you about Martin and everything.'

'Martin and everything?' I questioned, lost for words.

'Yes, and you talked about doing a soft swap. Remember?'

'But you were supposed to check with me,' I said gruffly, '

'I'm sorry,' replied Angie, 'it's just that you've been hard the whole time, and I think watching me with Marcus actually excites you, but you're just too Catholic to enjoy it.'

'Yeah?'

'Yeah,' said Angie, before telling me she loved me, and only me.

'Is that right?' I retorted sharply.

'Of course, silly,' insisted my wife. 'This is just a bit of naughty foreplay with no penetration. That's reserved just for *you!*'

'Just for *me?*' I questioned.

'Yes, just for *you*,' said my wife. 'But it's up to you,' she added, her pleading eyes locked onto mine. 'C'mon,' she hurriedly urged, 'they're waiting for us, and it's getting embarrassing!'

With a face full of tension, I urgently considered *my* woman's unashamed want to have sex with another man. Everything but penetration. But could I allow that? And did I want to do the same with Natalie? Then, in the midst of my contemplations, I observed Angie widen her eyes at Natalie and then very deliberately and slowly turn her head to my throbbing hard-on. Natalie instantly manoeuvred herself onto all fours so that her face was by my nether regions.

'I hope you don't mind,' she said, sotto voce, before immediately taking hold of my cock to guide it to her mouth.

I knelt up straight to project forward so I could watch Natalie sucking me. Partly driven by revenge, I enjoyed watching my wife looking on from her kneeling position, almost like I was giving her a dose of her own medicine. But then, when she looked up at me and smiled, genuinely pleased that I was having a good time, I felt bad.

Even though I kind of felt like I was being led by my dick, I found Natalie's sensitive touch incredibly exciting. Way more so than I'd imagined. She then slowly slid her lips up and down my throbbing shaft. This sent me wild with passion for her. Now my heart wanted Natalie. I was filled with a strange mix of close, warm intimacy, combined with hardcore sexual desire. I knew I couldn't penetrate her, otherwise Marcus would do the same to Angie, and I just couldn't handle that. With the way things had unfolded, I was happy swapping for foreplay, and then, like Angie said, penetration would be reserved just for me.

Pleased that Black Dog hadn't raised any objections to my plan, I lifted Natalie's face off my penis with my fingers, and drew her head to mine. She willingly obliged, whilst looking at me with her beautifully alluring big, blue eyes. With the two of us kneeling face to face, I slid my hand round the back of my playmate's neck and pulled her lips to mine. I then kissed her hard with the passion that had built-up in me, whilst my free hand instinctively found her soft breasts. By this time, my wife had taken me into her mouth, exciting me beyond belief.

With the devil in me now in total control, I relinquished my moral code in favour of the dirty, lustful, debauched filth that had found me. It was different. It was exciting, and I was turned on like never before.

After a few minutes, Marcus positioned his head next to Angie's. Now we were four people in very close intimate contact. Natalie and I were still kneeling up and kissing, whilst Angie continued to suck me, with Marcus looking on at close quarters.

In amongst the excitement of it all, I suddenly became aware that Angie had stopped sucking me. I looked down. She looked up at me questioningly. Overwhelmed by the thrill of it all, I nodded agreeably at my wife who smiled, first with relief, and then with wickedness. The naughty game was now on, leaving me excited, jealous, and angry in equal measure.

At this point in the proceedings, Natalie took hold of my cock again and began massaging me back and forth. Now she and I both looked down at Angie and Marcus.

With Angie now propped up on one elbow next to Marcus, the pair began kissing. They were up close and personal – literally! I watched my wife's tongue working in and out of her lover's mouth, whilst she massaged his erect penis. I was angry because my wife's erotic kissing was loving and intimate, and should have been reserved just for me. Yet I had no right to be angry. My thinking was illogical, because I too had just kissed Natalie like that. And, if I was being honest with myself, alongside my anger, watching my wife and Marcus was incredibly erotic. So in a strange way, all this slow caressing and warm erotic kissing was quite beautiful. Not something I expected to encounter in a sex club.

Leaving my wife to it, I returned my full attention to Natalie and resumed my kissing, before then slipping my hand between her thighs to find her wet, soft, silky-smooth opening. In that moment, my heart skipped yet another beat. Even whilst kissing my playmate, that brought a wicked half smile to my lips, because I was free to do anything and everything with Natalie, apart from vaginal penetration.

Having been lost in my blissful embrace with Natalie for quite some time, I emerged from my dreamlike erotic state and, upon opening my eyes, noticed that Marcus and Angie had knelt up from their half-prone position.

Now we were two couples kneeling side by side, kissing, caressing, and massaging each other's partners in an amazing sexual dance. Incredibly, Black Dog was still cool with everything, presumably overridden by the wonderfully wicked pleasure I was enjoying with Natalie, on a tit-for-tat basis. At this point, Natalie reached across to massage one of Angie's breasts. That was amazing to watch. Soon after, the girls eased away from Marcus and me to kiss and caress each other once again. I watched them as they slowly laid down beside each other, leaving Marcus and me kneeling each side of them, both slowly stroking our appreciative erections. I was wide-eyed and intense, whilst Marcus's smile was almost smug, like he was proud of a job well done.

Riveted to the spot, I watched Natalie run her hand down my wife's body, and over her gathered dress, to find her opening. She parted her legs to welcome Natalie in. In response, Angie slid her hand down Natalie's exposed tummy, and then followed the curve of her smooth mons pubis to her vulva. Both my wife and Natalie wriggled their hips in response to each other's touch. Such a beautiful and exquisite vista; gentle, loving, and softly sensual.

Marcus and I continued to watch the girls at it for a while, until Marcus caught his wife's eye. Then, with a flick of his head, he gave her some sort of instruction. She whispered something to Angie, and then rose up onto all fours.

'You girls need fucking!' insisted Marcus, with a naughty smile.

'Oh God yes,' sighed my wife.

Natalie then looked up at me and locked her eyes onto mine, before then crawling to the edge of the platform like a lioness. Angie followed her. They then both placed their knees at the edge of the mattress, thighs wide apart, overhanging calves splayed, and arses poking out.

Marcus got up off the platform and stood for a moment. Natalie, still looking at me, instructed me to follow suit with her eyes. Marcus and I were now standing side by side facing the girls. I looked down at our two beautiful women with their heads tipped back looking up at us. They were utterly gorgeous. Four full, soft breasts hanging down, and four deliciously curved hips melding into beautifully round arses. These two women were, without doubt, the very epitome of womanhood.

I was now desperate to be inside my wife. I needed to sexually possess her. With my cock standing big and proud, I walked round the mattress to get behind my woman. But, just as I was passing Natalie, she turned toward me and took hold of my hand. She then pulled my face down to hers. Her kiss, as before, was passionate, warm, and loving all rolled into one. I loved it and responded in kind, drawing her tongue into my mouth, and biting her lips. I then straightened up to continue on to Angie, but was again stopped by Natalie, who, this time, grabbed my hard-on and squeezed me tight.

'Fuck me, Rich!' she whispered urgently, in a low sultry voice as she looked up at me. 'I want this gorgeous, big, hard cock of yours inside me!'

Natalie excited me beyond words, and made me feel like a real man. I was completely drunk with desire for her.

Still on all fours, she arched her back downwards and presented her beautiful arse and voracious vagina to me with a sensual wiggle. I positioned myself behind her. There I was, standing tall and dominant, hands on hips, legs wide apart, raging boner protruding. Marcus was now standing beside me and poised ready behind Angie. He was also tall, hard, and rampant!

There they were, our two women on all fours, side by side on the edge of the mattress. Two gorgeous, sensual, and erotic women looking sexy as fuck.

Marcus had paused just millimetres from my woman's vagina. I too had paused just millimetres from a new and exciting opening, which beckoned me at a base, primal level. I hadn't expected to want this so badly, but I did. My heart pounded in my chest as I contemplated penetrating the forbidden fruit that was Natalie. With the feeling that I'd be breaking my marriage vows, I forced myself to resist, and just remained motionless at the gates to both heaven and hell. I then looked down and compared my manhood to Marcus's. I was bigger. I felt more powerful as I lifted my gaze and stared at him with testosterone-fuelled aggression. I was somewhat disarmed by his warm, friendly smile. At this point, I once again lowered my eyes down to the girls for a moment, before lifting them back up to Marcus. We were two red-blooded males staring at each other, both primal and rampant, yet he was politely waiting for me to give him the green light. It was a quid pro quo moment. He would only insert his penis into my wife's vagina, the most intimate of acts, if I did the same to his wife. He was waiting for my permission, and the moment I sank into Natalie, he would have that permission.

Still riveted to the spot, I was swamped by a feeling that I would one day regret this outrageous indulgence too far. Penetration was the ultimate betrayal in any marriage. A moment later, I told myself I was doing this for Angie's *forgotten me.*

Are you fuck? Countered demon voice, you're doing it for you! With a look of self-disgust on my face, I stared down at my woman who was wiggling her arse wantonly, excited by the anticipation of a new and different cock, and unashamedly begging for it. I remembered her words, "if you're gonna fuck, then fuck! Anything goes." Her sentiment tipped the already tipped balance fully to the side of self-indulgent immorality. And so, without further ado, I pushed my entire throbbing, wanton length up inside Natalie, in one slow deliberate motion, accompanied by a low, guttural 'arghhh!'

Natalie sighed appreciatively and then just one second later, Marcus pushed up into my wife, and she too let out a loud appreciative moan.

I was blown away by the physical sensation of pumping in and out of Natalie. And, in amongst this wild, new sexual experience, I immediately thought it felt much the same as when I slid up my Angie, but yet this was so much more exciting and exquisite. But why?

I'll tell you why, said my demon voice, as I continued to move in and out of my playmate, it's because it's going to bite you on the arse, because it's wrong, immoral, and downright dirty. And that's why you're fucking loving it!

With my stupid deliberations now complete, I tuned into Natalie's provocative chanting, which was perfectly timed to the slap, slap, slapping sounds of my pelvis meeting her gorgeous round arse.

'Fuck me, fuck me, fuck me,' she panted. 'Fuck me with that gorgeous hard cock of yours!'

My playmate once again made me feel like a man. She made me feel desired. And even though she wanted me and I'd already entered her, I felt I needed Marcus's approval to continue. I looked at him. He gave his approval with a satisfied smile before dropping his gaze. I followed his eyes and watched as he slowly and purposefully withdrew his length, inch by inch from my wife. He then grabbed the base of his erection and thrashed it about for a moment, almost as if to prove his dominance over my woman.

A moment later, he rubbed his cockhead up and down her engorged opening, before slowly slipping back up inside her. I watched every inch of him disappear into my wife, and listened as she sighed with appreciation.

As my strong jealous response eased a bit, I suddenly became vengeful at the sight of my wife unashamedly enjoying her extra marital fucking right in front of me. A second later, I realised I couldn't judge, because like demon voice said, I was fucking loving it! Loving penetrating a new and exciting woman. And on top of that, as I continued to watch another man penetrating my wife in clear close-up vision, I was surprised at how incredibly aroused I was. That was accompanied by an equal measure of anger. Yet my anger seemed to heighten my arousal, which in turn drove me to embrace the utter filthiness of this debauched soirée.

With Marcus having settled into a rhythm, he suddenly held my wife's arse cheeks wide open so I could see more of the action. I could see her labia clinging to him on his out strokes, and then being pushed in again as he thrusted back up inside her. I watched intently as he repeatedly pumped in and out of her opening. I never thought, not in a million years, that I'd ever witness my wife being fucked by another man. No husband would ever think such a thing, yet here I was. And I was locked into some weird caveman competition with Marcus, and felt I had to outperform him in every way. Be bigger, stronger, and filthier than him. The whole thing was surreal.

With my mind racing, a sudden extra surge of adrenaline ran through me, which made me thrust really hard into

Natalie. So hard in fact, that her arms collapsed, causing her head to drop down onto the mattress. That made her look even sluttier, driving me to pump in and out of her with everything I had. Marcus matched my pace with Angie. I was a sex-crazed machine, the likes of which I'd never known before. After a lot of panting and heaving, Marcus and I both slowed as our stamina faded. Soon after that, Marcus withdrew from my wife with an affectionate slap of her arse, and muttered something about lube before disappearing.

With Marcus gone, Angie dropped her head onto the mattress so it was beside Natalie's. As they kissed, Angie wiggled her bum, flaunting her puffy, reddened opening in my face. I automatically slipped two fingers inside her. Realising that another man had penetrated her just seconds earlier, both excited and disgusted me at the same time. I watched my Angie pushing back in perfect time to my finger thrusts, and in perfect time to Natalie's pushing back along my length. My unbelieving eyes zoomed in on my wife's opening, and then shot over to my cock sliding in and out of Natalie. I then took in the whole vista of two gorgeous women. The very epitome of womanliness, beautiful, sensual, erotic, and sexually perfect. And I was having my wicked way with both of them. My sexual senses were maxed out, and my heart raced like mad at the surreal excitement of it all.

After a few minutes, Marcus returned with some lube. He watched for a while whilst the girls and I continued our bizarre, yet strangely graceful sexual dance. He then moved closer to Angie and stood there with his handsome, wanton erection pointing up to the ceiling. Why handsome? Because it was dark and straight, and his balls were shaved and tight, not saggy and wizened. And yes, I was excited by it. It was like watching live porn.

With my eyes wide and staring, I watched intently as Marcus gripped my wife's hip with one hand, before aiming his cock at her opening with the other. Concentrating, he carefully pushed himself inside her alongside my fingers. I certainly hadn't expected that, but was damned if I was going to be forced out of my own woman, so kept my fingers inside her as a defiant gesture of ownership.

'Arghhh, fuck!' sighed Angie, having eased her mouth away from Natalie's, 'what are you two doing to me?'

As Marcus pushed in and out of my wife, his cock rubbing against my two fingers as he went, I got even more aroused, just when I thought there were no more sexual thrills to be had. Feeling Marcus hard for my wife made me proud of her. Proud that she had aroused him, and that he was young and good-looking.

Both tense and wickedly wanton, I continued pumping in and out of Natalie whilst I watched the scene play out. My eyes were fixed on another man's cock penetrating my wife's vagina alongside two of my fingers. I had never in my life touched another man's penis. Just the thought of it was abhorrent to me, but now, at this very moment, it seemed right.

Needless to say, the air was filled with sighs and moans of pleasure from our two women. I liked that, because it meant we were doing right by them, satisfying them. It was a matter of pride.

Whilst still sliding in and out of my Angie at an angle which accommodated my fingers, Marcus squirted some lube onto his hand. He then rubbed it on my wife's anus, before gently easing his forefinger inside her.

'Oh my fucking God,' panted Angie breathlessly, as

Marcus slid his finger in and out of her anus in time to his rhythm. 'What's happening to me?'

Feeling that I'd proved my ownership of my wife to Marcus, I withdrew my fingers from Angie before affectionately slapping her arse in appreciation. I then returned my gaze to Natalie, who was pushing back onto me with perfect timing. After a few minutes, she suddenly stretched her arms away from herself like she was doing yoga. Angie followed suit, and they joined hands by interlocking their fingers. They then kissed each other again. A warm and beautiful moment, I thought to myself, amongst the debauchery.

'God, you two are very naughty boys,' sighed Angie, having eased away from Natalie's mouth.

'And you two are very naughty girls,' Marcus declared in a loud whisper, 'who deserve whatever you get!'

'We're worse than naughty, Marcus,' replied my wife. 'So what are you going to do about that then?' she goaded.

'I'm gonna squeeze your nipples really hard, Angie,' replied Marcus, before instructing her to push herself up with her arms. He then bent forward and reached under her chest.

As I looked down, I watched him forcefully massage my wife's breast. He then took hold of her nipple and said …

'Once you get past the initial pain, the pleasure will go straight to your pussy! Do you want me to squeeze?'

'Yes,' whispered a nervous-sounding Angie. 'Squeeze me.'

I watched as Marcus squeezed and twisted Angie's nipple, contorting his face in some primal, dominant way as he did so.

'Arghhh!' moaned my wife, half in pain, half in pleasure. 'Oh God, oh God, oh God,' she chanted, as she wiggled her hips round Marcus's erection in appreciation.

Looking on wide-eyed, I became angry again. I never knew my Angie loved being squeezed so hard, and clearly, neither did she. Inadequacy ran through me. I hated that she'd had that first with another man. Desperate not to be outdone by Marcus, I slapped his hand out of the way, and pinched my wife's nipple.

'Much harder than you think,' whispered Marcus, before slipping his finger back up Angie's anus.

'Do you want me to squeeze harder?' I demanded.

'Yes,' whispered Angie.

Excited by pleasuring my wife in a new way, and at the same time angry at Marcus for telling me how to do it, I squeezed really hard.

'Ow, ow, ow,' panted my wife, whilst once again wriggling herself onto Marcus's cock with pleasure.

With my anger subsided, I returned my attention to Natalie, who had now raised her top half off the mattress, perfectly mirroring Angie. Still turned on like never before, I delighted in looking at my hard, beautifully aching cock going in and out of her. She was mine this very moment, and I loved it.

From our standing positions, Marcus and I continued our easy rhythm, spurred on by non-stop sighs, grunts and moans of pleasure from the girls. They too were lost in our wild sex orgy, but at the same time, also appeared to be trying to outdo each other.

Marcus and I slowed to a near halt. The girls then resumed kissing. The beauty and eroticism of the whole scene was totally intoxicating.

Feeling rested, I took hold of Natalie's soft hips and picked up the pace. Marcus shadowed my movements. As I fingered my playmate's anus in time to my vaginal thrusts, I sensed Natalie's orgasm starting to build. Moments later, I felt her tighten round my shaft and finger. I smiled with satisfaction, pleased I was performing well. Performing better than Marcus.

'Fuck me, fuck me, fuck me!' chanted Natalie.

Incredibly, Angie's breathing suddenly quickened, like she was in competition with Natalie. She too began chanting …

'Oh God, oh God, oh God!'

She went still and rigid. She was getting ready to come. Marcus clearly knew that and increased his pace until his playmate cried out …

'Arghhh, arghhh, arghhh,' as she then writhed and moaned with pleasure.

Natalie's orgasm followed seconds later. She was different to Angie. She wriggled as she came, and tried to pull off me as the intensity became almost too much to bear. I held her hips tight and slowed my thrusts down. She stopped wriggling, and then let her head drop onto the mattress, whilst panting like an exhausted greyhound.

I slapped her arse affectionately, before withdrawing my penis and falling to my knees. Having caught my breath, I kissed my playmate's opening like it was her mouth. When I'd finished kissing her, I eased back in readiness to stand up and resume penetration. Before I stood up though, I was inexplicably drawn to watch Marcus going in and out of my wife. Up close and personal. I was literally millimetres from his cock, and could see, hear, and smell the sex. It was mind-blowing.

After a short while, I suddenly noticed Marcus picking up speed. He was now slamming into my wife really hard and really fast. At this point she began chanting, 'Come in me Marcus. Come in me, come in me, come in me!'

Before I could formulate my want for him not to come in my wife, he shot his semen into her. Thrust and stop, thrust and stop, thrust and stop. Grunting as each thrust hit home. He then pumped deep into my woman one last time, leaving his cock in up to the hilt.

Black Dog was now antagonised beyond belief, eliciting an all-consuming urge in me to come deeper and harder in my wife than ever before. I sprang to my feet and bumped Marcus aside. Natalie turned and looked on wide-eyed. She then smiled knowingly, before settling down on the mattress with her husband, who had joined her, to watch the action.

I pushed my cock up my wife's saturated vagina as hard and as fast as I could. I then slapped her arse with all I had, before watching red handprints develop with satisfaction.

'Owww!' she yelped.

'You deserve that!' I said gruffly, 'for telling Marcus to come inside you.'

'Slap me,' ordered my wife. 'I'm a slut!'

Whack! I slapped her arse again, before pumping in and out of her vagina in a furious sexual rage.

Then, suddenly feeling the need to see my wife's face, I withdrew from her. I then forcefully manhandled her onto her back, and pushed her knees up by her face, causing the round of her bum to rise off the mattress. Still standing, I plunged my rampant cock into her open vagina as hard as possible. My woman yelped and moaned in response.

I was getting ready to come, and come harder than

I'd ever come before. I was pumping my wife furiously, filled with anger and a strange overwhelming competitive reaction. That reaction was made even worse, when I noticed Marcus's creamy semen oozing out of *my* wife, past *my* cock. At this point, I once again felt compelled to get my semen deeper into my woman than my competitors. Having straightened her knees, I hugged her legs tight to my chest. Then, whilst still moving in and out of her, I repeatedly kissed her calf. An involuntary loving gesture, in the midst of primal sexual dominance.

Feeling my release building rapidly, I took hold of the back of my woman's knees to bend her legs again. Having pushed her thighs wide open, I kept her arse raised off the mattress for maximum penetration. I then slammed into her even harder and faster than before; again and again, to displace more of my competitor's ejaculate.

After a couple of minutes of furious fucking, and with sweat pouring off me, an extra surge of adrenaline ran through me. At this point, I felt my cock begin to tense in readiness for my much-needed release. It remained charged for a while, like a powerful longbow having been drawn back. It stayed that way much longer than ever before, as I powered into Angie with everything I had, driven by raw, primal need. With my chest heaving, I gripped my wife's legs like a vice to keep her still. I then rammed right up into her as my orgasm finally began. I shot rapid fire bursts of semen from my cock under maximum pressure, whilst grunting like an angry gorilla, with my head tipped back. I then withdrew from my wife, before then slamming back into her one last time. I remained deep inside her until the last of my semen fired into her.

Mentally and physically spent, I collapsed onto my wife

like a dead weight. Then, panting like a steam train, I rested my head on her breasts. A moment later, I gradually came out of my altered state, as my senses slowly returned.

CHAPTER 19

As soon as we left The Hub, I turned my phone on. There was a text from Livy from a while back confirming that the little ones and Connor were fast asleep. She said she was in bed and hoped we were having fun. It felt weird getting back to ordinary family life, having just had sex with another couple, in a debauched den of iniquity.

'Livy texted to say the little ones and Connor are asleep,' I reported, 'and she's gone to bed herself.'

'Oh good,' replied Angie.

'Shall I text her back?'

'Probably best not to,' replied my wife. 'We don't want to wake her.'

Not in the mood to chat, I simply nodded in response. Then, once at the car, Angie and I climbed aboard in silence.

Twenty minutes into the drive home, my wife and I still hadn't spoken a word to each other. Yet when I was at The Hub, I was on a massive high; the craziest, most exciting walk on the wild side, ever!

It was only after my wife and I left the club, well past midnight, that our wrongdoing began to weigh heavy on my mind, in what you might call, the cold light of day. I was confused and angry at myself for dishonouring my marriage in thought, word, and deed. I can only liken my feelings to cheating on your spouse … you get caught up in the moment, but feel terribly guilty afterwards.

Driving home, I deliberately fixed my gaze on the road ahead to avoid eye contact with Angie. Needless to say, the events of the evening kept going round and round in my head. Sadly not in a good way.

Instead of celebrating a great night out, I kept reproaching myself and my wife for our actions. I felt guilty for bringing her down with my undue, unspoken judgements, yet I couldn't seem to stop myself. Perhaps this was the bite on the arse demon voice had spoken of. What is it they say? You often get cross with the one you love, when you're actually cross with yourself.

In an effort to put things into some sort of perspective to lighten my mood, I reminded myself that tonight was part of God's plan. A plan to make Angie blossom into her true self, so we could live happily ever after as a family. And maybe the evening was about my blossoming too. Either way, tonight had to play out the way it did, so as to make God's plan actually work. Bizarre as this may sound, once I'd figured all that out, my angst and regret left me, and I felt much happier.

In the sure knowledge that the Almighty always makes me work for the good he bestows upon me, I figured my emotional response was part of him working in mysterious ways. He was teaching me how to manage my emotions and overcome negative controlling behaviour. Once that thought had come and gone, I then began to wonder how I was going to make it up to my lovely wife. I felt especially bad because there were no recriminations or moral judgements from her whatsoever.

To make things right, I looked at Angie and smiled.

'Wow!' I sighed excitedly, 'we just did something completely crazy!'

She glanced at me with a troubled look on her face, and then nodded and turned away. Clearly in need of help to make things right and to assuage my guilt, I silently asked God to send me the right words to undo my wrong. I then rubbed my Angie's thigh reassuringly and told her I loved her more than anything in the world. She shot me a sideways glance, accompanied by a quizzical look that said, 'you've got a funny way of showing it.'

With my face contorted in a pained contrite grimace, I told my wife that I was really sorry for acting like a complete dick.

'Sorry?' she muttered, shaking her head.

'Please forgive me darling,' I pleaded, 'it was complete emotional overload back there. I was in some sort of altered state, like I was on drugs!'

Having nodded in response, my wife then told me she totally got what I was saying. Apparently, she too was in an altered state – completely overwhelmed by the moment. What she didn't get though, was why I felt the need to slut-shame her.

Despite asking for the right words from God, I wasn't man enough to fess up to my wrongdoing, and so deliberately appeared vague.

'Stop pretending you don't know what I'm talking about, Rich,' my wife insisted. 'You looked me up and down with utter disgust written all over your face in the car park. Remember?'

Realising I'd been sussed, I thought it best to finally man up, rather than adding insult to injury by proffering pathetic excuses. I owned up to my wrongdoing and said sorry, hoping that would draw a line under things, but it didn't.

'You made me feel dirty and ashamed Rich,' continued Angie crossly, 'but I didn't shame you, did I?'

'No,' I replied softly, 'you didn't, and I'm sorry for doing that sweetheart.'

'So you should be,' retorted my wife, sounding a little less cross.

Taking my eyes off the road for a second, I nodded agreeably. I then suggested that neither of us had anything to be ashamed of.

'We haven't Rich,' insisted my wife, 'but yet as a woman, I'm made to feel bad, but as a man, you're made to feel proud. And somehow,' she continued forcefully, 'you're seen as a stud, whilst I'm seen as a slut!'

Nodding in response, I told my wife that society did view things that way.

'And that's not fair,' I continued. 'But just so you know,' I added, 'I love you without judgement, and I'm so glad you had the confidence to do what you wanted to do this evening.'

'But do you really think that though Richie?' asked a doubtful-sounding Angie.

'Yes,' I replied resolutely, knowing not to leave any doubt in her mind, despite not being a hundred per cent sure of my answer.

'And what about you?' questioned my wife, sounding more relaxed. 'How did you feel about this evening?'

'Black Dog went crazy for much of the night,' I replied, 'and that made me angry and vindictive.'

Looking at me quizzically, my wife wanted to know what I meant by vindictive. I told her that I wanted to get back at her for having sex with Marcus.

'But our sex at The Hub was totally transactional,' she retorted. 'We all knew what we were there for!'

Whilst nodding in response to my wife's succinct statement, I mentally admired her emotional detachment to swinging sex. Then, as I was just about to tell her that, she told me that I wasn't to worry about being angry or vindictive.

'I read that emotions can run wild,' she added.

'You can say that again,' I replied, wide-eyed and nodding. 'It was weird. I got very possessive, especially after Marcus penetrated you, even though I was doing the same to Natalie. I think it was a combination of lust, and the jealous devil inside of me.'

'That's sort of a fault on the right side,' suggested Angie, 'because it shows you love me.'

'I suppose,' I replied, even though I knew I could never do it again.

With that said, we fell pleasantly silent for a while as we both processed the bizarre, yet profound events and emotions of the evening. Then, having reflected on things, and keen to lay Black Dog to rest, I asked Angie what she liked about the evening.

'What *I* liked about the evening?' she replied cautiously.

In view of her response, I again reassured my wife that I was totally cool with everything, and reminded her that we *both* did things at the club. I then glanced at her and was pleased to see her smiling.

'Well if you're sure,' she said, wriggling her bum into the back of her seat.

After a short pause, she told me that the excitement started when she called Lydia to talk about checking the club out.

'Okay,' I said, 'and then what?'

'Then the anticipation of it all kicked in a couple of days ago,' she replied. 'You know, choosing what to wear, the colour of my nails, having my hair done, etcetera.'

'Oh wow Angie,' I exclaimed, not having picked that up at all. 'I had no idea.'

'And I was all excited on the way to the club,' she continued, before adding that the whole thing was so different, so naughty, and so downright dirty.

Having nodded in reply, I waited for my wife to continue.

'By the end of the evening,' she said, 'I felt liberated and unshackled from my own misplaced chains of morality, despite your unspoken judgements.'

Keen not to get bogged down with the issue of my undue judgements any further, I once again reassured my wife that my behaviour was down to my insecurities, and had nothing to do with her at all. Having explained myself, I asked her if she was happy and glanced at her for confirmation that all was well. She nodded and smiled.

Pleased that all was well between us, I returned my wife's smile and felt myself go hard at the prospect of hearing how she felt about her naughty night at The Hub. I then asked her to continue.

'Well,' she said, 'my eyes were everywhere.'

'Eyeing up the guys?'

'Yes of course,' replied my wife, 'to see if they were checking me out, and to see if I fancied them. I also looked at the women to see how I compared.'

'And how did you establish if you fancied a guy or not?' I asked.

'God Rich,' responded Angie, 'you really do ask the most detailed of questions.'

Having gone red in the face from embarrassment, I told

my wife that I loved knowing everything about her because I loved her.

'And the more I know about you,' I added, 'the more there is to love.'

With her head tipped to one side, Angie smiled her warm, loving smile and then told me she could smell bullshit.

'I love it though,' she added, before telling me that she sort of looked at the whole person first. 'Height, face, build, etcetera, and if I liked him, I made eye contact. And then,' she added dramatically, 'I'd watch his eyes drop to my tits, and then down my legs and back up again, followed by an approving smile.'

'Did you like that?'

'God yeah,' sighed my wife, 'made me feel sexy and desired.'

'And what did you do in response?'

'What do you think I did, silly?' said Angie. 'I very obviously looked at their bits before widening my eyes and smiling back at them. Then later, once I'd found my confidence, I could feel guys looking at me, but I didn't return their gaze. Instead, I just strutted my stuff whilst quietly enjoying the attention.'

'But when you did return their gaze,' I said, 'what if you didn't fancy them?'

'Then I didn't look at them beyond my initial glance,' replied my wife, 'and therefore had no interest in their sexy bits whatsoever.'

At this point, I suddenly wanted to know if my wife was more inclined towards a bloke with a big dick, and asked the question.

'God yeah,' she replied. 'But if I don't fancy him, then it's a complete non-starter, no matter how big his dick is.'

'But if you met a guy in the pub and fancied him,' I said, 'would you be disappointed later if he was only small?'

My Angie chuckled in response, before telling me that, like most guys, I was clearly obsessed with penis size. She also said that she'd read somewhere that over eighty per cent of men wanted to be bigger.

'So clearly size does matter,' she continued. 'And before you ask,' she added warmly, 'you've got nothing to worry about in that department. It's just all the other departments,' she quipped.

Feeling reassured, I chuckled in response to my wife's funny. I then pressed her on the question of fancying someone who turned out to have a small dick.

'I would be disappointed when he took his boxers off,' she replied, 'but that wouldn't be a relationship deal-breaker, especially if he was naturally sexy. And just to clarify,' she continued, 'at The Hub we were just there for sex, so normal attraction criteria didn't apply.'

'But what does that actually mean though?' I asked.

'Well, The Hub wasn't about a meeting of minds,' replied Angie, 'it was just about sex provided you liked them. So if a guy was sexy and attractive with a big dick, I would have been more interested in him, than an equally attractive guy with a small dick.'

'Why?'

'Because a bigger cock fills me up and stretches me, which is more satisfying,' said my wife. 'Simple as that. Now stop obsessing about penis size,' she insisted, before quickly adding that in a survey, over seventy per cent of sexually active women felt that size mattered, and that it wasn't just her.

Having nodded in acknowledgement of my wife's

statistic, I asked her to humour me.

'So if you saw a guy with a sexy bod and an okay face,' I said, 'then what?'

'I would go with him, yes.'

'Really?'

'Yes, provided I got a good vibe from him.'

'Sure,' I said with a nod, before listening to Angie explain that he's not someone she'd want to wake up to every day.

'He's just sexually attractive,' she continued, 'which is of the moment, and for the moment.'

'And if the face was really attractive but the body was average?' I questioned.

'That's fine too, because it's just about the sex,' replied Angie, before adding that if the face and body were both rough, that would be a no.

Having nodded in reply, I asked my wife what happened when she saw a guy who was the whole package.

'I explored all his body,' she replied. 'And yes, before you ask, my eyes did linger on his bits. Especially if he had a hard-on. It's a natural, primal response, Rich,' she added, before admitting that she also checked their arses out after they'd walked by.

Somewhat surprised by that, I responded by saying that I thought only blokes did that sort of thing. Laughing, my wife told me that I didn't really know women at all. Having nodded in agreement, yet another question came to mind. Infuriated at my obsessive need to know my wife's every last thought and feeling, I nevertheless asked her if she wanted to make a move on any of the guys at The Hub.

'God yeah,' she replied, 'and even though women have now taken control of their sex lives, we still don't *actually* make a move, we just send out signals.'

When I asked my wife what she meant by that, she explained that throughout nature, males always pursue the females, and that it was no different with people.

'But in a sex club,' she added, 'women can be completely obvious, unlike in the outside world.'

'And did you send any signals out?'

'Like I said,' replied Angie, 'I did check guys out, but because we were with Marcus and Natalie, I couldn't really send any signals out to anybody else.'

'I suppose not,' I said.

'It helped that I fancied Marcus right from the off,' added my wife, 'so I really loved watching his reaction to my signals.'

'You mean watching him go hard?' I retorted a tad sharply, clearly suffering from a bit of residual jealousy.

'Well yes of course, but there were other responses as well.'

'And what sort of signals did you send out?' I asked, trying hard to rein in my jealousy.

'You know all this Rich,' said Angie, 'you were there.'

'Tell me anyway,' I said.

'Well, when we were in the bar,' continued my wife, 'I crossed and uncrossed my legs and let them linger apart. And I loved flirting with my eyes.'

Although, as Angie pointed out, I'd seen her teasing Marcus, I loved hearing her tell me about it. It excited me.

With my residual jealousy now faded, I asked Angie what would have happened if we'd intended to have sex with other people from the outset.

'Oh,' she sighed excitedly, 'there were quite a few guys I could have had some fun with. Two younger guys in particular, both of whom went erect whilst looking at me.'

'Oh wow!' I responded excitedly, as my hard-on throbbed with unexpected pride. 'Spontaneous erections! What did you do to make that happen?'

'Just what I said before,' replied Angie. 'A sort of flirtatious exchange where I just looked at them in a sexy way and smiled.'

'And how did seeing them go instantly hard for you make you feel?'

'Oh God Rich!' sighed my wife, 'watching a guy get an instant hard-on for you is so fucking hot! I felt so incredibly desired and sexy. I felt like I'd still got it. Even more so than when I was younger.'

'Well you did look sexier than ever,' I responded. 'Absolutely drop dead gorgeous!'

'Do you really think that though, Richie?' asked a slightly doubtful Angie.

'For sure,' I replied, before telling her that she didn't need my validation, because she'd had independent confirmation of her sexiness from two young studs.

My wife caught my gaze and looked at me with her gorgeous loving Bambi eyes. She didn't say anything to me. She didn't have to. Her look said it all. I was so pleased to see so much love for me in her eyes.

With the moment passed, I excitedly pressed Angie as to what she would have done if we'd intended to have sex from the outset.

Smiling a naughty smile, she explained that she would've told me which guys took her fancy.

'Like the two younger blokes who went hard for you?' I suggested.

'Yes. Then you could have invited them to join us.'

'Do you mean the two guys and me all together Angie?'

'The two guys yes,' she replied, before then grimacing apologetically, 'but not you.'

'So you kind of fancied cuckolding me then?'

'Yeah, because you could have watched me being fucked senseless from the bar on the big screens.'

'For my excitement?' I questioned.

'If I'm honest,' replied Angie, 'I like the idea of being fucked by strangers. It's naughty, dangerous and forbidden. And they can do what they want to me without you being there to influence them.'

'Sure,' I responded, as a jealous surge of adrenaline ran through my body, causing my erection to throb even harder.

'And I'd feel safe because you'd be watching over me,' continued my wife, 'but I wouldn't feel bad because I'd know you'd be going wild with excitement.'

Pleased my beloved wanted me to watch over her, I nodded in bizarre appreciation. At the same time, it hadn't escaped my notice that her swinging fantasies were entirely about her. But because I'd be way too jealous and possessive to allow such a thing, I wasn't too bothered. I was curious though about her thoughts on the full swap scenario which played out with Natalie and Marcus.

'That was a completely different dynamic,' she responded. 'And even though Natalie was amazing, if we had the evening again I think I'd rather have been shagged by Marcus and those two younger guys, while you looked on from the bar. Does that make me a bad person?'

I unequivocally told my wife that she wasn't a bad person, and that I absolutely loved her honesty.

'So many people don't tell the truth in their marriage,' I added, 'and that's a recipe for deceit and disaster.'

'It is,' agreed my wife. 'And whilst monogamy's a

beautiful idea,' she added, 'it's really hard to ask just one man to represent the whole of manhood for you, and vice versa.'

Having glanced at my wife for a bit too long, I began to wonder if she'd completely scratched her swinging itch after all. Then, suddenly appearing to want to move the conversation on, she quickly asked me how I checked people out at the club.

I explained that I looked at the ladies' sexy bits, and lingered on the ones I found attractive.

'And strangely enough,' I added, 'they weren't always the prettiest ones.'

'No?' questioned Angie.

'No,' I replied, 'they just seemed to have a sexiness about them … their look, their smile, their demeanour.'

'So it wasn't all about big tits then?' retorted my wife, half seriously.

'God no,' I replied, before explaining that it was about a certain *je ne sais quoi*. 'Which, just so you know,' I added, 'is something you've got by the bucket load!'

Smiling broadly, my wife thanked me for being so lovely. Then, breaking the short silence which followed, I asked her if she felt sexually objectified at the club.

'Not in the least,' she replied, 'I was on show for sex. The men were on show for sex. Part of swinging *is* sexual objectification,' she added. 'It's both primal and natural.'

I responded with a thoughtful nod, before telling my wife that I could see the sense in what she was saying.

'Swinging isn't like porn,' she continued, 'where women often appear to be there for men's pleasure. It's like Marcus said, the ladies control everything, and I certainly felt that the men were there for me, as much as I was there for them.'

Impressed with my wife's no-nonsense outlook, I prompted her to share more of her sexual feelings with me. I was aroused by them, driven by a healthy jealousy that made me want her even more. I was also pleased that my jealousy wasn't the unhealthy, disrespectful kind, which had accompanied Black Dog earlier.

Still clearly buzzing from the high induced by The Hub, my wife delighted in telling me that it was 'sensation overload' with Natalie and two sexy men playing with her at once.

'Especially when Marcus pushed into me alongside your fingers,' she added, shooting me a guilty glance.

Hearing that aroused me even more, and made my heart skip an incredibly jealous beat. Sensing my wife's guilt at enjoying such an encounter, I quickly reassured her that we both went a little crazy. I also explained that I got possessive, which is why I kept my fingers inside her, and then got extra turned on when Marcus entered her as well.

'You got extra turned on?' repeated my wife, as a smug smile slowly grew across her face. 'Was it a bit of a bi experience for you then?'

'Not bi,' I insisted in a deep voice, 'I was proud that's all.'

'Why?'

'Because you got a fit young guy totally rampant for you,' I replied.

'Yeah, and so?' questioned my wife, almost as if she was fishing for compliments.

'So,' I replied, 'you were breathtakingly beautiful, disgustingly dirty and amazingly amazing! And,' I added firmly, 'most importantly, you were *my* woman!'

With that said, there was a short pause, and when I

glanced over to the passenger seat, my Angie was looking at me with big, brimming eyes, beautifully illuminated by the full moon.

'Oh Rich,' she sighed, shaking her head, 'what a lovely thing to say. I feel so loved by you, and so not judged.'

'If I'm honest,' I replied, trying to hold back unexpected tears, 'I hadn't really articulated those feelings until now, but that's what it all comes down to.'

'I'm so lucky,' said my wife, as she wiped her tears away with the back of her hand.

Having completely re-focused on the road, I smiled to myself. I was pleased I felt that way about my wife. And then, needless to say, my curiosity as to how she felt about both me and Marcus being inside her at once, overwhelmed me. When I asked her about it, she told me it was way beyond her sexual imagination.

'And I loved being submissive and being used for yours and Marcus's pleasure,' she continued, 'not to mention how incredibly intense and disgustingly exciting it all was, alongside the eroticism of playing with Natalie.'

I nodded in thoughtful agreement. We fell silent for a moment, and as I felt my erection subside, I thought how wonderfully close I felt to my Angie when she shared her innermost feelings with me. All in all, I concluded that The Hub had done us a lot of good. That pleased me no end, and made me realise that we needed to go through the angsty bits, in order to unlock our deeply soulful emotions.

'So what about you, my big man?' whispered Angie, bringing me out of my musings. 'You liked Natalie, didn't you?'

'God yeah,' I sighed, 'but I felt guilty about breaking our marriage vows, especially when I wanted to penetrate her.'

'Aww Rich, that's so lovely,' said Angie. 'I felt the same when I first wanted Marcus.'

'When was that?'

'Well, like I said, I was attracted to him straightaway,' replied my wife, 'but it was only when we'd had a drink at the bar, that I started to hope for something more than just a recce.'

'Why?'

'Because he was really good-looking and charming. Not to mention the fact that he had a massive hard-on for me. Plus,' she added, 'he was looking at me desirously and I kind of got pussy lust for him.'

'Oh wow,' I exclaimed, 'so you wanted sex quite early on then?'

'Well yeah,' said my wife. 'A woman knows these things pretty quickly. And being truthful,' she continued, 'those feelings of guilt were soon overwhelmed by my debauched desires.'

Hearing that made my heart sink momentarily, until I realised that I too sidelined my guilty feelings about breaking my marriage vows, in order to indulge my decadent depravity.

With a hundred and one questions still racing around in my head, I suddenly wondered what specifically excited my wife about Marcus. When I asked the question, she chuckled in response, before telling me that I was weird for wanting to know every last nuance of her thinking.

Mirroring my wife's chuckle, I agreed with her. I then glanced at her expectantly, and listened intently as she explained that she was overpowered by her desire for the forbidden.

'What do you mean exactly?'

'I just wanted Marcus to fuck me senseless,' replied my wife. 'I wanted to feel his big, stiff, throbbing cock deep inside me,' she added breathlessly, 'pounding me hard – every which way!'

At this point, my penis immediately reacted to the unashamed, wanton hussy that was my wife. Freud's Madonna-whore complex had clearly kicked in, but without any disrespect on my part.

'Wow!' I sighed, as my jealous hard-on throbbed away between my legs, 'that's very naughty, Angie.'

'It is indeed,' she replied, shooting me a knowing glance. 'And I bet it went straight to your cock,' she added, before reaching over to see if I was erect.

Holding my wife's gaze as she squeezed my hard-on, I watched a smug smile slowly grow across her face. She then sighed heavily with delight.

'Thought so,' she said, releasing her grip on me.

Having returned my gaze to the road, I then began to wonder if my wife said these things to excite me, or even to control me. Or, was she just sharing her true feelings with me, whilst delighting in my response? For some reason, I needed her feelings, wants and desires to be genuine. If they were contrived, then I wouldn't react. Why that was, I didn't know. With uncertainty playing on my mind, my erection subsided.

After a moment's silence, I asked Angie if she'd deliberately expressed her thoughts in a graphic way to excite me. Or, was that actually how she felt.

'It's actually how I felt, Richie,' she replied, sending me hard again, 'and because I know you like my unfettered thoughts in graphic detail, I can be a complete slut with impunity. And because it excites you,' she added, 'it excites me even more, if you see what I mean?'

Pleased with my wife's honesty, I smiled and nodded. I then asked her if she'd signalled to Natalie to suck me when we were talking about doing a soft swap.

'Yes, if I'm honest, I did,' replied my wife. 'I was so excited and wanted to carry on. Plus I wanted you to have the pleasure of two women at once.'

'Oh wow,' I exclaimed, 'you were thinking of me?'

'Of course,' replied Angie, 'and I was strangely proud of you, because Natalie told me she wanted you to fuck her, and asked if I was alright with that.'

Swelling with pride, a smug smile involuntarily spread across my lips. A few moments later, I asked my wife if she'd agreed to me having sex with Natalie because she, Angie, wanted a full swap.

'Exactly right Richie,' she replied. 'I did say yes to Natalie so I could have full sex with Marcus, but I was still jealous. Then Natalie told me to follow her lead.'

Having nodded in response, I then suggested that Marcus wasn't wrong when he said that the ladies controlled what happened at The Hub.

'We certainly do,' said Angie, as she again reached across to squeeze my throbbing hard-on. 'You men are all led by your dicks!'

'You scheming little thing you,' I whispered, through a half smile. 'You're a naughty one!'

'As I said before,' responded my wife, 'if you're gonna fuck, then fuck! Anything goes!'

'And my God Angie,' I replied, 'anything did go!'

With that said, a short comfortable silence followed. As I contemplated the evening still further, I thought it odd that we both thought that kissing, sucking and licking were acceptable, but when it came to penetration, we felt we were crossing the line. I then articulated all of this to Angie.

'At a primal subconscious level,' she said, 'penetration is the bit that makes babies.'

Nodding in agreement, I then told my wife that being honest with each other was emotionally refreshing, and made me love her all the more. She responded with a smile. We then fell silent again. This time my thoughts drifted to the beautiful vista of the girls kissing and caressing one another. That prompted me to ask Angie if she enjoyed Natalie's attention.

'God yeah,' she enthused, 'I loved it. It was warm, loving and erotic, yet so naughty, dirty and debauched! And she was the best kisser ever!'

'Was she?'

'Yes. And when you and Marcus were taking us doggy whilst Natalie and I were kissing, it was … I dunno, just like a wild sex party!'

Desperate for more details from my wife, I remained both silent and erect, in the hope that she would continue. She duly obliged.

'No offence about the kissing, Rich,' she suddenly piped up, 'it's just that us women know what other women like. And, just to be clear,' she quickly added, 'you're the best man kisser I've ever had.'

'That makes me really happy,' I said, 'unlike when you suddenly sucked Marcus without asking me!'

'Sorry, my big man,' responded Angie, 'I was completely immersed in the moment.'

Having acknowledged my wife's apology with a nod, I then asked her why she liked sucking Marcus.

'Feeling your lover grow big in your mouth,' replied a

slightly breathless Angie, 'tasting his saltiness and feeling his balls bashing against your chin, is incredibly exciting.'

Unable to articulate a response, because my cock was throbbing away with wild, perverse, jealous excitement, I simply sighed and nodded.

'And turning Marcus on,' continued my wife, 'turned me on. Made my pussy wet in readiness to receive his big hard cock!'

Having regained my composure, I asked my wife if she would have preferred me to fuck her instead of Marcus. I think I was looking for yet more reassurance, whilst at the same time secretly wanting my wife to make me jealous.

'No, not really,' came her reply.

'Why not?'

'I wanted someone new,' explained Angie, 'someone exciting and different. No offence, but that's the whole point,' she insisted. 'Like I said, I wanted Marcus inside me. Wanted *him* to fuck me every which way.'

My wife's words, although bizarrely welcome, unexpectedly rattled Black Dog's cage this time. That soon subsided though, when she told me she liked me fingering her whilst I was *fucking* (she emphasised) Natalie.

'You naughty boy, Rich,' she added, wearing a disapproving school ma'am look, as we caught each other's eye.

'Yes I am a naughty boy,' I announced proudly, for some unknown reason. 'I mean fancy fucking Natalie whilst fingering you?'

'I liked it though,' said Angie, 'because I liked Natalie, and could tell she was enjoying you, and that you were enjoying her.'

Pleased to hear that, I turned to my wife and responded

with a huge grin of thanks.

'Watch out silly!' she said, turning my face back to the road with her hand, 'or we'll have an accident.'

Still pleasantly aroused, I focused on my driving. I then smiled in anticipation of making love to my wife when we got home. My musings were interrupted however, when she suddenly piped up, 'This evening was so unusual and so different,' she said. 'I can't stop thinking about it, and it just makes me want to talk about it to the point of obsession.'

'Welcome to my world,' I quipped through a smile.

'And mine too,' said Angie, before asking me what I thought of the evening.

In reply, I explained that I felt a bit inadequate, and so needed to outdo Marcus, or at the very least, match him. My Angie told me that she totally got that, because she too wanted to be as good as Natalie. Better even.

'I wanted to drive Marcus wild,' she added.

'And did you want him to, erm …'

'Come in me?' asked Angie, completing my sentence. 'Yes of course. Every woman wants her lover to come in her.'

'But I didn't want him to come in you,' I sulked, 'that was supposed to be special for us.'

'I know,' said my wife, 'but we both got caught up in the moment. I mean you didn't want us to kiss playmates,' she added, 'but yet *you* kissed Natalie.'

Having nodded in agreement, I then wondered what my wife liked about her lover coming inside her. Feeling like this was a question too far, I tried to put it out of my mind. As I fought to suppress my curiosity, I wondered why I needed such a detailed debriefing about the events of the evening. I then remembered Julia telling me that some people wanted to know every last detail of their partner's infidelity (which is what The Hub sort of boils down to) whilst others didn't want to know any details at all. On top of that, there was my embarrassing cuckold-type response, even though tonight was a swap.

After a painful quiet minute or so, I gingerly asked my wife what she liked about her lover ejaculating into her. She looked a little taken aback by my question and held my gaze. Feeling like my perverted probing was just too much, I told her I'd completely understand if she didn't want to answer.

'Don't be silly,' retorted my wife. 'All we're doing is talking about an everyday act. And because people generally don't mention the graphic details of it all, doesn't make our discussion perverted in the least. To the contrary,' she added, 'we're liberated freethinkers.'

Pleasantly surprised by my wife's willingness to answer my ridiculous question, I listened intently as she told me how she loved the *anticipation* of Marcus coming deep inside her, as he began to fuck her harder and faster.

'I loved him gripping me tight,' she continued, 'pulling me onto his cock as he thrusted into me, panting and sweating. Arghhh!' she sighed, as an involuntary shiver of excitement ran through her body.

Hearing such an enthusiastic account of another man ejaculating into my wife, made me incredibly jealous. That in turn made my cock throb with competitive desire.

With my eyes on the road, I told my wife that I loved hearing about how she felt. I also told her that her honesty made me feel closer to her, and made me want her even more. However, I didn't say that I felt inadequate, otherwise she wouldn't share her true feelings with me. That would deprive me of my perverse excitement, as well as foster mistrust.

'So go on then sweetheart,' I urged, 'tell me more.'

'Well, and I know this will sound stupid,' said my wife, 'but I felt really smug at having done a good job when Marcus came for me.'

'So what about when we make love?' I asked gingerly, as my jealous arousal subsided.

'When we make love,' said Angie thoughtfully, 'it's the same act but very different.'

'How?' I asked.

'Our sex is close and intimate,' she replied, 'and even if it's just a dirty fuck,' she added, 'it's still emotionally fulfilling.'

When I asked my wife what that actually meant, she told me that she got immense pleasure from our spiritual connection, and didn't even mind not coming.

'I just love our closeness,' she added.

Hearing her extol the virtues of our spiritual connection really lifted me, because no other man could provide that for her. However, my ego still needed reassuring, so I asked my wife if I was better than Marcus.

'We can never reproduce tonight at home, Rich,' she replied, 'because it will just be the two of us.'

'So what exactly was tonight then?' I asked.

'Dirty, hardcore porn sex,' responded Angie, 'with fantastic, mind-blowing orgasms!'

Whilst I appreciated my wife's honesty, her answer bruised my ego and made me insecure. In an attempt to allay my concerns, I again asked her if I was better than Marcus.

'It's not a question of better,' she replied, 'it's more a question of different.'

'Is it?'

'Yes,' said my wife, 'Marcus is different to you, not better.'

Hearing that explanation seemed to mollify my ego. Then, having smiled at my wife, I listened to her describe me as a man possessed.

'I could see it in your eyes,' she continued, 'and I loved you looming large over me – pounding me like your life depended on it.'

'I kinda felt like it did,' I remarked. 'And like I said, I wanted to outdo Marcus.'

'I'm glad,' responded Angie, 'because I thought you were gonna come in Natalie, and I didn't want that. I wanted your cum in me,' she added, leaning forward so as to make eye contact.

Buoyed by my wife's desire for my semen, I held her gaze and smiled. Then, turning my eyes back to the road, I asked her what specifically made her want me to come inside her, rather than Natalie. She told me she was jealous and possessive. That made me feel good.

After a short silence, yet another weird curiosity got the better of me. I then proceeded to ask my wife if she enjoyed me and Marcus ejaculating into her, one immediately after the other.

'I did,' whispered my wife. 'Is that wrong of me?'

'No,' I replied softly, when I really wanted to say yes for some unknown reason. 'What exactly did you like about it?' I asked casually, trying not to sound upset.

'Being desired and in demand,' responded Angie, 'and outdoing Natalie, even though I really liked her. Plus, 'she added, 'I felt empowered because I made a random, good-looking guy come. Also, it's just dirty and slutty, and that's me all over I'm afraid.'

Still frustratingly fixated on semen, I asked Angie if her desire for my semen differed from her desire for Marcus's.

'I usually want you to come in me to make babies,' she replied, 'even though we're not having anymore. But tonight, I wanted you to come inside me, born of possessiveness. I always smile when you leak out of me,' she added enthusiastically, 'when I remember how it got there.'

'And how about right now?' I asked.

'Right now, I can feel *both* of you leaking out of me,' replied my wife, 'and that makes me smile even more, because it's taboo, and there's a thrill in that.'

With that said, my wife slipped her fingers up her dress and felt between her legs.

'Honestly you two,' she sighed, before wiping her fingers on a tissue she'd pulled out of the glove box, 'I'm absolutely dripping with your combined cum.'

Hearing that sent a massive jealous and competitive surge through me. With my heart pounding in my chest, all I wanted to do was to stop the car and penetrate my wife, to possess her and to own her.

'Fuck Angie!' I said in a whisper, 'that's gone straight to my cock!'

'I knew it would,' she replied smugly, before opening her legs and lifting her bum off the seat. Then, having wiped herself with the tissue she still had in her hand, she told me I would have to wait until we got home to top her up. 'In the meantime,' she added, 'relax and tell me what you thought of tonight.'

'In amongst the angst, anger and excitement of it all,' I began, 'I was weirdly proud of you sweetheart. You got heads turning and Marcus was mad for you.'

'Oh Rich,' sighed my wife, 'you don't know how much it means to me to hear you say that.'

'I love you my sweetheart,' I said warmly, 'but I'm not

convinced The Hub is my kind of thing to be honest with you.'

At this point, Angie turned on her bum, took my left hand off the steering wheel and clutched it to her heart.

'You're my one and only love Rich,' she said, 'and you always will be. You do know that, don't you?'

'Yes, I suppose I do,' I replied, feeling reassured.

'And anyway,' she said in an upbeat tone, 'your cock's plenty big enough, and you're bigger than Marcus.'

'I guess I am,' I responded, swelling with pride.

'I didn't have the best tits in the house,' added Angie, 'and I think we both need to lighten up a little.'

I nodded in agreement, as I momentarily caught my wife's eye.

'And FYI,' she continued, 'you've got a great body, and were in better shape than most of the guys there. No belly, tall and muscular. Plenty of women were checking you out.'

I once again nodded in agreement with my wife, and then smiled thoughtfully. She returned my hand to the steering wheel before relaxing back into her seat. And even though she'd reassured me that I was a contender, I still knew I had a long way to go to be like her. Once that thought had come and gone, I relaxed back into my seat and left my autopilot to it, whilst I continued to analyse the hell out of everything.

My contemplations were suddenly disturbed when Angie blurted out, 'I know you liked Natalie, Rich, but she ain't all that. I mean she's a bit pear-shaped and her tits are a little saggy!'

Surprised at my wife's undue put-down, I nevertheless smiled contentedly, pleased at her apparent jealousy.

'I know she hasn't got your body my love,' I said, 'but she's got a certain niceness about her which I liked.'

'You're not supposed to get emotionally involved, Rich!' insisted my wife. 'Did you feel close to her? And be honest!'

'Yes I did,' I replied, 'but it was just a fleeting emotion. Is that odd?'

'I know what you're like,' said Angie, 'but you mustn't have caring feelings for women. Okay?!'

'Okay,' I agreed contritely, secretly pleased to have been told off.

Then, having settled further back into my seat, I drove on feeling happy. I no longer had the urge to fuck my wife senseless, like I did a moment ago when she scooped another man's semen out of her vagina. Now, all jealousy, insecurity and twisted sexual arousal had left me.

Feeling relaxed and calm, I now wanted to be spiritually and physically close to my wife. A moment later, I turned off the main road into a narrow country lane. Here, I soon found a secluded farm track. Having parked up, I cupped the back of Angie's head in my hand and gently pulled her face to mine. Kissing her softly for a while, I savoured the warmth of our mouth-to-mouth embrace, whilst enjoying the depth of emotion I felt in my heart.

After a few minutes, I backed away from my soulmate with a thoughtful look on my face.

'Do you know what?' I whispered, 'I kind of get what Natalie meant about how amazing she felt when Marcus made love to her afterwards.'

'Me too, my big man,' said Angie, cupping my face with her hand as she looked deep into my eyes. 'Guilt without regret,' she added with a smile.

I nodded in response, before sliding both front seats forward. I then took my shoes off before climbing over the centre console into the back seat of the car. Lifting the release catch, I pushed the back seat down flat. I then extended my hand to Angie, my eyes wide with adoration.

'I need to make love to you my sweetheart,' I whispered, choking a little. 'Leave my love inside you. Not fuck you like at the club.'

'Oh yes, Rich,' sighed my Angie, as she too climbed over the centre console to join me. 'I want that so much.'

Having slipped my chinos and boxers off in one fell swoop, I set about removing my wife's dress. She lifted her bum off the seat to assist me. Once I'd pulled her dress over her hips, she raised her arms so I could take it off completely. With her arms enveloped by her dress over her head, I looked at my woman's breasts sitting beautifully on her chest, before then slowly running my eyes along her now exaggerated sensual curves. The curves from her torso to her waist, and then the curves from her waist to her hips.

'Wow!' I sighed involuntarily, before removing her dress completely, 'you are just so fucking beautiful!'

My wonderful wife smiled warmly in response. Then, after gazing meaningfully at each other for a moment, I gently laid her on her back. With no knickers and bra on, she was completely naked, save for her high heels and hold-up stockings. Bathed in the soft blue moonlight which streamed through the windows, my Angie was a perfect picture of exquisite beauty.

I then knelt on the floor beside my wife and kissed her soft lips tenderly. She parted her mouth and drew me in. Before long, I eased away from her to gaze into her eyes. I then proceeded to deliver a myriad of mini kisses down her neck, until I reached her soft breasts and proud nipples. Here, I lingered for a while, before continuing my kisses down my wife's tummy to her inner thighs. At this point, I would usually kiss my wife's vulva, before then slipping my tongue inside her. But on this occasion, I did something different. I instead slipped two fingers inside my woman and massaged her g-spot with a "come hither" motion. I was surprised at the quantity of semen in her vagina. Mixed with her own love juices, it was silky smooth to the touch, and produced an intoxicating sex aroma, which was incredibly exciting.

After a few minutes of enjoying the intimate vista and feel of my wife, I bent her leg at the knee, and pushed her open. I then eased my head down to her opening, but then paused at the thought of Marcus's semen inside her. You've always kissed her here, Rich, I told myself, and that shouldn't change just because you *both* had a swinging experience. And anyway, I knew if I didn't lick my Angie as usual, she would feel cheap, like I was judging her, and I certainly couldn't allow that to happen.

Having taken a deep breath, I pushed my tongue into my wife, and then retched in silence at the taste of another man's semen. I'd tasted my own semen many times before, which of course, was no different to Marcus's. Realising that my reaction was all in my head, I set my silly thoughts aside, and got on with the pleasure of making love to my wonderful wife.

At this moment in time, my Angie began to wriggle her hips a little, whilst moaning and sighing with pleasure. Keen to give her a blended orgasm, I slipped two fingers back inside her and began massaging her g-spot again. I then started sucking and licking her clitoris. After a few minutes, my Angie tightened. She was ready to climax. I picked up the pace with my fingers and tongue. She then let out a prolonged soft sigh, as she involuntarily gyrated her hips with pleasure.

With my soulmate satisfied, I knelt up straight and explored her beautiful moonlit face with my loving eyes. After a short, meaningful silence, I climbed onto the seat and positioned my hips between my woman's thighs, my erection poised at the gates to heaven.

'I feel so very close to you Angie,' I said. 'Closer than ever before.'

'Me too,' she whispered.

Then, still looking deep into her eyes, I slipped my erection into my woman, and delighted in her heartfelt welcoming moan.

'Mmmhh,' she sighed, smiling at me.

'I wonder why we feel so close to each other at this moment?' I whispered.

'I dunno,' whispered Angie in reply. 'Maybe it's because we both realise that there are other people who are interested in us. And perhaps,' she added, 'that stops us taking each other for granted.'

Having nodded in thoughtful response, I then focused on the physical feeling of sliding in and out of my woman. It was sublimely warm and beautiful, because it was so profoundly meaningful. An intimate reconnecting of two symbiotic souls.

Feeling the need to be even closer to my woman, I wrapped my arms around her shoulders and pulled her body to mine. I then resumed our sensual kissing. I felt an incandescent love for my wife like never before. Perhaps this was part of the emotion Natalie was talking about when she and Marcus made love after their swinging sessions. As I lifted my head, my eyes locked on to Angie's. I continued my slow, gentle rhythm for a few minutes, until I felt myself getting ready to come. Changing up a gear, I began pumping in and out of my Angie with a sense of urgency.

'I want your cum deep inside me,' she whispered, as she gripped my hips with her nails and pulled me into her.

One last hard thrust, and then my semen began shooting out of me, deep inside my woman.

'Love you, my big man,' she whispered, still looking into my eyes as I pulsated inside her.

'Love you too,' I whispered back, gazing into the windows of my woman's soul. 'Until I die,' I added, before collapsing on top of her.

As I laid on my wife enjoying our special moment, I contemplated the fact that we'd both had sex with two random strangers just an hour ago. I was pleased that didn't bother me in the slightest. And I was pleased that the physical presence of another man's semen inside my wife, and her momentary desire for it didn't bother me either. I smiled at the absence of Black Dog. I guess he was absent because, all said and done, tonight was a quid pro quo event. Whatever my wife did, I did too.

Angie and I remained still and quiet for a moment. I could hear her breathing sweetly in my ear. I could feel her softness against me, and I could feel her heart beating next to mine. I felt warm and fuzzy beyond belief.

With a feeling that my marriage was stronger than ever, I gently eased myself out from Angie's embrace. We both got dressed. Then, as I drove home, tears of joy quietly filled my eyes at the realisation that my wonderful wife and I were back together again, as one combined entity, mind, body, and soul.

❖

CHAPTER 20

In the wake of our date with debauchery nearly a week ago, Charles Dickens's profound opening to *A Tale of Two Cities* kept going round in my head … "It was the best of times, it was the worst of times, it was the age of wisdom, it was the age of foolishness … It was the season of light, it was the season of darkness, it was the spring of hope, it was the winter of despair …"

Sitting at the very end of Inspiration Point, seventy metres into the sea and fifty feet high, I watched my old mate Mr Blue swelling, crashing and splashing around me, playing his relaxing melody as he went. With my chin on my knees, I pondered Dickens's insightful words of a hundred and sixty years ago.

'The best of times,' I whispered.

Definitely. The most amazing, crazy animalistic sex ever, followed by unparalleled feelings of love and adoration. Incredibly profound and intense.

'The worst of times,' I muttered in a low voice.

Sadly, yes. Despite the wonderful soulful feelings my Angie and I had for each other after The Hub, something about that night still troubled me. Plus there was the hurt I caused the family by losing my business. And when you add in the pain of uncertainty, and the undue sanctimonious judgements I made on my wife, you can see why "the worst of times" plays its part too.

'And what about the age of wisdom?' I asked myself.

Wisdom has certainly helped. I mean, loving my Angie for who she is without judging her, and helping her blossom, is unquestionably the right thing to do. An absolute must to keep the family together.

'The age of foolishness?' I said thoughtfully.

Yep, definitely that, beyond any shadow of a doubt. Disrespecting myself, my marriage, and my wife, by watching her have dirty, base sex with a complete stranger, whilst I did the same, was foolish beyond belief.

'The season of light and the season of darkness,' I whispered.

I've seen more darkness than I care to mention, I mused.

'But then again, Mr Blue,' I said out loud, 'in a weird way, the darkness has actually shown me the light!'

How is that? I hear you ask. Well, with the massive stress of running a multimillion-pound business behind me, I have found time to stop and smell the flowers. And, another way in which darkness has shown me the light, is the wonderful connection my Angie and I now have after The Hub.

'And what of the spring of hope,' I said out loud, 'here in Hope Harbour?'

Is that gonna happen? Or is an even worse winter of despair yet to come?

Despite my usual optimism, a negative niggle persisted in my head. Something I couldn't quite put my finger on, which stopped me from placing my trust in a spring of hope. That unfathomable niggle, together with my personal life experience (where I always received a kick in the bollocks just when I thought things were going well), made me sceptical.

Not wishing to contemplate these matters any further, I shook my head. I then rose to my feet and carefully plotted my way along the rocks of Inspiration Point back to the beach.

As I walked home, and despite trying not to, I began to unpick the mass of conflicting considerations I'd been brooding over. With my head fit to burst, and still unable to find any answers, I decided to somehow park The Hub episode as best I could, and move on. What else could I do? I knew there could be no recriminations, no regrets, and no judging of either of us, by either of us. At the end of the day, we both partook of forbidden pleasures of the flesh of our own free will. The one consideration that made complete sense to me though, was that swinging wasn't for me. My emotions just weren't in tune with its philosophy.

'The Hub was a one-off Richie boy,' I said out loud, as I paused on the beach. 'You knew it was wrong, but you did it anyway.'

Yes I did, I thought to myself, but I mustn't let that undermine my marriage. Walking on, I pondered Angie's "guilt without regret".

'You must feel that way too,' I told myself, 'until your Catholic conscience stops judging you.'

I figured the best way to achieve that would be to accentuate the most obvious positive from The Hub. That is, the incandescent love I now feel for my Angie. As I nodded in agreement with myself, the old adage came to mind … you don't know what you've got until you've lost it. My wife's de facto infidelity (where I momentarily felt that I'd lost her to another man) certainly brought that home to me.

'And now that you appreciate what you've got,' I told myself, 'you have a heads-up. So use it wisely.'

As I continued to walk along the beach, I wondered how The Hub could be God working in mysterious ways, when I had to battle against my Catholic conscience. The answer to that question soon became clear to me. God's mysterious ways are just that, *mysterious*. That's why he made swinging part of his plan to save our marriage by making Angie's sex fantasy come true. And now she's scratched that itch, we can move forward with a clean slate!

* * *

Upon my return home, I decided to take five in the sitting room to gather my thoughts before catching up with Angie. She was in the outhouse office getting on with her bits and pieces. As I sat on the sofa, I wondered why she'd gone quiet about the whole swinging thing. I thought it might be down to my initial reaction to her after The Hub. Or perhaps, now that she'd scratched her itch, so to speak, her interest in swinging was satisfied. Whatever her reasons, it was now time to discuss that particular elephant in the room, because, despite feeling totally loved-up, I was a bit fretful that Angie wasn't a hundred per cent alright with me. And even though I concluded that a major part of her *forgotten me* had blossomed at The Hub, I needed reassurance that she was okay with me. With that in mind, I jumped up from the sofa and purposefully headed to the office.

* * *

'Hey sweetheart,' I said, having closed the office door behind me.

'Hey,' replied Angie, whilst beckoning me with her fingers without looking up, 'come here,' she said, 'I want to show you something.'

'I will in a minute,' I replied, taking my seat.

'What's up?' she asked.

'We need to talk about the elephant in the room,' I said.

'The Hub?'

'Yes,' I replied, 'The Hub.'

'I'm glad,' said Angie, having spun her chair round to look at me, 'because I thought you were a bit off with me about it.'

Having laughed out loud with relief, I told my wife that I wasn't off with her at all, and that in fact, I thought *she* was off with me. I then went on to say that I'd stupidly built up a negative picture in my own head.

'Same here,' she said. 'Aren't we silly?'

'We are,' I replied, before adding that what's done is done, and that we should focus on the positives and leave the rest behind.

'Agreed,' responded Angie, before asking me what I got from The Hub.

'Well,' I replied, 'I now realise how much I love you.'

'Oh Rich, that's so lovely.'

'I also appreciate what I've got,' I added, 'and will never take you for granted again.'

Sighing, with what I can only assume was relief, my wife told me that I'd made her really happy, and that she felt even more positive, because I was positive.

'So are we all good then my love?' I asked, widening my eyes questioningly.

'More than all good,' said a smiling Angie.

Really pleased that all was well, I just sat there grinning like a Cheshire cat. We both had our backs to our desks, and with just a metre and a half between us, I could clearly see the joy in my wife's eyes. Still smiling, I wheeled my chair over to her with my heels, before then leaning forward to kiss my soulmate on her lips.

'I love you Angie,' I whispered.

'I love you too,' she whispered back.

I then took hold of her hands and held them to my chest.

'So what have you taken away from our night of naughtiness, Angie?'

'Well, apart from the excitement of eating forbidden fruit,' she replied, 'The Hub has also taken our sex life to another level.'

'How exactly?'

'Well, we've been at it like rabbits since,' she replied, 'and every time I think about it, which is a lot, I get horny.'

'Me too,' I said.

'And I've had loads of plays,' she added, having gone red in the face.

Then, looking at me thoughtfully, she told me she was too embarrassed to say anything before, but now felt able to tell me everything. Pleased to hear that, I squeezed my Angie's hands that much tighter to my chest, as I contemplated telling her that I'd also had loads of plays as well. Then, too embarrassed to admit to that, I released her hands back to her, and instead asked her why she now felt able to tell me everything.

'Because you just said you realised how much you loved me,' she replied, 'and appreciate what you've got, and would never take me for granted again.'

I nodded and smiled in response, and then listened as my wife told me that she really liked telling me stuff.

'Especially because it makes me feel closer to you,' she added, 'and excites us both.'

Nodding in agreement, I then said that it was weird how we'd both been thinking about The Hub so much, and how it had brought us closer together. Angie totally agreed with me. She then told me that, now we'd talked about the elephant in the room, she felt we had a special connection.

'Things don't feel wrong or awkward between us,' she added, 'and we can do and say anything together!'

Smiling and nodding enthusiastically in agreement, I told my wife I felt the same way. I then asked her if she took any more positives from our night at The Hub.

'Well, if I'm honest,' she replied, 'our sex is even more exciting when I think about specific things.'

'What sort of things?'

'Touching Natalie all over and her eating my pussy,' replied Angie.

'What? When I'm making love to you?'

'Yes,' she said, 'but mostly when I have a play.'

I nodded and smiled, as I momentarily thought about my wife and Natalie at it. I guess every guy dreams of watching his wife making out with a beautiful woman. Only my dream came true.

'And when you do me doggy,' continued Angie, 'I think of how Marcus stretched me open like never before, when he pushed into me alongside your fingers.'

Hearing that made Black Dog bark. Spurred on by an adrenaline rush, a surge of jealousy ran through me, bringing an angry erection with it.

Now on the edge of my seat, I asked my wife, without

realising, what else she thought about.

'Well, also when you do me doggy,' she whispered sexily, as she leaned in towards me, 'I think of Marcus fingering my anus. I really loved that!'

'Sure,' I said, desperately trying not to be provoked into an angry fuck.

With our noses nearly touching, I looked deep into my woman's eyes as a feeling of inadequacy ran through me. Inadequacy at her need for imagery of Marcus whilst having sex with me. Especially when I thought I'd been doing such a good job by myself. As we were openly talking about things, I mentioned my upset to my wife.

'Remembering Marcus is not a poor reflection on you,' she replied. 'It's just that he's a new stimulus. Something new to bring to *our* sex party. And anyway,' she added, 'you said you've been thinking about it a lot as well, and that's made you horny.'

'Well yes,' I responded, 'I keep thinking about Marcus and you, and it makes me want you even more, and I get sexually possessive.'

'Well there you are,' said Angie, 'you think of Marcus too, but in a different way.'

Feeling reassured, I straightened-up in my seat and smiled. I then felt able to say that I'd been playing a lot as well.

'What? In addition to shagging me twice a day for the past week?'

'Yes,' I replied as I felt my face flush.

'You sexy, sly old dog you. Why didn't you just come and have your wicked way with me?'

'Well, you were mostly on the school run. And as soon as I thought of Marcus shagging you senseless, and your wanton desire for him, I became jealous and sexually possessive.'

'Oh wow!' sighed Angie, 'that's so fucking sexy. Its exciting to know I have that effect on you.'

She then told me she could tell that Black Dog had gone into one about Marcus, and pointed out that, by comparison, Black Dog didn't even bat an eyelid when she mentioned remembering sex with Natalie.

'Probably because she's not a threat to you.'

Utterly gobsmacked at my wife's incredible insight, I nodded in acknowledgment. She then asked me how I actually felt about Black Dog.

Having taken a deep breath, I sighed heavily as I wondered how to best describe my feelings without appearing to find fault with Angie. With my considerations fully formed, I told her that I had two similar responses.

'First there's Black Dog,' I began, 'who's fuelled by insecurity, jealousy and feelings of inadequacy. That drives me to angry sex with you.'

'Why?' asked Angie.

'To make sure you still want me,' I replied, 'and to prove myself to you as a lover, compared to my male competitors. Plus I get possessive,' I added. 'And I know I push our sexual boundaries, but only if you're okay with it.'

'Like I said before,' responded my wife, 'I love it. I feel desired and it's really primal and hardcore. And then you calm down,' she remarked, 'and become loving and warm again.'

'Yes,' I said, before adding that Black Dog morphs into my possessive lion response.

'So what's that exactly?' questioned Angie.

'It's a competitive sexual jealousy,' I responded, 'where

I'm driven to see off other males, claim you for myself, and mark my territory with my semen.'

'Semen?' repeated Angie.

Feeling my face redden with embarrassment, I explained how I felt the need to outperform my rival's semen, at just the thought of Angie wanting another man's ejaculate inside of her.

'Stupid I know.'

'It's primal,' said Angie, before adding that Black Dog and Lion were sort of similar.

'Unusual for a cat and dog,' I chuckled.

'Yeah,' responded Angie, mirroring my chuckle. 'So with Lion,' she continued, 'you wanna fight guys off, secure me for yourself, and make me pregnant?'

'Yes,' I said, nodding in agreement.

'I kind of like being fought over,' replied a slightly red-faced Angie, before suggesting that I was a bit of a Jekyll and Hyde character.

'I guess so,' I said.

'And then when Mr Hyde has had his wicked way with me,' she continued, 'the Good Doctor returns and you hold me close.'

I responded with a nod, and then smiled broadly as my wife told me that she really loved my Jekyll and Hyde persona.

'Because I feel taken and used by you,' she added, 'yet safe and protected because it's you.'

'And I feel like you've controlled me by my dick with your naughty girl persona,' I responded.

Laughing a wicked laugh, through an equally wicked smile, my Angie did admit to being a bit flirtatious sometimes.

'A bit,' I exclaimed. 'More like a total prick teaser!'

'Nooo!' she responded, tongue-in-cheek.

'No?' I playfully questioned. 'So what about bending over in front of Ryan with your pouting vajayjay barely covered by your knickers?'

'Did I actually do that?' questioned Angie.

'Yes,' I replied. 'And presenting your vulva like that is incredibly naughty and sexy. Not to mention the postie,' I added, 'you know, when you got your tits out for him.'

'Yes alright then,' retorted Angie, pretending to be cross at being rumbled, 'I'm a prick teaser. But you love it!' she insisted, wearing a coquettish grin. 'Don't you?'

As I nodded and smiled in response to my wife, I again realised that a perverse part of me enjoyed being teased. I guessed it was because I felt like a man when I took sexual control of my woman, in response to her sexual goading. Plus the sex act itself was totally base and way more exciting than when I made love to my Angie. It was ALL about the physical. No warmth of emotion, and no soulful connection. Angie also enjoyed this hardcore sex, and had told me that her new sexual feelings were amazing beyond belief. She also said that, but for the fact that I encouraged her to talk about her fantasies, she would have gone through life without fully exploring her sexuality.

Despite all these considerations, I was nevertheless concerned that I sometimes lost control a bit too much, and was a bit too sexually dominant. With that in mind, I asked my wife if she felt it wrong, in this modern age of feminism, for me to dominate her sexually and take her like a wild animal.

'No,' she said, 'like I said earlier, I love it when you sexually dominate and control me. And that doesn't make me any less of an independent woman,' she added, 'not in the least.'

'But am I being controlling?'

'Not at all,' replied my wife, 'you take *control* Rich, but you're not *controlling!*'

'Sure,' I sighed, 'but it's not exactly women on top, is it?'

'Some feminists would definitely have a go,' countered Angie, 'because they don't like men taking control, and they don't want to be submissive to a man in any way. But they're over-the-top! And ironically,' she continued, 'they actually control other women, who don't agree with their thinking.'

'Wow,' I exclaimed, 'that was some oration!'

'Well,' sighed my wife, 'only feminazis think giving any control to a man is weakness.'

As I smiled in response to my wife's particular brand of feminism, I thought how interesting it was to be discussing the experience we had at The Hub one minute, and then having a deep and meaningful discussion about feminism the next. I concluded that was the impressive nature of our connection. We could literally talk about anything and everything. I then told her that we should use Black Dog to our advantage now and again. She agreed.

Then, feeling like we'd talked the elephant in the room to death, I pushed my chair back to my desk with my heels. Once there, I suddenly remembered that Angie wanted to show me something when I came into the office. I asked her what it was. She looked at me with a sheepish smile.

'Come over here,' she said, before spinning her chair round to face her desk.

Following my wife's instruction, I stood up and stepped

over to her desk. As I stood behind her chair, she woke her computer up to reveal a swingers sex site.

'Swinging?!' I exclaimed, as Black Dog instantly reared his ugly head, despite my consideration that we could use him to our advantage just seconds ago.

'No, not swinging per se, silly,' dismissed my wife, 'they have competitions.'

'Competitions?' I repeated.

'Yes, ones where the wives get their tits out for the boys,' she said, hovering the cursor over "wife of the month".

There was a photo of Anna from Latvia naked on a sun-lounger with 'WorldWideWife – Wife of the Month' written above her head. She was leaning back with her palms planted behind her. With her feet together to force her thighs wide open, she looked like she was in labour. *Everything* was on show.

'So what's this got to do with you then?' I asked crossly, as my negative default setting for anything new kicked in.

'With proper photos,' replied Angie, 'I reckon I could be wife of the month.'

'Wife of the month Angie?' I questioned with a screwed-up face.

'Yes,' she replied, swivelling her chair around to look up at me. 'And I'll win fifty euros!'

Good God Almighty, I screamed in my head, how can she want to aspire to that? At this point, I realised my marriage hadn't actually exorcised its demons. And even with proper management, I now doubted that life would get back to normal anytime soon. I was finding it hard to let my wife be who she wanted to be, despite knowing that the secret to success in any marriage, is to never change the person your spouse is.

Angie returned her gaze to the screen and waited for me to say something. I suggested that she didn't want to be wife of the month for money.

'No, it's not for the money, Rich,' she replied thoughtfully. 'It's probably because The Hub has raised the benchmark of expectation. And anyway,' she added, 'whatever happened to us using Black Dog to our advantage, and you realising how much you loved me?'

Completely ignoring my wife's question, I just said that The Hub was a one-off.

'I know,' she replied, 'but I really enjoyed it, and posting on WorldWideWife will be fun too.'

'So do you think posting pics is a substitute for The Hub?'

'Well, as you want to focus on the positives and leave The Hub behind,' replied my wife, 'I suppose it must be.'

'But why do you actually need to post photos at all, Angie?'

'If I'm honest,' she replied, 'it's attention-seeking naughtiness, and it makes me feel good.'

'Yes, but why?'

'Perhaps I don't want to be invisible anymore,' suggested my wife with a shrug of her shoulders. 'You know, just being another ordinary mum and wife trapped in a life without any meaningful self-determination.'

'But you're not just another ordinary mum and wife,' I protested.

'I am!' insisted my wife. 'And thanks to you,' she added with a look of disgust, 'I can't work till I'm out of my bankruptcy. I'm not even sure I'll be any good as a barrister anymore anyway, even if I could find work!'

'You'll be fine,' I retorted sharply.

'It's not just about being a good barrister, Rich,' declared my wife. 'I need to prove myself. I need to be me and have some much-needed fun!'

With that said, she dropped her gaze to her lap and folded her arms defensively. Still standing beside her chair, I straightened up to my full height and sighed heavily. I then told her that her reputation as a barrister would be in tatters if WorldWideWife ever came to light. She immediately lifted her gaze to meet mine and reminded me, yet again, that it was my fault she couldn't practise. Needless to say, I felt like shit after hearing that, because the truth hurt. Having bowed my head in shame, a sense of guilt then weighed heavily on my mind. That thought was soon overtaken though, as the possibility of Livy and Connor coming across pornographic pictures of their mum suddenly struck me. I immediately shared my concerns with my wife, and added that her family, my family, and our friends could also stumble across her pictures.

'Most people view porn at some time in their life,' I continued, 'even if it's just to satisfy a passing curiosity.'

'Rich!' sighed an exasperated Angie, 'please credit me with some intelligence. The possibility of people we know seeing my pictures was a worry to me initially. But then when I thought about it, I realised they were never going to see me, because WorldWideWife is a swingers site.'

'I know that,' I replied, 'but ...'

'No buts about it,' interrupted Angie. 'If people want to look at porn online, they look at videos.'

'Yeah, but all the porn sites post each other's porn,' I responded.

'You're surprisingly well informed on these matters, Rich,' retorted a cross-sounding Angie, 'but what you haven't taken into account is that I'm only posting photos, and photos are not shared across porn sites, only videos are.'

Unable to challenge my wife's argument, I just remained quiet and considered what else I could use to dissuade her.

'How are you gonna find time for all this?' I suddenly demanded. 'Life is pretty full on with the children as it is.'

'This is not going to affect my time with them,' insisted my wife. 'I love being their mum, and they will always take priority. We can do the photos when they're at school, and I'll do all my online stuff, which won't be much by the way, when they're in bed. It's just a bit of fun,' she added, before reminding me that she wasn't allowed to practise as a barrister and so had plenty of time on her hands.

There was that nasty little snipe yet again. Deliberately side-lining the guilt-trip my wife was trying to put me on, I immediately countered by suggesting that the children might stumble upon her online activities or her computer history.

'Don't be so bloody silly!' she retorted. 'We have sex all the time and the children don't stumble upon us, do they? We know how to be discreet. And as for my computer history, my laptop and office computer are password protected, *and* the children have their own computers.'

'Well yeah, I guess so,' I reluctantly replied.

Then, having run out of counter-arguments, I momentarily contemplated letting my wife do her thing. A second later though, I was reviled by the thought of a load of pervy blokes masturbating over intimate photos of her, and told her as much.

'Just moments ago you were saying how much you loved me,' responded Angie. 'You said we were close, but now you're judging me and using every trick in the book to slut-shame and control me. I'm disappointed to say the least.'

'I'm not trying to shame or control you,' I replied, 'all I'm saying is that blokes on here won't respect you.'

'Why wouldn't they?' demanded my wife, drilling her stare into me. 'They're not all pervs and misogynists you know. They're just ordinary red-blooded males who appreciate a woman's form.'

'Of course they are!' I retorted sarcastically.

Still staring at me, my wife told me that it was interesting how I didn't view the increasing number of women who use porn, the same way as I did men.

Unable to counter the sense in my wife's argument, I turned my gaze away from hers to gather my thoughts. I realised I wanted to judge the women on WorldWideWife as immoral. With that consideration in mind, I stopped looking at my wife in a bad light. However this didn't mean that I felt able to support her going forward.

With the silence becoming difficult to bear, I lowered my gaze. There was Angie looking up at me with tear-drenched eyes. And, with her head tipped pathetically to one side, she looked sadder than sad.

'WorldWideWife is nothing like The Hub,' she piped up. 'There's no sex or anything. Just a few naughty pics, that's all!'

'I know Angie but ...'

'Rich!' she interrupted through a dramatic sigh. 'I've lived my life in chains, and never even knew I had the key!'

'Had the key?' I questioned.

'Yes, the key to free myself from undue moral chains,' replied Angie, 'and from just being your wife and the children's mother. I need to be recognised in my own right!'

'Recognised in your own right?'

'Yes,' she replied. 'I mean, when we were in business, I was always introduced as your wife, even though I was a director of the company too.'

'So?'

'So, I lost my identity.'

Not really understanding what my wife was on about, I just looked at her and shrugged my shoulders.

'You say you love me Rich,' she said, 'and you say you'd do anything for me, but you won't, will you?'

'I will,' I insisted.

'Richie,' sighed an exasperated Angie, as she wiped her tears away with her hand, 'I thought we had an amazing connection where things didn't feel wrong or awkward between us. You know, like I said earlier, where we can do anything together.'

As I searched for the right thing to say, my wife seized the conversation. She reminded me that I'd said we should take the positives from The Hub. She then also reminded me that I was cool with her flirting, and clearly very happy with how it excited me in the bedroom.

'Teasing anonymous guys online,' she continued, 'isn't even real life!'

Having looked away from my wife, I reluctantly agreed with her argument. However, the better part of me couldn't quite go with it. Why? Because, despite my desire to give my wife whatever she wanted, and despite my perverse desire for jealous sex, I didn't know for sure if WorldWideWife was going to be the tip of some debauched, marriage-wrecking iceberg. So yes, my feelings were conflicted.

In the absence of a reply from me, Angie told me that it

made her feel really sexy and desired, when good-looking men found her attractive.

'And that makes me want you even more,' she continued. 'So everyone's a winner!'

With neither of us willing to comment further on the matter, we remained silent for a bit until Angie suddenly dropped her head in her hands and began crying again. I perched my bum on the edge of her desk and gently lifted her face with my fingers.

'I probably couldn't compete anyway, Rich,' she sobbed, before slapping my hand away. 'I mean look at me,' she added, gesturing to herself, 'I'm a forty-six-year-old middle-aged woman with wobbly bits!'

With my bum still perched on Angie's desk, I took hold of her hands and held them to my lap. She then stared up at me expectantly. She looked like a little girl lost, which made me want to gather her up in my arms and protect her.

'The way I see it,' I began, 'is that you like attention from men because it stops you feeling invisible.'

'Yes.'

'And turning them on excites you, and makes you want me even more?'

'Yes.'

'And flirting,' I continued, 'helps to restore your self-esteem, which I robbed you of?'

'Yes.'

'And being "wife of the month" will release you from undue chains of morality and boost your confidence?'

'Yes.'

With my summing-up complete, and still holding her hands, I looked deep into my wife's Bambi eyes. My heart felt the need to make things right by providing for her in some way, especially as I wasn't providing for her financially anymore. Weighing against that desire, was my concern that WorldWideWife could be the tip of some disastrous iceberg.

Then, a moment later, having finally weighed up all the pros and cons in my head, I decided that a few naughty pics would do my wife and my marriage the world of good. And, knowing I could never handle Angie having sex with another man again, WorldWideWife was a walk in the park by comparison.

With a massive smile on my face, I lifted my wife's hands to my lips and kissed them. Then, holding them to my chest, I told her that I would support her efforts to be wife of the month.

'Do you really mean that though, Richie?' she asked.

'Yes,' I said positively, before adding that I'd always fancied myself as a photographer.

'Oh Rich,' sighed my wife, 'you don't know how much this means to me!'

'I'm so pleased my love,' I said, returning her hands to her. 'Just as long as it's not the thin edge of some disastrous wedge?'

'Don't be silly,' came Angie's immediate reply. 'This is *all* I want.'

With my happy grin still glued to my face, I watched my wife turn to look out of the window to gather her thoughts. I could hear the cogs going round in her head.

'I'll create an account on WorldWideWife in readiness for my "debut" posting,' she announced excitedly. 'And oh!' she quickly added, turning sharply to look at me, 'I'll need to get in better shape, so you'll need to increase my workout.'

My wife's whole demeanour had now changed. She

suddenly oozed confidence and was a woman on a mission.

'And I wanna be ready in three weeks,' she continued with considerable urgency. 'Can you do it?'

'Of course!' I replied. 'I've got just the thing.'

'Great!' said Angie, before standing up to kiss me full on. Pleased to see my wife so happy, I responded enthusiastically.

'Ooh baby,' she whispered, having eased back from my embrace, 'you're turning me on!'

'Good,' I said, before picking her up in a cradle lift to resume our kissing.

A moment later, I let her feet drop to the floor. I then eased her down so she was sitting on the carpet. Kneeling beside her, I unbuttoned her light floral frock, before sliding the shoulder straps down her arms so that her dress gathered round her waist. I then unclipped her bra and tossed it aside. Having grabbed my back support cushion from my desk chair, I laid my wife flat and deftly placed it on the floor in time to meet her head. As I stroked her body, and dreamily watched my fingers running over her porcelain skin, she reached up to unbutton my jeans, but I diverted her hand away.

'I just wanna look at you,' I said in a low voice, 'like people do a beautiful work of art.'

'Ahhh,' sighed my wife, 'what a lovely thing to say.'

'You should be hanging in the National Gallery, Angie,' I whispered, 'like Rubens's *Samson and Delilah*.'

'Ahhh,' she again sighed, looking at me adoringly, making me feel loved.

'Delilah got her boobs out centuries ago,' I continued, 'and put Samson under her erotic spell. You've done the same to me.'

'Only you haven't got the hair,' quipped Angie, bringing a smile to my face. 'Plus it didn't end well for him,' she added, laughing so much that her breasts wobbled on her chest.

Really amused by my wife's humour, I too began laughing. Now we were both in fits of laughter, just being ourselves and having fun.

'Well you certainly know how to ruin the moment,' I said, having finally caught my breath.

'Sorry,' chortled my wife, 'but you really set yourself up by choosing that painting.'

'I know,' I said. 'I should have gone for the *Judgement of Paris*. The Goddess Aphrodite actually looks like you. She won the beauty competition and was presented with the golden apple by Paris.'

From her Rubenesque prone position, my Angie looked up at me and smiled.

'I'm honoured to be your goddess,' she said, before telling me that she'd need to show off more than just her boobs to win wife of the month.

Smiling in response, I told my beloved that I would show her off as beautifully as any Rubens. Quite incredibly, that warm thought made my penis grow to full size.

'And will you be proud of me when I'm wife of the month?' asked a doubtful-sounding Angie.

'Of course,' I responded, as I admired her entire body from my kneeling position.

'I love you with all my heart Richard Rowe,' declared my wife, 'and I'm the luckiest woman in the world to have you. And all this stuff we're doing will make our marriage stronger,' she added. 'It already has!'

Having widened my eyes in agreement, I brushed my

Angie's hair off her forehead. I then traced my fingers down her face and stroked her softly from her neck to her breasts and back again. I could see her pretty face relax as she closed her eyes. I then gently caressed both her breasts. I loved the closeness and warmth of her smooth yielding flesh, giving way in my big warm hands. At the same time, my eyes savoured the sight of my woman's erect nipples popping up between my fanned-out fingers, as I ran them across her softness.

'You've hit the jackpot there,' she whispered. 'That's gone straight to my pussy.'

'Hmmm,' I sighed, before leaning over to run my tongue round and round the areola of her left booby, taking extra care to avoid her nipple.

I knew my Angie loved the anticipation of me filling my mouth with as much breast as I could, before then concentrating on sucking, tonguing, and biting her nipples. Before long, I did just that. My Angie sighed and moaned with pleasure. That sent extra excitement to my pulsating penis.

With my mouth still locked on to my wife's beautiful softness, I slid my spare hand down over her gathered dress and onward to her thighs. I then slid my hand back up again, bringing her dress with it so it was gathered round her middle. I always knew to do this, because even though my Angie knew I loved her mummy tummy, she was a bit self-conscious about it. So, being confident about her thigh/arse/pussy combo, as she called it, she felt sexier and more sexually empowered with her tummy covered-up.

Kneeling up a little straighter, I again surveyed my pretty wife lying there in her M&S big girl white knickers, ankle socks and blue and white pumps. To me, she portrayed the very essence of carefree innocence. And, despite her forty-six years, she hadn't lost her inner girl, and I loved that.

Licking my lips in anticipation, I pushed my woman's thighs apart. She loved me doing that because it felt like I was taking her. I knew what she liked, and took pleasure in providing it.

As I ran my hand up and down Angie's mons pubis over her knickers a few times, I watched her eyes moving beneath her eyelids as she savoured my touch. Observing her exquisite half smile, I took hold of her big girl pants. She lifted her bum, and I slipped them off.

Pausing to look closely at my wife's delicious womanhood, I felt my caged penis pulse out yet more pre cum. Leaning forward, I kissed her smooth opening lightly without pushing my tongue inside. Then, sucking each of her lips into my mouth in turn, I pulled them up a little before releasing them. I repeated this process many times before French kissing her vagina like it was her mouth. My tongue inside her, probing and searching whilst enjoying her taste and scent. Then, holding her open with my fingers, I licked her clitoris until it was stimulated and proud. To intensify her pleasure, I slipped two fingers inside her and massaged her g-spot at the same time.

As my Angie neared orgasm, her hips began gyrating. I matched the rhythm of her gyrations with my tongue and fingers. With my mouth locked onto her body, I moved in complete harmony with her pelvic movements. She then lifted her bum high off the carpet. With a reverse arch in her back, she let out a series of half sighs, half grunts …

'Arghhh! Arghhh! Arghhh!'

With each involuntary moan, she squeezed her thighs tighter still round my face, whilst trying to push my head away with her hands.

Knowing that my woman had orgasmed, I remained locked-on for a moment longer, licking and fingering at a slower pace, before then easing away from her super-sensitive clitoris, once she had relaxed her bum back down onto the floor. Having then gently and lovingly kissed her vulva for a moment, the urge to be even closer to my wife suddenly overwhelmed me. Jumping to my feet, I kicked my trainers off and dropped my jeans. My penis pinged up with a sense of urgency. Angie smiled and then looked at me longingly. With our eyes locked together, I straddled her and slowly pushed inside her wet, warm vagina. She moaned with each inch of penetration.

'Love you, my big teddy bear,' she whispered, stroking the side of my face. 'Always will.'

'Love you too, Angie darling,' I whispered back.

Then, taking hold of her hands, I placed them above her head and settled into an easy rhythm. With excited eyes, I watched her breasts wobble with each soulful penetration.

After a few minutes, I switched to a kneeling position, so I could enjoy the vista of my physical connection with my woman. Pushing her ankles over her head, I re-entered her. I was in heaven. I just couldn't get enough of her. I wanted her Rubenesque image painted on the walls, so I could see even more of her. Having slowed to a stop, I remained inside my woman and observed her soft sensual body. She opened her eyes.

'You're beautiful, my Angie,' I whispered urgently, whilst gazing into the windows of her soul. 'Every inch a woman,' I added. 'And every inch a goddess.'

'Aww,' she sighed, reaching up to stroke my face, 'you really do know how to make a girl feel special.'

I smiled at my wife, exuding warmth and affection.

'I wanna ride you, my big man,' she suddenly whispered. 'I wanna pleasure you; do the work and watch you enjoying me.'

With that said, she then bucked her hips up a little to prompt me to move. I dismounted. She knelt up straight. I then laid down on the floor. With my proud erection waiting to be ridden by the most beautiful woman in the world, my heart skipped a beat. Having straddled me, my wife's warm eyes locked onto mine. I was transfixed. Her hand then found my cock and drew it over her lips, until it reached her opening. With a firm grip on my shaft, she slowly sank onto me.

'Arghhh,' I sighed with pleasure. 'Fuck that feels good!'

Looking at me with wicked eyes that said more than words could say, my Angie slowly rode me, with her back beautifully straight, like she was doing the rising trot.

A few minutes later, I closed my eyes and focused on the amazing sensation of being fucked by my woman. A while after that, I felt her hands on my chest and opened my eyes. I observed her gorgeous, tousled hair swinging back and forth with each rise and fall. Our eyes again locked together, until the gentle sway of my woman's glorious hanging breasts caught my attention. I wanted to suck and gently grip her big nipples with my teeth, like a dog does your hand in love. But being pinned down and unable to partake of the hanging fruit, I happily contented myself with watching them sway in time to our sex rhythm.

My woman's dulcet sighs, the touch of her body on mine, and the scent of our sex filled up my senses to overflowing. This erotic, sensual and spiritual moment, took me to a beautiful place, where the focus was holistic.

Mind, body, and soul.

Taking her palms off my chest, my Angie straightened up and continued her rising trot. I reached my big hands up and caressed her breasts, whilst at the same time synchronising small, upward pelvic thrusts in time with her rhythm. I now longed to see the point of our most intimate union, and so traced my hands down my woman's soft body, past her tummy to where we met. Having raised my head, I stretched my wife's tummy up so as to view our physical connection.

'You want to see more, my big man?' my lover asked in a husky voice.

'Yes,' I whispered. 'I can't get enough of you!'

With a wickedly smug smile on her face, Angie closed her eyes and leant backwards. She then gripped my ankles. Now I could clearly see her opening impaled on me. Looking both beautiful and dirty at the same time, she replaced the rising trot, with a to and fro motion. Watching her take control like a femme fatale was amazing. I reached over and rubbed her proud clitoris with the tips of two fingers.

A few moments later, my lover suddenly sped up. I instantly picked up the pace of my clitoral massage to match her speed. After a short time, my huffing and puffing Angie began moaning in time to her rhythm. Then, panting from exertion, she suddenly let out a huge 'Arghhh!', whilst writhing in ecstasy.

'Oh wow,' she finally whispered, having allowed her torso to fall onto my chest, 'that was amazing!'

Smiling with pride and contentment, I slid my arms round my wife's back and cuddled her tight. I then asked her, without knowing why, what she was thinking of.

'Honestly?' she panted.

'Of course honestly,' I replied.

'I was thinking about Marcus.'

My wife's response instantly antagonised Black Dog, wiping the contentment right off my face, as a visceral surge of jealousy ran straight through me. With my heart banging in my chest at an almighty rate, I demanded to know why my wife would think of Marcus, when I was the one making love to her.

'It's like I said before,' she replied. 'It's exciting.'

Angry at her admission, despite being grateful for her honesty, I drilled my stare straight into my woman's eyes. She stared right back at me with a knowing half smile on her face. A millisecond later, I bucked her off me and forcefully flipped her onto her front. Then, having slid my hand under her tummy, I pulled her up onto all fours and knelt behind her.

'Oh but Richie,' she protested mockingly, 'you said we should use Black Dog to our advantage and take positives from The Hub!'

Angry and incensed, I grabbed the base of my throbbing shaft, and drew my cockhead along my wife's labia until I found her opening.

'What exactly were you thinking?' I demanded gruffly, as I rammed into her.

'Ahhh,' she moaned, 'nothing.'

'Tell me!' I insisted, before again ramming into my woman, this time accompanied by a hard slap to her big round arse.

'Well, if you must know my private thoughts,' replied a slightly breathless Angie, 'I was thinking about Marcus fucking me doggy, and about when he squeezed my nipples really hard.'

'Yeah?' I questioned.

'Oh yeah,' goaded my wife, 'and it went straight to my pussy,' she added, 'just like he said it would.'

'And do you want Marcus here now to squeeze your nipples, Angie?' I demanded through clenched teeth.

'God yeah,' she sighed. 'And the rest!'

Now outraged and completely overwhelmed by my lion response, I bent forward and slipped both my hands around my woman to find her hanging breasts. Whilst continuing my pumping action, I angrily told her that I was going to teach her a lesson.

'I'll fucking show you Angie!' I declared, as I pinched both her nipples really hard.

'Ow, ow, oww!' she yelled, as she wriggled onto me with pleasure, just like she'd done with Marcus.

After keeping the pumping and pinching going a few minutes longer, I suddenly asked my wife whose cock she wanted.

'Marcus's,' she replied. 'And you love that,' she added, 'because you wanna be cuckolded, don't you?'

'No!' I insisted, with a slap to her arse.

'Yes!' retorted Angie. 'You loved seeing Marcus stretching me open,' she continued, 'and I loved feeling him building up to come deep inside me.'

'He shouldn't have done that,' I responded gruffly.

'Oh yes he should have,' insisted my wife, 'because I excited him so much that he shot his cum right up me. He filled me up before you did,' she added, 'and so what are you gonna do about that then?'

'I'm gonna come deep in you right now,' I declared through clenched teeth, 'deeper and harder than anyone else, that's what I'm gonna do about it, Angie. Do you understand?'

'Yes,' she whispered.

'And am I stretching your pussy open more than your lover did?' I demanded to know.

In the absence of a positive reply from my wife, I released her nipples and slapped her arse vengefully. I then re-gripped her hips to control her. She responded by wriggling back onto my cock with pleasure.

'Yes,' she finally replied, 'you're stretching me open more than Marcus did.'

'You see,' I growled, 'size does matter!'

With an absolute imperative to shoot deeper into my wife than anyone else could, I pounded her with all I had, whilst at the same time pulling her onto me for maximum penetration. I kept this up for a good few minutes, huffing, puffing, and grunting as I went. With my body tense, sweaty and nearing exhaustion, I felt my mate tighten around me. She then began chanting, 'No, no, no.' She was coming. It was intense for her. And despite her no's, she didn't want me to stop. And anyway, I wasn't going to, because I was building up to come in her, deeper, much deeper than her lover did.

'Do you want my cum, Angie, or Marcus's?' I demanded gruffly, as I gripped her hip fat hard with my fingers and rammed into her at speed.

'I want both,' she panted, 'just like at The Hub.'

'You're just gonna get mine!' I insisted, before again ramming hard into my woman as the first wave of semen spurted out of me. Then, having pulled out of her, I again rammed home as another wave of angry, primal ejaculation hit me. One more hard, deep thrust to release the remainder of my semen, and I was done.

Fixed to the spot, I panted like a dog, as the tension in

my body slowly dissipated. With my fading erection still inside my wife's vagina, I leaned forward and kissed her back lovingly.

'Jesus Richie,' she whispered breathlessly, 'that was off the scale!'

Having said that, she then collapsed from her doggy position to flat on her tummy, taking me with her.

After a quiet moment, I rolled off my wife. She was face down; I was face up. We remained in this easy quietness for a while, as we both caught our breath. Then, having found the energy to move, Angie repositioned herself onto her side, and rested her head on my chest. She then bent her leg at the knee, before laying it across my crotch. We were now in our favourite snuggling position.

'You alright my love?' I whispered.

'Oh yes,' sighed Angie softly. 'I feel all peaceful inside.'

'Do you really?'

'Absolutely. And I feel loved, safe and protected.'

At this point, Angie and I fell into a momentary silence, until she asked me how the sex was for me.

'Incredible,' I replied. 'You were amazing!'

'I'm so glad.'

'And do you actually like thinking about Marcus?' I asked. 'And when you tell me about it, is that just to get me going sort of thing?'

'Well, yes I do like thinking about Marcus,' responded my wife. 'He adds to my excitement. And yes,' she continued, 'I tell you about him because it gets you going, and that excites me even more. Plus I feel sexually empowered. It's like you said, this is us taking advantage of Black Dog and The Hub. Everyone's a winner!'

Satisfied with my wife's explanation, I nodded in

response. I then savoured the beauty of our spiritual and physical closeness, just like I'd done in the car after The Hub. I was once again deeply moved by the act of physically loving my woman; albeit warmly and soulfully to begin with, and then rampant like a lion at the end. I thought I'd known sublime love with my Angie before, but since The Hub, I'd discovered a new level of emotion. Hitherto, I never knew that two people could feel so deeply connected, just by the sheer force of love they felt for each other.

Overwhelmed by my beautiful epiphany, I felt tears forming in my eyes. Then, with the next blink, I felt them cascade down my cheeks. With a soft sigh and a contented smile, I snuggled my Angie that much closer to me. I then silently offered thanks to the Almighty, for the exquisite love he'd most graciously sent me.

CHAPTER 21

Nearly three weeks had passed since Angie had decided to go for wife of the month. She was a woman on a mission who was dieting and exercising with a purpose. She had a real spring in her step.

It made me happy beyond measure to see her so full of the joys of life. There was no doubt in my mind that she would still be down in the dumps and unfulfilled had we not discovered the wilder side of life.

Without wishing to go on about it, my wife's freedom to be who she wants to be without judgement or reproach, has been the making of us.

With my more liberated approach to love and marriage, I felt much lighter of heart. Now, I could support my Angie's quest to be wife of the month with pleasure.

Giving love to your wife is such a joy, especially when she returns that love manyfold and is so appreciative. Plus, I get to take naughty pictures of the sexiest woman I know. What could be better than that?

Angie had uploaded a few face pics to her profile page on WorldWideWife. She was very pleasantly surprised at the number of friends requests she had from guys who really fancied her just from the look of her pretty face. These 'friends', as she called them, were really excited to see her first set of photos and had been discussing the sort of poses they wanted to see. Apparently, they got very horny just talking about her photos. My beautiful wife was really excited and flattered by this, even though the whole wife of the month thing gave her butterflies.

* * *

'I'm just gonna take a quick shower,' announced Angie, as she handed me a steaming mug of tea. 'I won't shave my bits though,' she added, 'as there isn't time.'

As I wrapped my welcoming fingers round my mug, I nodded and smiled at my wife, without really understanding why she'd mentioned shaving her bits. She then turned on her heel and disappeared into the ensuite. A second later she popped her head round the door and reminded me that we were going to Truro today.

'Truro?' I questioned.

'Yes, you remember?' replied Angie. 'I couldn't find what I wanted when I went with Livy. And anyway,' she added, 'it was a bit embarrassing shopping for lingerie with her.'

'Oh yes,' I said slowly, as the penny finally dropped.

'I'm nervous but excited,' remarked Angie.

'Nervous?' I repeated, wrinkling my nose, 'you're only buying a bustier.'

'Yes, but it's the thought of posing in it that gives me butterflies.'

'You're absolutely gorgeous sweetheart,' I insisted enthusiastically. 'They're gonna love you. No doubt about it!'

'Hopefully,' said an irresolute Angie, before disappearing

back into the ensuite.

Having sighed heavily, I sunk back into my pillows and sipped my tea. The doubt in my wife's voice troubled me. Why? Because crazy though it sounds, her self-esteem and confidence were at stake over wife of the month. I therefore knew that failure wasn't an option. Angie had to be a wife of the month, and that was that.

All you need to do Richie boy, I thought to myself, is make that happen.

'Simples!' I whispered, before gulping down the rest of my tea.

* * *

With Angie showered, dressed, and getting breakfast, I headed to Phoebe's room, salivating at the smell of cooking bacon as it wafted upstairs. My wife was amazing; she often kept several plates spinning at once … bacon on; wake the children; turn the bacon; make the butties; do the packed lunches; and so it went on. And always with a smile on her face.

On a school day, my job was to get the children dressed and ready by the back door with whatever they needed for that day. This included sports kit, homework, show and tell, parental permissions and money if required.

Having drawn the curtains aside in Phoebe and Archie's room, I paused to look out of the window. Admiring the view, I smiled with contentment as I once again appreciated the beauty and joy in my life. I figured this extra appreciation and newly acquired capacity to be in the present, was as a result of nearly losing my marriage, after Angie's revelations about her past.

Also, you would've thought that most spouses would have ongoing issues having seen their partner at it with someone else. But no, contrary to normal expectations, I now loved and valued Angie more than ever before, and she loved me even more as well.

All in all, I viewed the ill effects of my wife's revelations and the blossoming of her *forgotten me*, as a blessing in disguise. Why? Because I now knew her better than ever before. In addition to that, our marriage nearly failed when she called for divorce in the car, and I went mad. Nearly losing my family ensemble was a valuable wake-up call to me. Thankfully, I was lucky enough to realise that, and was now determined to seize my second chance with both hands.

Coming out of my strange reverie, I wiped my unexpected tears away with my sleeve, and knelt down beside Phoebe's bed. I looked down at her lying there with her mouth slightly open, and a lock of hair stuck to her cheek with dried dribble. Smiling, I gently gathered the wisps of hair in my fingers and swept them behind my little girl's ear. Looking closely at her beautiful repose, I paused before disturbing her slumber.

'Wakey wakey Phoebe darling.'

She opened her eyes in response and smiled at me. She then snuggled the duvet tight under her chin.

'Do you want a bacon butty for brekkie?' I asked, beaming at her.

Having closed her eyes, she nodded enthusiastically.

'And do you want one of Dadda's special banana milkshakes?' I asked, 'with chocolate sprinkles on?'

My Phoebe again nodded without speaking. Then, before I could respond, I was caught by surprise when Archie jumped on top of me and unbalanced me, causing us both to land in a heap on the floor.

'Now you're in for it Archie!' I growled, rising to my knees. 'The *claw* is gonna get you!'

The claw was a rip off from Jim Carrey's *Liar Liar* – mine and Angie's favourite comedy. Bending my arm at the elbow, I made a claw of my fingers and relentlessly pecked at Archie. As I did so, Phoebe joined in the affray. I pecked and tickled the pair of them until they eventually overpowered my arm.

'Okay! Okay!' I pleaded in my Captain Sam Brady's pirate voice. 'I give in. Now let the claw up, and he'll leave you alone.'

Captain Sam Brady was a character I created to fit with the pirate theme in Devon. The children loved hearing stories about him. He was a good, but mischievous pirate who loved children.

'Do you promise to leave us alone?' asked Phoebe, as she and Archie continued to pin my arm to the floor like their lives depended on it.

'Promise hearties,' I replied, sobbing like a broken man.

Showing mercy, my two little ones released my arm.

'Well helps your old captain up then, shipmates,' I said.

Jumping up, my two little ones pulled me to my feet. And then, before they knew what was happening, I scooped them both up at the same time, one under each arm.

'Aa ha!' I cried. 'I lied me hearties! Now I'm gonna clamp you in irons and steal you away in the *Golden Pearl*.'

Phoebe let out three shrill, ear-piercing screams as she and Archie flailed around wildly, just because they could.

Having thrown the two of them onto the bed, I left them with instructions to clean their teeth and get dressed.

Upon leaving their room, I again encountered the

smell of sizzling bacon, and was subliminally drawn to the kitchen. En route, I came upon Connor on the landing looking frustrated.

'This is ridiculous,' he said, looking straight at me with his sparkling green eyes, 'I've got toothpaste on my jumper.'

'This is indeed ridiculous,' I responded, keen to repeat his latest word. 'Just wipe it off with a damp flannel and it will be dry by the time you get to school.'

With that said, I grabbed him round the neck with my forearm, and kissed the top of his head in a rough, laddish way.

'Daaad!' he protested, before disappearing into the family bathroom.

Pleased to have been of help, I continued on to the kitchen.

At the bottom of the stairs I literally bumped into Livy. She looked concerned.

'What's up big girl?' I asked, as I wondered why even just the smallest thing was always such a big problem for my teenagers, particularly on a school day.

'My skirt's not dry, Dadda,' she replied, holding it up in front of her.

'Don't worry,' I whispered, taking the skirt off her, 'I'll iron it dry.'

'Well if she'd put her uniform in the laundry basket,' said Angie from the kitchen, sounding a little cross, 'we wouldn't have this problem!'

'Wow, you've got superhero hearing,' I said, genuinely surprised at being overheard.

Wearing a big grin, I playfully mocked Angie by screwing my face up and mimicking a jabbering mouth with my fingers. Olivia smiled a knowing conspirator's smile, before scooting off to her bedroom.

'Livy gets her carelessness from me,' I said, having ventured into the kitchen.

'That's all well and good,' retorted Angie, 'except, unlike when you were a boy in Africa, Livy hasn't got servants to pick up after her!'

Not inclined to get into a debate about my untidiness with my slightly stressed wife, I simply smiled agreeably before disappearing into the utility room. Then, having ironed Livy's skirt dry, I delivered it to her bedroom, and returned to the kitchen. Standing by the back door, I smiled as I watched my wife gliding towards me with a bacon butty in one hand, and a steaming cuppa in the other.

'You're poetry in motion, Angie darling,' I said, smiling.

'I know,' she replied, before thrusting my breakfast into my hands.

Having washed my bacon butty down with my tea, I quickly made two milkshakes with chocolate sprinkles on, and placed them on the table for Phoebe and Archie. Angie had already put orange juice out for Livy and Connor, and was just finishing the bacon butties.

With the food on the table, I called 'Breakfast!' up the stairwell. The children soon arrived and took their seats at the dining table. They then wolfed their breakfast down in record time.

With everyone marshalled out of the back door, I set the alarm and locked up. I loved this morning blast of frenetic family activity. It made me feel I was living life!

As we proceeded slowly down the long farm track towards the main road, I slipped my hard rock CD into the sound system. I then paused it in readiness for some fun en route to school. Then after a few moments, Phoebe suddenly suggested I do the register.

'Yes, do the register Dadda,' enthused Archie, clapping his hands.

Taking the register first began, tongue in cheek, after we almost left one of the children behind in the chaos of a rushed morning. After calling each name, I would add a bespoke witticism or simply insult the little ones with toilet humour, which they of course loved.

'Ridiculous Rowe?' I bellowed like a public school master.

'Of course I'm here, Dad,' he said, 'don't be ridiculous!'

'Archie farty poo head?' I called out.

'You're a farty, poo, bogey and wee head, Dadda,' he replied, pleased he'd delivered his superior insults with gusto. 'So there!'

Impressed with my son's retort, I caught his eye in the rear-view mirror and smiled. He smiled his big beaming smile right back at me, warming my heart in the process.

'What about Mum?' said Phoebe.

'Oh yes,' I replied, 'what name shall we have for mum? How about, yummy mummy with her muffin-top tummy?'

'Harsh!' said Livy.

'Harsh?' I questioned.

'Yes Daddy,' said a smiling Angie, 'harsh!'

Smiling in response, I told Angie that, in common with most discerning men, I adored her womanly curves.

'You've got all the right junk in all the right places,' I enthused.

'Oooh, very hip Dadda,' chuckled Livy.

Pleased to have impressed my big girl, I went on to insult her and Phoebe with renewed enthusiasm. They loved it and enjoyed hurling insults right back at me.

With the register out of the way, I became preoccupied with my own thoughts. As the sound of animated chit-chat faded into the background, I admired the ever-changing vista which unfolded before me. Brown, yellow, and green fields, tall leafy hedges, long stone walls, birds of prey swooping nearby and today, deep blue skies. Richard Rowe, I said to myself nodding with satisfaction, you're a lucky, lucky man.

Feeling the need to thank the Lord for his kindness, I began praying in my head. Thank you for all the beauty you have bestowed upon me. Please let me be a successful trader so that I can build a secure future for the family. And please let Angie's first posting be a resounding success, to restore her confidence and self-esteem. I know the church won't approve, but my Angie's needs must come first.

* * *

With the school run done and dusted, we set off for Elite, Truro's premier lingerie and sex toy shop, because they were doing twenty per cent off everything.

Sitting beside me in the passenger seat, Angie flapped her thighs open and closed. She often did this when she was both excited and nervous at the same time.

'I'll be alright won't I?' she said, wearing a pained expression.

'Of course you will!'

'You're right,' said my wife, 'I shouldn't be put off by those skinny Eastern European bitches.'

'What do you mean?' I asked, widening my eyes questioningly.

'They dominate the top ten,' replied Angie, 'and one of my boys reckons they somehow vote for themselves to win the prize money.'

'It doesn't matter what they do sweetheart,' I responded, 'because you've got a certain sexiness which totally trumps size zero!'

'You're just saying that to make me happy,' retorted a cross-sounding Angie.

'I'm not,' I insisted firmly. 'I can only tell you what I know from personal experience and what my male friends say in our inner sanctum.'

'Which is what exactly?'

'Which is,' I replied, 'that we don't find skinny model types particularly attractive. They don't have proper womanly curves. Women like you give us blokes a stonking hard-on because you go in and out in all the right places. And before you go on about your tummy, a washboard stomach is not sexy. The curve of a mummy tummy is sensual and erotic. Curves are kind of what God intended women to look like,' I added, 'but as usual they're not happy and they want to look like someone else.'

'Well that told me,' responded Angie.

'Good,' I said, 'because you're gonna win wife of the month, because I know how sexy you are, and I know exactly how to capture that with my camera!'

Angie held my gaze whilst wearing her beautiful warm, broad, even smile. I smiled back at her and then focussed on the road ahead. We both fell comfortably silent.

Whilst alone with my thoughts, I became a little concerned at my wife's contempt for the competition. I then concluded that her hostile competitiveness was her way of actually being confident. With the matter settled in my mind, I relaxed into my seat.

As I drove steadily on, the calm of the countryside was slowly replaced by an ever-increasing muddle of cheek-by-jowl buildings. I mused at how my mind often went from calm to muddled as well. Today was no different. It dawned on me that "talk" was easy. And even though I was happy for my wife, now that we were getting closer to actually posting explicit photos of her online, I suddenly became scared and felt out of control. Why? Because by comparison, at The Hub, it was me and Angie together. But with WorldWideWife, she would mostly pursue this by herself. It was her thing.

Angie caught sight of my troubled look and cleared her throat nervously. She then asked me if I was alright with everything. I nodded enthusiastically because I didn't want to appear negative. She wasn't convinced.

'You promised to do whatever it takes to let me be me,' she said, like a spoiled daddy's girl.

'And I will,' I replied, before asking her if she thought she might regret WorldWideWife in time to come. Putting it like that, was my way of subtly backtracking on my categorical assurance to support my wife.

'I won't regret this,' she replied. 'And if you hadn't noticed,' she added, 'I've been working really hard and I'm very happy.'

'Sure,' I said. 'But do you really think that posting is the way forward?'

'Rich, I'm not getting any younger,' responded my wife. 'I'll be fifty in a few years. My inner thighs will be wrinkly, and my boobs, bum and tum will sag like sloppy dough, and my face will be even more wrinkled than it is already!'

'Sweetheart,' I responded warmly, 'you're gonna look

fab at fifty!'

'I won't,' snapped my wife. 'I need to prove myself right now,' she insisted, before adding that it was alright for me, because I'd be like a silver fox who is still attractive to younger women.

Pleased at my wife's assertion, I smiled broadly before asking her if she really meant what she said.

'Oh Rich!' she sighed, 'this isn't about you. This is about me feeling that life's passing me by!'

Keen not to upset my wife any further, I said sorry, and then told her that the 'young studs' on WorldWideWife were gonna love her.

With that said, I took hold of her hand and gave it a reassuring squeeze.

We then both relaxed and left each other to our own thoughts.

A few minutes later I glanced over to my Angie and was pleased to see her glowing with a sense of achievement yet to come, tempered by a certain trepidation that it might not.

After a few more quiet minutes had passed, Angie broke the silence.

'I told my boys I'd be doing my debut posting soon,' she said.

'So?'

'Well, one of my friends, called Soldier Boy,' she replied, 'suggested I send him, and the rest of my inner circle, my best pics.'

'Why?'

'So they can each select their top ten.'

'Oh, I get it,' I said, 'and then we can post the most popular ones. Right?'

'Exactly!'

'Do it!' I insisted enthusiastically. 'Let's get the best possible result!'

'Yes, let's,' replied Angie. 'I couldn't handle a poor response. That would kill me.'

Having nodded in reply, I pulled into Cathedral car park and drove straight into a parking bay.

Angie got the parking ticket and placed it on the dashboard. As I watched her, I sighed a big sigh and smiled. You're married to a beautiful, sexy woman, I told myself, and all you have to do is capture that with your camera.

* * *

With our eyes wide and everywhere, we wandered round Elite in search of bustiers.

'Hi!' came the voice of a thirty-something pretty blonde assistant with "Chelsey" on her name badge. 'How are you guys today?'

'Good thanks,' replied Angie.

'Can I help at all?'

'Yes please,' I responded assertively, taking charge of the conversation.

For some weird reason, I needed people to know that Angie and I were doing WorldWideWife together, so that I didn't look stupid.

Chelsey looked at me expectantly. I cleared my throat, and told her I was going to take some sexy photos of my wife, to send to her soldier friend who gets lonely on duty.

'Helping a lonely soldier,' replied Chelsey in her twangy Cornish accent. 'Aww, that's so lovely.'

'Thanks,' said Angie, smiling appreciatively. 'I'm looking for a bustier to smooth my middle and accentuate my bust.'

'Do you want full cup or half cup?' asked Chelsey. 'Personally, I love getting my puppies out for the boys.'

'I wanna get my puppies out for the boys too!' said Angie, through a laugh.

'Great,' said Chelsey, turning to the rail on her right. 'We have these half cups here, and this one,' she added, pulling out a turquoise bustier, 'has got waist control. Do you like the colour?'

'Oooh yes!' said Angie, before taking the bustier from Chelsey and stepping over to the mirror.

With her head tipped down and to one side, she pursed her lips (as she always did when she was deliberating over clothes) and studied her reflection whilst holding the bustier against herself.

'Why don't you try it on, sweetheart?' I suggested.

'Yes, why not?'

'And it comes with matching lace knickers,' announced Chelsey.

'Oooh, this just gets better!' declared Angie, before trailing behind Chelsey to the changing rooms.

Left to my own devices, I drifted aimlessly round the shop until I came across a wall full of vibrators. Good God, I exclaimed in my head, there must be over fifty different types here. There was Rampant Rabbit, finger vibrating clit stimulator, the Trumpeter Swan vibrator, vibrating nipple pumps, cock rings with vibrator attachment, and Mr Dick vibrating dildo. I was particularly intrigued by the Lover's Lust strap-on dildo, and even more so by the double-ended vibrating dildo.

Feeling a bit pervy, I continued to loiter around the sex toys in a world of my own, until Chelsey's voice suddenly startled me.

'Your wife wants you,' she said, pointing to the changing rooms.

I thanked Chelsey, before then threading my way through the vast array of sexy outfits to the far side of the shop. I then rounded a corner and came upon a row of changing rooms. All the doors were open except for one. I assumed Angie was in the locked changing room, and so knocked on the door.

'Angie, are you in there?' I asked.

'Yes,' came her reply, as she opened a small, eye-level flap in the door to look at me.

'Aren't you gonna let me in then?' I asked.

'I can't babe, they don't allow partners in.'

'What?! That's mad!'

'Yeah, I know,' replied Angie. 'Apparently people have been having sex in here.'

Keen to take a peek at my wife, I stepped forward and peered through the six-inch square opening.

'Wow,' I exclaimed. 'You've literally just gone straight to my cock!'

Angie smiled in response, before asking me if I thought she looked a bit lumpy-bumpy.

'Don't be silly,' I insisted. 'You've got a slight yummy-mummy tummy, which is very sexy.'

'Good,' she said, before asking me to get her a red bustier from where Chelsey got the one she was wearing.

'What size should I get?'

'Fourteen,'

'Sure,' I said, 'I'll ask Chelsey.'

'If you like.'

'But what if I can't find her,' I said anxiously, 'or she's with a customer or something?'

'Oh Rich!' sighed an exasperated Angie, 'I forgot you were a man. I'll go!'

With that said, she snatched the matching turquoise knickers off the bench, and removed them from their plastic bag.

'I'm gonna buy this bustier,' she said, stepping into her new knickers.

Then, having slipped her feet into her high-heeled street shoes, she confidently strutted out of the changing room, and straight into the store. She had now morphed into her "femme fatale" persona. There she was, in full public view, wearing just her turquoise bustier with matching knickers. Her tits were well on show, and her vagina lips and arse were easily visible through her lace knickers.

As I followed her with my eyes, I noticed a man position himself behind his wife so that he could check my woman out. She looked over at him. He smiled at her and widened his eyes. She then returned her gaze to the direction of travel. That silent encounter seemed to exude dirty sex, just like at The Hub. That observation sent my heart pounding in my chest and reignited my hard-on.

Even though this episode had aroused me, I kind of wanted my wife to be outraged at being stared at, but she wasn't, and I knew why. It went back to something she'd always said. If a woman likes a man, she quite likes him checking her out, and even staring at her tits. But if she doesn't fancy him, then it's an unpleasant, creepy experience which disgusts her.

Despite my adrenaline-fuelled jealous response, I was really pleased that Angie's confidence was growing. I was doing my job by supporting her. I loved doing that, and realised it was my *raison d'être*, alongside caring for my children.

Having arrived at the rail, Angie selected a red bustier, and then strutted back to the changing room. Her admirer followed her every move, but this time though, she didn't return his gaze. Again, this was just like at The Hub. Once she knew she'd caught a man's attention, she would ignore him.

At the changing room, Angie stepped inside and shut the door behind her. I busied myself on my phone for a few minutes until she emerged.

'How did you get on?'

'The bustier fits perfectly,' she replied.

'Oh good,' I said, before gesturing to her to lead the way.

At the till, we settled up with Chelsey. We then left Elite with a naughty spring in our step.

* * *

Having walked out into a glorious sunny day, we strolled into the open space directly in front of Truro Cathedral. I was admiring the beautiful round, stained-glass window, when I was disturbed by Angie tugging on my arm.

'I'm hungry Rich,' she said. 'Do you fancy something to eat?'

'Don't mind if I do,' I replied. 'How about there?' I said, pointing to a chalk board outside Cathedral Bistro.

'A pulled pork bap,' said Angie, reading the special, 'with stuffing and a coffee for £3.99 – perfect!'

Having finished our snack in double quick time, I drove home with all haste. I was keen to get down to the clandestine and strangely exciting business of taking sexy pictures of my wife, for other men's pleasure!

❖

CHAPTER 22

Once home, Angie stripped off, before carefully putting her shower cap over her hair. Whilst she was in the shower, I set about preparing everything for her very first photo shoot.

I immediately drew our bedroom curtains wide open and hooked them onto the curtain pole ends to maximise daylight. I then switched on all the lights and repositioned my bedside lamp to counter shadows and illuminate specific areas. Two fluffy white pillows rested against the tall brass bed head, lending a boudoir feel to the set.

Rather pleased with my studio preparations, I popped into the shower room to let Angie know I was ready. She thanked me in a slightly anxious voice, and then told me that the anticipation of doing the shoot was both exciting and nerve-wracking at the same time.

'Oh dear,' I replied, looking at my wife through the glass shower door, with a sympathetic grimace.

'So anyway,' she said, in a sudden upbeat tone whilst continuing to shave her legs, 'what exactly have you got in mind?'

'I was thinking of some shots of you in your short cocktail dress,' I responded, 'to show off your hourglass figure. We can use that to tease them with first.'

'Maybe.'

'Definitely!' I said. 'Especially if you lift your dress up to reveal your bum. You know, like in the tennis poster.'

'Yes,' said Angie. 'With no knickers on, that could work.'

Buoyed by my wife's positive response, I then suggested I take some shots of her standing, legs apart, in her bustier and stockings.

'With my heels on,' she said, as she rinsed her razor under the shower.

'Yes,' I replied, before turning my gaze to the window.

Then, having tuned into the *pshhh* of the shower, I desperately tried to come up with some more tasteful, yet exciting poses.

A moment later, my thoughts were disturbed when Angie suddenly announced that she needed to ensure she was extra smooth today. I turned round to face her.

'Men don't like stubble,' she added, pulling her vulva taught to draw the razor over it.

Chuckling in response, I stepped back into the bedroom. Suddenly feeling both anxious and excited, I sat on the corner chair and contemplated my impending actions. I couldn't believe I was actually doing this, but I knew I had to.

A few minutes into my muddled musings, Angie appeared with her towel fastened above her boobs. She stood in front of the full-length mirror and leant in to take a closer look at her face. Placing her fingertips on her temples, she pulled her skin tight, and then stared at herself for a bit, before allowing her face to return to normal. This was followed by a concerned grimace.

'Hmmm,' she sighed, 'a little lift wouldn't go amiss.'

Taking a step back, my wife removed her shower cap

and unhooked her towel. Having tossed those items into the ensuite, she again scrutinised herself in the mirror. I watched her smooth out her lumps and bumps by pulling her stomach taut. She then announced that she wanted a tummy tuck when I was back in the money.

Having whisked her black hold-up stockings off the cheval mirror, my wife stepped across to the bed. Sitting on the edge of the mattress with her legs crossed, she eased her clenched fist down one stocking and positioned the toe correctly. Having gathered the complete stocking in the fingers of both hands, she leant forward and slipped it over her pointed toes, before slowly unrolling it up her shapely leg as she elevated her calf. She then sensually ran her hands up her leg to the top of her thigh, trailing her long smoothing fingers behind as she went. As I watched, I went hard.

At this point, I realised there was something very erotic about watching my woman morph into her femme fatale alter ego. From my viewing spot in the corner, I admired the sensational contrast of her white skin against the red of her stocking tops, complete with red seam. She looked so incredibly sexy. I was aroused by her beauty, her soft womanly curves and her assertive, yet seductive demeanour. Alongside these feelings, I was also anxious. Sensing my unease, Angie smiled at me lovingly. Feeling somewhat reassured, I decided to give this WorldWideWife thing my best shot, and enjoy the forbidden excitement of it all.

'And now for the little black number!' announced my wife, before rising to her feet to wriggle into her short Lycra cocktail dress. It had a deep V-neck, so her cleavage was well on show. Having slipped into her red Jimmy Choo "come fuck me" heels, she stood tall with her legs apart.

I nodded and smiled in approval, and then watched my sexy model of a wife apply her lippy in front of the mirror, before adjusting her hair to perfection. The atmosphere was now sexually supercharged.

In sharp contrast to the doubtful look she wore just a few minutes ago, Angie now had a purposeful glint in her eye, and exuded confidence. Her femme fatale persona had completely emerged. She was gonna do this, and she was gonna do it well. I admired her ability to overpower her negative body issues, and put herself out there. I knew that, in spite of my perverse excitement, I would need to lay my deep-seated moral demons to rest, to meet my wife's needs. I concluded that this was the loving self-sacrifice Julia referred to.

'How are you feeling sweetheart?' I asked.

'Like I said, excited and nervous,' replied Angie, as she fussed over straightening her stocking seams.

Sitting forward in my chair, I unwittingly suggested that most women would feel objectified with men looking at them purely in a sexual light. Angie, sounding a little irritated, stood in front of me and explained that objectification had nothing to do with it. It was all about how people made her feel, both men and women.

'I'm sorry to be such a buzzkill,' I said, 'when we're just about to get down and dirty.

But I sort of need to understand how your mind works. If that makes sense?'

'I get it,' replied Angie. 'You need to get past your ingrained moral Catholic thinking.'

I nodded in reply, and then listened as she explained that objectification is looking at people's bodies in a sexual light, and not at the person as a whole.

'Women do it to men, and men do it to women,' she continued. 'That's often how an interest starts. And then you either get to know the person and pursue them or not, or just have sex and move on.'

Still clearly annoyed with me, Angie continued with her diatribe. She insisted that objectification was a misplaced notion where feminists judge women who enjoy that sort of sexual attention.

'And I'm not going to let the feminazis make me feel guilty or bad about myself,' she added. 'They pressure you to think that you're being objectified because you like exciting men. It's undue.'

'I agree entirely,' I said, having realised that it would do no good to engage with her on that point any further. I instead asked her if she was okay with guys she *didn't* fancy looking at her through sexual glasses.

'I'm not bothered in the least,' said Angie. 'I know that some fat old pervs will be wanking over me, but good luck to them. I'm putting myself out there to be enjoyed. I'd obviously prefer to know that good-looking guys are excited by me. That's flattering.'

Barely pausing for breath, my wife then went on to explain that no matter where you were; on a plane, train, in a meeting or at a party, and no matter how you dressed it up and hid behind formality and moral constraints, nature inherently drove sexual interest between men and women.

'The point I'm trying to make,' continued my wife, 'is that men and women sometimes become sexual objects to each other, and there's nothing wrong with that, so long as there is mutual respect.'

'Mmmhh,' I sighed, 'I kind of see what you mean now that you put it like that.'

'And when us girls check out a guy's arse,' added Angie, 'that is sexual. The same as blokes check out a girl's boobs. It's often just fleeting, but you think mmmhh, sexy.'

In an attempt to bring this animated conversation to a close, I told my wife that I totally got her point.

'Good,' she responded, before asking me if we could get on with the photo shoot. 'This is supposed to be a bit of sexy fun!' she added.

'You're quite right,' I said, rising to my feet. 'Let's get this party started!'

'Now, how do you want me?' asked Angie.

'Erm, I thought of another pose,' I replied. 'How about you luxuriate on the bed half prone, with your legs crossed showing your stocking tops?'

My wife duly obliged, and I began snapping away purposefully. To make the photos arty, I took them from low down and then reviewed them with Angie whilst sitting on the bed.

'Oh no,' she exclaimed, 'that angle makes my legs look bigger than my body. That's not flattering at all.'

'It's all a bit trial and error to begin with,' I insisted, excusing my crap photography. 'How about you sit on the bed with your dress ridden up?'

'Oh Rich!' sighed my wife, 'you're so naïve. You have no idea, have you?'

'Okay then smarty pants,' I retorted, 'you come up with something!'

'Okay then, I will,' replied Angie, jumping to her feet.

She stepped away from the bed, and with her back still to me, bent forward a little with her legs straight and together. Poking her arse out like a porn star, she pulled her dress up and over the curve of her bum, accentuating its perfect roundness. She didn't have any knickers on. I jumped up and snapped away.

A few moments later, my model wife bent further forward so that her head was at waist level. I again snapped away. Then, she parted her legs, leaving absolutely nothing to the imagination. Half squatting, I continued to photograph Angie from the left, then the centre and then the right. Widening her stance even more, she put her head between her legs and pouted at the camera. And, just when I thought it couldn't get any more hardcore, she swung her arms behind herself and pulled herself open.

Despite my surprise at her explicit poses, I knew I couldn't judge my lovely wife. And anyway, I had a raging hard-on for her, so who was I to judge? And on top of that, I wanted to give her what she needed, so she would feel properly loved and wouldn't feel the need to leave me. That said though, my actions were driven by love, as opposed to fear.

Moving my eye away from the viewfinder, I looked directly at my slutty wife. The contrast between her labia and her inner pinkness was very apparent. She was opening herself up to invite the viewer in. It was graphic, powerful, and exciting.

Having recovered my composure, I dropped to my knees and resumed clicking.

After a minute or two, I'd exhausted all the various angles and stopped. Angie stood up straight and turned round.

'Well? What do you think?'

'You're a bit contrived!' I replied a little sharply, suddenly unhappy at the thought of perverts ogling intimate images of *my* wife.

'A lot of men like these sort of contortionist shots,' countered a slightly irritated Angie.

'Erm … well yeah, of course,' I replied, whilst trying to wrestle my negativity to the ground.

'Rich!' sighed my wife. 'You're not getting into this, are you? I mean, whatever happened to your motto?'

'Motto?' I questioned.

'Ask not what your family can do for you,' she began, 'ask what you can do for your family!'

I'd always been inspired by JFK's words about how Americans should support their nation, and had adopted that sentiment for the family. Angie was right, I needed to stand by my own motto. With that in mind, I put a big smile on my face and assumed a porn photographer's persona.

'Right, you sexy fucker,' I enthused, having gotten into character, 'let's get those gorgeous tits out for the boys!'

'Okay,' replied Angie, wearing a pleasantly surprised look.

'Pull your dress down to show more cleavage,' I ordered, 'and hoick it up just short of your vag.'

Following my instructions, my Angie revealed the round of her breasts to her areola. She then pulled her dress up to show a tantalising peep of pussy.

'Yes, that's great!' I enthused, snapping away. 'Now pull your top down a bit more,' I demanded, 'and give me that sexy smile!'

Angie duly obliged, whilst I bobbed and weaved around her like a pro seeking out the best angles.

'Sexy as hell,' I said. 'Now do your own thing,' I instructed, 'you're a natural!'

Following my direction, Angie pulled her boobs out, cupped them in her hands and looked down at them with an unsmiling sultry face. I snapped away some more, but was stopped in my tracks when she declared that her nipples weren't big enough.

'Suck 'em out Rich,' she demanded anxiously. 'Fuckmaster's desperate for my big nipples!'

'Fuckmaster?' I questioned, as Black Dog appeared.

'He's one of my boys,' replied a slightly out of breath Angie.

Even though facilitating another man's desires really got to me, I did the necessary, and then continued to snap away with an angry hard-on throbbing in my jeans.

'Take good shots for Fuckmaster, Rich,' insisted Angie, 'he's gonna come all over my tits and post it!'

That was a comment too far for Black Dog. He bounded forth with teeth bared. I tossed the camera onto the chair without thinking, and pushed my wife onto the bed. She landed with a heavy bump and then froze, her mouth open and her eyes wide, with both surprise and desire.

There was a momentary pause whilst Angie and I looked at each other. Two seconds later, I lunged forward, and slapped her knees apart, before thrusting my fingers inside her.

'Am I wet or what?' she demanded.

'You're sopping!' I replied gruffly, 'because you've been thinking about exciting Fuckmaster!'

Reaching up, Angie undid my jeans and massaged my excited cock roughly, whilst I continued to finger her. After a short while, I had the uncontrollable urge to eat my wife's pussy. I wanted to taste her body fluid, and pleasure her, to prove myself as a lover. Then, and only then, could I rightfully have my selfish wicked way with my mate, to satisfy my lion response.

'I'm gonna eat you now Angie,' I declared gruffly, my angry eyes still firmly fixed on hers. 'Do you want that?'

'Yes!' she replied urgently. 'Eat my pussy!'

Having completely removed my jeans and boxers in one go, I pulled my wife's bum to the edge of the bed. I then slid her dress up to her tummy, before pushing her thighs back to scrutinise her sexy, exciting orifices, framed by her soft, white, smooth skin.

Kneeling on the floor, I held her labia open with my fingers. With her hands behind her legs, my woman pulled her knees up by her ears, so that she was wide open.

Excited to be overwhelmed by desire, I proceeded to lick my wife's fragrant, engorged opening upwards, with long strokes of my tongue. I felt like a slightly angry, yet passionate artist working on his masterpiece. Having continued with my long paint brush strokes for a while, I then focused more on my woman's clitoris, whilst pleasuring her g-spot with a come hither fingering motion. I relaxed into that for a few minutes. Angie then started to rub the back of my head. That was my cue to synchronise my licking and fingering to her pace. She then began to writhe with an increasing range of movement. I continued to keep time with her now quickening head rubs, with my mouth firmly engaged with her vagina. We moved in perfect harmony.

'Oh, fuck you Rich!' whispered my wife, as she tightened round my fingers.

Then, after a quiet moment, she let out a massive 'Arghhh,' as she gyrated her hips wildly and tried to push my head away with her hand. 'No more,' she insisted, squeezing my head between her thighs.

Despite her calls for no more, I carried on pleasuring my

woman a moment longer. Then, when she was on the cusp of being way too over sensitive, I stopped all activity. She went still, and, with a heavy sigh, released her powerful thighs from around my head. Now free to move, I sprung to my feet, before then kneeling beside my wife on the bed. As I knelt above her, with my cock hovering over her head, I was both disgusted and aroused in equal measure – just like at The Hub.

'Suck me!' I ordered, thrusting my hips forward.

My wife responded by pushing herself up onto one elbow. Then, with her mouth at the right height, she opened wide and went to work. After a few minutes, I suddenly needed to be deep inside my woman's body, so as to mark her as mine. With that in mind, I quickly pulled out of her mouth, making a popping sound in the process, and manhandled her into the middle of the bed. I then pushed her legs open and mounted her with considerable urgency. Having penetrated her vagina with my wanton, throbbing penis, I began pumping vigorously. There was no romance involved, just a dirty, sex object fuck.

'Don't come in me, Rich,' insisted my wife. 'My boys wanna see cum on my tits!'

Hearing that really upset me.

'Cum on your tits for other men?' I growled, increasing my pace. 'Is that what you want?'

'Yes,' whispered my wife. 'Give me your cock and I'll wank you to ecstasy.'

'Do it then!' I insisted, in a gruff voice, as I reluctantly withdrew from my woman's vagina and straddled her in one uninterrupted move.

Then, with my cock hovering over her chest like a demonic snake, I watched my wife adjust her dress so it laid evenly under her breasts. She was clearly conscious of the shot she wanted, which made me wonder if our sex was just some sort of act as far as she was concerned. I completely dismissed that consideration the moment she grabbed hold of my erection. To me, she was sexing me of her own free will, so her motives were academic.

Looking down, I watched my sex goddess of a wife slide her hand up and down my shaft. She had cleverly positioned her thumb on the underside of my helmet to augment my pleasure, whilst rimming me with her free hand. I observed her face locked in a tense purposeful grimace, and then turned my gaze to her gorgeous breasts. I watched them wobble in time to her hand action. All this wasn't enough for me though. I needed more dirty sex vistas. Leaning back, I pushed three fingers into my woman's engorged opening and watched them speeding in and out of her, pushing and pulling her labia back and forth with each motion. I needed total debauchery to excite me to my angry and vengeful climax.

Feeling my orgasm building as my muscles tensed, I focused all my concentration on releasing the near painful tension that was racking my body. I needed to fire my cocked and fully loaded gun all over my wife.

'Jesus Christ!' I grunted gruffly, as I picked up my fingering pace, 'I'm coming!'

With Angie's action matching the speed of my fingers, I returned my gaze to my cock and let out a loud 'Arghhh' through a tight grimace, as I began to explode all over her chest. She then rubbed my cockhead over her nipple as every last drop of hot semen shot out of me.

As the tension in my whole body began to ease, I gently removed my fingers from my wife and relaxed my bum onto her tummy.

'Wow!' she sighed, looking down at her chest, 'look at all the cum you've made for me.'

I nodded in reply, strangely pleased that my wife wanted to impress 'her boys' with the prodigious amount of ejaculate I'd just shot all over her chest. She always felt that the volume of semen was testimony to how excited she'd made me. I felt that as well. I also felt that lots of cum was manly and, in this instance, would prove as much to her random men friends.

'Quick Rich,' whispered my wife, 'take some piccys!'

I dismounted, stepped over to the chair, grabbed the camera and snapped away. Angie confined her poses to semi vertical so my cum didn't run off her chest. For her last pose, she picked up a globule of semen on her finger and held it by her mouth. She then poked her tongue out, giving the impression she was going to lick it off.

I had no idea how my wife was so well informed about the sort of explicit and sordid photos men wanted to see, but she was. To be honest that didn't bother me; I was pretty much over the initial shock of it all now.

After I'd put my boxers and jeans back on, and Angie had cleaned up, we sat side by side on the bed and began reviewing the photos on the camera screen. Before I could even articulate my thoughts on the very first photo, Angie blurted out …

'Oooh no Rich! Look at my double chin!'

'Looks okay to me,' I quickly replied, before swiftly moving on to the next shot.

'This one's even worse,' exclaimed a very upset-looking Angie. 'Look at my pussy lips sagging and gaping.'

'Don't be silly,' I insisted, 'it's just that you've never seen yourself bending over.'

'That's a stupid thing to say, Rich,' snapped my wife.

'I'm sorry, I was just …'

'Of course I haven't seen myself bending over,' she interrupted, 'but I have seen those skinny Eastern European bitches pose like that!'

Not quite sure what to say, I just nodded and grimaced sympathetically as my wife got angrier and angrier about the skinny competition.

Having finally gathered my thoughts on the matter, I once again reminded my wife that a lot of men didn't find very skinny, younger women sexy because they didn't have proper womanly curves.

'You have all the right junk in all the right places,' I continued enthusiastically, 'and are naturally sexy. And I'm not just saying that because I love you,' I added. 'I mean remember Marcus, he went mad for you!'

Somewhat reassured, my wife smiled at me and then returned her gaze to the camera screen. Then, in an attempt to progress matters, I suggested that we simply delete the photo and move on.

'I can't,' she replied. 'I promised Soldier Boy I'd do a shot from behind for him, but I don't like the sag and gape. And look at my stupid fat tummy,' she added crossly, whilst tapping the offending bit on the screen.

The image showed Angie on all fours, her thighs spread apart, her bum stuck out like she was going to be taken, and her pussy wide open with lips hanging down. Her tummy hung low in the background. It's not what anyone having sex with her would ever see, but I could understand why she wanted it gone.

Looking both pensive and troubled, Angie sat quietly with her head bowed. I hated seeing her so upset. I felt sad for her; she obviously didn't expect to see what she saw.

'Angie my darling,' I began, putting my arm round her, 'you've given birth to four ten-pound babies, things are bound to be a little …'

'A little what Rich?' she demanded angrily. 'A little saggy, is that it?'

'No, not saggy,' I responded, 'mumsy. Where a certain Rubenesque tummy curve is incredibly sexy. And anyway,' I added, 'there are *loads* of other fantastic shots we can use!'

'I don't think so!' snapped my wife, 'I told you I need shots of me bent over. My Soldier Boy is desperate for them. I can't have this sag and gape, and hanging tummy crap, *OKAY!*'

A gut-wrenching jealous reaction suddenly struck at me from nowhere, probably because Angie said *my* Soldier Boy. Anxious and erect, I breathed in deeply to calm myself. Two minutes ago, I thought I was okay after I'd marked my territory, but now this. I released my deep breath along with my misplaced jealousy. And then, flaccid and calmer, I told Angie I could fix the problem.

'How?'

'Bring your thighs slightly closer together,' I replied, 'and when you're bending forward, just lift your tummy up with your hand so it won't be visible.'

Angie then got onto all fours and pulled her tummy up. I bent down level with her arse to take a look. Unfortunately, she was still sagging and gaping. Weirdly, holding her labia open was a turn-on for guys, but somehow a natural gape wasn't. I couldn't really work that one out.

'Well Rich?' questioned Angie, in the absence of any activity from me.

'Your tummy's gone now,' I replied, 'so we just need to

deal with the gape.'

'Oh,' sighed my wife, resigned to failure.

After a moment's silence, I asked her if we had any honey.

'Honey?' she repeated, having turned round to face me. 'Yes, why?'

'Maybe we can stick your lips together,' I suggested, 'to keep everything tidy.'

'Sounds like a plan,' she said, appearing happier, 'anything to get rid of that sag 'n' gape!'

* * *

Having returned to the bedroom with Asda's finest clear honey, I discovered Angie lying on the bed, still in her black dress.

'Ready?' I said.

'Yes,' she replied, before pulling her dress up to expose her nether regions.

As I stood by the bed looking down at my slightly anxious wife, I shook my head and then burst out laughing. Her face relaxed as she joined in the laughter.

'If we ever told anyone what we'd been up to,' I began, trying to suppress my laugh, 'they'd never believe us!'

'I know,' replied Angie, 'because truth really is stranger than fiction! And here you are,' she continued, 'creating the perfect shot to make me wife of the month!'

'Art should know no boundaries sweetheart,' I declared.

'Art?' repeated Angie, furrowing her brow quizzically. 'You're very kind, but this is hardly art.'

'C'mon my love,' I said encouragingly, 'let's get that shot.'

With that said, I squeezed a dollop of honey onto my

middle finger before smearing it on the inside of Angie's labia. I then glued them together. My Angie's delicious vulva was now compact. Just the way she wanted it to be.

With my model properly prepared, I quickly set to work with the camera and captured some amazing images. Once Angie and I had reviewed them, she took her dress off and slipped her bathrobe on. She then insisted on making me a cuppa by way of a thank you for a job well done.

Whilst my Angie was downstairs in the kitchen, I dug out the deep-red throw from the airing cupboard and laid it over the duvet. Then, alone with my thoughts, I began to ponder the crazy world I'd just ventured into. I walked over to the window and thoughtfully gazed across the countryside to the sea beyond. I tried to work myself out, and mused at how I was fine with all this one minute, and then really anxious the next, when jealousy and anger took hold. Then, I would go wild and rampant for my wife. But once my lion response had been satisfied by marking her as my own, I relaxed and wanted to support her. I sometimes thought she used this response to her own advantage.

The one thing I knew for certain though, was that when my lion response kicked in, I didn't feel emotionally fulfilled. Not like when I 'made love' to my Angie. This troubled me deeply, but I decided to punch on and continue to expose myself to her sexual wants. I felt sure that I'd eventually become desensitised, just as she'd predicted. And anyway, everything was fine when I was relaxed about it. Fun even.

As I was contemplating that consideration in more detail, the bedroom door suddenly swished open. I turned away from the window and watched Angie walk in with a tray of tea and toast.

'Oooh Rich! It's very boudoir in here,' she said.

'You likey?'

'Likey muchy,' replied my smiling wife.

Having walked across the room, I took a piece of toast off the tray she'd placed on the bedside table. I munched on it and sat on the bed. I watched her slip her bathrobe off, before hanging it over the edge of the mirror she was standing in front of. With only her stockings on, my wife scrutinised her reflection wearing a very serious face.

'Look at this stupid muffin top!' she said crossly, before turning to look over her shoulder. 'And this horrible back fat.'

'Stop right there!' I insisted firmly. 'You've barely got any fat. And please don't aspire to be a stick insect model. They're not representative of real women!'

'You say that,' scoffed my wife, 'but blokes seem to like women with a see-through gap at the top of their legs.'

'You're totally wrong there,' I retorted, 'trust me. You women think men like only that, but we don't mind either way.'

'Do you actually think that though, Rich?' asked Angie through a questioning grimace, 'or are you just saying it for my benefit?'

'Yes, I actually do think that.'

'Really?'

'Yes!' I said, before insisting that we focus on the positives. 'You've lost loads of weight,' I added, 'and look sensational!'

Looking more relaxed, Angie turned from side to side, whilst keeping her eyes firmly fixed on the mirror.

'Not too bad for my age, I suppose,' she said thoughtfully. 'And considering I gave birth to four huge babies; your fault,' she added, 'the man determines the size, I'm not doing too badly.'

Then, without notice, my wife turned on her heel, strutted across the room and pulled her red bustier out of the posh Elite bag which was hanging off the corner chair. Having stepped into it, she slipped her red stilettos on and walked over to me.

'Can you tighten the laces please,' she said, turning her back to me, 'I need my tummy squeezed in.'

Having stood up, I pulled the bustier laces tight, making sure they were straight and central. With that done, I leaned back to take a look. The sight of my woman's gorgeous round arse, framed at the top by her bustier, was so irresistible that I bent forward and bit it.

'Don't Rich,' she insisted, pushing my head away, 'you'll leave a mark.'

Feeling like a schoolboy who'd been admonished by the sexy headmistress, I smiled to myself. I then watched as my Angie attached the bustier suspender clips to the tops of her hold-ups. Her look was even more erotic now, with the bustier cutting high over her hips. This accentuated the length of her shapely legs. She looked simply delicious, and I couldn't wait to see her from the front.

'Turn around sweetheart,' I insisted urgently.

Angie obliged with a flourish.

'Oh yes!' I enthused, truly taken aback by her sensual beauty. 'Fucking amazing!'

Staring at my wife, I took pleasure in observing every last detail of the vista before me. Her breasts, lifted by the half cups, were seductively round. Her silky smooth shaven opening beckoned me. She was sexy as hell. I just knew she wasn't going to wear her matching knickers, and now I could see why. I was horny for her again, but this time in a loving way.

'Right! What's next?' I asked in a business-like voice to distract myself from my erotic thoughts.

'How about this?' Angie immediately replied, as she flopped onto the bed, leaving her legs dangling over the edge.

She then parted them, rested on her elbows, and pushed her chest up toward the ceiling.

'Looking good!!' I said, as I grabbed the camera off the bedside table and began snapping away.

Once I'd got the shots I wanted, I called 'Next!'. Angie responded by putting her high-heeled feet on the deep red throw. She then lifted her bum off the bed and held herself open with her fingers. After I took twenty or so shots from varying angles, my wife slipped two fingers inside herself and looked straight into the lens like a professional. I snapped away at speed, squatting, bending, and darting around her, just like I was on a proper porn shoot.

'That's great! Sexy as hell,' I enthused. 'Yes, loving it!'

I continued to click away. My wife now sat bolt upright, pushed her chest forward, tipped her head back a little and pouted.

'Yes, looking good,' I whispered encouragingly.

'Shoot me from the front now,' she ordered, 'doggy with my tits out – my boys will love that!'

Having deftly positioned herself on all fours, she popped her breasts out of her bustier and looked up at the camera with her head at a jaunty angle. She was wearing a come-fuck-me smile. I snapped away from various directions until I was satisfied. I then called 'Next'.

Over the following few minutes, Angie struck pose after

pose with gay abandon, like an experienced sex model. There she was lifting her breasts up towards her mouth with her tongue out. Then she was pouting directly at the camera with her head up. Then, head to the side, bending forwards, bending backwards, smiling face, serious face, legs apart, legs together, etcetera, etcetera. She was the very epitome of a pro. She was brimming with confidence, no doubt helped by her bustier tummy control, accentuating her womanly curves. She was, without question, a naturally beautiful woman, who photographed amazingly well.

After a while, my wife suddenly stopped posing. She then drew a deep breath and flopped onto the bed with a huge sigh. Wearing a pleasantly exhausted, yet satisfied look, she raised her head a little and regarded me with a warm smile.

With the photo shoot finished, I climbed onto the bed and laid down beside Angie. I then cuddled her close to me.

'Love you for doing this for me, Rich,' she whispered.

'And I loved doing it for you too, my angel,' I whispered back.

CHAPTER 23

The next morning I awoke in an instant. It was just before six. Feeling well rested, I carefully got out of bed without disturbing Angie. I then slipped into yesterday's clothes, before quietly passing through the half-open door onto the landing. Keen not to disturb the children's slumber on a school day, I avoided the creaky floorboards and stairs with the stealth and dexterity of Spiderman.

Once in the kitchen, I clicked the kettle on and contemplated the glorious day ahead. And was it a glorious day because we had something exciting planned? No. It was a glorious day because my wife and I had discussed our "swinging" elephant in the room, and had cleared the air. Now we were all set to live happily ever after. That included Angie competing in wife of the month. That way she could be herself and do what she wanted to do. I wasn't controlling her or suppressing the blossoming of her *forgotten me*. On the contrary, I was actively supporting her for who she was, as any good husband should do for such a loving wife. This was testimony to our ability to manage our relationship with love and care for each other. And now, with our marriage built on a solid foundation of love, honesty, and trust, we could simply get on with living life in the here and now, with no more emotional distractions.

As I poured hot water over my teabag, I reflected on my Angie's desire to be wife of the month. That made me smile because her self-esteem and confidence had clearly returned – big time! It must take real balls, I thought to myself, to go up against these thirty-somethings, who haven't had any children. Clearly Ryan, The Hub, and her sexy online friends had all played their part in bringing my wife to such a great place.

'And you Richie boy,' I whispered, 'must do your part too.'

All you have to do is capture your wife's abundant beauty in ten sexy pics every month. That will stop her feeling invisible, allow her to be herself, and win her fifty euros.

The thought of fifty euros made me chuckle. Not so long ago I would have spent that in Starbucks on a family brunch. Now, it would actually come in handy, and wasn't to be sniffed at!

With my cuppa in hand, I forced my feet into my laced-up trainers, unlocked the door to the garden, and sauntered out into a bright summer's morning. Standing on the patio, legs wide apart and head skyward, I took a deep breath to draw in as much of the fresh sea-scented air as I could. I then tuned into the abundance of mellifluous bird song, as I slowly exhaled.

Observing the gorgeous open vista before me, I smiled like a Cheshire cat at the uncompromised happiness that enveloped me and my beloved family. That prompted me to remember my dad's simple, but profound aphorism; you don't appreciate good times, until you've had bad times. I never really got that until now, probably because I'd only ever known good times, until the recession knocked me down and I lost everything. Thankfully, with the bankruptcy complete, my fear of further court proceedings and thug-like debt collectors had passed. I was now set to rebuild our finances with my trading. And crucially, Angie and I were back on track.

Still smiling, I ambled over to our rickety wooden bench, which nestled cosily by a mature laurel hedge in a secluded corner of the garden. Upon arrival, I wiped the dew off the seat with my hankie, before slowly sitting down without taking my eyes off the wondrous view. The bench creaked and wobbled under my weight. Having sipped my tea, I then placed my mug beside me. Lifting my bum a little, I reached into my jeans back pocket and pulled out my Post-it note pad and betting shop pen. I then began jotting.

You have journeyed life's arduous road
Eyes now a different world behold

Your darling Angie, your amazing love
In her world she puts you above

And so what if she's an unusual creature
It's not for anyone to judge or tease her

And so if at times my pain her pleasure
It's what I want, 'tis my gift of treasure

With our children all happy and content
We made their world exactly as dreamt

My family ensemble secure and well
Ha ha Beelzebub we've avoided hell!

Having read my poem out loud, I then laughed whilst shaking my head.

'You can't show this to anyone,' I whispered to myself, 'it's like an infantile rhyming couplet from the Disney Channel!'

Feeling embarrassed, I decided to write a more sophisticated poem. Deep in thought, I picked up my tea and sipped it whilst looking at the dew-laden laurel leaves. I then massaged one between my fingers.

'Daphne!' I said out loud, 'the very antithesis of Angie!'

Now there's a thing, I thought to myself, as I remembered the story of Apollo and Eros from my classics class at school. Apollo insulted Eros. Eros then shot Apollo through the heart with a golden arrow, so that he loved and lusted after Daphne, the daughter of the river God Peneus. Eros then shot Daphne with a leaden arrow, so that she would always reject Apollo.

Wanting to retain her virtue in the face of relentless unwanted attention from Apollo, Daphne asked her father to change her form. He turned her into a laurel bush. Having never taken Daphne as his wife, Apollo wore a wreath of her leaves, and decreed that wreaths of laurel be used to decorate the heads of statesmen.

I smiled as I recalled seeing the beautiful statue of Daphne and Apollo in Rome, when Angie and I were on our honeymoon. Daphne is gracefully trying to escape Apollo's pleading attention. I could never have imagined, not in a million years, that Angie would be the exact opposite of Daphne. More like Rodin's *The Kiss*, in fact, where another man's wife gives herself to her lover.

'I'll be ironic,' I whispered, trying to sound scholarly. Then, a moment later, I committed pen to paper.

This laurel casts a pondering shadow
Like Daphne who, pursued into exhaustion,
Transferred her virtue into triumphant wreaths
I uprooted my own Daphne
And bedded her in Devon soil
Where she now longs to be pursued
To hang triumphant wreaths
On every man who picks her ripened fruit

As I nodded thoughtfully at a job well done, I decided to dedicate my poem to Angie in recognition of the beautiful and complete person she'd now become. With that in mind, I went to the office to make it her desktop background, so she'd see it the moment she turned her computer on. With her machine fired up, I went to click on settings, but was distracted by a new email notification at the bottom of the screen from Dave Dancer. Staring at the notification, I hovered the mouse over it.

'Hmm,' I sighed, 'who's this Dave Dancer?'

Is that his actual name I wondered, or is it someone called Dave who dances. In a moment of sudden realisation, I became engulfed by a sinking feeling. This must be salsa Dave. You shouldn't jump to conclusions, I told myself. And you shouldn't open your wife's personal emails.

At this point I tried to convince myself that it was wrong of me to assume anything untoward. A battle then ensued between good cop and bad cop. Most of me wanted to do the right thing by not making any assumptions. Then I could perhaps ask Angie who Dave Dancer was at some later point.

Demon voice then entered the debate by insisting that I'd got every right to look at my wife's emails, because she was probably up to no good. Just click it open, I told myself. If she's completely innocent, then you'll know for sure and no harm done, except she'll go ape shit when she sees I've been snooping around. Willing to face the consequences to clear my head, I took a deep breath and clicked on the email. As I exhaled long and hard, my eyes widened at the unbelievable content which hit me in the face.

'Jesus Christ,' I exclaimed angrily, as my heart went from nought to sixty in a millisecond. 'What the fuck?'

By now, Black Dog was absolutely furious. With my breathing quickened and my eyes glued to the screen, I re-read the email out loud to get my head round what was going on.

My darling Angela,

I know you said not to email, but what I have to say is too long to put into a text. Please forgive me.

Since I saw you on Thursday, you have rekindled my feelings for you like never before. After we met in February, I thought about you every day, but after seeing you last week, I have thought about you every minute of every day!

It's like you said, ours was a special time for those three years, but I was with Jane and you were with Rich, and the time was wrong. But when you told me things weren't going well with Rich, I knew *our* time had finally come.

I spoke to my lawyer today, and he confirmed that Jane had agreed to a fair settlement. I don't mean to be presumptuous, but this means we'll be financially secure going forward. I know that might sound like a crass thing to say, but it is an important practicality.

My sweet Angela, you know I love you, and I know you love me, but it will take planning to do the things we talked about. I think we both know that we are destined to be together!

I know Rich is a great dad, and I wouldn't presume to take his place, but I just want you to know that I will certainly be there for the children.

Your husband is a good guy, but as you say, your window of life with him has closed. And I know you weren't being unkind when you said he was a spent force financially.

When I held you in my arms with your head on my chest and you told me you could be like this for eternity, that really meant something to me.

Take courage my darling Angela. Life is too short not to be with the one you love.

I can't wait to be with you to plan the rest of our lives together.

Tell me when you can get away again, and I'll be down to Plymouth in a heartbeat.

Sending you oodles of kisses from my lips to *all* of yours. Wow, just the thought of that has made Mr Longfellow throb with excitement! 😈

Love, your Dirty Dancer, Dave 🖤🖤🖤

Jesus, every time I think I'm set to live happily ever after, something always kicks me in the bollocks.

'Why do you do this to me God?' I demanded, looking skyward. 'I mean, I think I'm a good person, and I try to do the right thing, so why do you test me like this?'

With a heavy sigh, I dropped my chin to my chest. It's not God, I told myself. He gives us free will. This is Angie's free will. She's the one who chose to see Dave at least twice since we moved down here, not God.

And she didn't just see him for coffee, scoffed demon voice. No, he added, she was up to her old bump and grind with Dirty Dancer Dave in his hotel room!

That thought instantly gave me an angry, competitive erection.

'What the fuck is wrong with you?' I whispered gruffly, as my face reddened with heat. 'How the hell can you want sex with your wife when she's been shagging another man behind your back?'

The infuriating need to see off my rival by sexually securing my woman for myself, really got to me.

'What sort of a sick bastard are you?' I demanded crossly.

Unwilling to contemplate the workings of my twisted mind, I instead wondered how Dave could think he and Angie were destined to be together, when she appeared to be so happy with me. Plus she was over the moon when I agreed to support her foray into WorldWideWife. This just doesn't make any sense.

'It doesn't need to,' I told myself. 'Not anymore. This is it!' I declared boldly, 'it's time to stand up and be counted like a proper man.'

With that in mind, I printed off Dave's email before rising sharply to my feet. I then strutted purposefully towards the house. The time had come to confront my wife and tell her we were over. And yes, that would mean judging her badly for what she'd done.

And even though I knew God was testing my unconditional love for my wife, I wasn't going to be sweet-talked by her lies. I couldn't let her use my love for her as a weakness, and I wasn't going to be manipulated into being Samson to her Delilah. I wasn't going to buy into the 'innocent explanations' which she would no doubt spin in response to being caught out.

If Dave thinks they're supposed to be together, then

they can fucking well be together! I've had enough.

'You've been well and truly fucked, matey boy,' I said angrily, as cockney demon voice took over my vocal chords, 'and now it's time to bite the hardest bullet of your life. No two ways about it!'

THE END

T O   C O M E ...

DESIRED

T W O   H E A R T S

B O O K   2

I just stood there in the heavy, awkward silence trying to get my head round things. Then, having taken a deep shaky breath, I exhaled long and hard.

'So you love another man,' I whispered. 'Huh, fancy that.'

'Yes, but I love you first and foremost,' insisted my wife, 'and Aron is second to you. It's like I've got two hearts, a small one I've grown for him, and my main, big heart that is always for you.'

'Is that right?'

'Yes. I'm not going to cheat on you Rich,' said my wife, 'I'm asking you. I want to have a complete and full life. I like to love and be loved.'

She then went on to say that when people have affairs, it doesn't mean they don't love their spouse. They mostly do it because there's something missing. And often, when that need is fulfilled, it strengthens their marriage.

'And you think you loving Aron is going to strengthen us?' I said, with incredulity etched on my face.

'Yes!' responded Angie, before stepping forward and taking hold of my unwilling hands. 'You silly man,' she added anxiously, her eyes imploring me to believe her, 'can't you see how much I love *you*? You're my hero, my knight in shining armour, my big protector.'

'Something doesn't add up here!' I declared resolutely.

'It does add up Rich,' responded Angie, 'loving one man romantically doesn't stop you from loving another man the same way. It's just like loving more than one child.'

'It's not like that at all,' I countered.

'It is,' insisted my wife, 'it's called polyamory, and it's more common than you'd think.'

'But we're swingers,' I said, 'and you have lots of sexy online fun, which we both love. Where did polyamory suddenly come from?'

'I think Aron has just happened in response to a need.'

'A need?' I repeated. 'He's not reality. He's all about the fun, sexy bits; not the everyday married, and sometimes boring bits. He's the stuff of fairy tales.'

'You can have someone else as well,' enthused my wife. 'This is what our marriage needs,' she added. 'This is what *I* need.'

Unable to articulate a single clear thought, I just dropped my head into my hands.

'I really don't know how I can possibly do this,' I said. 'This is all just too much.' …

❖

Printed in Great Britain
by Amazon

55617393R00212